THE
REBORN

BOOK ONE:
SYNTH

P. J. MARIE

Anxious Bean Publishing

SYNTH

First Edition

Book Cover Design by Alex Albornoz

ISBN: 978-1-7780028-4-7 (*paperback*)
ISBN: 978-1-7780028-5-4 (*hardcover*)
ISBN: 978-1-7780028-3-0 (e-*book*)

Anxious Bean Publishing
ON, Canada
https://www.anxiousbeanpublishing.com

For Dan.
Thank you for always believing in me.

CONTENTS

Synthetic (adj)
    – produced by humans rather than natural processes.

Gorski

It was early.

Traces of sunlight could still be seen in the sky as dusk began to creep through the air. My watch beeped to signify sunset, but I had been up for hours. I hadn't been able to sleep. Truthfully, I hadn't been sleeping properly for weeks—not since I'd completed my exams and applied to the open detective position within my precinct. I hadn't heard anything back yet, which I'd expected, but that didn't stop my impatience from getting the better of me.

I was young by traditional standards. I'd only *just* met the requirements to complete the exams. My application was unlikely to be accepted, but that wasn't a deterrent. If anything, it only motivated me to push harder.

I didn't care that I only had ten years' experience, which was the bare minimum required, and I didn't care that most officers typically waited until they had fifteen or twenty years under their belts before bothering to apply. I had never been one to let traditions stop me. If I had, I wouldn't be a cop working in the largest and most prestigious precinct within Carneth.

Instead, I would probably still be in school, completing a first or second doctorate degree. I would probably be in a relationship.

7

I would probably be doing something better suited to my smaller stature and "non-physical intellectual capabilities". I would probably have a better relationship with my parents. I wouldn't be driving to work before sundown to get started on filing my paperwork while sporting a 9mm semi-auto pistol on my hip and carting blackout gear in the rear of my car with the sunshield up.

But for me, this had never been an option. I wanted to help. I wasn't entirely sure how or why, but the feeling had always been there, inescapable and etched into my bones. I couldn't ignore it. I wanted to change the world and make it a better place, and the obvious solution to satisfy that desire was joining the Carneth Police Department—or the CPD, as we call it—to stop crime and make Carneth a safer city.

So that was exactly what I did.

I had been obsessed with cop shows as a child, and I told my parents that I wanted to be a police officer when I was only eight years old. At the time, they had shrugged it off, thinking it was cute while expecting me to grow out of it. They figured my goals would change, and I would become something more "reasonable". Something better suited to the family's academic standing and tradition of pursuing higher education. Had they understood just how serious I was, perhaps they would have tried harder to keep me away from it. Perhaps they would have rethought my requests to take self-defence lessons and stopped letting me watch "those ridiculous and unrealistic movies".

Funny enough, they weren't entirely wrong.

The movies were unrealistic.

Being a police officer was a hell of a lot more paperwork than I could have ever anticipated and a lot less action and high-speed chases. But I didn't mind, and I certainly didn't regret applying to the Academy after graduating from university. It was worth it. I loved it. I didn't care that my parents thought I was wasting my brain away in what they considered to be a menial beat-cop job—I had always preferred doing something ahead of just thinking about it.

A life of pure academics and research wasn't for me, even if I could manage it.

I snorted as I carefully changed lanes and made my way onto the highway. My parents had looked devastated when I'd told them that I was accepted to the Academy. It had resulted in a lot of pleading, yelling, and arguments over the years. It wasn't that being a cop was considered a poor career choice by Reborn in general. Officers of the law had an important role in society—maintaining order, keeping civilians safe, and bettering the community—and some titles within the CPD were actually quite prestigious. It was just that my family, and those like them, who came from scholarly backgrounds focused on scientific advancement, thought municipal law enforcement was a waste of valuable tax dollars. They probably would have given me less of a hard time if I had applied to the Federal Investigation Agency, but I thought it was better to start local.

Initially, my parents chalked my decision up to misplaced aspirations based on false pretenses, and they assumed that I would get bored of the night-to-night grind, then give up after a year or two and return to university to complete a law doctorate. They assumed I would become a lawyer, perhaps a professor, something more respectable in their eyes. Three years in, they started to realize that they were wrong. By the fourth year, they stopped talking to me about my career choice altogether, and by the fifth year, they had begrudgingly made peace with the idea without truly accepting it.

We just didn't talk about it anymore.

But then again, my father was a theoretical physicist stemming from a long line of multiple PhD holders who all worked in academic research. My mother was an engineer who had her doctorate in aerospace science. She was currently working for a company developing space flight systems with goals of reaching the moon. And my brother was a software engineer working for a massive financial institution. It was difficult for them to understand me. I was, and always had been, the odd one out in the family.

Well, the odd one out in most situations. It had bothered me when I was younger, but I learned to ignore it and push ahead because I liked being a police officer, and it was the nearest I'd ever come to feeling like I belonged.

By the time I reached the downtown core and exited the highway, darkness had finally settled in, and the city began to wake. A slow trickle of cars entered the streets. Shop signs turned on, and figures could be seen strolling down the pavement without blackout gear to obtain their first coffee of the night. I slowed as I looked at them.

I knew that my coworker and often assigned partner, Lexie Grace, would be in early tonight. She was going on vacation for two weeks with her husband to celebrate their anniversary early starting Monday, and she had a bunch of paperwork to catch up on that I had promised to help her with.

I eyed a few of the pedestrians carrying steaming paper cups in their hands and bit the inside of my lip thoughtfully. Tonight would be the last night that I would see her for a while, and we could use the caffeine to get through our reports. Checking my mirror, I quickly changed lanes and headed toward the coffee shop just a few blocks from the precinct.

I didn't exactly have spare cash, what with earning my beat-cop salary, as my brother loved to call it, but I could spare a few dollars to treat myself and Grace to a nice, steaming cup of coffee. Besides, it was a Friday shift, and this week had been long—why not celebrate it being over?

I pulled into the empty drive-thru tunnel and made my way up to the ordering screen, quickly scanning the options and scoffing at the absurd prices on some of the more eccentric beverages.

"Good evening! Welcome to Grindz. How may I help you start your night?"

"Can I get two large black coffees made with synth, please?" I called out through my open window. Getting takeout coffee was one thing, paying for real blood was another, and I could not afford that. Especially not for coffee, where you could hardly even taste the difference.

"Of course!" The female voice crackled through the speaker. "We now offer RealTECH synthetic groupings as part of our regular menu. For fifty cents more, you can pick between synth A and O, or for a dollar more, you can pick synth B or AB. Would you like to give that a try?"

"No." I let out a quiet sigh. That would make it nearly as expensive as real blood. "Just regular synth is fine, thank you."

"Alright, two large coffees made with regular synth. Anything else I can get you to start your night?"

"No, thank you," I responded, watching the overpriced total appear on the screen. "Just the coffee."

"Perfect, drive up to the next window, and we'll have those ready for you!"

After handing over my loose change to pay for the coffees and securing them in my two cup holders, I exited the drive-thru tunnel and made my way back onto city streets. It was still quiet outside. One benefit of coming into work so early, I got to miss the late-evening traffic and evade the nonsense of idiot drivers going to work or school. I smiled as I leaned my elbow on the open window frame and felt the warm summer breeze ghost over my pale skin.

A few more turns and one exceptionally long red light later, I reached the precinct and drove into the underground parking garage, quickly rolling up my window to prevent the stale smell of gasoline from filling up my vehicle—this building was incredibly old, and the ventilation in the garage was terrible.

"Evening, Gorski!"

"Evening, Hawthorne!" I called back, placing the two coffees on the roof of my car so I could haul my duffle bag out of the backseat.

"Ooh coffee – must have been quite the week if you're buying," Hawthorne said, a small chuckle leaving his lips. I watched him weave his way through the cars toward me. "That second one for me?"

"Not a chance," I said, slugging the duffle bag over my shoulder; it was nearly as large as I was. "It's Lexie's – besides, you hate coffee."

"I wouldn't hate it if you bought it for me." Hawthorne winked, and I rolled my eyes at him. "So when are you going to give up this game and start calling me by my first name?"

"We work together." I grabbed both coffees again before he could reach for them. "That would be unprofessional."

"You call Officer Grace Lexie," Hawthorne pointed out, frowning as he fell into step by my side.

"That's different."

"How on earth is that different?" he asked, pressing the button for the ancient elevator and crossing his arms over his chest.

"Because Lexie isn't trying to sleep with me," I quipped, grinning up at the look on his face. "And I only do it outside of work. The second I step inside this elevator, she will become Officer Grace. Besides – you call me Gorski."

"*That* is because I respect you as a fellow police officer. I value your opinion. I think you are a huge asset to the force, possibly one of the best officers that we have ever had, and thus, I hold you in the highest regard."

"Sure, alright." I gave him a disbelieving look. "I'm still not sleeping with you."

"Even if I told you that you're the most beautiful woman I've ever laid eyes on?" Hawthorne teased as the elevator finally dinged to signify its arrival.

"That would just be workplace harassment," I said. "Didn't you go to the HR training session last week? I would have thought that Mallick would have you front and center for that."

"Hmm," Hawthorne hummed, stroking his cheek as he pretended to think about his answer and followed me onto the elevator. We both swiped our passcards, then he pressed the button for the eighth floor. "I was there… but I was pretty distracted—"

"Don't say it."

"—by the instructor."

"You're a pig," I said, closing my eyes and letting out a sigh as I leaned back against the elevator wall. He was a lost cause, and some days I wondered why we were friends. I turned to look up at his amused smile, the minty scent of his shampoo improving the usual hint of hydraulic oil and grease that lingered in the elevator. Then I elbowed him sharply in the ribs. "Honestly, I have no idea how you're still employed – you're a lawsuit waiting to happen."

"It truly is one of life's greatest mysteries," he mused, ignoring my jab and leaning against the wall by my side.

He towered above me. At just a hair under six feet tall, I was by far the shortest person in the precinct, so I had to crane my neck to roll my eyes at his seven-foot-nine frame.

"But I'll have you know, despite what you and everyone else here think of me, when I do take someone out on a date, I am quite proper. I would never be this blunt and indecent."

"Really?" I arched a brow, studying his traditionally handsome bone structure and innocent expression. "So am I just a joke to you then? Practice? An object for your amusement?"

"Careful." He grinned, his pale green eyes crinkling with his lopsided smile. "You almost sound upset that I might not actually want to sleep with you."

I turned my eyes away from him and let out a huff.

"You're lucky I've known you since the Academy," I muttered. "And that I know what you're really like."

"Charming? Intelligent? Handsomely good-looking?"

"A degenerate who would make any mother ashamed," I shot back, and he snorted at my words. "But utterly harmless, and a surprisingly talented ballroom dancer."

"You swore you would never tell anyone about that – you know what the guys are like here."

"And I never have." I turned to look up at him once more, and my eyes narrowed at him. "So why are you here this early anyway? You hate waking up."

"Ughhh." He let out a breath and pinched the bridge of his nose. "I lost a bet with Hernandez, and now I have to finish our paperwork – which I'm behind on."

"Behind? Paperwork is the one thing you're good at. How did that happen?"

"I got stuck on crowd control for the last four nights," Hawthorne groaned. "The protests downtown got a bit larger than they anticipated, and they needed an extra crew, so Hernandez and I were added to the list."

I frowned as I looked at him, truly looking this time and taking in his exhausted appearance. There were slight bags under his eyes, and he looked paler than usual. He gave me a weak smile, and my gaze locked to his teeth as he closed his eyes and let out a heavy breath. His fangs were a bit more prominent than usual. As with the other signs of fatigue he showed, it wasn't overly noticeable, but I had always been attentive to detail, and they were definitely longer and more pronounced, which was never a good thing.

"Hawthorne," I said, my voice low as the elevator slowed. "When was the last time you ate?"

He cracked an eye open to look down at me and shrugged. "I dunno, sometime the other night? I think I forgot to eat dinner. I just went right to bed when I got home."

"Here." I shuffled the coffees in my hands to reach for my vest as I followed him off the elevator and onto our floor. I paused just off to the side and flicked open one of the many pockets, pulling out a small silver packet. "Take these. They're not fancy like the ones that Grace stocks. It's just a cheap synth mixture, but it will tide you over until you can grab some proper food."

"Gorski, you don't have to. I can just grab something from my desk and—"

"We both know that you don't keep anything at your desk," I said, thrusting the two sealed tablets into his chest. "And once we get in there and you get started on those folders, you're going to have a hell of a time trying to leave to go pick up food. I don't need you going depraved on me or having Mallick think you're draining. You could lose your job over that."

He snorted again, but his eyes softened as he smiled down at me. "Thanks, Gorski. You're always looking out for me."

"Someone has to."

I rolled my eyes as he clapped me on the back and took the tablets from my hand. It was a habit he had developed during our days at the Academy, and I had never really understood it.

"So, did anything happen when you were there at the protests?"

"Thankfully nothing too bad," Hawthorne said, unwrapping the first gelatin cube and popping it into his mouth as we started to make our way across the empty floor toward our desks in the northeast corner. Day shift was still out on patrol, so there would be another solid hour of silence before night shift started to arrive and shift change began.

"It was tense, though," he said. "A group of counter-protestors turned up on the second night, and a few fights broke out. Honestly, the counter-protestors were a bigger problem than the protestors – they were baiting them, trying to get them to react. They were the ones that caused all the problems. They also made it hard to clear the square before morning. Two people got second-degree burns. A few officers had to use mace at one point to disperse a brawl that got out of control, but it never got worse than that."

"That's good." I nodded in understanding. No officer enjoyed crowd-control duty, and they certainly never wanted things to escalate past mace. Or, as in the infamous case of the hunger strike twenty years ago, full military support to control a horde of depraved who had slipped into bloodlust. The Academy used that horrifically historic day as a case study for trainees, and just the memory of it was enough to make me uneasy. "Any idea how long it will keep up?"

"No idea," Hawthorne said as we cut across a few empty bullpens and then moved down a row of cubicles. "The ag-gag law was proposed just over a week ago, and the human rights groups haven't gone anywhere yet. They seem pretty determined, and they've upped their antics – we had to take a few signs away because the mayor's office got so many complaints from bypassers about the grotesque images. But unless they start blockading streets or obstructing people from going about their night, I can't see that anything will be done. They're not breaking any laws by being there. So aside from taking away the worst of the signs or maybe trying to restrict the space for their demonstrations, there really isn't anything else that the CPD or city can do, no matter how much the public complains."

"That makes sense," I said as we reached our bullpen. I placed the coffees on my desk while Hawthorne popped the second gelatin cube into his mouth. "They've never really been a problem for law enforcement before. They're a small group – human rights activists don't typically get much support. It's only in the last few years that they've gained any traction, but even then, despite being tenacious, most of the groups are against violence, so they rarely ever get charged with anything. They'll likely move on in a few nights and go back to handing out pamphlets and camping out at farms until the law is passed."

"Maybe," Hawthorne said, and when I looked up at him, his gaze was fixed on the silver wrapper in his hand. His expression was unreadable, but he paused after he swallowed the remains of the cube in his mouth. "You said this was synthetic, right?"

"Yes." I nodded, dropping my duffle bag to the ground by my desk as I tried to make sense of his strange expression. "Why?"

"No reason," he said, then he quickly crumpled the wrapper and tossed it into the trash. Before I could open my mouth to say anything else, I heard footsteps, and a familiar voice rang out.

"You know, Valya, when I said meet me here first thing, I didn't mean get to the office before the sun goes down."

"I wanted to beat the rush. Otherwise, getting these would have been too much of a bother. But for the record – the sun was down before I got here."

I turned to face the tall, elegant-looking figure who had just entered the bullpen on the far side and grabbed her a coffee, holding it out. She was nearly a full foot taller than me, and she was always put together, makeup done, clothes pressed, nails immaculate, and the faintest hint of petunias clinging to her perfect skin. I had no idea how she found the time to do it, but there was never a hair out of place on her head.

"Whatever." Officer Grace waved her hand and quickly closed the distance between us to grab the coffee. She took a long sip, and I could see her thin body relax as the caffeine flooded her veins. Her pale blue eyes creased with pleasure, and then she groaned. "*Uggghhh* – damn, it's so good. You're a lifesaver."

"And you're bordering on inappropriate with those noises," Hawthorne remarked, pulling out his chair and collapsing at his desk. "I should report you to HR for indecent moaning."

"Oh, shut up, Theo," Grace sneered as she made her way over to her desk on my right. She pulled out her chair, setting her coffee down before carefully running her hands over her hair to make sure that the long blonde locks were still perfect. "You're just jealous you didn't get one. Why are you even here? It's so early."

"Lost a bet," he replied without bothering to look up.

"Hmm," Grace hummed, nodding in approval of her coffee again as she took a seat. "Hernandez must be pleased."

"I bet he is," Hawthorne muttered as he stripped off his standard-issue vest and tossed it onto the small filing cabinet beside his workspace. Then he started up his computer and grabbed the topmost file from the stack on the corner of his desk.

I followed his lead, turning my own computer on and pulling out my chair to sit down as I tugged off my vest. Sitting in the garment all night was uncomfortable, but wearing it was mandated outside of the office while on duty or when entering the building to start your shift. Tearing it off the second that you got to your chair had become second nature for most in the precinct. As I draped the heavy attire over my own filing cabinet and scooted my chair closer to the grey keyboard as the machine slowly came to life, I found my gaze lingering on Hawthorne's hunched form.

He looked thinner.

I hadn't noticed it when he was in full uniform, but now, as he leaned over the open folder with a look of concentration on his face, it was clear in the way that his dress shirt hung from his body that he had lost some weight. My brow creased as I stared at him, typing in my password by touch memory before slowly opening the case file on my desk. I had known Hawthorne since our training days at the Academy. We'd met the very first day of orientation, and he wasn't the type to get bothered by stress.

Frankly, it could be difficult to get him to take anything seriously, so I couldn't imagine that work strain was the cause of his slimmer frame. Regardless of the reason, it was concerning. Like many of the other officers, he put a lot of effort into maintaining his muscle mass to be larger than a typical civilian, so I couldn't imagine him throwing all that effort away by choice, and I knew he would never drain. Even he wasn't that irresponsible, so something else was going on.

"Valya, are you still good for the 24th?" Grace asked.

"Yes." I nodded, knowing she was talking about her anniversary party.

"Great." She grinned, shuffling through a few folders before turning back to look at me. "Do you have the Miller file?"

"Uh, yes." I glanced back at Hawthorne as I started to dig out the folder, wondering if I should try to talk to him about whatever was going on. "Right here – this one was pretty messy, though. You sure you want to start with it?"

"I'd rather get it out of the way," Grace said, getting up from her desk to come grab the thick folder that I pulled from the pile. "Then I can push it down into a dusty corner of my mind and convince myself that it never happened."

"Honestly, I'll probably do the same." I grimaced, handing her the file.

"Miller?" Hawthorne said, leaning back in his chair to look at us. "Isn't that the asshole who had someone in his trunk?"

"Yes." I nodded in confirmation, a sickening feeling sinking in my gut at the memory.

Awful as it had been, situations like these were why I loved being a cop. That night, we had saved someone's life. It had been a routine traffic stop, except that when Grace and I were running his plates through dispatch, we heard a thumping sound from his trunk. Long story short, his stepdaughter was bound and gagged in the rear of his vehicle, and his wife was later found dead at their home. The case had been turned over to a pair of detectives from our precinct, per standard procedure, but we still had to finish the paperwork for our portion of the arrest.

"He was a monster," I said, watching as Lexie opened the case file.

"He was degenerate scum – a damn *vampire* is what he was," Grace spat, and I stiffened at the word. Even Hawthorne went still, but we all jolted as a deep voice filled the small bullpen.

"*Language,* Grace!"

"Captain Mallick," Grace breathed, her eyes growing wide. She stood and straightened to her full height, quickly turning to face the approaching broad-shouldered man. "I'm so sorry, sir – I – I didn't realize that you were there."

"Clearly," Captain Mallick said, his tone low with disapproval as his gaze skimmed around the small bullpen. His eyes darted to the clock on the wall before shifting back to Grace.

"But that's no excuse for using *that* word in this precinct. We have a zero-tolerance policy here, Officer Grace, and I take that seriously. Now, lucky for you, you're technically off the clock, and there isn't anyone else in yet to hear it, so I won't write you up – but don't think for a second that that sort of language is acceptable in the CPD."

"No, sir." Grace shook her head. "It won't happen again."

"It better not," Captain Mallick said, stepping closer and glaring down at her. He was thick with muscle for a Reborn, and it was even more apparent next to Grace's trim frame. "Because if it does, regardless of when or where it happens, you're suspended without pay. I don't care how deplorable Mr. Miller is – that sort of language and behaviour is *unacceptable*. You're an officer of the law, and everything that you do reflects back on this precinct and your peers. You're a role model. A leader. A professional. You're expected to act like one at all times. Understood?"

"Yes, sir." Grace nodded as her grip on the folder tightened. "Understood. I will strive to be better and uphold the values of the CPD, sir."

"Good," Mallick said. He stared at Grace for a moment longer, then his gaze shifted to meet mine, and I noticed the paper in his hand. "I wasn't expecting you to be in this early, Gorski – I was going to leave you a note on your desk. Get your paperwork done, and swing by my office during the break. I need to speak to you before you go out on patrols."

"Yes, sir."

We all watched in silence as Captain Mallick turned and left the bullpen, and I wondered why on earth he might want to see me.

"You could have told me that he was there," Grace hissed as she turned and glared at me.

"Me?" My mouth fell open in surprise. "I didn't know he was there – I didn't even hear him come in. You shouldn't have said that word, Grace. You're lucky you didn't get written up."

"Whatever." Grace rolled her eyes and let out a sigh. "It's just a word – besides, we were all thinking it."

I watched her move back to her desk and shook my head in disbelief. It wasn't the first time that I had heard Lexie Grace use that word, but it was certainly the first time that she had ever uttered it inside the office. It wasn't like her to be so careless. Maybe it was just the stress of going on vacation next week or the memories associated with the Miller file, but either way, she wasn't entirely wrong—I had thought it. The difference was I wasn't stupid enough or cruel enough to ever say the word out loud. It broke the rules, and the rules were there for good reason.

I glanced over at Hawthorne and noticed that his strange and pensive expression was back. His gaze was locked on something in the distance, and he seemed to be deep in thought.

"So, what do you think Mallick wants with you?" Grace asked as she dropped into her seat again and cracked open the folder once more.

"No idea," I said, making up my mind and grabbing a scrap piece of paper from my desk. I scribbled a quick note onto it, then crumpled it into a ball and threw it at Hawthorne's head, which seemed to startle him out of his thoughts.

"What are you, five?" Hawthorne groaned, picking up the paper from his desk as Grace laughed.

He moved to throw the ball into the trash but paused when I cleared my throat. He stared at me, then his eyes narrowed. I watched as he slowly uncrumpled the paper and read the message.

I could see confusion cross his face as he looked back at me in disbelief. When I didn't laugh or react in any way to suggest that it was a joke and simply arched a brow in question, he stilled. His eyes flicked to Grace, who now had her head buried in the Miller folder and wasn't paying us any mind. Then he met my gaze once more, nodded, and tucked the paper into his desk drawer.

Promotion

"You wanted to see me, sir?" I asked after knocking on the open door to get the captain's attention.

"Gorski – yes, come in. Shut the door behind you and sit down."

I nodded as I entered Captain Mallick's office, noticing the familiar hint of cedar as the door clicked shut. His voice was always stern, but this time it made me a bit uneasy.

Mallick had never been particularly friendly, but I could hardly blame him for his rigid and to-the-point attitude. He'd had a long career and endured a lot. He was in the third tier of command, only ranking below our chief of police and commissioner. He was one of seven different captains within this precinct, and he was constantly swamped and sought out for advice because his experience was unrivalled. He was a shoo-in for promotion when the chief retired in the next ten years, and even though Mallick had never been a ladder climber, he would not refuse the role. Instead, he would take it without complaint like the professional that he was, while continuing to be a shining example of what it meant to be an officer of the law within the 33rd Precinct of Carneth.

I respected the man beyond measure, but I would be lying if I said that I wasn't also intimidated by him. Especially right now. Despite pondering it all evening, I had no idea why he wanted to see me. I hadn't forgotten to file any paperwork. I never did. My firearms licence had been recently renewed. I had completed my mandatory HR training modules and aced all the accompanying tests. I wasn't behind on any of my reports, and I didn't have any pending vacation requests.

I fought the urge to outright ask as I sank into the uncomfortable chair and watched the man before me as he shuffled some papers around on his desk but remained otherwise silent.

"You graduated top of your class," he finally said as his hands settled on a tan folder.

It wasn't a question, so I refrained from answering. I simply nodded as the captain flipped the folder open, and I saw the name on the front. It took me by surprise when I realized that it was my file, and his pale brown eyes were skimming over the details almost assessingly.

"You've worked mostly in patrol, a few crowd-control duties, and made several small-scale arrests. Except for your involvement in the high-profile Miller case, you have minimal experience with investigations. Your drug tests are all clean, your marksmanship is, quote, "excellent", and your reports are always completed on time with perfect details. There are no civilian complaints lodged against you, no internal harassment claims, no documented suspicions of draining, and no issues with gear returns. You're a model officer and a promising asset to the CPD.

"Yet you have zero experience working alongside homicide – except for providing supplemental support on two occasions where you patrolled a barrier. You have yet to shadow a senior officer, you only have minimal surveillance background, and you're shy of five to ten years of experience that we would normally expect to see. So, Gorski," Captain Mallick said as he dropped the open folder down on the desk and met my gaze. "Tell me – what made you think you were qualified to apply to the open detective position at the largest precinct in Carneth?"

I blinked at him and struggled to find my words. I was completely caught off guard. I had never even considered that my application might come off as arrogant or potentially even insulting to Captain Mallick, given that he ran Patrol and Street and had nothing to do with the Detective Unit.

"I have wanted to be a detective since I applied to the Academy, sir," I said quickly, trying to make sense of the unreadable expression on his face.

I couldn't tell if he was angry, annoyed, or simply indifferent and doing his job. Perhaps I had crossed a line—upset Captain Vogle, who led the Detective Unit here, and I was going to be reprimanded for applying inappropriately. Yet, I struggled to believe that could be the case since I had not broken any rules.

"I completed all the exams and paperwork – and the position opening stated that those either with a current pass or awaiting results could apply."

"Yet you know we typically only promote those who have double your experience," he said, his tone blunt.

"Yes, sir."

I gripped the fabric of my pants tightly, wondering if I had just unknowingly made a massive mistake. Perhaps there were unspoken rules among the captains? Or something that I had missed as I reviewed the handbook.

"Are you trying to take a shortcut, Gorski?" Mallick asked as he sat back in his seat and fixed me with another unreadable look. "Or are you unhappy in your current position?"

"No, sir." I shook my head. "I'm not trying to take a shortcut, and I'm very happy with my current position. I apologize, sir – I should have told you that I applied. I didn't mean to catch you off guard or have it come off in any way rude or disrespectful. I wasn't trying to hide my application. In all honesty, sir, I assumed my application would be passed over because my experience only met the bare minimum requirements. I never expected to hear anything back – I didn't even think that I would pass through the electronic screening."

"Then why bother applying?"

"For practice?" My voice sounded unsure, and as I saw his eyebrow twitch at my response, I quickly tried to clarify. "That was poorly worded. I took the process very seriously, sir – I didn't apply for fun. I want the position; I just didn't expect to get it or even hear anything back about it. But I thought if I applied now, maybe it would help me in the future. On the off chance that someone did see my application, I thought that they might keep me in mind for a future opening because when I applied again, they would know that I was serious – since I had applied before. It also gave me some insight regarding the application process and the sort of questions asked on the forms, so my next application will certainly be even better, but I never meant to—"

"Relax, Gorski," Mallick said as he let out a sigh and crossed his arms over his broad chest. "You're not in trouble – but yes, you should have told me that you applied."

"I'm sorry, sir." I felt the disappointment heavy in my gut. "I genuinely didn't think you would even see it."

"Yes, well, I was caught by surprise when Captain Vogle stopped by my office to ask about you," Captain Mallick said. I cringed at his words, but he raised a hand as if to wave my discomfort away. "To be honest, I was more bothered by Vogle than by you blindsiding me. You're young and ambitious – I don't fault you for that. If anything, it just shows how serious you are about this career. You're not the first junior to apply to a position well above your years, and you're not wrong either. I typically don't hear about it because those applications don't make the cut. If they do, I don't take it personally, and I don't stand in the way of my officers when they want to progress their careers. I know that you want to make detective – you've been very forthcoming about that since you got here. But I was serious about the question, Gorski. Why do you think you would be a good fit for that position based on your current experience?"

"Because I'm a quick learner," I said, and the words fell easily from my mouth. I didn't need to make up a response. I had already thought about this a million times. "I work hard, and I train even harder, sir. I notice things that other officers don't. I have good intuition. I know I'm short on experience, but I can make up for that with academic knowledge. I have been actively studying to become a detective since I graduated from the Academy. It's why I applied to the 33rd in the first place, because the Detective Unit here is unrivalled. It's the training center for the other units.

"I've read every book out there," I continued. "I know all the procedures from memory. I know how the department works and where each jurisdiction ends. I'm even familiar with their paperwork, forms, and legal requirements. Detectives work in pairs – if I were to be paired with a more senior detective, I could learn from their experience and be moulded into what they need. I know I'm young by comparison, but I'm motivated. I'll work harder than anyone else ten or twenty years my age, and I'll pick things up more quickly than my partner will be able to teach them to me. I know I can do it. All I need is a chance, sir."

Captain Mallick looked at me for a long moment, and I could have sworn something sad shifted behind his eyes—though I didn't understand why. Then he let out a sigh and sat forward in his chair to rest his elbows against his desk.

"Captain Vogle seems to think the same thing," Mallick said, and my chest tightened at his words. "The 24th Precinct had a lot of success when they brought in five younger candidates. Apparently, it can be quite difficult to untrain bad habits out of older applicants, more so than it is to train good habits into younger ones. So, naturally, Vogle wants to give it a try here. After all, he's supposed to be the one leading the charge in training and churning out good results for the other precincts to follow suit. Thus, you're his top candidate. He came to me looking for a character recommendation."

"I see." My voice was hoarse, and I struggled to keep my face straight. "And – and what did you say, sir?"

"I told him he couldn't ask for a better officer – but that I thought you were too fresh," Mallick answered without hesitation, then he let out another sigh. "That didn't deter him. He wants you on his team."

"I – I don't know what to say, sir," I whispered as my hands began to tremble in my lap.

"Well, don't thank me yet," Mallick said, though even his gruff voice could not sober my excitement. "I didn't say that he could have you – but I did agree to give this a trial run. You're one of my best young officers, so I'm not going to give you up that easily. However, as I said before, I won't stand in the way of you progressing either. My unwillingness to let you go is purely because I believe that there are still valuable things for you to learn while under my command in this unit, not because I selfishly want to keep you here longer than you need to be.

"But," Captain Mallick said almost reluctantly, "Vogle seems to think he can make this work. So, he and I made an agreement. You'll be loaned to his department for the next three months. Think of it as a probationary period to test the waters and see how you perform. If it goes well, we will extend it for another three months, then another and so on until you complete a full year. During that time, you will technically still be under my command, but you will report to Vogle functionally and follow the orders of your senior partner night-to-night."

"Yes, sir," I breathed, clenching my pant legs once more to stop the exhilarated shaking. Though it was clear Mallick knew I was barely controlling myself, because he gave me a look and leaned forward to meet my gaze.

"Gorski," Mallick said, his voice stern once more. "I know you're excited, but I need you to listen very carefully to what I'm about to say."

"Of course, sir." I nodded, straightening my back and sitting up in my uncomfortable seat.

"Becoming a detective may be your dream job, but the position is not for everyone," Mallick said as his gaze grew very serious. "That isn't to say that I don't think you can do it. Quite the opposite, I know you can do it. The question will be, do you truly want to. Detectives in this precinct work longer hours than any other officer, department, or unit within this city because our jurisdiction spans the largest area. Precincts 31 through 40 have the highest crime rates in Carneth, and *we* are the ones that respond to those calls for investigation support. As a result, Vogle and his unit get more cases than any other precinct in this city. And those don't include the cases we get asked to consult on by the Provincial Police, or the other three Detective Units in Precincts 7, 15, and 24 when they need additional resources.

"We are the main hub, and as a result, the job is hard, Gorski," Mallick said. "Not just physically, but mentally as well.

You will see things that will affect your sleep and change the way that you view your fellow Reborn. It will affect your personal life. It will affect your health. Statistically, yes, you are safer from injury as a detective than you are in any other position, such as working patrol – but the dangers you will be exposed to are greater on a different level, and they are much more violent. You might not break a leg from a hit-and-run during a traffic stop, but you will constantly be injecting yourself into extremely unpredictable situations with exceedingly dangerous people.

"Detectives die and go missing in this precinct, Gorski," Mallick said, and I felt the air around me grow still at the low tone of his voice. "They handle everything from homicide to kidnappings – gang violence to grand larceny. And as a result of that, they are often bribed, pressured by gangs, run off their feet, and tormented by influential and prestigious members of our society. It makes doing your job difficult, and while I would never doubt your integrity as an officer of the law, I know how quickly the stress takes hold, and it's a side of the city you've never had to see. It is a long and exhausting career. You will rarely be thanked, and you will often find yourself reaching dead ends as leads dry up or key witnesses suddenly become silent. Our precinct solves less than thirty percent of all reported crimes from our ten-precinct jurisdiction, and those numbers drop further when looking at the worst categories. I'm not trying to convince you to give up on your dream, but I did it for fifty years, and I can tell you, I came out the other side different from how I went in.

"So if at any point during your trial run you change your mind and no longer want to be a detective – tell me," Mallick said. "I won't ask you for an explanation. I won't ask you what happened. I won't tell Vogle or any of the other officers, and you can come back to the Patrol and Street Department with no questions asked. I won't abandon you over there to get sucked into the abyss, but I can't help you if you don't tell me honestly how it's going. Do you understand?"

"Yes, I understand, sir," I said. "I promise – I'll let you know if I change my mind."

"Good." Mallick nodded, then he sat back in his chair. "Then I'll tell Grace you're not on patrol with her for the late-night rounds. She'll be paired with Officer Tilson."

"What will I be doing instead, sir?"

"Vogle already has your partner picked out," Mallick said, and the hint of reluctance returned to his voice as he reached for another thick folder on his desk. "He's a vet – as senior as can be and harder than stone. Randall Hakim."

"Wait." I faltered, struggling to believe his words. "Sir – Randall Hakim – the same Detective Randall Hakim who caught the eastside strangler and busted the child trafficking ring two years ago?"

"Yes," Mallick said, and my mouth fell open in awe. "Close your mouth, Gorski."

I snapped my jaw shut, and Mallick fixed me with another one of his stern looks.

"He doesn't like gawkers or kiss-asses, so don't fawn over him, or you won't even last until dawn. His partner went missing one month ago, and you would do well not to ask him about that."

I nodded but didn't dare say a word. I knew perfectly well why mentioning Randall Hakim's missing partner was off-limits. That should be common sense, but then again, knowing Grace, she would probably ask Detective Hakim about it outright, so I couldn't blame Mallick for the warning. Especially after my gawking.

But I wasn't going to ruin my shot at becoming a detective by asking Hakim if the rumours were true—if he really had worked his partner so hard that the man became a degenerate drainer who got so loaded up on drugs he skipped right over slipping into a bloodlust and wound up in a coma instead, then died somewhere in the sewers of Carneth from starvation.

The rumour had begun circulating the precinct right after Detective Lavoie had gone missing one month ago. At first glance with no other context, the story might sound insane, but rumours of Detective Lavoie's draining and deteriorating health had started long before he'd gone missing, and rumours surrounding Detective Hakim's intensity had been around for even longer.

"I know the media and this precinct like to paint Hakim as a hero," Mallick continued. "But in reality, Randall Hakim is as bitter and unsympathetic as they come. He's seen the absolute worst that this city has to offer, Gorski, and he has been doing this for nearly as long as you've been alive.

"This is the case file that you two will be working on." Mallick handed me the thick folder. "It's a Provincial Police file, but they asked for local assistance given the situation and anticipated requirements. Take it home with you and learn as much as you can. I have no idea how much work Hakim has done so far, but knowing him, he already has a plan, and he probably won't be too happy that he got saddled with you. Shadow him. Do as he says and watch how he works, but don't get in his way. If he doesn't like you, he won't hesitate to kick you back to the office and tell Vogle to get lost."

"Yes, sir." I nodded, taking the folder that he held out to me and clutching it to my chest.

"Now let's go – I need to get this introduction over before my meeting starts in half an hour."

"Yes, sir," I said again, standing from my chair as Mallick rose from his seat.

I followed him to the door, fighting to control my excitement as we left his office and made our way through the bullpens toward the elevator. I caught Hawthorne's eye as we walked by. He looked at me curiously, but I shook my head and didn't say a word. I would tell him everything that happened later when I got the chance.

The elevator ride up to the main floor of the Detective Unit took several long minutes, and when the doors finally opened on the eleventh floor, the quiet was quickly replaced with the hustle and bustle of bodies and typing fingers. We made our way down a long, wide hallway by a row of desks in a massive open space. We passed countless offices along the way, and I assumed that they must belong to the most senior detectives, but I honestly wasn't sure. I had never been on this floor. We made a right turn before I heard a low voice, and suddenly, Mallick was slowing to a stop before the open corner office door.

"And here I was thinking that I would need to come find you. Did you forget how to find your way up here, or were you trying to change her mind before she even started, Mallick?"

"As if you gave me any choice in the matter," Captain Mallick replied as he made his way into the large room. I followed him inside, lingering awkwardly by the door. "You know how slow the elevator in this building is."

"It really is criminal." Captain Vogle smirked as he sat perched on the front edge of his desk. "Though I doubt they will ever fix it."

"Well, they keep saying that we'll be getting a new building."

"But we all know that's a bureaucratic lie," Vogle replied. "Especially if Constance gets her way with Precinct 24."

Captain Mallick nodded as Vogle's eyes shifted to me. I had never met the man, but I recognized him from the photos on the main floor. He was older than his image – maybe by a decade or so, though he still looked young. Probably younger than Mallick. If I had to wager a guess, I'd place him around eighty, but it was always so hard to tell.

"I'm sure the right decision will be made," Mallick said as he shifted to the right and turned back to look at me. I moved to stand by his side, a nervous smile on my lips as the captain introduced me. "I don't have time for niceties – Vogle, this is Officer Gorski."

"Captain Vogle." I shuffled the large case folder in my arms so I could reach out to shake his hand as I stepped forward. "It's an honour to meet you in person, sir."

"Goodness, you really are fresh." Vogle laughed as he pushed off his desk to stand and take my hand. He was strong. Trim like most Reborn and incredibly tall, even taller than Hawthorne. He easily pushed eight feet, and his grey eyes were paler than my own. "I've never been a stickler for formalities. You're much shorter than I expected – can you manage hauling your own gear?"

"Yes, sir. My height has never been an issue." I released his hand and fought the urge to frown. Height had nothing to do with strength, and I had never been able to figure out why everyone here always assumed I was weaker just because I was short.

"I doubted it would be, but Hakim won't help you even if it is," Vogle said as he stepped back to perch on the edge of his desk once more. He gestured his head toward the left side of the room, and it was at that moment I realized there was a fourth person standing in the large space.

He was eerily silent, maybe an inch or two taller than Mallick. The second my eyes landed on his still frame, I felt discomfort shifting down my spine. It was hollow and much more sinister than anything I had experienced before. I had seen his picture in the newspapers, but seeing him now in the flesh, I realized just how poorly film captured his essence. His skin was ashen like Captain Mallick's, but that was where any similarity between the two men ended.

Randall Hakim was thin and lanky like most civilian Reborn. He hadn't tried to bulk up as most officers do, but he was clearly in good shape. His shoulders were broad and undoubtedly covered in lithe muscle from the way his standard-issue shirt was fitting, and he held himself with a sort of confidence and placidity that I had never seen before. All Reborn were quiet in their movements, but he gave off an aura of deafening silence.

His left eye was almost entirely white, while the right remained pale blue. He could have been born that way, or it could have been lingering damage from an injury in the field. I doubted that I would ever know the answer to that question, but just by looking at him, I immediately understood what Captain Mallick had tried to tell me. Detective Hakim was not nice, nor would he hold my hand or walk me through this. He was quiet and controlled, and he was here to do his job – not to make friends or be a mentor. He didn't have time for useless young officers tagging along behind him looking for instruction, and I got the distinct impression working with him would be an uphill battle.

"Hello, Detective Hakim." I forced the words from my lips as I moved toward him, my legs suddenly feeling stiff and reluctant. "It looks like we will be partners. It's a pleasure to meet you, sir."

I outstretched my hand to him, and he stared at it. I could practically feel his gaze burning into my pale skin as his eyes swept up my arm, over my face, and down my body. Then something like a scoff left his thin lips, and for a horrifying moment, I thought that he would ignore my hand and walk out of the room. To my surprise, he didn't; instead, he took my hand and gripped it tight.

"We'll see about that."

His voice sounded like gravel, and I had to fight not to tremble under his unnerving stare as he squeezed my hand even tighter. It was Vogle's friendly laugh that pulled me from the pale vortex of his gaze. I felt my hand fall to my side as Hakim let go, and I turned to look back at the two captains.

"Ignore Hakim," Vogle said with a grin as he shook his head. "He's like that with everyone. He's skeptical of my plan, but I've read your application and seen your file – you'll be just fine."

"Thank you, sir," I said, clearing my throat as I instinctively took a step back from Hakim. "Is this contingent on my exam results, sir? I know the opening said a pending pass could apply, but I still haven't seen my final score."

"I've got them right here," Vogle said, tapping an envelope on the corner of his desk. "You'll probably get an email about it this weekend, but I'll spoil it for you – you passed with flying colours. This isn't contingent on anything but your performance."

"Alright – introductions are over. I still need to tell Officer Grace that she will be pairing up with Tilson for late-night patrol duty," Mallick said as he checked his watch. "Vogle, Hakim – she's all yours. But remember, she's on loan, so don't break her. I expect her back in one piece each dawn until she is formally transferred to your department."

Vogle waved his hand in dismissal as Hakim remained silent. "Yeah, yeah. I never took you as the type to have favourites, Mallick – you're really shattering my beliefs here. Go do what you need to do. Hakim, Gorski – get out of my office and sort yourselves out. I need to go speak to Lieutenant Antonov about some issues on ten, and I want to get out of here early. They've set up a new open season in mid-July, and I want to try and get tags before they sell out.

"Hakim is leading this case, Gorski. So do as he says, no questions asked. Become his third arm, so to speak, and this will work just fine," Vogle said as he stood from his desk once more.

"I'll touch base with you next week to see how things are going but otherwise, if you have any questions, ask Hakim first."

The dismissal was abrupt, but I nodded and thanked Vogle without complaint, turning to leave the office behind Mallick as Hakim trailed silently behind me—my initial excitement fading as I turned and tilted my head to look up at my new partner.

"What would you like me to do before dawn, sir?" I asked as he closed Vogle's door behind us and turned to meet my gaze. "Mallick pulled me off patrol, so I'm all yours. Is there anything you want me to get started on?"

He stared at me, his mismatched eyes lingering on my face for a long and uncomfortable moment while I resisted the urge to fidget until he finally responded.

"How old are you?"

My brow creased. It wasn't exactly a question I was expecting, nor was it proper etiquette to ask, even if it didn't break any rules.

"Thirty-four, sir," I answered.

I watched him carefully to gauge his reaction, but he didn't have one. His face remained blank as he stared at me a while longer, making my discomfort grow. It felt like bugs were crawling under my skin, and I didn't like it. I would have just preferred that he outright make a snide remark about me being young and useless.

"Go back to your desk and read that file," he finally said as he crossed his arms over his chest and looked down at me. "Get familiar with the contents of it front to back and memorize it if you can. If you have questions, write them down and work to resolve them on your own. I'm not your babysitter. Be here early for your Monday shift – Sunday evening before sundown, level two of the parking garage. We'll be going to the scene, so bring your gear bag, and you had better be able to carry it."

With that, Hakim turned on his heel and walked away. I watched him grow smaller as he made his way down the long hallway toward the other side of the building.

Everything about him was unwelcoming—even his walk.

He moved like a stealthy predator on a mission. He gave off the impression of having little regard for anything or anyone around him, and yet I knew that couldn't be the case. His eyes were piercing. He was observant. Unnaturally so. It was why he made such a great detective and why he hadn't mysteriously gone missing or been injured while on the job.

Mallick was right. He was hard as stone—jaded, unsympathetic, and unhappy about being partnered with me. However, there was one thing Mallick hadn't identified about Hakim. It wasn't as obvious, because it was more of a feeling than a fact, but I was certain that working with him over the next three months would prove my intuition correct. I would've bet my entire measly yearly salary on it.

The reason why Hakim had such a successful career as a detective was that he was just as dangerous as the criminals that he was hunting.

Hawthorne

"I can't believe I'm in your apartment," Hawthorne said as he stepped into the living room, and I hung up his coat. "I've been trying to get in here for years."

I rolled my eyes at him, regret brewing in the pit of my stomach, as he turned to give me a mischievous grin. Even I couldn't believe that I had invited him over for dinner. I followed along behind him as he moved into the center of the room and watched him look around the small space, silently taking it all in as I grew uneasy.

I didn't have many visitors. When Grace and I got together, we always went to her place because she owned a house in the western suburbs, which was a lot nicer than my cramped one-bedroom apartment, and I had certainly never considered allowing Hawthorne to come here in the past. Prior to reading my scribbled address on the scrap piece of paper I'd thrown at his head, he hadn't even known where I lived. Now, here he was, standing in my living room, eyes trailing over all my belongings with interest.

There wasn't all that much to see. I wasn't at home very often, so I didn't own as many things as most people did.

His gaze shifted over my old couch and vintage chair—which was just a polite way of saying I'd gotten it second-hand. Then his eyes moved past the coffee table, television, and grey computer that sat on a tiny desk near the window before shifting to the kitchen. It was open to the living room, separated by a small half-wall. I didn't have space for a large fancy dining table and half a dozen chairs like Grace did. Instead, I just had a small table in the living room pushed up against the wall with two exceedingly old wooden chairs. It was usually covered in mail and notes from work since I used it as an extension of my desk and ate at the small bartop counter that divided the room, but I had cleaned it off before Hawthorne got here.

He turned, his eyes trailing away from the kitchen back over the living room once more, past the closet where I had hung up his coat, to the small hallway that extended down toward two doors – one open, one closed. That was intentional. I had closed my bedroom door before buzzing him into my building because I refused to give him any sort of indication that this was a promiscuous visit. Though that didn't stop the slow smile that crept across his face as he eyed the closed door, then turned to look at me with an amused expression.

"Bedroom?" he asked, and I could tell that he was enjoying himself.

"Don't be gross," I said, pushing past him toward the kitchen. I could hear him chuckle behind me as he turned and followed. "I'm not above tossing you out and keeping your food for myself."

"You're so cruel," he said, smiling as he pulled out one of the chairs at my small table and took a seat while I grabbed the paper bag on the bartop counter and brought it over to unpack.

"I hope you don't mind cheap takeout," I said, pulling the first container out and sliding it across the wooden surface toward him.

I already knew that he didn't. Like most men in the CPD, Hawthorne was somewhat similar to a garbage disposal, and I had seen him eat countless questionable things over the years. When RealTECH synthetic products first hit the market, they were expensive, and the company nearly went under. But over the last few years, prices had gone down, their products had improved, and organic food had become more expensive. Since we didn't exactly have the salary to support fine dining, cheap now often meant low-grade, but still edible, synthetics in the fast-food industry, which was exactly what this food was.

Though, in this case, I had bought it intentionally for another reason.

"Not at all," he said, grabbing the container and taking the fork that I handed to him. He eyed the lid curiously, then slowly popped it off. "Where's it from?"

It was an innocent question, and he tried to ask it nonchalantly. Anyone else might not have questioned it, and had I not grown concerned about him earlier at work, I wouldn't have spared it a second thought.

"Albert's," I said, taking out my own container. I pulled out the other chair and sat down across from him. "They have the best shawarma."

"They do," Hawthorne agreed as he dug his fork into the food, then looked up once more. "So, you going to tell me what this visit is really about? Are you planning to confess your love for me now or later?"

I exhaled, sitting back in my seat and crossing my arms over my chest. He looked amused with himself, which was a rather typical expression that could be found on his face, but I refused to give him an out or let him run away from this. I had known him too long, and he'd become one of my best friends, even if I didn't always understand how that had happened. Then again, I suppose it may have been unavoidable after the water training fiasco back in our Academy days.

I pushed the thoughts aside, refocusing my attention on the current problem. There was something wrong, and I wasn't going to let him risk slipping into a depraved state over it.

"I think you're the one that needs to tell me what's really going on," I said, fixing him with a stern stare.

"What do you mean?" he asked, dropping his hold on his fork to sit back and look at me. "You invited me over."

"Yes, because I'm worried about you. What's going on, Hawthorne?"

His brow furrowed, and I could see the muscles beneath his shirt starting to tense. "Nothing – I'm just tired."

"Tired?" I pressed. "I've seen you tired before – this isn't tired."

"Nothing's wrong, Gorski," Hawthorne said, an unfamiliar edge creeping into his voice as he shifted in his seat. "I have no idea what you're on about."

"You're my friend, Hawthorne," I said. The words were low and laced with concern, and he stiffened as he met my gaze. "Maybe no one else has noticed it, but I know you're not okay. You're paler, you're thinner, your fangs are at *least* four millimetres longer than they usually are, and you've lost a bunch of the muscle that you obsessively worked to maintain. Lie to me all you want and blame the crowd-control shifts, but I'm not stupid. You're clearly not sleeping. You're not eating enough either, but it's more than that, isn't it? Something happened."

I watched him shift again in his chair as I held his pale green gaze. He looked like he wanted to leave. He looked more uncomfortable than I had ever seen him, and I wondered if he was debating getting up and just walking out.

"What's going on, Hawthorne?" I asked again, softer this time. "I know you would never drain, so what happened?"

He stared at me, unmoving yet nearly twitching as he fought some kind of internal battle. Then, after a long moment of hesitation, he cracked, and it was like nothing I had ever seen before. His lighthearted and friendly mask fell away to reveal a tormented look of anguish that I didn't know he was capable of possessing. He let out a heavy sigh, leaning forward to brace his elbows on the table before dropping his head into his hands.

"Nothing is wrong," he said, but his voice sounded broken. "I just – I don't know."

He let out another deep exhale, his fingers running through his short, wavy hair before he forced himself to sit up once more, and he looked at me almost desperately.

"Don't you ever wonder about all this?" he asked.

"Wonder about what?"

"About this," Hawthorne said, waving his hand as if to collectively point at my apartment. "About everything. About all of it. About what we do. Where we live. Don't you ever wonder about the food you buy? Where it comes from, or how it's processed? Don't you ever think about any of it?"

I stared at him, not really sure what to think as I shifted in my seat.

"Not really," I admitted, watching as he let out a breath and shook his head. Clearly I didn't understand whatever he was trying to get at. "What do you mean, Hawthorne? What are you thinking about it?"

The last of his restraint fell away as he sat back in his chair and let his shoulders drop. He looked lost. His eyes stared at the wall, unfocused, and his fingernail absently scratched against the surface of my table.

"I don't know," he said, his voice distant as he shook his head again. "I don't know what I think anymore. I just – I just don't know."

He swallowed, his eyes dropping down to the table. Then the words poured unfiltered from his mouth as if they had been eating him alive.

"When I was working crowd control three nights ago, there was this young woman there protesting. She couldn't have been much older than eighteen. Maybe twenty, but I doubt it. Anyway, she was being heckled by some asshole on the other side of the protest line, so I went over to make sure she was okay. A fight had broken out the night before, and the last thing I wanted was some naive kid getting caught up in the middle of it, but she was holding her own. It was actually rather impressive. She remained calm the whole time, no matter how rude the heckler got. I managed to get him to leave, and she thanked me. I'm not sure how it happened, but somehow that turned into a conversation. She said she had been there since the protests started and that she volunteers in the Wildlife Preservation Programs – you know, the ones for making sure the human population is stable?"

He glanced up at me, and I nodded.

I knew exactly what program he was talking about. It was run through the government and had been around for decades. They were always complaining about never having enough funding, while other organizations and businesses constantly lobbied to cut said funding. Yet no matter the back and forth, the programs would always exist to some extent because the factory farming industry had discovered ages ago that keeping humans together closely was a breeding ground for disease.

It was no different than keeping any other creatures too close together – even hospitals faced disease outbreaks on extremely rare occasions. It was just worse because humans were naturally weak and susceptible to infection. So it was critical to sustain wild populations. Not only were they hunted during open season by avid hunters for recreational sport and population management, but they would also be occasionally caught to supplement farm stocks because wild humans tended to be a little more sturdy.

So, just like they did with deer, bears, wolves, and other natural wildlife, the government had developed conservation efforts and put programs in place to ensure that humans were not overpopulated, hunted illegally, or accidentally driven to extinction.

"Well," Hawthorne continued as a strange look crossed his face, "she said that she met one."

"Met a wild human?" I asked, disbelief evident in my voice.

"Yeah," Hawthorne breathed, nodding in understanding of my reaction. "I didn't believe her at first either. Apparently, she ran into the girl while repairing an alarm sensor along the edge of the wildlife reserve, but – the more I talked to her, the more convincing she was. Did you know that humans have best friends? That they can do maths and think critically – and that they speak?"

I didn't know what to say. I had honestly never thought about it before or paid attention to any of the human rights activist propaganda.

"Apparently, they're very well-spoken if taught how to speak," he said, and suddenly the pieces started to fit together in my mind. "She said they're incredibly clever and resourceful. They're smaller than us and weaker, and they don't live nearly as long, but cognitively, they're no different."

"Hawthorne," I said, struggling to keep the skepticism out of my voice. "Are you saying that you think we are keeping a sentient, intelligent species with cognitive functions comparable to our own as food?"

"I know it sounds crazy," he said, running his hand through his hair again, making it even messier than before. "That's why I didn't say anything."

"I'm not saying you're crazy," I said, letting out an uneasy breath as I tried to wrap my head around this. I leaned forward, bracing my elbows against the table and watching him all but glare at his food.

"I'm just saying that those human rights groups are pissed off because of the ag-gag law, Hawthorne. It's no different than the fiasco that happened with the environmentalists who were pissed off about that dam that was constructed five years ago. They falsified data to try and show that an endangered species of bird was living on the river beds to delay construction. It wouldn't be the first time that they or any other extremist group embellished truths to try and push their agenda. Don't you think the whole concept is a bit absurd? If humans were intelligent, they would have laws in place to protect them."

"I know," Hawthorne acknowledged. "But the data they're citing is older than this ag-gag law, Gorski. The studies that she told me about are from decades ago – pre-tech days. I looked through the information she gave me when I got home, and they have been preaching this stuff for ages, but a lot of the data they're citing is incomplete because the papers referenced are physically damaged, so no one takes it seriously. But their message hasn't changed in decades. They've just been getting louder about it because of the law and because they think the conditions that humans are being kept in are continuously getting worse. Look – okay, you know how in school they taught us that we descended from humans, that we're the next evolutionary stage?"

"Yes." I nodded.

"Well, she didn't disagree with that," Hawthorne said, the words coming out quickly. "We did descend from humans and we are the next stage, but what she's saying is that the split happened much further along in the evolutionary chain."

"What do you mean?"

"What I mean is – the basis of everything we have now came from them. That's her theory. She's working on it with some people in the activist group, but they haven't published it yet because they're still researching it and they're dealing with a bunch of lawsuits. But that's what the group she's a part of is starting to suspect. The world we live in, the cities we inhabit – they were human cities originally. According to this girl, humans built this world, and we just took it over. Large parts of it were destroyed and lost in a war, but her point is, humans aren't stupid like monkeys. We're much more closely linked," Hawthorne said, and his words made my stomach curl in discomfort. "She said that the human girl she met was friendly and curious, and that she wanted to know how the sensor worked. Apparently, we're really not that different at all – except that they can live without us, but we need them."

I stared at him, completely lost for words. I had suspected that being involved in the protest crowd control had something to do with his recent aversion to real blood, but I figured he was just unsettled by the images on the signs he had taken away or that perhaps he was second-guessing the contents of the ag-gag law. I had never imagined that this was what was causing him anguish, nor had I ever even thought about these things before.

"So what are you saying?" I asked him after a long silence had stretched between us.

He snorted, shaking his head and letting his body slump. He looked so different from how I had ever known him to be. His confident exterior had wholly crumbled away to reveal cracked concrete and bent steel – like he was an old building two seconds from collapsing under its own weight.

"I don't know," he said, the words sounding just as lost as he looked. "I have no idea what I'm saying, Gorski. Not a clue. I'm just—"

He paused, sucking in a tight breath and holding it for a long moment before he let it all out and dropped his head into his hands with a heavy sigh.

"I'm just so confused," he murmured. "I don't know what I'm doing anymore. All I've ever wanted was to become a police officer, and my only goal for the last few years has just been to not get fired. Now, I feel like my mind is tearing itself apart. I don't know what to think anymore. I don't know if that girl was lying or not. I don't know if it's just conspiracy theories or what; I just know that I can't stop thinking about it."

I watched him sit there, feeling completely out of my depth.

"Please don't tell anyone," he whispered, slowly raising his head to meet my eyes once more. "At the office – or anywhere. Please don't repeat this. I don't want people thinking I've gone and lost it or become some human-loving bleeding heart."

"I won't say anything," I said, and I meant it. "You're my friend, Hawthorne – and this has nothing to do with work. I just worry about you."

A small smile touched his lips, and I could see him piecing together his usual carefree exterior.

"I always knew you had a thing for me," he said, his tone shifting back to his normal joking vibe. "It was only ever a matter of time."

"Right." I scoffed, but I couldn't help but smile at him. "You'll be waiting indefinitely for that."

"Oh, come on," Hawthorne said, pushing back in his seat and crossing his arms over his chest. His eyes trailed over my form, and he arched a brow at me suggestively. "You're not even just a little bit curious? You don't want to try it once to see if you'll like it? You're missing out, you know."

"I can't miss it if I've never had it," I said, picking up my fork before I fixed him with an appraising look. I let my eyes scan over his body in assessment, just as he had done to me, then I scrunched my nose. "Besides, you're not really my type."

"Ouch." He placed a hand over his heart with a pained expression. "You're so cold, Gorski. It's your loss."

"I'm alright with that," I said, feeling a small flicker of relief as Hawthorne picked up his fork and took a bite of his food.

"Oh!" he said after he had swallowed his first mouthful and taken a drink of water. "I can't believe I almost forgot – congratulations on making detective, Gorski. Nicely done."

I groaned, closing my eyes and letting out a breath. "I cannot believe how fast news travels in our precinct given the size of it."

"It really is rather impressive." Hawthorne nodded. "I think I knew about twenty minutes after you left."

"So right when Captain Mallick came back to the floor, huh?" I pushed my shawarma around with a frown. "I'm surprised he announced it. It's only probationary for three months. I would have thought that he would keep that quiet until he knew how things went for the first few nights at least."

"Well—" Hawthorne's fork stilled, and I glanced up at him in question.

"Well, what?"

"Technically, Captain Mallick didn't announce it. Lexie did," Hawthorne said. "She was a bit pissed that she was put on patrol duty with Tilson."

"Tilson?" I looked at him in confusion. "Why would Lexie be pissed about being put on patrol duty with Tilson? Tilson is great."

"I know Tilson is great," Hawthorne agreed. "She's always on time, super nice, brings in homemade snacks from her wife – her paperwork is impeccable."

"You really do have a weird fascination with paperwork," I muttered, and Hawthorne shot me a dirty look.

"I just like things organized," he said, his tone slightly defensive. "That's not the point, though. I don't think that Lexie has any real issues with Tilson."

"Then why was she pissed?"

"You know what she's like," Hawthorne sighed. "She doesn't like being caught off guard, and she's probably just jealous that you made detective so young."

"I agree she doesn't like change, but why would she care about me making detective on a probationary status?" I challenged. "She doesn't even want to be a detective."

He smiled, shaking his head as he looked at me.

"What?"

"As smart as you are, you still have your blind spots," Hawthorne replied. "She doesn't want to be a detective. She's just pissy that you have something she doesn't. You know what she's like. Remember what happened last winter holidays?"

"Maybe," I said, thinking back. My mother had gifted me an unnecessarily expensive scarf, and Grace had promptly gone out to buy an even better one, but I hadn't thought much of it at the time. I took another bite of my food as Hawthorne did the same. I knew Grace could be a bit jealous at times, but I doubted she actually cared. "She's probably just stressed about going on vacation."

"Maybe," Hawthorne said, taking another drink before his voice grew excited. "So – what's your first case?"

"Uh—" I took a long drink of water as I tried to decide what to say.

"Wait," Hawthorne said, his intrigue only seeming to grow as he leaned across the table toward me. "Is it top secret? Is it confidential? Are you going to save the world?"

"You really are just a big child. You know that, right?" He laughed, and I couldn't help but grin. Then my smile faltered when my mind shifted back to the question, and I dropped my gaze to the table. "My case isn't confidential. I checked it when I got home, so talking about it isn't an issue. I just—"

"Just what?" Hawthorne prompted when I remained silent.

"I'm not sure what my partner would think of me talking about it."

Hawthorne slowed, his fork dropping back to his container as his eyes traced over my face.

"Wait," he said, and my body involuntarily stiffened. "Who's your partner?"

"Hakim," I said, and I watched his body react. His eyes went wide, his body grew still, and he stared at me in disbelief.

"Hakim?"

I nodded.

"They partnered you with Detective Hakim."

"Yes."

"The Randall Hakim who—"

"Yes, yes – *the* Randall Hakim who caught the eastside strangler, busted the child trafficking ring two years ago, has more closed files than any other detective in our precinct, and allegedly drove his partner to become a drainer and OD on drugs. Yes, him," I said, fighting against the tightness of my voice. "And I'm pretty sure that he hates me. So this whole thing is going to be a disaster, and when he kicks me back to Patrol and Street, the entire precinct will know that our best detective doesn't like me, that I wasn't good enough, and my entire career will be over."

Hawthorne stared at me for a moment, and I knew he could see the fear behind my eyes. I had never been one to doubt myself, and he knew that, which was probably why he looked so uncertain.

"Okay," Hawthorne finally said, his voice slow but steady. "First – wow. Talk about an incredible partner to have. Second – he is terrifying. I had to share an elevator with him once, and I don't think I breathed the entire time. Third – I'm sure he doesn't hate you."

"You weren't there for the introduction, Hawthorne," I said as I leaned back in my chair. "He was the farthest thing from excited about working with me."

"I bet he's like that with everyone," Hawthorne countered.

"Captain Vogle said that, too, but I'm not sure it's the same," I said doubtfully. "He seems to think I'm a burden. He made it exceptionally clear that he has no interest in mentoring me, working with me, or even being around me. I'm pretty sure that he will be actively looking for any excuse to cut me loose."

"Then don't give him one," Hawthorne said, and I scoffed at his words.

"Obviously, I don't plan to give him one. You know me, I won't make any mistakes or give him the chance, but that won't stop him from looking for one regardless. He told me that he wasn't my babysitter, and I'm not even sure if he thinks I'm competent enough to carry my own gear bag."

Hawthorne frowned. "Why, because you're short?"

"Yes," I said, and my voice was clipped.

"Well, that's just ridiculous," Hawthorne said. "You can carry your gear bag just fine."

"I know I can," I said in exasperation. "Just like I know I can be a good detective. I know I can do this, Hawthorne. I'm not doubting my own capabilities – my point is that Hakim has already decided that I'm incompetent."

"But you're not incompetent. Everyone in the precinct who knows you knows that, and more importantly, Captain Mallick knows that."

"I know." I let out a sigh and closed my eyes. "If I didn't think I could manage this, I never would have applied, but if he doesn't like me and he sends me back, they may never promote me again. Even with the rumours, Hakim is one of the best detectives in Carneth and people love him. They respect him. His opinion matters, and if he says I'm not good enough, then people will believe that."

I opened my eyes to look at him, finding a genuinely empathetic expression across his face.

"You're not going to fail, Gorski," Hawthorne said, his voice soft. "I know you, and I know how tenacious you are. You might have to work harder – and he probably won't make this easy for you, but you can do this. Do you have the case file?"

"Yes."

"So, study it this weekend."

"Already started."

"Memorize it – we both know you can. Then prep for Monday and just be ready. Anticipate everything that he might ask you, and don't let him walk all over you. That's all you can do," Hawthorne said, then he looked at me thoughtfully before speaking once more. "And if it really goes that poorly or he's setting you up to fail—"

"I'm sure he isn't going to break policy. He's the best detective we have."

"But if he does – or if he's being unfair and sabotaging you, tell Mallick."

"Hawthorne—"

"I'm not saying go tattle on him." Hawthorne cut me off. "Just tell Mallick it isn't a good fit. I know you refuse to give up, but it would be better to step out yourself with a plan to come back later than have Hakim kick you to the curb and ruin your reputation before you even get the chance to start. After Lexie groaned about it, Captain Mallick made it abundantly clear that it was a temporary position to fill a hole. He made it sound like you're on loan to them because they're short on resources and needed the extra help. So if you come back to patrol before your probation is over, no one will think you failed out."

"I guess," I muttered, but my shoulders sank at the idea of just admitting defeat and walking away. "Mallick did say he had my back."

I stared at the table hard, my fingers curling into the somewhat rough material of my black uniform pants as I thought through everything that had been bothering me. I wasn't sure that I was willing to allow a single person to crush my dreams of becoming a detective simply because they didn't like me or thought I was too young – even if that person was the best detective in the precinct. I knew I could do this; I just needed a fair shot, and I already knew that I would never complain to Mallick unless Hakim broke our code of conduct. Even if Hakim turned out to be the rudest partner ever and the rumours about his insane work ethic proved true, I wouldn't complain. I refused. I would just have to find a way to make this work.

I let out a breath, forcing the doubts aside and glancing back up at Hawthorne.

"I'm sure it will be fine."

"It will," Hawthorne said, giving me a reassuring smile as he picked up his fork. "So, what's the case?"

"You're persistent, you know that?"

He grinned at me, and even though I still wasn't convinced it was the best idea, I told him about the case. I left out the key details and kept it high-level, mostly telling him information that was available to the public and that had been reported on the news, which was that several factory farms had been targeted by protest groups and human rights activists. At first, it was minor vandalism, which, while annoying, really didn't warrant a full-scale investigation. However, in the last month, the attacks had escalated to include outright property damage to the fenceline and the equipment used at the facilities – and Hakim suspected the attackers might be interested in the human stock.

Which was concerning for a number of reasons. First, it affected the farm's production. A human's gestational period closely matched that of a Reborn, and it took a lot of time and effort to breed new stock. Second, it violated federal human trafficking laws and ownership legislation. It was illegal for any Reborn to own a human, keep them in the cities, or release them into the wild because it impacted conservation efforts. Only agricultural facilities and food processing plants were allowed to handle and hold humans.

The first attack at the start of the previous month hadn't been too bad, and even though the corporation which operated the farm was angry about it, they hadn't been too concerned. The losses were covered by insurance, and they moved forward thinking that the attack was a one-off.

They were wrong. Two weeks later, it happened again. Then the following week, thousands of dollars of damage was done in a single day.

Since the farms were located just outside Carneth, the investigation technically fell under the jurisdiction of the Provincial Police, but the case was handed over to our precinct a week ago when it became apparent that they needed feet on the ground at the site on a regular basis. The Provincial Police weren't set up to support an operation like this. They handled highway patrols and specialized in traffic collision investigations and speed traps. Their nearest office was over two hours away, closer to Holton City.

So, as per protocol, the files were sent to the main precinct in the nearest city for support, and Hakim had been working on his preliminary investigation for the last few nights while he closed up other cases. Reading through the copy of the case file, it seemed like he was ready to start taking action, and that was why I would be driving out to the farms with him Sunday evening.

"It's going to be a long drive," Hawthorne said, and I nodded in agreement. "Do you think he'll talk to you?"

"I doubt it." I grabbed the empty food containers from the table and brought them over to the sink to rinse them. "I have a million questions I want to ask him, but honestly, the more I think about it, talking to him might be worse than just sitting there in silence."

"No kidding," Hawthorne said as he casually leaned against my counter, glancing out the tinted window where the sun was already well into the sky. He looked far too comfortable standing there for having only ever been to my place this one time. "It's getting late."

"It is," I agreed. "I should probably go to bed. I have so much to read tomorrow and a bunch to get ready for Monday's shift."

He nodded, pushing off the counter to move toward the door. I followed behind him, grabbing his jacket from the closet while he pulled on his shoes. Then he stood, towering above me once more as his lips twisted into a smile.

"Thanks for dinner, Gorski." He clapped me on the back in his usual fashion, and I couldn't help but smile. "I appreciate it."

"Of course," I said. "I'm glad you agreed to come over."

His eyes creased as he looked at me. Then, as if he could no longer handle the sincerity of the situation anymore, he took a step forward and arched a suggestive brow.

"So," he all but purred, "you still sure about this only being dinner? Or are you interested in some dessert, because—"

"Ughh," I groaned and rolled my eyes, shoving his jacket into his chest and reaching past him to open the door. "Get out of my apartment. I regret ever inviting you over."

"But you just said that you were glad I came!" he sputtered as I shoved him out the door and into the hall. He stumbled as he turned to look back at me, grinning widely.

"Yes, well, I lied," I said, gripping the door firmly in preparation of shutting it in his face. "Go home and take a cold shower. You need to cool off."

I heard him laughing as the door closed, and I had to fight not to smile as I locked the deadbolt, then made my way to the bathroom to get ready for bed.

Hakim

I scrunched my nose, trying to ignore the pungent smell of gasoline that filled the underground parking lot beneath the precinct. If we didn't get a new building soon, surely someone would get sick down here from lack of oxygen. In the meantime, I was left standing in the stink waiting for my ride. I glanced around the large, empty concrete space, making a mental note of each car and wondering if one of them belonged to Detective Hakim.

I couldn't imagine that he would drive a jeep, so my eyes quickly skimmed past it to look at the others. A van—probably not his. A regular sedan—possibly, it was black and nondescript, which had detective written all over it. There was an SUV next to it and a truck further down. I couldn't imagine him driving a truck either. I glanced over my shoulder, spotting three more nonspecific, normal-looking cars. Any of those could be his, or he may have parked on a lower level.

Along the far wall were the CPD vehicles designated to the Detective Unit, and a few were already missing. My heart sank as I looked at them, and I wondered if maybe Hakim had already come and gone and left me behind.

If that were the case, I would be back to Patrol and Street by sunset.

I forced the concern aside, glancing at my watch and rechecking the time. It wasn't even 7:30 pm. The sun didn't set until 8:45 pm tonight, and I had already been here for fifteen minutes. I had arrived well over an hour and a half before sunset because I refused to give Hakim any reason to doubt me or my dedication. He'd said to be here Sunday evening before sunset, so I had made damn sure that I was. I didn't even waste time going up to my desk. I had come in last night to grab anything and everything that I might need instead, and my gear bag had been packed and ready to go before I'd gone to sleep. Now it sat on the ground by my feet, stuffed with supplies.

I hadn't slept, not well at least, which wasn't good, but there was nothing I could do about that now. Though that detail probably didn't matter. My excitement and nerves would keep me wide awake even if Hakim was silent for the entire drive. Besides, I had lots to think about to keep my mind occupied for the hour it would take us to get to the first farm. I'd already looked at the map and memorized the case file. I knew nearly every single detail by heart, and I'd even flipped through a bunch of the procedural books for our precinct as a refresher.

Sure enough, Captain Vogle had been correct. I had gotten an email from the training board first thing Saturday evening informing me that I had passed my exam. I knew that I knew my stuff, and I had the grades to prove it—now I just needed to show Hakim I wasn't useless.

I frowned, looking around the underground parking garage once more and wondering if maybe he really was going to set me up to fail as Hawthorne had suggested. I wasn't expecting him to be nice to me after our rough introduction—hell, I wasn't even expecting him to be decent. But I had assumed that a man of his professional reputation was above blatant sabotage.

The elevator dinged just as the thought hit my mind, and I turned around to see Hakim step out of the doors with his gear bag slung over his shoulder. His mismatched gaze instantly found me, but he didn't react to my presence; he simply walked toward me with a set of keys in hand.

"Vehicle number 403," he said as he got closer, and I nodded and picked up my bag.

He didn't say anything else, and I followed him to the large SUV. He remained silent as he unlocked it, popping the trunk to throw in his gear bag and leaving it open for me as he walked around the vehicle to the driver's door. Swallowing down my discomfort, I tossed my bag in alongside his and then closed the trunk, making my way to the front seat to get in the car as the engine roared to life. I closed my door, fastened my seat belt, and glanced down at my watch, barely managing to keep the unimpressed expression off my face.

"Is there a problem?"

His rough voice sounded to my left, and I turned to look at him. He was watching my face carefully, something unreadable behind his eyes as his wrist hung loose on the steering wheel.

"No," I said, keeping my expression carefully blank before shifting my eyes to look out the front window. "I'm ready."

I could feel his gaze lingering on my face. Then, after a moment passed, he shifted, putting the vehicle in drive. I let out a breath as he drove us to the exit without another word. At least he seemed to be a good driver; that might be his only redeeming quality because it was 7:32 pm—a full hour before sunset—and I got the distinct impression that if I hadn't been standing there waiting for him, he would have left without me and not spared it a second thought.

Apparently, he wasn't above sabotage, and I didn't know how to feel about that.

I glared out the window as we drove along the highway, and the sun started to set. I was wrong. The quiet was awful. He didn't speak to me. He didn't look at me. He simply drove in silence, and I was left with the same horrible feeling that I'd had the night I met him.

I wished he would just outright say that he didn't like me. I wished that he would just say what he was thinking instead of ignoring me so completely it was as if I didn't even exist. Then again, maybe I didn't exist in his mind. Maybe I was so beneath him and so utterly incompetent in his eyes that he didn't think anything about me at all.

I wasn't even worth his dislike.

I swallowed, forcing the thoughts aside and running through the case file details instead, focusing on what was to come. If I couldn't keep my head right, then failing would be no one's fault but my own. It was exactly like Hawthorne had said—I just had to be ready. Anticipate what's coming and be prepared for anything. Show him that I know what I'm doing and that I'm worth more than cold silence.

The drive out into the country seemed to take forever. Each minute ticked by more slowly and painfully than the last as I tried to prepare myself. There was hardly anyone on the road at this hour, and after forty-five minutes of silence on the highway, Hakim took an off-ramp, and we made our way onto old country roads. I knew it would be another twenty minutes or so before we arrived. The sun was nearly fully set, so Hakim lowered the sunshield and rolled down his window, and I breathed a silent sigh of relief. At least it provided noise and some fresh air, but I didn't dare move or touch anything in the car myself. I just sat there stiff and uncomfortable until the trees and farmland changed, and a long stretch of fence came into view.

I couldn't help myself. I sat up straighter and turned to look out the window. I had never seen a factory farm before, and the case file didn't have any pictures in it.

I wasn't sure what I was expecting to see, but this wasn't it. The fence that ran around the perimeter was tall and topped with razor wire. Inside the fenceline there was nothing but long white buildings with rounded roofs. Dirt with tire tracks looped each building, but there was absolutely nothing in sight to suggest that anything lived here. The land was barren within the fencing, and if not for the Dolan's Agriculture company symbol painted on each unit, I would have had no idea what this operation was.

We passed at least seven long buildings before Hakim finally started to slow, and I saw the gate come into view. There was a tiny guardhouse at the break in the fence. It looked old and needed paint. There were two large cameras pointed at the road, but they looked nearly as aged as the guardhouse.

Tearing my eyes away from the fence and nearest white building, I reached for my badge, holding it up like Hakim as he rolled to a stop at the gate. A lanky guard named Raymond came out to greet us. He told us we were early, checked our badges, then instructed us to drive in toward the main building, where Carl would meet us in fifteen minutes. I nodded, making a note of the name. It matched the operations manager listed in the case file for this facility, but I didn't say anything and just put my badge away as Hakim drove inside toward the smaller white building near the back of the muddy lane.

It took nearly another two whole minutes to get there, and that short duration felt as long as the drive out. When the vehicle finally stopped, and Hakim rolled up his window, it was all I could do not to bolt from the SUV just to get away from him. I unbuckled my belt, let out a breath, and reached for the door handle, only to freeze when I heard the car doors lock.

I stiffened, slowly turning to look at him.

"We're early," he said, not bothering to so much as glance at me as he spoke. "We wait in the car until Carl comes out."

"Alright," I said, tracing through the procedures in my brain before confirming that this was not one of them.

He didn't seem to have anything else to say, so I shifted my gaze and stared out the front window. He didn't move. He didn't speak. He didn't review any case file notes or tell me his plan. He just sat there for seven whole minutes in silence. I struggled not to fidget as I wondered why the hell we couldn't just wait outside the car until his voice startled me.

"I read your personal file this weekend."

I turned to look at him, but he was still sitting there, calmly staring out the front window, arm draped casually over the wheel as if this awkward tension didn't bother him at all.

"Double major in criminology and law." His voice was slow and indifferent—quiet, and yet it filled the car and made me want to squirm in my seat. "Graduated in the top ten percent of your class, top marks in the Academy, perfect marksmanship scores, and you didn't get a single question wrong on the detectives' exam."

I didn't say anything. None of these were questions, and I found myself tensing as he finally turned to look at me and fixed me with a piercing stare.

"None of those things will help you here."

It hit like a physical blow, and I immediately wanted to take back my earlier words. I didn't want to know what he thought of me. I wanted him to go back to being silent and dismissive. But it seemed like he was determined to make me eat my own thoughts as if he'd known all along exactly what I was thinking.

"You're too young. Too inexperienced. You have no idea what you're doing, and book smarts aren't going to save you if we run into problems. Precinct 24 might have had some success by recruiting younger candidates, which makes us look bad since we're supposed to be the main precinct in Carneth, paving the way and supporting the others, but what Vogle forgot to mention is that two of those new recruits are currently in the hospital. One of them is in life-threatening condition. And they are all at least five years your senior with previous experience assisting on investigations. You are woefully out of your depth here, and assigning you to this case not only puts the investigation at risk, but it also puts me at risk," Hakim said, and even though his voice remained calm and level, I could feel the undertones of anger laced in his words. "You put my life at risk because you are simply too inexperienced to know any better, and regardless of how prepared you think you might be – you are going to make a mistake. And when that happens, you're not going to know how to react.

"I have no interest in working with you. I have no time to mentor you, and I most certainly am not going to end up dead because of you and the decisions being made by Vogle and the board of directors," Hakim continued. "What they teach you at the Academy doesn't prepare you for the real world. Things work differently in the field, and being on the side of the law doesn't always keep you safe – often, it places a giant target on your head."

I heard a door close, and I glanced out the front window to see someone approaching the car, but Hakim didn't move. His gaze remained locked on my face, and his eyes took on a serious glint.

"And I have neither the time nor the inclination to keep you from stepping on your own inevitable landmines." His voice had taken on a dark edge, and this time, I couldn't stop the tremor that ran down my spine. I knew that he saw it, but I forced myself to hold his gaze as he continued to obliterate my confidence. "So, you will watch, take notes, listen, do exactly as I say when I say it, and try to learn something. Don't touch anything. Don't do anything unless I tell you to do it. Don't waste my time with pointless questions. Think before you ask, but if they're critical to this case and what we're doing – you ask me. The last thing I need is you making decisions based on something that you read in a book. This isn't a game. This isn't a roleplay assignment at the Academy to test your knowledge of procedural processes. I don't need to see a demonstration of your leadership skills. I need you to stay out of my way, carry your own gear, and try to make yourself useful. Otherwise, you will be right back at your patrol desk tomorrow evening, and I promise you, you will never leave it."

He stared at me hard, his gaze all but burning into my own.

"Do you understand?"

I felt my head nod.

"Perfectly," I whispered, hating how weak my voice sounded.

"Good." His hand moved, and I heard the doors unlock. "You ever been to a factory farm before?"

"No," I said stiffly, watching as he pocketed his keys and opened the door.

He paused, turning back to look at me as something cold and ruthless flashed behind his eyes.

"Well, there's a first time for everything," he said, a dark smile crossing his lips. "Apparently, some find it a bit unsettling. I hope you didn't eat too much breakfast, Gorski."

With that, he got out of the vehicle, leaving me inside it in silence as he made his way around to the trunk. I could feel my fingers knotting into the fabric of my pants as I stared at the empty driver's seat and struggled to breathe.

How the hell was I supposed to work with him after that? Why should I even bother? He'd already made up his mind. Chances were, no matter what I did tonight, he would return me to Mallick with a stamp on my forehead that read "Rejected".

I could feel my hands shaking as the seconds ticked by, and my mind raced with his words.

What a complete and utter asshole. More than that, how stupid of me to think that I actually wanted to know what he thought. How stupid of me to think that this could ever work or that I stood a chance. I had just wasted my entire weekend preparing, studying, doing everything that I could to be ready, and none of it would matter.

I heard the trunk door open, and I turned my head to look between the two seats at him as he opened his bag to get something out. He looked so calm. So confident. So totally unbothered. So entirely indifferent. So uncaring that my career was sitting in his hands, and he could crush me in an instant. I could feel everything spinning and building in my chest like a wave—a bunch of tiny little doubts I had never considered collecting together and threatening to tear me apart as my body trembled.

Then, I stilled, and my eyes narrowed.

"I don't think so," I whispered, turning in my seat and yanking open the door.

If this asshole was going to reject me and send me back to Mallick, then he was going to have to work for it. I had come too far and pushed too hard. I'd worked my ass off to get this opportunity, and I knew I could do it. I shut the door with more force than necessary, rapidly making my way around the vehicle and grabbing the trunk hatch seconds before he shut it.

He froze, his hand gripping the metal above mine as he turned to look down at me. He didn't look surprised—his face was far too controlled for that—but there was something there dancing just out of reach, and I knew in my gut that he hadn't been expecting me to get out of the car. He'd made that speech on purpose. He was trying to make me give up. So I smiled at him, pushing the hatch up higher before I ducked beneath it to grab my gear bag.

"I need my notebook," I said, forcing my voice to remain polite as he stood there watching me pull out my stuff. I double-checked that my pens were still in my vest pockets before I stepped back from the trunk and fixed him with a level stare. "Otherwise, how will I take notes and learn?"

If he thought he could chase me away and scare me off, then he didn't know me at all. He may have read my personal file, but he had no idea who he was dealing with. His eyes creased ever so slightly, then they trailed up and down my form before he tilted his head toward my bag.

"Got everything?" he asked, and I nodded.

"Yes," I said, tucking my notebook under my arm and straightening my back. "I'm ready."

"Then let's go." He shut the trunk, shouldering his smaller bag and moving swiftly around the car.

I followed him in silence, staying exactly two feet behind him on the right as he made his way toward the tall figure waiting for us. I didn't speak until he introduced me, feeling strangely pleased that he seemed to be just as curt and unwelcoming to Carl the facility manager as he was to me. It was good to know that Hakim wasn't sexist—he just didn't like anyone.

"So, where do you want to start?" Carl asked after he had shaken my hand.

"I need to see the most recent attack location," Hakim said as his eyes trailed over the nearby buildings. "It had the most damage, correct?"

"Yes, that's right." Carl nodded in confirmation, the annoyance clear across his face. "This isn't the first time that we've dealt with minor vandalism, pranks, and young idiots trying to sneak in to poke at our stock and 'see a human'. But this isn't kids – this is organized, and it's a problem. We'd best drive out there, though. They attacked and damaged building six, and it's at the back."

"Alright," Hakim said, his gaze shifting back to the building behind Carl once more. "Is that your office?"

"Yes."

"You have maps? More recent ones?" Hakim asked, reaching into his pocket and pulling out a folded piece of paper. "The documents collected by the original responding provincial officers aren't nearly good enough. I need a facility map – the full layout, including any existing security measures you have and any changes that you've made in the last year.

"I need stock counts per building by age, copies of your security footage for as far back as you maintain it, a list of your equipment, where it's located, and any servicing that it's had in the last few months. I need a copy of your logbook showing who has come and gone through the gate in the last year – including shipping and receiving. And a register of your employees, including names, addresses, and employment records, a copy of their shift schedules for the last year, and the shift schedules you have planned for the next few weeks."

"You think one of my employees did this?" Carl said in disbelief. "The crew I have working here are top-notch. They've all been with Dolan's for five years or longer."

"I never said that they did anything," Hakim said, his tone flat as he turned to look at Carl. "But you reported the incident, and now I'm here to investigate it. If you would rather handle this privately or have it transferred to Precinct 6 in Holton, I'll head back to the office and close the file now. But I was under the understanding that this investigation was required by your insurance company and that they are looking for a findings report and recommendations list on additional security upgrades. This isn't personal, and it isn't a commentary on the integrity of those that you employ. This is standard procedure. I'm here to do my job, and without that information, I can't do it."

I watched Carl's face falter, a deep frown crossing over his features before his eyes darted to me to see if I would say anything different, but I didn't. Instead, I inclined my head. Jerk or not, everything that Hakim requested was legal and within the rights of the investigation lead. Yes, Carl could refuse to provide it. That was his right, but it would only hurt the investigation and they were the ones that had requested it. Some of the stuff Hakim rhymed off might be a bit overboard—I wouldn't have thought to ask about equipment maintenance, but I understood why he was requesting it.

Hakim wanted to know exactly who had come and gone from this facility over the last six months because he must suspect that whoever was attacking had some inside knowledge of some sort—but that didn't necessarily mean an employee. It could have been a mechanic who came by to fix something. It could have been a truck driver who came through or an agricultural health inspector.

Hakim was being thorough.

Incredibly thorough, and it was hard not to be impressed.

"Alright," Carl said finally, though he didn't look alright with it at all. "All of that's in the office, mostly electronic, thankfully, but it will take some time to compile the full logs because the guardhouse still uses paper records."

"That isn't a problem," Hakim said. "I brought some spare disks. Gorski will come to pick up the logs once you've made copies, and she'll be available to grab anything else you find that might be useful."

With that, Hakim stepped forward, making his way toward the office building as I let out a quiet sigh and fought against the urge to groan. On the one hand, he hadn't kicked me to the curb yet. On the other, he had just designated me as his lackey, who would waste hours driving around to collect data instead of actually shadowing him. It wasn't ideal, and it wasn't exactly what I'd had in mind when I'd thought about becoming a detective, but if it made me useful to him and kept me from getting kicked back to Patrol and Street, I would do it without complaint.

Besides, it was an important part of the investigative process, and someone had to do it.

"Here," I said, pulling my card from my vest pocket and handing it to Carl, who looked a bit taken aback. "My email is on there along with my office phone number – I wrote my personal cell phone number on there, too, in case there's an emergency. You can let me know when you have information, and I'll come to grab it."

"Great," Carl said, his voice far from enthusiastic as he took the card and turned to follow Hakim toward the office building. "I'm so glad you're both here."

I followed along behind him, biting my tongue the whole way as he unlocked the office and let us inside. He started with the most recent facility maps, giving us hard copies to take with us before he unlocked his computer and inserted one of the blank disks that Hakim had brought. Then he began making copies of everything he had. As the disk burned and the security camera footage downloaded onto a spare hard drive, I looked over the map, my brows creasing in confusion.

"Is this it for security cameras?" I asked, glancing up at Carl. He was seated behind his desk, answering questions when Hakim asked them while continuing to locate the requested data. "There are massive sections of fencing without any coverage."

Hakim glanced up at me, then shook his head and dropped his gaze back to the logbook he was skimming.

"Lady – do you have any idea how much fenceline we have to monitor?" Carl said, turning in his seat to glare at me. "Do you have any idea how expensive that would be?"

"But doesn't the cost of the damage outweigh the cost of the cameras?" I couldn't stop the question. It fell out of my mouth before I could stop it, and Carl snorted and shook his head.

"No, it doesn't," Hakim said, and when I turned to look at him, he was still staring at the logbook on his lap. "Public and private security cameras act more as a deterrent to criminals than anything else – but it's the stickers reading 'warning security surveillance in effect' that do the work, not the cameras themselves. They have never been proven to be effective at stopping crimes. The majority of the footage obtained by them cannot be used for conviction in a court of law because the video quality is either too poor or too far away for it to show anything useful. Unless a camera manages to record a criminal's face, unobscured and with perfect indisputable quality, a judge would never allow it to be used in a court case as evidence to convict an individual specifically.

"All security footage does is gather intel on generics – where the attack occurred, what time it happened, and potentially the heights of the perpetrators. Though often, those taking part in crimes will combat that by wearing bulky clothes, lifted shoes, masks – they've gotten creative over the years. In addition to that, most security cameras are installed incorrectly," Hakim continued indifferently as his gaze travelled down the log entries, pausing at the bottom before he flipped to the next page. "Aside from banks and commercial store exits, most places don't bother installing any reference points – making the video even more useless since it can't be examined to determine the heights of the offenders.

"This facility has kilometres of fenceline, Gorski," Hakim said, finally raising his eyes to meet my gaze. "They would need to install thousands of cameras to fully monitor the entire perimeter and the buildings inside, and even then, the majority of it would remain useless. Cameras only range so far, and in order to get a decent image of someone's face, they would need to be low, angled correctly, and spaced even closer together. The amount of money it would cost to install that system, maintain it, monitor it, and store the video files would be astronomical – and it would be for little to no gain. It's not profitable, nor is it practical. The cost of the damage done from a rare event of vandalism for a facility of this size is a drop in the bucket in comparison to installing the security system required to monitor the entire fenceline."

"I see," I said, and my face flushed with embarrassment as Carl chuckled. "So – then what's the plan for stopping these attacks?"

Hakim stared at me. He didn't appear mad that I had asked, but it was clear that I had just cemented all his opinions about me in his mind. I didn't know anything. Not by his standards. I was inexperienced. Naive. I could feel unfamiliar doubts starting to creep back into my mind, but I shoved them aside, refusing to let them take hold. Instead, I clenched my jaw tight, holding his gaze with determination as I did my best to swallow down the embarrassment.

I was supposed to be learning, and that was precisely what I was doing.

"We anticipate the next target based on the evidence that we do have," Hakim answered. "Then we set up a monitoring system in those areas specifically. But just like this facility, we only have so much equipment. We cannot watch the entire fenceline. It's impractical. That's why we need all of this data. It's clear that these attacks will continue until stopped, so to stop them, we think like them, then we cut them off before they do it again."

"Well, at least one of you seems to know what you're doing," Carl said as he got up from his desk to go fix himself a coffee. "Better than those idiots from the provincial team that came by."

I swallowed, fighting the urge to react to the dig Carl had made as I held Hakim's gaze. He didn't say a word. His expression remained unreadable, then he turned back to Carl to ask something else. I took notes as they spoke, but I didn't ask any other questions. Instead, I just listened and looked over the map, familiarizing myself with the layout of the buildings and noting the attack locations.

It took nearly three hours in total to copy all the data that Carl had before Hakim was finally satisfied and stopped asking questions. Then, we went back outside and made our way to the vehicle. I let Carl sit in the front so he could direct us and took careful notes of the information he shared along the drive to the back of the facility. When we reached building six and got out of the car, Hakim handed me a camera from his gear bag and told me to take pictures. I didn't question it. There were already pictures from the initial reports, but it was quite clear that Hakim thought they'd done a terrible job, so I planned to take pictures of everything. I refused to give him any other reason to doubt me after what had happened in that office.

Carl led us around the building to show us the damage.

The fence had been cut, but it had been cut a decent way away from the building. Any tracks that might have been visible were long gone, but I photographed the damaged fence anyway and the surrounding area. There was no evidence. I knew from reading the case file that the initial crime scene investigation hadn't found even a single fingerprint, fibre, or footstep, so it was impossible to know how many offenders there were.

The door to the long white building had been damaged, and the alarm had somehow been bypassed, so now there was a hefty padlock installed as a temporary solution. I took pictures while Carl informed us that they were still using the building for livestock storage because they had nowhere to move them right now, but the blood-processing units were completely ruined, and the building was considered offline.

A total of six pumps had been damaged. One drum was punctured, two more had critical-level equipment knocked off, and several pipes had been cut. No humans were missing because this building housed mature adults, and past cases from several decades ago suggested that only the youngest stock would be targeted for theft, so the intent here had been property damage.

I let out an impatient breath as I waited for Carl to pull out his keys and unlock the door. When the click sounded, Hakim shifted, stepping back to allow me to move inside first, behind Carl. I wasn't really sure what to make of it, it was an unexpectedly polite gesture, but the second I stepped over the threshold and into the large building, I froze.

The smell was overwhelming.

I had noticed it when we arrived, but there was a breeze tonight and it hadn't been that bad, so I hadn't thought too much about it. Now, standing inside the door looking around the white building, I felt smothered in it. It was thick. It was rank. It was a horrible combination of blood, waste, and a pungent, musky scent I had never encountered before. I couldn't swallow. I couldn't seem to breathe as everything in my body went stiff, and my eyes grew wide at the unbelievable sight before me.

There were humans in here.

Hundreds and hundreds of humans, and it was like nothing I could have ever anticipated. Some of them were sleeping. Some of them were just sitting there leaning against the walls of their metal-barred stalls, staring into nothing. All of them had permanent PICC lines inserted into their arms or necks. They looked weak. Thin. Pale. Unnervingly similar to Reborn, except for their much smaller size and empty stares.

The one nearest to the door turned its head, its lifeless-looking eyes narrowing at me as its gaze travelled up my form, then stopped on my face. It stared at me. *She* stared at me, and I felt all the air leave my lungs.

She had pale green eyes, just like Hawthorne. And as his name came to mind, all his words from Friday morning quickly followed. An uneasy feeling started to slide down my spine. I couldn't look away from the human's eyes. I jolted as something touched me and turned quickly to see Hakim standing directly behind me, gripping my shoulder tightly as he leaned down and his low, gravel voice echoed by my ear.

"Get it together or get out," he murmured, then he let go of my shoulder, pushing past me to follow Carl toward the damaged equipment at the back of the building.

I made myself inhale the awful-smelling air, ignoring the dull tremble that seemed to be coursing through my body as I gripped the camera tighter. Then I let the breath out and made my legs move, following along behind my partner.

I could feel hundreds of eyes on my body. They were watching my every move, tracking each and every step I took.

I examined the equipment that Carl showed us as Hakim asked more questions. He remained entirely unfazed and unbothered by our surroundings. I took pictures. I took notes. I paid attention and listened to everything they said, but I didn't look at any of the humans again.

I couldn't.

Humans

I stared out the window into the growing night, watching the trees whip by as my mind wandered.

Working with Detective Hakim was both more difficult than I could have ever imagined and easier than I'd dreaded it would be. What made it easy was that he didn't talk to me unless there was a purpose or he was giving me directions, which meant that I wasn't forced to share personal information about myself to make conversation. I had never particularly enjoyed that aspect of work, as it always felt like a waste of time, so it was nice that neither one of us had to pretend to get along. He wasn't interested in being friendly and making small talk, and he was incredibly comfortable with sitting in silence, which would make any normal person tense.

What made it challenging was trying to reconcile the enormity of the gap that existed between us. He was so much more skilled than I had anticipated, and keeping up with his work ethic was a challenge, because Hakim was a monster.

He didn't stop.

He just kept going. I had been told by my instructor at the Academy and by Captain Mallick several times over the years that I needed to slow down. I was used to being told that this wasn't a sprint, that personal health was important and required to function in this job, and that, yes, the working hours did apply to me, and I needed to comply with them. Officers were only allowed to work so many hours in a week, and after several very dangerous incidents had occurred in the past, the CPD had started taking that seriously and monitoring shifts more closely.

Apparently, those same rules did not apply to the detectives.

And further still, they didn't even exist in Hakim's world.

I felt like I was running full tilt, sprinting as fast as I could, and yet, still, I was ashamed to admit that I could not keep up with him. After finishing our work at Dolan's factory farm on Monday, which had involved going to see all the other break-in locations, taking more photos, and walking a few sections of the fenceline to get a lay of the land, we finally returned to the precinct. I followed Hakim up to the eleventh floor, ignoring that it was well past sunrise and our shift was officially over, and proceeded to spend the next several hours working in a large boardroom that had been converted into his office.

He gave me the largest printed map, told me to pin it on the wall and plot out the exact locations of each known entry point, damage, camera location—everything. Then he told me to add in any significant reference points outside the fenceline. That was my job. If we knew something about the physical location of anything, it was to go on the map, so that was precisely what I did. I spent over two hours painstakingly assembling our map on the wall, cross-referencing the reports with the coordinates and double-checking the scale with a ruler to make sure that I plotted it correctly. When I was finally done, I took a picture of it for backup and printed a copy to keep in my files for reference. Hakim glanced at it, said nothing, then told me to use the spare computer Vogle had IT bring in to start scanning through security footage for the dates on which the attacks had occurred.

While I watched a bunch of blurry, useless footage, he started to cross-reference employee names and information to their shift schedules, checking for patterns or anything to suggest that there may be a suspect on the list.

There wasn't.

The shifts were consistent but not suspicious. Given the location of the attacks compared to where the employees were known to be located at the time, there was nothing to suggest that they had helped in any manner. They may have given out information about the facility and assisted in the background, but they certainly hadn't participated during the events of each attack.

I lost track of time as the video played by and I kept a list of each file reviewed. As Hakim had suggested while we sat in the office with Carl, nothing on the tapes showed anything. Even if someone had walked directly in front of the camera, they would have just looked like a blurry blob because the technology was so old and the placement was so poor. It wasn't until Hakim stood up, grabbed his jacket and bag, and told me to leave and be back the following evening so we could go out to the next facility that I finally stopped working.

Except this time, I asked him specifically what time he planned to leave. His eyes creased at my question, and I knew that he knew that I knew that he would leave without me if I wasn't there on time, and this would all be over.

"7:30 pm," he said, shutting the door to the boardroom behind us and locking it with his key.

I ended up leaving the precinct with him, riding down the elevator in silence as he remained unbothered by everything, including my presence. I was so tired; I didn't even watch to see what vehicle he moved toward.

After tossing my gear bag into the backseat, I somehow managed to drive myself home, immediately going to shower as I tried to block out the smell of the farm from my memory. I forced myself to eat, then crawled into bed, falling asleep before my head even hit the pillow.

I genuinely don't think he believed that I would come back to work with him for a second night. For a brief moment, I even wondered if that was why he had pushed so hard. Perhaps, similar to his cutting speech in the car, he was trying to deter me—trying to make me give up by making it seem like the job was impossible.

I was wrong.

The second night was just as brutal, and Hakim made no indication of needing to nor wanting to slow down. I got out of bed at precisely 6:00 pm, showered, ate, packed, and made my way to the precinct. Hakim exited the elevator at 7:29 pm, and we got into vehicle number 403 at exactly 7:30 pm.

Apparently, he was above blatant sabotage; he just wasn't willing to give me anything for free. A lesson I learned very quickly and kicked myself for not having realized it the night we met. I could have asked him during our introduction what time he *specifically* wanted to meet, but I hadn't. If I had shown up late and he'd left me behind, that would have been my fault. This was his case, and I was just an unwanted little pest trailing by his side. So if I wanted to continue to be present, I would need to step it up and ask where I needed to be and when.

Tuesday shift, the drive was just as silent as the first. He didn't say a word, and I didn't move in my seat. When we arrived at the second facility, which was another few kilometres further northwest, I didn't try to get out of the vehicle while we waited for the operations manager to come to meet us. Instead, I sat there, staring out the window until our host exited the office building, and this time, Hakim didn't lock the doors or say anything. We got out of the SUV, made our way to the trunk, and he waited for me to grab my notebook and gear before closing the hatch.

I followed him to meet Jonathan, and we repeated the same process as the night before, except this time, I knew better what to expect. This time, I didn't say anything about the lack of security cameras. I just collected all the information that Jonathan had and took as many notes as I could. I paid closer attention to the facility layout as Jonathan directed us around and gave us a tour. I even looked at the surrounding area outside the fenceline, gauging how far away the forest was while making a mental note that this operation was closer to the Norhaven Wildlife Reservation.

We finished up at the second factory farm much more quickly because there was no damage to examine, and we returned to the precinct before sunset. Yet despite this, and despite our shift being nearly over, I followed Hakim back upstairs, ignoring the curious glances that I got from passing officers, then spent another long morning crawling through data with Hakim.

Wednesday shift was more of the same—a third night spent entirely in the office crawling through information until sunlight traced through the sky.

I found absolutely nothing useful in the security footage from the dates of the attacks. I ran rapid background checks on the maintenance crew who had come in to repair a pump the month prior and found nothing but clean records, but I submitted them for an extensive review regardless. Then, Hakim gave me half the guardhouse logbooks and told me to "check them". If not for having observed him working on the employee records and shift schedules the night before, I'm not sure that I would have completed this new task to his standards. But, having seen him work, the first thing I did was create an electronic spreadsheet— making a note of every unique name that had been to the facility, when they had visited, and for how long.

It took hours to get the data entered, and I knew it would take hours more to comb through it and find anything useful. It was tiring, and for the first time in my life, I started to question my own capabilities. Yet despite this, I felt proud.

I had made it through three nights of working with Hakim. He hadn't sent me back yet. He hadn't told me to get out, and I was starting to realize that if he looked at my work and remained silent, it meant I had performed adequately enough to remain in his presence. I never got compliments, nor was I ever told that I had done something well. I knew that he would continue to push me and try to make me leave, but if I could keep this up and continue to be useful to him, then I might just stand a chance.

I might actually get to remain a detective, and if I could survive Hakim, then I could survive anything.

I straightened in my seat as the familiar fenceline came into view, but this time, Hakim drove past the gate when we reached it. He continued on for another five minutes down the road before turning onto an old dirt path that ran along the facility on the outskirts of the fence. The SUV rocked on the uneven ground as we made our way further and further from the main road to the back corner of the property. Then, Hakim stopped, and we got out.

"Keep your radio on at all times," Hakim said, tossing me one from the trunk as he pinned his own to his hip. "Follow the map and use the GPS device if you need it. Make sure you don't get lost and put the sensor sets at the exact coordinates that I told you to and make sure the cameras are properly connected. Each sensor pair can't be more than twenty feet apart, and you need to make sure they're hidden from view, assuming a northerly approach. Don't mess it up. Check each set before you move to the next location because I don't want to have to come back and fix your mistakes."

"Got it," I said, grabbing my small supply bag and looping it across my chest before taking the larger gear bag stuffed with sensors and pulling the straps over my shoulders.

I double-checked that I had my compass and extra battery pack for the GPS device. The last thing I wanted to do was get lost in the woods; that would be immediate grounds for Hakim to send me back. Then I grabbed my notebook and made sure I had my paper map and cell phone safely tucked into my vest. I wasn't sure if there would be much service out here, but I figured it was better to bring it than not.

"And watch your footing," Hakim said as he closed the trunk, locking the vehicle before he hauled on his own gear bag and set out into the woods. "If you get caught in a trap and can't get yourself out, I'll leave you there until I'm done with my section."

"A trap?" I asked, my brow creasing as I followed along behind him. "You think that they put traps up around the edge of the fenceline? What would be the point?"

To my surprise, he stopped mid-stride and turned to look at me fully.

"Not the attackers, Gorski," he clarified. "The operations manager and local hunters."

"But trapping is illegal," I said, stopping alongside him to meet his gaze. "If there are wild humans outside of the reserve and a hunter was caught poaching them or other wild animals, they would be charged. It's illegal to hunt outside of open season. That's a serious federal offence, and if the operations manager of this facility was found to have been laying traps – even if it's to protect their facility from attackers – they would have a lawsuit on their hands."

"And?" he challenged, his voice taking on a dark edge as an unnerving glint shone in his eyes. "We're in the country, in the middle of a forest; there's no one around to see or hear anything. Do you think the activists planning this would be foolish enough to report it if they got caught? How do you expect we would prove those traps were laid by the operations manager? Or link them to a hunter poaching humans? Better yet – do you think anyone would care? Losing a few dozen wild humans to poaching each year doesn't damage their population. It's not our concern."

I stiffened, and an uneasy feeling tugged through my chest.

"Illegal as they may be, traps are an effective deterrent that will leave behind ample physical evidence. So, watch your feet," Hakim said, turning and moving forward once more. "A foothold trap won't kill a Reborn, but they are difficult to pry open, and you'll be left with a nasty scar. We have eight hours until sunrise, don't be late."

I swallowed, forcing myself to follow along behind him as I fought the urge to frown. Even though he had turned away, I could hear the dark amusement in his voice.

We parted ways another thirty feet into the woods. Hakim made his way west while I made my way east toward the first location that he had identified as a potential entry point. I placed my sensors eighteen feet apart, confirming the coordinates with my GPS device and making sure that the laser was unobstructed before I connected the corresponding camera, which would be activated only when the sensor was tripped. Then I tested the set and moved on to the next location.

The process was incredibly tedious and unexpectedly tiring. The two gear bags were heavy, and carrying them together was cumbersome. I made sure to take my time, carefully hiding each sensor behind a tree, log, or rock—low to the ground, so it was unnoticeable—all while watching my feet.

A part of me wanted to believe that Hakim was just trying to frighten me away again and that the illegal traps were a lie. It was difficult to imagine someone of his position being so dismissive of federal laws, but the deeper into the woods I went, the quieter it seemed to get. There was nothing but the rustle of leaves. I was keenly aware of just how alone I was, and doubts started to form.

'Gorski.'

I jolted, my hand reaching for the radio on my hip as my pulse spiked at the jarring noise.

"Yes," I said, pressing the button to transmit my voice.

'I'm finished with the western segment and on my way back,' Hakim's voice crackled in response. *'Just under two hours until sunrise. You had better be done.'*

"I'm setting my last set now," I said, glancing at the large oak tree which I planned to use to hide my final sensor. It was twenty feet away from a massive rock formation, which I made a mental note to mark on our map.

'Get a move on.'

"Yes, sir," I said, putting the radio back on my hip and letting out a sigh.

I set the sensor as quickly as I could, double-checking that it was functional before connecting the camera and shouldering the empty gear bag. Then, I turned around and made my way back to our starting point. I moved as quickly as possible while still being careful as the sounds of morning started to ring out through the trees. Birds were chirping. A dim glow was working its way through the sky. My watch beeped to let me know I only had an hour left until the sun was up, and I swallowed down my discomfort. I knew I could push the limits—I wouldn't get burned until roughly an hour after the sun peeked over the horizon, but I picked up my pace just the same.

For all I knew, Hakim would just leave me in the woods if he got to the SUV before me, and that thought only spurred me to move even faster. I would die out here without my blackout gear unless I could find enough shade to last the entire day.

Following my GPS device and map, I jogged along the final stretch of ground for twenty minutes until I saw the fenceline. Then I slowed, letting out a breath of relief. I could just make out the SUV in the distance through the growing light that was making it harder to see, and Hakim was leaning against the bumper, looking over a large map.

He hadn't left. He was actually waiting—so maybe I wasn't giving him enough credit. That or he figured that dealing with the paperwork of leaving me to die was too bothersome.

"Cutting it close," Hakim said as I neared the SUV and unshouldered my two bags.

He rapidly folded the map he was looking at and stuffed it into his vest, then reached out to take my bags. The gesture was unexpected and caught me off guard, but I let him take them as he gestured with his head for me to get inside the vehicle. I moved toward the passenger side door as he quickly opened the trunk and tossed my stuff inside.

"Sorry, sir," I said after he had closed the trunk and climbed into the vehicle by my side. "I had some trouble with sensor set four; it wasn't synching."

"Did you get it?" he asked, starting the vehicle and putting the sunshield up.

"Yes."

"Good."

He didn't say anything else, and I closed my eyes and sank into my seat. We drove back to the precinct in silence, parked in our usual spot among the row of CPD vehicles and then made our way to the elevator. I marked the rock formation and a few other key details on the map using the GPS coordinates I had scribbled down, then watched through a few more hours of useless surveillance footage before Hakim called it a night.

"Gorski."

"Yes, sir?" I turned to look at him as I grabbed my gear bag from the floor by my chair.

"Take this home and start looking it over," he said, stepping toward me and holding out a thick file. I took it from him, my eyes narrowing at the confidential stamp that crossed the cover of the manila folder.

"What is it?" I asked, looking up to meet his gaze. He stared at me silently for a moment, then arched his brow as if I were an idiot.

"Another case file," he answered, and I felt my shoulders sag. "Or did you think detectives only worked one thing at a time?"

"No, sir." My voice was quiet as I pulled the file tighter to my chest. "I'll get familiar with it this morning."

"Good," he said, grabbing his own bag from the ground before moving toward the door. "Because you will be running background checks this weekend and compiling a timeline of the bodies."

I nodded, because I didn't have anything to say. I followed him from the boardroom, waiting for him to lock the door before we both made our way to the elevator in silence. When we reached the parking garage, I watched him move toward a car along the far wall, noting that it was black, nondescript, and just as unnoticeable as I had expected it to be. Then I got into my own car and fought the urge to yawn.

I wasn't used to feeling tired, and the drive home felt long. My legs were sore from trekking through the woods, and I realized that I would need to find time to start exercising again if I wanted to keep up with him. I had no idea how he'd been able to get back to the SUV so quickly when his section had three more sensor sets than mine did. Perhaps he was just quicker at setting them up because he had used them before, or maybe he was in even better shape than I had thought.

I groaned, dropping my head on my hand as I pulled into the underground parking garage of my building.

I parked in my designated spot, grabbed my gear from the backseat, and then made my way to the elevators. I didn't feel like cooking, so when I finally got inside my apartment, I just ate six gelatin cubes before collapsing at my table to review my notes. Yet no matter how many times my eyes trailed over the pages of my notebook, I couldn't seem to see the patterns that Hakim saw. I wasn't sure why he'd picked the area that he had for us to monitor. I could understand the western front where he had gone to set sensors because it was closer to the outbuilding that housed the youngest humans, which we suspected were a target, but I had no idea why he'd had me move so far east.

Maybe he'd just wanted to give me something to do.

Letting out a frustrated groan, I pushed my notes away, grabbing the new case file that Hakim had given to me before I'd headed home. I couldn't help but grimace at the images and details when I flipped it open, and I wondered if I would ever get used to seeing things like this.

Then I wondered if I should.

If anyone ever should.

It was a case file for four dead bodies scattered throughout the southeast side of Carneth, which had been initially discovered by officers in Precincts 38 and 40. With both precincts being in our jurisdiction and neither having their own Detective Unit, the cases were passed to us to handle as per regular protocol. The most recent account had happened nearly a month ago, but the recorded case data was vague at best and seemed to be tossed into the folder with little care.

How had Captain Mallick done this for fifty years? How had Detective Hakim done it for over thirty? I knew that not every investigation dealt with factory farms or violent murders, but still. How did they sleep? How did they go home to their families and have any sort of normal life after seeing these things?

Actually, I wasn't sure if either of them even had families...

I frowned, my stomach knotting as my eyes lingered on the image of a body with lifeless eyes—an unidentified young female, according to the notes in the file. It unsettled me for multiple reasons, some of which I didn't know how to process. Yet I couldn't stop looking at it, and I wasn't sure that I would have put the image down if not for the knock on my door.

Jerking in my chair, I turned to look at the thick, dark wood. "Who the hell?"

I stood, taking a moment to quickly tuck the photos back into the folder and close it before I made my way over. Then I paused, hesitating a moment before looking through the peephole, only to groan out in annoyance.

"Hawthorne," I said, unlocking the deadbolt and yanking the door open. "What the hell are you doing here?"

"Gorski!" He grinned as he leaned against the doorframe. "I just got off patrol; thought I'd swing by."

"You know, just because you know where I live now doesn't mean that it's an open invitation to stop by."

"Not even if I bring tea?" he asked, holding up two large paper cups.

"It's 12 pm," I sighed. "A bit late for tea, don't you think? And who even let you in the building at this hour?"

"Some nice old lady with a red bag," Hawthorne answered, and I mentally cursed Mrs. Bailey for being fooled by his charm. "But that's not the point. It's decaf, I haven't seen you since last week, and I heard that Hakim is working you to the bone. So I figured you could use a break. You want the tea or not?"

I stared at him, willing myself to send him away, but the scent of fresh tea filled my nose and his familiar, kind, and genuinely happy smile was comforting after having faced nothing but Hakim's abrasive edges for the last four nights.

"I want the tea," I said, opening the door wider and waving him inside. "Now get in here before one of my neighbours sees you and thinks this is some kind of inappropriate midday rendezvous."

"You make it sound like you would be embarrassed if people thought we were together." He laughed, stepping inside and turning around to face me as I closed the door. His smile faltered at my expression. "Wait a minute – you'd be embarrassed if people thought we were together? Why? I'm a great catch!"

"Don't be dramatic." I grabbed one of the teas from his hand and made my way toward the small table to sit down. "You know perfectly well that anyone would be embarrassed to be dating you."

He snorted, and I turned back to see him grin.

"So, how's it been?" Hawthorne asked, pulling out the same chair he'd sat in the last time. Then he collapsed into it like he couldn't bear to stand any longer.

"In a word," I said, popping open the tab to take a drink of the warm beverage. "Brutal."

"That's not good," he murmured as he opened his own drink.

"Nope. But at least he hasn't kicked me back yet. What about you? Why are you getting off shift so late?"

"We had trouble clearing the square before sunrise," Hawthorne said, his expression weary as his shoulders slumped. "Had a bunch of paperwork to file afterward as a result."

"They put you on crowd control again?"

"Yup."

"It's getting worse, isn't it?"

"Yup," Hawthorne sighed, taking a long drink from his cup. "Three people were sent to the hospital with severe burns and sun poisoning, and more than half a dozen small fights broke out."

"That's not good."

"Nope." He met my gaze and gave me a weak smile. "So tell me – in detail – what's it like? What's he like?"

"He's cold," I answered, leaning back in my chair as I thought about how best to summarize Hakim. "Uncaring, detached – he works like a machine. I've never seen anything like it. After going to the factory farm the first night, we came back to the precinct, and he brought me up to a boardroom that he uses as an office, and then we set up for the case. We worked for hours, Hawthorne. Hours and hours, crawling through the data. Then finally, at 1 pm, he told me to go home and be back at 7:30 pm so we could head back out to the neighbouring facility owned by the same company to gather their data as well. He didn't even stop to eat – he never stopped once. If not for the tablets I'd packed and the mints in my desk, I would have had nothing, and who knows what state I'd be in.

"Then," I said, meeting Hawthorne's gaze. "It was the same thing the next night. Nothing but data crunching. And tonight, we went out to set up monitors at the first location where Hakim suspects the facility might be targeted."

"That's intense," Hawthorne said, and I nodded in agreement. "How are you holding up?"

I scoffed, shaking my head before I dropped my elbow against the table and leaned my chin on my hand.

"I don't even know anymore," I whispered, staring blankly at the dark, wooden surface. "He gave me another case to look at. It came from 38 and 40, dead bodies found on the southeast side. I was just taking a look at it before you got here – there isn't much information. I don't think the responding officers really put any effort into it. They barely took any photos and seemed to want to pass it off as gang violence, but all the victims appear to be female. I'm not sure what Hakim plans to do with the case given the lack of data and leads, but I don't know how or when we'll fit it in.

The factory farm attacks already take up all our time and yet he seemed completely unbothered by the additional work. He's not like anyone else I've ever worked with. He's on a different level, and I'm not sure I can keep up."

Hawthorne scoffed. "Don't sell yourself short, Gorski. You work incredibly hard."

"I know." My voice came out softer than I wanted it to, and I could feel the same strange sensation that had been bothering me these last four nights tugging across my chest again. "I'm not selling myself short. I know I work hard, Hawthorne. It's just—"

I hesitated, swallowing hard as the sensation continued to grow.

"He's just so much more experienced than me," I whispered. "I knew this would happen. I knew there would be a learning curve. I just – I didn't realize how much I didn't know. I guess I'm just wondering if I might be in over my head and about to drown."

I couldn't believe I'd said it out loud, but as I looked at him, I could see the understanding in his gaze.

"Then I guess you had better learn how to swim," Hawthorne said, and I couldn't help the small laugh that left my lungs as I shook my head. He was the only person who knew how true that was. "You'll regret it if you give up."

"I know." I nodded, straightening in my chair once more. "And I never would – I guess this is just the first time I've ever wondered if my best will be enough."

"Welcome to my life," Hawthorne muttered, and I smiled at him. "It will be okay, Gorski. Worst case, you get fired, I'll quit, and we can go start a business."

"Is that so?" I arched my brow as I took another sip of tea. "And what would we do?"

"No idea." Hawthorne grinned as he took another drink from his own cup. "So, Hakim being an unstoppable force of nature aside, how's the case going?"

"Alright," I said, and I tried to focus on the positive, which was that we had already made some progress. "We're going to be going out to check the sensors every few nights for the next three weeks. Based on the past attacks, it seems like the frequency is increasing, but there's been a lull after the last one – probably because it was so big, and they know law enforcement is involved now. So we're expecting the next attack to hit in a week or two. Hakim is following up on some leads in the city, and Dolan's Agriculture, the company who owns the facility, is sending in some more monitoring equipment at the end of this week. We're going to set them up first thing next week at the second facility to try and better our chances. Unfortunately, it's sort of a game of cat and mouse at the moment. The more they strike, the more data we'll have and the better we can anticipate their moves, but the more they strike, the more pissed off the company will get and the more pressure we'll be under to stop this.

"We're going to a third site tomorrow, one much farther east to gather their information too. Despite being a more inconvenient location to attack, Hakim thinks that whoever is behind this might try anyway just to make it harder to track and anticipate their movements," I explained. "So, for the next foreseeable future, we'll basically be monitoring set locations, checking sensor data, and then adjusting based on the findings. It's obvious that each operation is meticulously planned, and they're scoping out the facility beforehand. If we have the next target locations correct, they should trigger our cameras before they actually attack, and we'll be able to isolate the next areas of interest and hopefully be there to stop them in the act."

"So a lot of crunching data, making assumptions, long awkward car rides, and tramping through the woods?" Hawthorne said.

"Pretty much." I nodded. "And now in between that, I get to run background checks on the list of potential suspects Hakim gave me for these murders."

"You know, I think Lexie might have the right idea," Hawthorne said after taking a long drink. "Stay on patrol and push papers."

I snorted, taking another sip of my tea and wondering if that was maybe why some officers never progressed. I had always assumed their stagnant careers were due to them being incompetent in some way. I had never even stopped to consider that their positions might be voluntary.

"So," Hawthorne said, his voice sounding almost hesitant. "Did you see one?"

"Did I see one of what?" I asked before taking another drink.

"A human."

I stilled, the tea lingering in my mouth as I struggled to swallow. The scent of blood and waste flooded my nose as images of the large white buildings filled my mind. I could nearly taste the musky odour that had clung heavily to the air. It was salty, almost bitter, and I had come to learn from Carl that it was the smell of sweat. I had almost forgotten just how rank the air had been. I hadn't let myself think about it. I hadn't even had the time, what with barely getting any sleep and being Hakim's shadow for the last ninety-six hours as I crunched through seemingly endless piles of data so he could statistically analyze where the next hit might be. So it was startling just how quickly and accurately my body recalled the foul memory.

I forced myself to swallow, and the tea didn't taste nearly as good anymore.

"Yes," I answered, my voice quieter than I wanted it to be. "I saw lots of them."

"What were they like?" Hawthorne asked, and even though he kept the question simple and lighthearted, I knew it was a loaded gun. Just as I knew that this tea was made from synth.

I hesitated, and I felt like I could taste the smell of the facility in my mouth as my gaze dropped to the table once more.

"They were exactly like they looked from the pictures at school," I said, and I could see him looking at me intently from the corner of my gaze. "And they were nothing like them at all."

I stared at the table, my eyes creasing as all the thoughts that I had been shoving aside started to bubble up. I knew he was watching me. I knew he wanted more details. I knew he wanted to know exactly what it had been like, but I wasn't sure I was capable of describing it to him because I still wasn't sure what my thoughts were. I forced myself to look up at him, knowing that he would be able to see the discomfort in my eyes.

"They're small," I said finally, my words slow as I tried not to sink into the uncomfortable thoughts that had been shifting just beneath the surface of my mind. "Smaller than I expected. They look weak and fragile, but – they watch you when you move. And... it's unsettling."

I gave Hawthorne a weak smile, then we both dropped our gaze. My eyes lingered on the paper cup in my hand before me, and even though it was still warm and I was still thirsty, I couldn't seem to make myself drink it, because after spending four nights wandering around factory farms with Hakim, crawling through the data, and reviewing the photos moments ago, it was all starting to blur together.

Our similarities were disturbing... and I wasn't sure what to make of it.

Ensnared

"Gorski!"

I froze mid-step, the paper I had just grabbed from the printing room in my hand, and I turned around to see Captain Vogle making his way toward me.

"Sir," I said, nodding my head in greeting. "Good evening."

"Vogle is fine, Gorski," he said, waving his hand in dismissal and stopping just a few feet before me. "You don't need to be so formal. Where's Hakim?"

"At his desk." I gestured over my shoulder and stopped myself from saying sir once more. "We were just about to head out."

"Then it's a good thing I came in early tonight, isn't it." Vogle grinned. "I meant to catch up with you both last week, but things have been crazy – two murders in city centre – worst week we've had in months. Anyway, I need an update, and I have some good news. Tell him you're both to stop by my office on your way out. Oh, and congratulations on making it two weeks. He's not an easy partner, but he is the best. I knew you were a good candidate."

With that, Vogle turned and made his way back to his office, leaving me standing in the empty hallway in silence.

"Okay," I breathed out, turning on my heel to make my way down to the boardroom.

We had been following the same pattern for the last few days after setting up the additional sensors provided by Dolan's Agriculture on the 13th. We met at the precinct early, worked for an hour, reviewed the plans for checking over the sensors, then grabbed whatever gear we might need before jumping in vehicle number 403 at precisely 8:30 pm to head out. After checking the sensors, we always came back to do more work and follow up on dead leads related to the unsolved murders, and I suspected that Hakim wouldn't be overly pleased about having his schedule hijacked by his captain.

"Hakim," I said as I entered the large room that served as our base of operation. He didn't look up at me, but I saw his head tilt, so I knew he was listening. "Captain Vogle asked that we stop by his office on the way out. He wants an update, and he said he has good news."

My partner nodded, the motion slow as his eyes rapidly consumed the information on the page before him. Then he stood from his seat.

"Get your stuff," he said, grabbing his bag off the floor. "We're checking the first set of sensors tonight, and it always takes the longest – we need to get back in time to file surveillance request forms."

"Alright." I dropped the papers I had collected from the printer on my new desk and grabbed my smaller bag. Then I followed him back out into the hall to Vogle's office.

"Ah, perfect timing," Vogle said, grinning as he got up from his desk to come perch on the front of it before us. "Just got an email from the chief, so I need to head upstairs. Give me an update – find anything useful yet?"

"Nothing yet," Hakim replied, dropping his bag to the ground. He didn't sit, so neither did I, but I kept my gear bag on my shoulder. "We're monitoring the areas most likely to be targeted, and I expect we'll see something soon. I had Corban run some half prints I found on the pump, but nothing came up."

"What about the employees?" Vogle asked, crossing his arms over his chest. "Anything promising?"

"No," Hakim said. "There's nothing to suggest they assisted the night of, and I have nothing to use to get a warrant. One had a parking ticket, but no judge would think that's grounds for executing a search."

"You don't think it's them," Vogle sighed.

"It is unlikely. They've all been there long enough that it would be unexpected for them to do something like this now. They're paid well, have good benefits, and after asking around, it seems like most of them like their jobs."

"So, what do we have?" Vogle asked as he leaned back on his desk.

"Additional equipment provided by Dolan's," Hakim answered. "Because of that, we're able to monitor two facilities at once. Now it's just a matter of time."

"Alright." Vogle nodded. "What about maintenance or truck drivers – anything unusual with facility access?"

Hakim turned to look at me and arched a brow. I stood there in silence for a moment before I realized that he was waiting for me to answer.

"Oh – no, sir – Vogle – sorry," I sputtered as my temporary captain's face split into an amused grin. "I checked the logbooks and cross-referenced everything. I haven't finished going through them all, but everything in the last month appears consistent with the last two years. I ran everyone through the Federal ID Archive, and they all checked out. Full background checks came up clean too, and as Hakim said, these crews are regulars, and they have been working with this facility for years. I did some digging on Dolan's Agriculture just in case, but there's no history of any issues. No labour disputes, no grievances, no disgruntled employees – there's no reason to assume that anyone working there was involved at all. Based on the way the attacks progressed, it almost suggests that the offenders gathered the information themselves by checking out the facility through the fences, entering only after they found the buildings they wanted. I'm not sure that anyone who had access to the farm or company information leaked anything."

"At least not knowingly," Hakim added, and I nodded.

"Alright," Vogle said, standing up to move behind his desk. He pulled open a drawer and fished out three red plastic tokens. Each one was hanging from a thin chain and had white numbers printed across it. "I wasn't expecting you to have anything yet given the state of the case when it was handed over to our precinct; everyone knows the Provincial Police can't manage anything but road cleanup, but it looks like you have it under control, and that's what matters. Time for the good news – I was able to get four tags for this weekend. Hakim—"

He turned back to face us, tossing one of the rectangular tokens toward the tall man by my side. Hakim snatched it out of the air, glancing at it once before tucking it into his vest pocket.

"Now, Gorski," Vogle said, perching on his desk once more and holding up the two remaining tokens. "Want in?"

I faltered, my eyes pinching as I stared at the plastic that Vogle was holding. I read the numbers, but I didn't recognize them, and my mind drew a blank.

"In on what?" I asked, and I heard Hakim scoff as Vogle shook his head.

"You've never been hunting before?" Vogle asked.

"No," I said, my voice suddenly quieter. "I haven't."

"Ah, then you're in for a treat." Vogle grinned as he tossed me both tags. I caught them reflexively, but I struggled to find anything to say in response as Vogle stood up and began collecting documents from his desk. "There's nothing like it. Unfortunately, Stevens got called in for a double to cover another precinct this weekend, so he and his son can't come. It's your lucky night. Bring your boyfriend along. Hakim can give you the details."

"I don't have a boyfriend," I said as I stared at the tags in my hand. I didn't want to go hunting. I had never been interested in hunting before, and I certainly wasn't interested in the idea now.

"Then bring your life partner or a friend," Vogle said, seemingly entirely unaware of my discomfort as he continued to gather stuff for his meeting. "I don't care who you bring – but it was a bitch to get those tags, so don't let the spare go to waste."

I turned to look up at Hakim, my mouth falling open as my mind latched to the only excuse I could think of. "I have to finish going through the surveillance footage this weekend and check the purchasing records."

"You can do that Monday," Hakim said, slamming the door on my excuse so quickly it was like he knew exactly what I was thinking. He grabbed his bag from the ground, fixing me with an intent stare as his voice dropped low. "Unless you're saying that you'd rather file paperwork than hunt?"

I stiffened, my entire body going rigid as I stared into his mismatched eyes and wondered just how much he could see.

"I—"

Whatever I was going to say was cut off by Vogle's laugh as he finished gathering his papers and shook his head in amusement.

"Of course she wants to go. Don't give her such a hard time, Hakim. You've been working her to the bone. Alright, get out." He moved away from his desk, herding us into the hall before him. "Message me if you find anything out there tonight – and Hakim, make sure she has my cell number too, just in case. Otherwise, I'll see you both this weekend. Don't be late. Gates open at 9 pm. Gorski, you can rent a firearm there if you don't have a personal one; just bring your licence with you."

With that, he made his way down the hall toward the elevator, leaving me speechless by Hakim's side.

"You'd better hang on to those and not lose them," Hakim said, his voice stern as he shouldered his bag and set off down the hall. "They're very expensive."

I stared at the two plastic tags a moment longer, then stuffed them into a vest pocket before following Hakim down the hall. He didn't say anything about the hunting trip until we were in the car and on our way. Even then, he kept it short and brief.

I was to wear dark clothing that I didn't mind getting ruined. I was to make sure that I wore good shoes and brought a fully charged phone. If I had a hunting knife—bring it. Otherwise, I could rent one of those too, and I was to wear the reflective safety band and emergency beacon they gave me at all times. Since hunting rifles used standard animal-grade ammunition, getting hit was unlikely to kill me, but it would still put me off work for a night or two if I was struck in a vital spot. So he warned me to be careful but not to activate the beacon unless I was legitimately lost or injured.

And he told me to be early.

"Get there at 8 pm," he said as we made our way out onto the highway. "Since it's your first time, you'll have to fill out some forms and get registered."

"Okay." My voice was quiet as I turned to look at him. "I'm not sure that I have anyone to bring since my friend is on vacation. Did you want the spare tag?"

"No." The reply was short, and when he glanced in my direction, my stomach knotted. "I prefer to hunt alone. Ask one of your fellow patrol officers."

"Alright," I murmured, turning my gaze back to the window while doing my best to ignore the subtle insult that he still considered me a patrol officer—not his partner—even though my employee access had been transferred over to that of a detective three nights ago.

I didn't know what else to say, so I just sat there in silence. It was clear that Vogle was an avid hunter, and he was really excited about this special open season; rejecting the invitation might screw me over long-term if it offended him. The fact that he had even thought to include me was a huge compliment, even if I had zero desire to go.

I had known that Officer Stevens hunted. He worked in the SWAT department, and when he'd run the firearms refresher this year, he'd talked about it quite a bit. But I had never considered where Hakim fit into the mix because he didn't talk about his hobbies or interests the way that many others in the precinct did. I was used to Grace, who talked about everything, and Hawthorne, who appeared as an open book. I supposed it wasn't all that surprising to find out that Hakim hunted, but I couldn't see how this was going to go well for me.

I let out a quiet sigh, shoving the thoughts aside and forcing my mind to focus on the case instead of the two hard tags securely nestled in my vest pocket. It wouldn't do me any good to worry about it now. I would figure it out later when I got home.

Hakim remained silent for the rest of the drive, though I felt his gaze on my temple twice. I ignored it, keeping my exterior as calm as outwardly possible until we passed the facility and reached the ever-increasingly familiar dirt road that ran along the fenceline.

It didn't take long to reach our usual parking spot, then we both got out and made our way to the trunk. I grabbed my bag, slung it over my shoulders and double-checked all my pockets to ensure that I had everything before pulling out my map and GPS device. I didn't need them. I had walked the route four times in the last two weeks, but it was always better to be safe than sorry.

"Alright," Hakim said, shutting the trunk hatch and shouldering his own bag. He glanced at his watch, a small frown touching his lips before he turned back to face me. "We have less time than usual, so be quick. I want to get out of here before sunrise. Same procedure as always – check the sensor and battery unit, then exchange the hard drive. If anything is out of place or you find something that needs to be bagged and tagged, call it in."

"Will do."

I followed him into the woods, and we split at the same point that we always did. I checked my first sensor set and found no sign of disturbance, but I exchanged the hard drive anyway. Then I checked my second sensor set and found nothing again. The pattern continued just like the last time until I reached the sixth set of sensors and groaned in frustration.

"Hakim," I said after grabbing my radio and pressing the button.

What is it?' came the crackled reply.

"Something chewed on the camera for sensor set six," I said, bending to examine the damage. It had very clearly been gnawed on.

'Is it still working?'

"No," I confirmed after checking the cord. "It chewed through the cord and dug up around the sensor. I'll exchange the hard drive anyway so we can look at the video footage, but I doubt there will be much. It was probably a skunk."

'See if you can patch the cord with one of the repair kits. So long as it works, it doesn't matter what it looks like. Don't waste too much time – you still have more to check.'

"Copy that," I said, sinking to my knees completely and taking off my bag.

I was able to detach the external hard drive from the device despite the damage. I had no idea how much footage there would be, given that the cord was chewed through, but I expected that I would catch a glimpse of something furry before the feed cut out. Taking out a set of pliers and wire strippers, I pulled back the casing of the damaged cord, then dug through my bag to find the clips and patch wire to fix it. It took me a few minutes to get it right, then a little longer to wrap each repaired strand with electrical tape.

I checked the connection, making sure that the camera still turned on and functioned with the sensor before I pulled the device from the ground and moved it to another tree a few feet away. All said and done, it took me nearly an hour to repair the damn thing, wipe off the mud, and get the two lasers realigned. Then I pulled my bag back on my shoulders and set out toward the next set of sensors.

I tried to move as quickly as I could to make up time, checking my watch every so often to ensure I wasn't falling behind. I no longer worried that Hakim would leave without me, but I knew better than to be late. I could already hear the odd bird chirping as the first signs of morning started to drift through the air; I was running out of time. It took nearly an hour and a half to get back at a steady walk, and the sun would be up in two hours.

I let out a groan, picking up my pace as my boots grew wet from the morning dew. I was just approaching the large oak tree before my last set of sensors when suddenly my nose flooded with a familiar scent, and I froze.

It was blood.

Human blood.

I stiffened, my eyes shifting through the trees, looking for any sign of movement. I inched my way through the grass, careful and silent until the massive rock formation came into view, and I stopped. Just before my set of sensors on the north side was a human, and its leg was stuck in a foothold trap.

I stared at it, and it stared at me.

It had been trying to pry the trap open to no avail, but had stilled the moment that I came into view. I could see it squinting at me through the fading darkness, trying to make out the details of my form. My eyes traced over its frame, and my mouth fell open in disbelief as my fingers, which were millimetres away from my radio, twitched, then hesitated.

This was a wild human?

I took an unconscious step forward, unable to look away from it as my heart began to thud against my chest. At my movement, the human shifted, hesitating for only a split second before it moved so quickly I could hardly believe it. I didn't know they were capable of being so fast. The ones I had seen at the farm were sluggish and listless, but before I could even process what was going on, the human drew a knife from its jacket pocket—and I instantly knew what it was going to do as the blade lifted into the air. It was going to do what any animal would do when caught in a trap, and before I could think, I moved, forgetting my radio completely as both of my hands shot out.

"Wait!" I shouted, my voice sounding desperate as I darted across the ground through the sensor line toward the trapped human. "Wait! Stop! Don't cut your leg off!"

It froze, the knife inches away from its calf, as I reached it and dropped to my knees. I had seen one of these traps once, way back at the Academy, when we briefly covered poaching laws. I had no idea how long the human had been stuck, but I knew I needed to pry back the springs on both sides to open the jaws, and I knew I needed to do it quickly. These traps cut off blood flow, and if the human had been here long enough, the damage could be severe.

Without pausing to think, I grabbed the cold metal. Hot blood covered my hands as my fingers curled around the spring tabs—it was bright red, vibrant, and nothing like the dull near-brown colour of my own. Pushing the trap into the ground, I shoved the springs on either side down, grunting at the effort and throwing all my weight behind it as the jaws started to open. The second they were wide enough, the human pulled their leg from the metal bars, and I let go—the clamp snapped shut with a sharp clank as I let out a breath of relief.

Then I looked up at the human and stiffened head to toe.

It was a male—and *he* was unlike any other human I had seen to date.

He looked nothing like the tiny lifeless creatures at the farm. He looked nothing like the humans from our school books. He was taller. Even with him sitting on the ground before me, I could tell that he was larger than I was. He looked healthy. Fit. Strong—with messy brown hair that nearly reached his broad shoulders. My eyes trailed up his form, and my chest squeezed tight.

His clothes were dirty and covered in blood. His skin was sun-kissed and tan. There was stubble on his face, something I had never seen before. Reborn didn't grow facial hair, and even if they could, it was considered inferior—something that only a degenerate would do.

I watched the shocked surprise slowly fade from his eyes as his gaze trailed over my face. Humans didn't see well in the dark from what I remembered Carl telling me. Maybe that was why he had hesitated when I'd called out for him to stop. Maybe he had thought I was another human because I was so small. But I was close enough for him to see me clearly now, and his expression twisted into one of pure hatred and disgust as his knife came up once more, and he scrambled across the ground to get away from me.

"Get back," he said, trying and failing to stand as I stood and staggered away from his hostile movements.

"You can speak?" I breathed, watching dumbfounded as he forced himself to stand with a groan and hobbled back another two steps.

"Of course I can speak!" he spat, pointing the knife at my face as he glared at me. "Is that what they teach you? That we're mute and incapable of cognitive thought? Unbelievable – fucking vampires."

I cringed at the word, my blood-covered hands shaking in the air before me as I struggled to rationalize what the hell I was seeing.

He was standing. This human was standing and trying to stumble away despite his injury. I could see blood dripping down his leg. The wound had yet to heal. I knew almost nothing about human biology, but I knew that having an open wound of that size couldn't be a good thing—especially out here. I glanced back up to his face, seeing beads of sweat forming across his brow. I could smell it. It was musky and laced with stress, but nowhere near as bitter and horrible as the odour that lingered through the farms.

"You're in pain," I whispered, my eyes dropping back to his leg. "If that doesn't heal, it's going to get infected."

I reached for my vest, my body acting on instinct before my brain could catch up. I pulled out the balaclava that I had started carrying on me after my first night out in the woods for protection in case I got stuck out in the sun instead of dragging my helmet along. It wasn't much material, but I didn't have much else. I didn't carry many medical supplies because they weren't really something that I ever needed—especially when in uniform. I had a few small bandages in my bag that could cover a moderate sunburn and some old antiseptic spray, but it wouldn't be enough for his injuries. I ripped off my bag next, dropping to my knees and wiping my bloodied hands on the grass before I reached inside and pulled out what little I had. I gathered it all up, then stood and stepped toward him.

He staggered back, nearly falling over as his injured leg gave out.

"You won't be able to walk on that," I said, stopping in my tracks. My watch beeped, signifying one hour until sunrise, and my body tingled as I looked around at the brightening sky. "Shit – I – I have to go."

I dropped the limited supplies on the ground, stepping back once more as I looked at him.

"If – if you wait here, I can bring you more stuff."

I staggered toward my bag, quickly closing it and hauling it from the ground. My legs were trembling. I couldn't think. He was staring at me with so much resentment and hatred I could feel it in my bones. It made me feel sick. I would take Hakim's cold cruelty over this human's revulsion any night. He looked like he was cursing my very existence with his gaze.

"I'll come back," I said, hardly believing the words as they left my lips. I forced myself to shoulder my pack, stumbling on the uneven ground as I struggled to breathe. "If – if you stay there by that rock – I'll be able to find you. I'll come back with more stuff in a few hours and fix your leg."

I was going to vomit.

I could taste the bile in my mouth.

Why did I say that?

What was I thinking?

I turned on my heel, glancing back at his motionless form before I darted away, only to stop when I saw the camera.

"Shit!"

I pulled off my pack again, grabbing the bottle of lens cleaner and pouring it over my hands to wash away the blood. I knew he was watching. I could feel his eyes on my body as I grabbed a water bottle from my bag and dumped that over my hands too, then wiped them off on the grass before grabbing the camera. I knew it had footage. It would have recorded everything that I had just done.

My throat started to burn as I stared at it. Then, before I could even think it over, I pressed the reset button on the back of the hard drive and wiped it clean before ripping it off and tucking it into my bag with the others. I replaced the hard drive with a new clean one, jammed the camera back into place, and scrambled to my feet again as I grabbed my bag. Then I took off at a sprint, running through the trees as fast as I could as my entire body started to shake.

I could still smell the blood. I could still smell his sweat. I could see his hateful gaze as I jumped over a broken log and sprinted another twenty minutes back toward the car. The birds were getting louder. Any second now, Hakim would be calling me on the radio to ask where the hell I was.

I sprinted even faster, closing the distance so rapidly it felt like my legs were going to leave the ground. Then I stopped, colliding with a tree and gripping it tight for support as I struggled to stand. I closed my eyes, forcing the air in and out of my lungs as they burned. Then I reached for my bag again, pulling out the very last water bottle I had. I sank to my knees, crumpling like a broken structure at the base of the tree as I carefully washed the last of the blood from my fingers. Then I grabbed the two small alcohol wipes from the repair kit and wiped my hands and vest clean.

I didn't stop until it smelt sterile, then I buried the used wipes in the dirt before I forced myself to stand and walk the rest of the way back to the SUV. I tried not to tense as Hakim came into view. He was leaning back against the vehicle, looking at his map like he always was, but at the soft sound of my feet, he glanced up.

"You're late," he said, his tone clipped but indifferent as I tugged my bag from my shoulders and tried to stop my hands from shaking.

"I know. I'm sorry," I replied, avoiding his gaze as he reached out to take my bag. I didn't want to give it to him. I hadn't checked it over thoroughly to make sure that there was no blood on it, but I had given it to him every other night before, so I held it out as I approached him. "I had a problem with the last camera that took longer than I thought; I had to run back."

"What was wrong with it?" Hakim asked, and he stilled as I got closer. His eyes trailed over my form, lingering on my face before his nose scrunched. "How much lens cleaner did you use?"

"All of it." I forced a fake scoff from my lips. "I didn't have time to call it in, but – the camera was covered in mud, took the whole bottle to get it clean. Something knocked it over and dragged it away. It took me a while to find it and get it set up again."

What was I doing?

Why was I lying to him?

He nodded. Taking my bag and repocketing his map. "Is it working now?"

"Yes," I answered. "I exchanged the hard drives, but I doubt there will be any data on it."

"That's fine," he said as the chirping of the birds started to grow louder. "That happens in this sort of environment, but you had better have relocated it so whatever was toying with it doesn't find it again."

"I did."

The lie came out easily, just like the others, but my stomach curled at the sound.

"Good." He jerked his head toward the car. "Get in."

I nodded, moving toward the passenger side door as he brought my bag to the trunk. I let out a breath and buckled my belt, eyeing his seat from the corner of my gaze as I heard the trunk close. I tried to act normal as he climbed into the vehicle beside me, started the engine, and put the sunshield up, but I couldn't seem to remember what normal was. My right hand kept twitching, so I propped it on the windowsill and dropped my head on my hand.

"We'll restock the lens cleaner when we get back to the precinct," Hakim said as he reversed the car and turned us around. "I used half my bottle tonight as well, and I need another patch kit because something gnawed through one of the cords. You can fill out a requisition form for some spare batteries when we get back too."

"Okay." I nodded, not at all caring that he was giving me more grunt work.

"Tonight wasn't a complete loss," Hakim said as the car bounced along the dirt road. "There was data on sensor set fourteen in my area."

"Oh?" I feigned excitement as I turned to glance at him. "That's good."

"It is." Hakim nodded. "And I found footprints heading to the north and a partial print on the fenceline. It was only ever a matter of time. Within the next week or two, they'll move, and we'll be there waiting."

"It will be nice to make some progress," I said, and he turned to glance at me, a dark glint forming in his eyes.

"Yes, it will."

I forced myself to smile at him as a shiver ran down my spine. He pulled the vehicle out onto the country road, and I shifted my eyes back to the front window. My heart was beating in my ears. My legs quivered as the adrenaline in my body finally started to fade and reality set in like a sickening wave.

What the hell had I just done?

Warren

I have never been one to do anything unexpected.

Yes, my parents were surprised when I applied to the Academy, but anyone who knew me well would have seen it coming from a mile away. My application? Flawless. Not a single detail missing. I spent weeks preparing it to make sure that it met all requirements.

The courses that I took as part of my undergraduate degree? Carefully handpicked to give me the optimal education for a career as a police officer. I knew what I would be studying at university before I had even graduated high school.

Inviting Hawthorne over for dinner? Not something that I ever anticipated doing, but still, that had been carefully considered even if I did make the decision quickly.

That's who I am. I plan and prepare with a level of detail and meticulous consideration that would drive most people crazy. I don't do things "just because".

Which was probably why my legs wouldn't stop shaking.

I gripped the strap of my gear bag tighter, staring at the elevator doors while silently urging the old metal box to move faster. I could feel Hakim's gaze lingering across my features. He had been glancing at me since we left the boardroom after working for another two hours upon returning to the precinct. I had done everything that I could to appear normal—transferred the footage from the hard drives I had retrieved, wiped them clean for the next changeout, filled out the requisition forms without complaint, submitted the orders for new patch kits, and combed through the limited data for the murder case that seemed to be going nowhere quick while discretely glancing through the factory farm information on human health to refresh my limited knowledge.

Yet the entire time I worked, a dull tremble shook through my hands, and it just kept getting worse.

My eyes felt glassy and unfocused. I had excused myself immediately upon our return to use the bathroom, washing my hands six times to remove any traces of blood while ignoring my reflection because I wasn't sure that I could look at myself. Then, at 8 am, when Hakim unexpectedly called it quits early and handed me yet another case file—another body found by Precinct 38 with trauma to the head similar to our other Jane Does—I grabbed my gear bag and followed him to the elevator.

Now, standing in the elevator clutching the new file to my chest, I was struggling.

My eyes darted up to the lights across the top of the doors. Only six more floors to go. If I could make it six more floors, then I could get to my car and figure this out. I had no idea what figuring this out would entail because I had no idea what the hell I was going to do, but I had to do something, and my window for admitting what I had done without massive repercussions that would impact every facet of my life was gone.

It had passed by the second I'd handed Hakim my bag, lied to his face, climbed into the SUV, and sat in silence by his side for the hour-long drive back to the 33rd Precinct. I still don't understand why I did what I did, but the damage was done now.

Which meant I had to do something else.

I clenched my teeth and watched floor three go by. I could feel Hakim staring at my temple.

Did he know?

Could he tell?

Had he smelled the blood through the stark scent of lens cleaner?

I didn't know. I didn't know anything anymore. I didn't even know who I was, and I could barely keep myself from visibly shaking as the elevator got closer to the underground garage. I watched floor two go by, then floor one. Perspiration was starting to form across my skin, which was not a normal thing for Reborn unless they were dying or pushing their bodies to the absolute extreme of their limits.

Was this how Hawthorne had felt after talking to that girl at the protests? Better question, what the hell would I have done tonight if not for Hawthorne?

I wasn't stupid. I knew the only reason my hand had hesitated by my radio was because of him and the little thoughts he had put in my head. Because of all those questions I had never considered before. Because when I saw that human, I stilled. The intrinsic instinct to do my job had melted away, and I reacted blindly in a way I could never have anticipated.

The elevator dinged as it reached B2, and I let out a breath, clutching the strap of my bag tighter and all but bursting from the doors. I made it three steps before I heard my name, and I instantly froze.

"Gorski."

I stiffened as the echo of my footsteps against the concrete of the nearly empty garage stopped. I forced my body to move, turning to face his typical indifferent expression as his rough voice rang out once more.

"I know"—my heart caught in my chest—"that murder cases aren't easy to swallow."

All the air in my lungs nearly came wheezing out as Hakim's eyes darted to the folder clutched tightly to my chest, but I managed to remain silent as he took a step forward and his voice dropped lower.

"Neither are a lot of other cases you're going to see, but they are the reality of being a detective that you will need to learn to deal with," he said as he gave me a cold look. "So find a way to deal with it and manage it. I won't tolerate you losing focus or slipping up because the parameters of this case are unpleasant.

You're expected to be able to handle whatever you're assigned, and if you can't, then you shouldn't be in the department. This job isn't for everyone. There's a reason why new recruit turnover is so high – everyone wants the title and the glory that comes with cracking a case, but most of them can't cut it."

I stared at him, hardly believing that this was happening as he continued on.

"Vogle doesn't play favourites. He's not going to stop assigning you these sorts of cases just because they make your hands shake, and you're going to see a lot worse before you even make it a year in this department. The world isn't a nice place. Traffic violations and petty possession charges are no longer your norms. Do you understand?"

"Yes, sir." I nodded. "It won't be an issue."

"Good," he said, slinging the strap of his bag over his shoulder. "Then be here tomorrow at the usual time. We have a lot to work through, and I promise you, it's only going to get worse."

I nodded again, watching as he turned away before forcing my shaking legs to move toward my car. I threw my bag onto the backseat, then quickly got in, waiting until Hakim had exited the parking garage before I let out a deep breath and closed my eyes.

On the one hand, I was lucky. I had gotten away with what had happened, and Hakim was unaware of my betrayal and blatant illegal actions. On the other hand, he still thought I was pathetic. He still thought I couldn't hack it as a detective, and he now believed that my shaking hands were linked to seeing photos of dead bodies from the murder cases I had been working on for the last hour of the day and the new case file sitting on the empty seat beside me.

Neither situation felt good, but if I had to pick, this was the best scenario—even knowing that it was all I could do not to panic as I started my car and exited the garage. I still didn't have a plan. I still hadn't figured out exactly what I needed to do, but I knew I needed to do something, so I drove in the opposite direction of my apartment as I thought it through.

I had promised that human—that man—that I would go back, but the thought of doing that just made me nauseous. Why had I said that?

Go back for what? And with what, exactly?

I didn't have anywhere near enough medical supplies at home to help him. There were a few medical cocktails available at the hospital, which helped save lives and stimulate healing after catastrophic injuries, but those drugs were heavily regulated. It wasn't like I could get my hands on them, and even if I could, for all I knew, giving humans one of those mixes would flat-out kill them. Hell, he might already be dead. Humans were weak, after all. Maybe he had bled out? Maybe some wild animal had gotten to him, or hunters had found him?

I let out a deep groan and resisted the urge to hit my own face against the steering wheel.

I had to go back.

Regardless of the human and his current condition, I had to go back because I had to wipe off that camera properly and remove any lingering blood.

I could hardly believe what I was thinking, and yet I knew it was the only logical solution. I had to go back and burn the alcohol wipes that I had buried. I had to remove the blood from the trap, too, and I had to get rid of any other evidence I'd left behind. If the human was still there, fixing him up and helping him was actually in my best interest because I needed him to get as far away from that farm as possible. I couldn't risk anyone finding him or finding out what I had done.

I let out a sigh as I stopped at a red light.

I had always thought of myself as a good person. A good cop. I had always assumed I would do the right thing in a bad situation. That I would maintain my integrity and follow the law, and yet here I was, rapidly trying to plan how to cover up my tracks as I intentionally drove away from my home.

But if I did find him again, maybe I could talk to him and figure out what was going on. Maybe this mess could somehow help me with the case, and I could turn this all around.

I took the next right, driving into a poorer area of the city and scanning the streets for a bank drive-thru tunnel. I went to the first one that I saw, taking out two hundred dollars in cash before driving another two kilometres to a twenty-four-hour pharmacy. I parked three blocks away, stripping off my vest, dress shirt, badge, and firearm in the car before yanking out a plain black shirt from my gear bag. I forced myself to put it on before pulling out my smaller bag and cramming my badge and weapon inside. I ran my shaking hands through my hair, then pulled on my blackout helmet and gloves and got out of the car.

The store was empty when I stepped inside, which was to be expected. I kept my face turned away from the old battered-looking camera and kept my helmet on even though it was considered bad etiquette. The lady at the cash register eyed me suspiciously as I grabbed a basket and made my way down the aisle toward the medical supplies, but I ignored her. I knew this area of Carneth from my first few years as an officer. The clerk was probably used to sketchy customers at all sorts of weird hours, and I was no different. So long as I paid for my stuff and got out without causing a problem, I would be fine.

My hands continued to tremble as I grabbed nearly every single medical item that they had available and piled it into the basket. Two wraps, a small package of bandages, and several tiny bottles of antiseptic and creams meant to help heal burns that lingered due to minor sun poisoning. It wasn't much, but no pharmacy had much by way of medical supplies. If you required legitimate medical care items, it meant that you had a preexisting medical problem that delayed your healing. That, or you were so injured you were on the verge of dying, in which case, you should be at a hospital. Not the local pharmacy.

I grabbed two bottles of water and some acetaminophen on the way to the register and paid for the order with cash. Then I drove another four kilometres away and repeated the process.

It took three stops to gather enough medical supplies and alcohol wipes. And at the third pharmacy, I added a small travel sewing kit to my order before paying in cash and getting back into my car. Tossing my helmet onto my backseat, I ignored a group of kids skateboarding on the street in cheap blackout gear and quickly made my way to the highway.

Somehow the drive seemed to take even longer than the horribly awkward ones that I endured with Hakim, but I tried not to think about him as I drove. I tried not to think about what he would do if he found out what I had done. My career would be over, that much was obvious, but I got the feeling he would take it personally. It had happened under his very nose, and that made me feel even more uneasy.

He didn't strike me as the type to be forgiving... and I knew he wasn't above underhanded tactics. But thinking about him just made me feel sicker, and bile burned at the back of my throat. I didn't want to think about what he would say or do if he found out—especially because he had been right. I was woefully unprepared for the real world. My education and training hadn't helped me when I'd found that human stuck in a trap. I had just made a massive mistake, and I didn't know how to handle it— just as he had said.

I hated that.

My grip on the wheel tightened as I finally pulled off the highway and made my way down the familiar old gravel road that led toward the farm, but I didn't take the usual route. I might have just ruined my life, but I wasn't completely stupid, and I sure as hell wasn't going to make my situation worse by driving by the scene of the crime and getting caught on the gate security cameras, which I knew captured the road traffic.

Instead, I drove ten minutes out of the way to approach from the opposite side—nowhere near any facility camera. Then, I pulled onto an old unused farm road and parked my car behind a thicket of trees. As of right now, we had never checked the area for tire tracks, but I wouldn't put it past Hakim to add it to our list of things to do. Luckily the ground wasn't wet so my tires didn't sink in, and though our Julys were typically dry, there was supposed to be a decent rainstorm this weekend, which would wash away any tracks and dilute the blood in the woods. Still, I wasn't taking any chances, and I made sure that my car was deep into the brush so it wasn't visible from the road before I started repacking all my stuff.

I put my vest back on, carefully tightening the straps so it was securely in place before I checked to confirm that my firearm was properly loaded with a standard black animal-grade magazine, then I strapped the weapon to my hip. I stashed the red Reborn-grade magazine, which was only to be used in emergency situations where regular ammunition failed to work as a deterrent, in my glove box—there would be no need for it in the woods. I jammed the last of my cash into one of the many pockets of my vest before pinning my badge in place, because it was better to have it than not. Worst case, if someone saw me out here, I could pretend that I came back to get something. I could claim that I had forgotten something in the forest. Though I sincerely hoped that wouldn't be necessary.

Next, I emptied my smaller bag and repacked it, stuffing it with the water, pain pills, medical supplies, and alcohol wipes I had just bought. I zipped it shut and pulled on my gloves, quickly examining my gear to make sure I was securely covered before tugging on my helmet and opening my door to step out into the sun. Then, I locked my car doors and set off into the woods.

It took me longer to navigate through the sunlight than I thought it would without my CPD GPS device. I could see through the visor of my helmet fine, but it wasn't ideal. The contrast was off, and it made everything look warped.

Which was why most Reborn refused to drive during the day and why I doubted anyone would be out here. The regular glass of the windshield had a UV filter, as did all glass, and it was enough to prevent you from getting burnt, but it didn't block out much of the light. So seeing through clear glass in daylight was near impossible, which was exactly why we had the sunshields and blackout gear helmets with tinted visors for daytime. But no one liked using them, and we avoided them if we could.

I glanced down at my watch as I cut through a thicket of trees. It was already 11:30 am. It would take me a solid hour to get back to my car, possibly longer. It would take me another hour and a half to reach Carneth on the back roads if I wanted to avoid the same path I had used to get here, and I needed to be back at the precinct by 7:30 pm to start work.

I wouldn't be sleeping much today, though as I made my way through the forest, I doubted I would have been able to sleep even if I had all the time in the world. My mind was too busy, trying to make sure that all my bases were covered and nothing would be left behind. I recited the limited amount of human biology I knew from the factory farm case. I scanned the surrounding trees for approaching figures while simultaneously checking the underbrush for more foothold traps. The absolute last thing I needed was to accidentally step in one of those.

I made note of two and their location, marking them on my map as best as I could without my GPS device before setting them off with sticks to dismantle them.

Then I grabbed a long, solid-looking branch that could be used as a splint and tied it to my bag just in case. I kept pushing forward. Never once slowing and never once allowing myself to truly think about my actions. Whatever was happening, whatever I was doing, it hadn't completely sunk in yet, and I knew when it did it would be difficult to swallow.

After ten more minutes of navigating the woods with my compass and map, the large rock formation came into view. I could smell blood, and the scent was stronger. Either the human was still here and still alive, or something else had found him. I carefully made my way toward the camera set first, pulling the long pole from the ground and moving it to the west by another twenty feet so it would be well out of my way before I disinfected the entire device and reset the memory one more time.

Carefully stepping around the sensor, I then made my way back toward the rocks, squinting through my visor and mentally cursing the material. Tinting technology had come a long way in the last few years, but my helmet was easily a decade old and not the best quality. I paused by the trap, wiping it down and rinsing it off with care before unhinging the latch and leaving it permanently disarmed in the bed of underbrush where it had been hidden. I tried to ignore the shake in my legs as I stood back up and finally approached the large rock formation.

The scent of blood grew stronger as I looked for where the human may have gone, but it wasn't until I had circled around to the northeast that I heard the rustle of movement and caught sight of him. He was sitting inside a small, deep cutout in the rock formation, leaning against the stone with a pained expression on his face.

He didn't look good.

Sweat covered his skin, and I could smell his stress from here. Blood coated his leg. He'd wrapped the balaclava around the wound, but it wasn't doing much to help, and even I knew that he was in trouble. He wasn't here because he wanted to be. The injury didn't appear to have healed at all, which made sense, given my quick review of Dolan's facility notes. Humans didn't heal. At least not quickly. Based on the files the factory kept regarding stock health, it would take days for this to heal—weeks if his bone was broken. Usually the farm just put humans down when injured since it wasn't worth the effort to get them medical attention because they picked up infections much too easily.

Yet despite this, despite the unbelievable amount of pain that he must be in, he lifted his knife into the air when he caught sight of me.

"Wait!" I said, raising my hands into the space before me. "It's – it's me. I came back like I said – with supplies."

He didn't lower the knife.

He didn't even move. He just continued to sit there and stare at me, eyes narrowed into a glare as he leaned harder against the stone.

I hesitated, then took a slow step forward. "Look, I – I'm not going to do anything. I didn't even bring my radio, and I can fix your leg."

He still didn't move, and I was starting to wonder how much he could really understand as I took another small step forward.

"Can—" My head tilted curiously to the side. "Can you actually understand me?"

He snorted, a look of disgust shifting across his sweat-covered face.

"Of course I can understand you," he said, his deep voice laced with burning hatred. "I'm not incompetent."

"Okay." I stared at him through my visor as I lowered my hands back to my sides. This wasn't going how I thought it would. Then again, I hadn't had a clue how this was going to go.

I glanced down at my watch, cringing at the time. I needed to get him out of here. Our coroners and the Forensic Department would be able to determine his time of injury and death. If Hakim or the operations manager, who I didn't doubt was regularly checking his traps, ever found his body, there would be no way that I could lie to cover it up. There wasn't a Reborn on the planet that wouldn't have noticed him in that trap while completing the sensor check, and there wasn't enough alcohol in the world to remove the scent of his blood from this area.

If Carl came out before the rain came this weekend, my life would be over.

"Look. I don't have a lot of time," I said, my patience fading as my irritation started to grow. I took another step forward, pulling the small bag off my shoulders. "I need you to get out of here. The operations manager of this facility set that trap, and if he finds you, I'm not sure what will happen, but I can promise you it won't go well. I didn't come all the way back out here to hurt you. So, you can either let me fix your leg and you can leave voluntarily on your own, or I'm going to knock you out and move you anyway. Your choice."

He stared at me, his eyes narrowing into such a dark glare that I could feel it in my bones. But then, he slowly lowered his knife, and I let out a quiet sigh of relief. I hadn't wanted to make any threats because I genuinely didn't want to hurt him. I didn't want to hurt anyone, and the last thing I wanted to do was knock him out and carry him deeper into the woods. I didn't have time for that, and more than anything, I just wanted all of this to be over.

I wanted none of this to have happened.

I wanted to go back in time.

Yet even as that wish crossed my mind and I made my way toward him, I knew going back wouldn't change anything. The course of my life had altered, and I felt like I was just along for the ride. I would probably end up here all over again even if I could go back, because for some reason, the idea of calling this in and reporting him made me sicker than what I was doing now.

And I wasn't sure what to make of that.

I stepped into the shadow of the small cutout, crouching so I could close the distance before I dropped to my knees a foot in front of him. I watched him eye me warily as I opened my bag and started pulling out my supplies. It didn't take long for me to get frustrated with my gloves, so I ripped them off. Then, cautiously, I unbuckled the strap of my helmet and pulled it off too.

I knew that removing it in the middle of the day was a risk, but I didn't want him to think that I was a threat. Besides, the cutout was deep enough to completely block the sun, which was already on the other side of the rock formation. So it was not only dark enough to keep me safe, I also had the advantage sightwise—especially with my helmet off—and this would go a lot faster if I could see what I was doing. And even with him being larger than me and nothing like the humans at the farms, based on what I knew, it wouldn't be difficult for me to win in a fight.

Reborn were strong, and he looked like he knew it.

That's why he was still gripping the knife in his hand even though he had placed it on the ground by his side. Even if he stabbed me, I wouldn't die. I was wearing my vest, which covered everything, including my neck, and it would take a devastating puncture through the heart or a complete decapitation to kill me. Neither of which were possible. My vest was designed to protect against attacks made by Reborn.

So I set my helmet on the ground by my side, then looked up once more.

He stared at me, and I stared at him.

His eyes traced over every single millimetre of my face, almost like he was searching for something or trying to memorize it. He had probably never seen a Reborn up close before, at least not like this, not with enough dim light for him to be able to see my features clearly. Reborn didn't venture out into the woods unless hunting, and any illegal poachers canvassing the area would be wearing helmets to avoid getting ID'd.

I watched his examination of my face closely, wondering what he was thinking as I took in his appearance. He looked exactly how I remembered him from earlier, sun-kissed skin, long messy brown hair—but now, I was calm enough to see all the little details of his face, even if my heart was beating abnormally fast.

A dusting of tiny, nearly invisible dots covered the bridge of his nose, which was mostly straight, except for the subtle bump that hinted it may have been broken and improperly healed a long time ago. Though it wasn't unattractive. His jaw was well-defined, the stubble along it matching in colour to the hair on his head. There was a thin scar that ran down his temple, cutting through his left eyebrow and stopping just shy of his eye.

His eyes were brown, but they were warm in colour. A deep and brilliant shade that I didn't know was possible. It was like they mimicked the rich, vibrant shades of the earth, and I found I couldn't look away. I watched the vivid colour circle over my face twice more before his eyes suddenly jerked back to my light grey ones, as if he realized what he was doing, and his expression grew tight.

"Fix it then." His voice was cold and toneless. "If that's actually what you're here to do."

I bristled, his words pulling me back to reality and quickly dismissing any fleeting thoughts I had about his anger and hatred being the result of fear toward his unfortunate situation. It wasn't. He was making that clear with his continued glare, even though I'd done absolutely nothing to hurt him since the second I had found him.

"That is what I'm here to do," I said as I dropped my gaze back to my supplies. "Why else would I be here?"

"Midday snack," he replied, and I stiffened at his words.

I could smell his blood so strongly it was almost nauseating. It did smell good—but the scent of blood wasn't irresistible. It wouldn't send me into a bloodlust. Not eating and becoming depraved for too long, whether intentional or not, was what sent Reborn into a bloodlust. At which point, yes, the smell of any blood would become overwhelmingly attractive.

But that wasn't something that happened. Reborn ate regularly. Access to food wasn't a problem, and intentionally becoming depraved, or draining, as it was commonly called, was not only irresponsible, it was illegal. Slipping into a bloodlust was incredibly dangerous, and it wasn't something that happened.

"Is that what you think we're like?" I questioned, distaste slipping into my tone.

I knew the old stories, the ones that kids would tell each other for fun and to get a scare. The old folktales that had originated the slur vampire, which this human had already thrown in my face once. So I assumed he must know them, too. I had never been a fan of the terrifying tales, myths, and legends, or anything else illogical.

"Insatiable creatures constantly on the hunt? Monsters from one of those old stories meant to scare kids?" I snorted, shaking my head. "Do you have any idea how ridiculous that is? We're not mindless beings that go crazy at the smell of blood, and we're not venomous predators stalking the night – our fangs don't have poison. We're Reborn."

He didn't say anything for a moment, but I could tell that he was watching me closely.

"Tell that to the ones that hunt us in the woods," he said, and his voice was dripping with so much acid it might as well have been a physical burn to my skin.

I struggled to come up with something to say in response. I had never been hunting before. I had no idea what happened out there in the woods, but the idea of Vogle or Stevens or Hakim or anyone else being mindless, bloodthirsty beings seemed unlikely and absolutely absurd—and even considering the thought made me uncomfortable.

So I pulled out my knife instead, dropping my eyes back to his leg and quickly cutting back the soft fabric of his pants around the wound before removing the balaclava.

"This is going to hurt," I said, reaching for one of the pill bottles by my knee. I cracked it open and handed it to him. "This is acetaminophen – given your size, you should be able to take one without any issues."

He took the bottle without a word, then he swallowed three pills. I stared at him in disbelief, wondering briefly if he had seen this medication before or if he was simply in so much pain that he didn't care. Based on the cold and lethal expression on his face, I doubted I would ever know.

"Alright then," I muttered, reaching for a bottle of antiseptic next. "Try to hold still."

He flinched as the fizzing liquid washed over his wound. Beneath the mess of blood, I could see two distinct lacerations, one on each side of his calf. It took three of the small bottles to get it clean, and despite his efforts to remain quiet, a grunt of pain left his lips when I pulled some leaves and grass from the wound.

I worked mostly in silence, using the thread and needle I had brought to carefully stitch as much of his skin back together as I could, all while trying to ignore how strange the warmth of his body felt to my hands.

He didn't flinch or pull away from my touch, but I could see his fingers digging into the dirt by his sides as I continued to patch him up. When I finished with the stitching, I cleaned my hands with a bottle of water and some wipes, then got out the small tube of cream I had brought to cover the wound and help it heal. I hoped it worked for humans too, but I genuinely had no idea. Then, as I added some wound closure strips in case my stitching failed, I couldn't help myself, I stole a few glances at his face and studied his body.

His lashes were dark, and his pupils, while small like his irises, appeared to be fully dilated. Yet he still squinted at me a little, suggesting human sight was even worse than I thought it was. His hair was damp from sweat, but it seemed like the medication was working now, and some of his muscles had relaxed. The hair on his legs, which was uncommon for Reborn, was black, and it was shorter and more coarse than the locks on his head appeared to be. I could feel his pulse beneath my fingers, and while the beat of his heart was steady, it seemed fast. Though, perhaps that pace was normal for humans.

I put the tube of cream back in the bag and grabbed the bandages and tape next, then started to wrap the lacerations.

"I thought you healed on your own."

His voice startled me, and when I glanced up mid-wrap, he was watching me.

"We do," I said.

"Then where did you learn to do this?"

"We're taught basic first aid at the Academy," I answered hesitantly. "On the off chance that an officer is hit with a Reborn-grade bullet, knowing how to close a wound, even crudely, can save a life."

"So, you are a cop," he said, and his eyes darted down to my badge.

I nodded even though it wasn't a question.

"Yes." I glanced back down and continued to wrap his leg. "But they don't teach us anything about humans. So – I don't know how well this will work."

He didn't say anything else, but he continued to watch me intently as I ripped off pieces of tape and started to fasten the bandages in place. I wanted to ask him something. I wanted to ask him why he was here and who he was. In the back of my mind, I was fairly certain that I already knew the answer to one of those questions—even if it did go against everything that I thought I knew. Even if it did seem unbelievable. But I couldn't seem to get the words to come out.

When I was done, I put everything but the tape back in my bag. Then I reached for the thin branch I had grabbed while walking through the forest, measuring it along the length of his calf before easily snapping it into two shorter pieces to fit what I needed. He remained completely still and silent as I started to tape them to his leg. I didn't know if the bone was broken, and I wasn't about to start twisting it to find out, so I figured it was better to be safe than sorry.

I blinked my tired eyes and forced them to focus. The adrenaline was beginning to wear off, and I was starting to struggle. Between the late mornings, early nights, working intensely with Hakim, and now this—I felt ready to crash.

I glanced up at the man again, then heard my quiet voice fill the silence.

"What's your name?" I asked, and his eyes narrowed. He didn't say anything, and I felt my discomfort with everything grow. "My name is Valya."

My hands faltered the second the words came out, and my eyes dropped down to his leg again as I wound the tape around the sticks to hold them in place. I don't know why I said that. That was incredibly stupid. If he was ever caught and questioned, he would be able to identify me not only by sight but also by name. Though, then again, my name was on my badge and stitched onto the small bag sitting less than a foot away because it was standard-issue from the CPD.

If he could read, he would already know it.

I should have thought of that…

"Warren," he said, and my eyes widened as I looked up at him.

He didn't look pleased with himself for saying it. In fact, he almost looked pissed off. Maybe the detail had slipped from his lips as it had done from mine. Maybe he was tired too.

He looked tired.

Or maybe he only said it because he knew how screwed I was—how screwed we both were if either of us were to ever get caught. He knew I could never give his name away.

"You're from the Norhaven Wildlife Reservation," I said, each word quiet as I held his hard glare. He hadn't let up on it since this started, and I wondered if holding that much hostility was part of the reason why he was still sweating. It must be exhausting. "Do – do you all speak?"

He didn't answer. Though I hadn't really been expecting him to. After uttering his name, his jaw had clenched shut, and I doubted that he would say anything else to me. Yet I pressed on anyway as I quickly finished the last wrap on his leg and tore off the tape, because I should at least try to learn something before I let him go.

"Are there a lot of you?" I asked, tossing the tape back in the bag with the other supplies before reaching for his leg once more to make sure everything was set. "Can you read too?"

If I thought that he was glaring at me in hatred before, I had been wrong. At my last question, his body seemed to grow impossibly still, and the disgust radiating from his gaze reached a level I didn't know was possible.

"You and your people," he said, enunciating each word with venom, "are the worst thing to have ever happened to this earth."

I stiffened.

I could feel my hands starting to tremble against the warmth of his skin. I shouldn't be afraid of him. I had no reason to be afraid of him, and yet for some reason, I could feel fear inching down my spine.

"I don't know what they teach you in your schools," he spat, "but you're nothing more than the by-product of a disease gone wrong."

My heart faltered in my chest.

"An abomination that should have been eliminated centuries ago," he continued as his voice grew dark with revulsion. "The worst parts of humanity. Soulless. Heartless. Entirely empty of anything good."

I opened my mouth. To do what, I wasn't sure. To argue? To refute his words? To ask him what he meant or why he thought those horrible things were true?

I wasn't sure what would come from my lips, but I didn't get to find out. Before I could blink, he yanked his bandaged leg from my grasp and lunged toward me.

I didn't even have time to process what was happening. He completely caught me off guard. His weight pressed heavy on my chest as my back thudded hard into the ground. My vest pulled against my shoulder and neck as the air left my lungs. He rolled off me before I could grab him, easily evading my startled fumbling.

I made to sit up as I heard him moving away, but my shoulder wouldn't lift. Then I realized what he'd done. He had jammed his knife through the loop of the fabric strap on my vest, embedding the blade into the dirt all the way to the hilt to pin me to the ground. With a quick yank, I tugged the knife free and sat up in time to see him hobbling out of the tiny cutout—with my helmet and small gear bag in hand.

"What the—" I scrambled to my feet, my eyes going wide as his arm swung back. "Woah, woah, woah! What are you doing!!"

I watched in horror and disbelief as he threw my helmet twenty feet out into the sun, rapidly following after it on his freshly bandaged leg. I chased after him, reaching for my firearm only to find the holster empty. My mouth fell open, a mess of emotions exploding in my chest.

He took my firearm.

He took my helmet.

He took my bag.

He took everything except my gloves in a matter of seconds.

I had underestimated him.

I had completely screwed up. Had this happened while on duty with a fellow Reborn, I would have been sent back to the

Academy to relearn my basics. I would have my firearms licence suspended, and I would be stuck on desk duty for a decade.

"Why would you do that?!" I yelled, my voice nearly breaking as I skidded to a stop at the edge of the rock formation shadow and squinted into the sunlight.

I lifted my hand to block the rays but hissed in pain and stepped back when the sunlight brushed against my skin. Without my helmet, I was stuck. I couldn't leave this tiny cutout, and he knew it. But what he didn't know was that I was going to be late for work. I was going to get fired. My entire life was going to be over after having already risked it to try and save him and hide this mess I had created. And that was assuming he didn't just shoot me now.

My hands clenched into balls at my side, my anger swelling as I watched him stop ten feet out into the sun and turn back to look at me.

"I just fixed your leg!" I yelled, struggling to make out his face in the bright light, though he appeared to have no trouble seeing me now. "I just saved your life!"

"Yeah, and I'll bet you've taken thousands of human lives without thinking too," he spat, and the disgust in his voice made my next words die on the tip of my tongue. "You've never even thought about it, have you? I can tell by the utterly bewildered and indignant expression on your ignorant face. You didn't even consider me a threat this entire time! You don't know a damn thing about humans, who you are, or where you come from – and you and your people aren't as smart as you think you are."

I stilled, watching as he easily removed the magazine from my firearm and racked the slide to clear the chamber without dropping my gaze. It shattered any faint hope I had that he might not know how to use it. Then he threw my pistol thirty feet to the west, emptied the rounds from the magazine, and pocketed each one before throwing the empty casing twenty feet to the east.

"I'll spare you today – but only because it will cause me more trouble if you go missing in these woods," he said, and my mouth went dry as he held up my small gear bag. "I'm taking this. I'm sure you can get another one without too much trouble. It's standard equipment, right? And I know you're not going to report this or say anything about what happened, because if you do, your life is as good as over. I'm sure you'll get creative and find a way to account for the missing rounds."

He slung my bag over his shoulder, looking completely calm and confident. Entirely the opposite of how I felt. I watched the way the sunlight and soft shadows from the trees above shifted across his tanned skin and strong frame. He watched me for another long moment, his eyes scanning over my face one last time, soaking in every detail before he pulled a second knife from his pocket and turned away.

"At least this way I know I've got a few hours head start before you can creep from your cave," he called, not bothering to glance back at me or spare me another second of his time. "If you follow after me – I'll kill you."

He didn't stop.

And I didn't say anything.

I watched him leave, standing there, motionless, helpless to the rays of the sun as he hobbled across the ground toward the north.

Hunting

I stared at the knife resting on the counter, feeling the seconds tick by as the murmur of other customers echoed behind me. It was the first time I had ever set foot in a hunting supply shop, so I knew I should be paying attention to the gear clerk because I had no idea what I was doing, but seeing the weapon had caused my mind to slow, stall, then jump back into the past...

The odd, detached numbness that had encased my body after Warren had ripped the world out from under my feet and left me abandoned in the shadow of the rock formation yesterday hadn't taken long to fade away. Once he'd disappeared from sight, I had backed up further into the cutout and collapsed on the ground in disbelief.

Even now, I could hardly believe it was real.

I had forsaken my duty as an officer of the law to help him and had been repaid with nothing but cruel words. I had sat there in the cool dirt, squinting into the streams of sunlight, watching them slide over my helmet as a soft buzzing noise rang in my ears.

Not only could humans speak, but they could also defend themselves, and Warren was the farthest thing from weak or primitive. In a matter of seconds, he had disarmed me, dismantled my firearm, and left me in the woods. I would have died if not for the shade of the rocks, and I knew in my heart, despite him saying I didn't have one, that he wouldn't have cared.

I had sat there in silence for what felt like forever, struggling to process the torrent of emotions that rushed through my veins. In reality, it was less than an hour, then I stood from the ground, pulled on my gloves, and unstrapped my vest. I used it as a sunshield to cover my face as I darted out across the forest floor to grab my helmet.

It hadn't been ideal. I could hardly see anything. I had to feel around with my hands, stumbling blindly and pinching my eyes as they burned in pain from the bright light until I finally felt the familiar shape of my helmet brush my glove. Then I staggered back to the shadow and safety of the cutout. It took a few minutes for my eyes to stop watering, at which point, I pulled my helmet on and then stared out into the forest once more.

A part of me had wanted to chase after him, find him, and demand answers. But it was already nearly 3 pm, and I needed to get back to Carneth. Besides, I was utterly speechless, and I wouldn't have had anything to say to him.

So I collected the pieces of my firearm and reassembled it. Then I walked back to my car. It wasn't until I got to my apartment, dropped my larger gear bag by the door, stripped off my clothes, and stepped into the shower that it all hit me—and it was like a wave.

A horrible, sickening storm that rocked through my gut and nearly made me throw up.

A part of me had wanted to just go straight to work and confess what had happened because I didn't know how on earth I was going to continue. Yet a much larger part of me knew I couldn't do that. My actions, if they were ever found out, would impact more than just me. They would impact my family. They would reflect poorly on Captain Mallick—on Captain Vogle and Hakim. Possibly even Hawthorne and Lexie because they had spent so much time working with me over the years. I couldn't just go admit what I had done. It wasn't that easy. The gravity of my decision hadn't sunk in when I'd been hopping between pharmacies collecting supplies. Nor had it fully sunk in when I'd mended Warren's leg and covered up my actions. I had, somewhat selfishly, only considered myself in the equation.

But reality had hit fully as I'd stood in the shower.

This was bigger than just me, and I could not undo it.

I was alone in this, but my actions impacted many.

I knew the only thing I could do was press forward and hope that when the rain hit this weekend, it took the last of the evidence with it. Even though Warren had given me no reason to trust him, I couldn't see that he would identify me if he was ever caught. It wouldn't gain him anything. In fact, I couldn't imagine him saying much of anything in an interrogation. He would probably remain quiet to protect himself and whatever else was going on.

And that was assuming he let an officer take him alive.

He had very nearly cut his own leg off to get away from me the first time. He'd fought back against me even when I'd shown him no harm. I really couldn't picture him being brought in for questioning without putting up a fight that would likely result in him winding up dead.

Maybe I was wrong. It wouldn't surprise me anymore… I had been wrong about so many things, apparently. But I knew I didn't have a lot of alternative options, and unless I wanted to ruin the lives of those around me, which I vehemently did not, I had to get myself together, and I had to continue. I had to fight my way through this. I wanted to fight my way through this, because no matter how many mistakes I had made in the last twenty-four hours, I wanted to be here. And I still firmly believed that I could make a difference in this world while working in the CPD.

So I had forced myself to straighten beneath the flow of water. I washed the unease from my bones and rinsed my hair. Then, I followed my usual night routine, brushing my teeth and braiding my long hair for work before I pulled on fresh clothes. I rummaged around my closet, looking for the old small gear bag that I had retired two years ago. I found it, wiped the thin layer of dust from the faded canvas, hoping Hakim wouldn't notice or question the change, and then packed it as I would have done any other night.

I ate an entire packet of gelatin cubes, ignoring the strange curl of my stomach as they slid down my throat. I texted

Hawthorne and spent a few minutes reviewing the new file Hakim had given me before downing two coffees and heading back into work. By the time I got to the precinct, my hands had finally stopped shaking. I had a plan—I didn't like it—but I knew what I needed to do.

I smiled at Captain Vogle, who had come in early for another meeting, as I stepped off the elevator on the eleventh floor. When he asked me if I was excited about the hunting trip, I lied and told him I was, then made my way to the boardroom to meet Hakim.

My reluctant partner greeted me with the same indifferent nod he gave me every morning, though his eyes lingered momentarily on my hands—probably checking to see if they were still shaking. I must have passed his test, because he didn't say anything, and I settled into my chair and got to work.

I checked on the status of our requisitions, then reviewed the sensor data from the night before. Sure enough, Hakim's camera had captured footage of someone walking by the day prior to our visit. The face of the individual wasn't visible, but I knew it was Warren. Hakim wouldn't know. Hakim wouldn't even realize that it was a human. The man on the screen looked too large and moved too carefully, but his broad shoulders and the confident way he carried himself was unmistakable, even if the hood on his jacket was hiding his hair.

I pulled still frames from the video, per Hakim's request, and added them to our system so we could keep an eye out for any Reborn activists who matched the physical description. Then Hakim had Corban enter the partial prints he had collected into the database and initiated a comparison check to see if we could find any leads.

We wouldn't.

Warren's fingerprints wouldn't be in the Carneth system or any other system for that matter. The print was useless. I knew this, and yet I said nothing and continued to work through the night. When Hakim called it quits at 10 am and reminded me not to be late for the hunting trip, I assured him I would be there. Then, instead of going home, I made my way down to the gun range for "practice".

At the range, I filled in the proper documentation and made my way over to the farthest target. There was hardly anyone else there. It was too late. Most officers practiced before work or immediately after, not at 10:30 am after working fourteen and a half hours. Stevens, who had been manning the cage, didn't seem to mind my late visit, and he eagerly handed me new rounds. He asked if I was excited to go hunting. I guess word had gotten around that Vogle had invited me, which only confirmed my theory that it was quite the compliment, so I lied and said that I was. He told me he was jealous he couldn't go.

Then I stood at the end of the range, pretending to fire my weapon until the appropriate amount of time and ammunition had passed.

It was the only solution I could come up with to account for the missing ammunition without blatantly stealing more. I was just lucky I hadn't taken my Reborn-grade magazine with me, or I would have had to find a way to replace those too, which would have been much more difficult.

I made it home just after 12 pm, barely managing to strip off my boots and force down more gelatin cubes before I collapsed on my bed and passed out. I slept for five and a half hours solid. I would have slept for more, which was concerning, but my alarm woke me, and I forced myself from bed because I knew I needed to get ready for the hunting trip.

Now, standing in the registration building that doubled as a gear store with Hawthorne at my side, I could feel my carefully cultivated calm starting to crack.

The tall man in front of me pulled out a second knife, placing it on the counter as he launched into a dissertation about the benefits of this more expensive but better and newer model. My eyes shifted between the two weapons, and my stomach curled. They both looked unnecessary—and unreasonably dangerous. It wasn't that I didn't know how to use them; we trained with knives at the Academy. I just hadn't taken to them like most of my peers, and I couldn't fathom why anyone in their right mind would want to go hunting and use this to catch their prey.

I swallowed.

The words tasted awful in my mouth even though I hadn't spoken them aloud because all I could hear was Warren's voice in my head over and over and over again.

Mid-day snack.

I stiffened.

Tell that to the ones that hunt us in the woods.

My nails dug into my palms as my hands balled into fists.

Yeah, and I'll bet you've taken thousands of human lives without thinking too.

I had never killed anyone. I had never even hurt anyone. Not when I was a kid, not when I was in school, and not even during the Academy when we trained in defensive hand-to-hand combat. Sure, I had landed a few friendly blows during sparring, but I had never caused injury because I never wanted to hurt anyone.

Ever.

I had only wanted to help.

That's why I joined the CPD. That's why I upheld the law. I thought that's what I was doing, but his voice and hateful eyes wouldn't stop haunting my mind.

...taken thousands of human lives without thinking...

My stomach lurched. My jaw clenched tight. I struggled to inhale as a third knife was placed on the counter—this one with a serrated edge—and I thought I might get sick.

"I think I'm good with just the rifle." Hawthorne's voice rang out, snapping me out of my downward spiral. I glanced up at him, seeing him smile at the man behind the counter before he glanced down at me. "How about you, Gorski?"

"I'm good," I said, perhaps a little too quickly as I turned back to the man and reached into my pocket for my wallet. "How much for the rifle and ammunition?"

We paid for our equipment rental, waiting patiently as the man photocopied our firearms licences and IDs and then explained the safety equipment. There was a reflective armband and a push-activated light beacon with GPS tracker that we could use if we got lost or injured. Both were to be worn at all times, and tags were given to mark the location of anything caught. We signed for the equipment, agreeing to pay for anything damaged before reviewing the waivers and signing them too. Then we made our way past the other hunters waiting to rent equipment and back outside into the low glow of the setting sun.

"You know," Hawthorne said, stifling a yawn behind his hand as we moved toward the small crowd of Reborn gathering near the gate a hundred feet away. "When you ask someone on a first date, you don't usually make them get up before nightfall and drive an hour to the middle of nowhere."

"This isn't a date," I said as I slung the rifle over my shoulder.

He smirked. "How is this not a date? It's two beautiful people spending time together and partaking in an activity."

"You're only here because I had a spare tag." I rolled my eyes at him, then dropped my voice lower. "Vogle invited me. I had to come, you know that."

"You texted me out of the blue and all but begged me to come here with you. Me," Hawthorne said, his voice taking on a deep and provocative tone. "You could have asked Tilson – but you didn't. You asked me, and I think you would have asked me even if Lexie was back from vacation."

"Do you get begged for dates often?" I asked as I glanced around the parking lot. There were a lot of people here—several that I recognized from the precinct. "Got a waiting list?"

"Mhmm." Hawthorne nodded. "And the list is long."

"Then why were you free?" I challenged, arching a brow.

He paused, and I stopped by his side to let a car go by.

"Who says I didn't cancel my plans for you?" he countered.

I snorted. "I wouldn't believe that for a second."

"Gorski!"

My head snapped up toward the gate, taking in the sight of Captain Vogle, who had raised his hand in the air in greeting. He was standing beside Captain Tan, who ran the SWAT department. Next to them were three other officers I recognized but didn't know the names of, and just off to the side stood Hakim—silent and unwelcoming as ever. I forced myself to smile, raising a hand back in greeting before whispering at Hawthorne through my teeth.

"Be good," I muttered as he raised a hand in greeting too. "I can't afford to mess this up."

"Relax, Gorski," Hawthorne whispered, his lips scarcely moving as we closed the distance to the others. "You look like your life is hanging on this moment. If your goal is to impress Vogle, at least pretend like you're excited."

I nearly scoffed. If only he knew how true those words were.

"You look nervous," Vogle said when we stopped before his small group.

"Excited," I corrected, letting out a nervous laugh as Captain Tan chuckled. "I'm not really sure what to expect."

"Well, with any luck, you can expect the most delicious meal you've ever had," Vogle said, his group breaking out into laughter with him as he outstretched a hand to Hawthorne. "And you brought a date!"

"Just a friend," I said quickly. "This is Officer Hawthorne – we worked together in Patrol and Street from time to time."

"Right." Vogle grinned in a way that suggested he didn't believe my words.

His smile exposed his fangs, and I had to fight the urge to blatantly stare as a prickle ran down my spine. They looked… longer. Far longer than what would be considered acceptable.

"Theo," Hawthorne said, taking over his own introduction. He gripped Vogle's outstretched hand firmly and gave it a shake. "I'm lucky you had two spare tags. Otherwise, I would have had to plan the date tonight. You really got me off the hook."

Vogle laughed, and I resisted the urge to punch Hawthorne in the ribs. Having Vogle think we were a couple wasn't the worst thing in the world, and the truth was, I owed Hawthorne. He wasn't exactly kidding about the begging. I did have to convince him to come here with me tonight, though neither one of us outwardly expressed the reasons for his apprehension on the phone. Yet, those unspoken words were exactly why I had texted him.

I had no interest in hunting humans. Not tonight. Not ever. And I was fairly certain Hawthorne didn't either. I had pitched this as a work event, an opportunity for growth and exposure. It would give him the chance to spend some out-of-office time with Vogle, Hakim, and any other officers who might show up. It would be good for his career, and because it was our first hunting experience, there would be zero expectations of us being successful.

In return, I would owe him a favour, which I agreed he could ask for at any time.

He had accepted the deal, and while I was apprehensive about finding out what his future favour might be, I was thankful that he had come. I wasn't sure that I could do this alone, and I certainly didn't want to get wrapped up in Vogle's hunting party if he did indeed hunt with partners. Maybe that was why Hawthorne was boldly insinuating that we were a couple, so the others would leave us alone in the woods.

I was disrupted from my thoughts when another officer arrived, and more introductions began. I shook several hands, chatting nervously and fighting to keep a smile on my face as I eyed their elongated fangs and nails. They didn't look right. And as the night started to get darker, an uneasy feeling in my gut began to grow. Then the wind started to pick up, and I could smell the rain in the air. I let out a sigh of relief, closing my eyes briefly as some of the tension left my shoulders.

Once the rain hit, I was safe.

Once the rain hit, this was closer to being over, and I could forget this mess and move on.

Precisely ten minutes before the hunt started, one of the organizers called for everyone to gather in front of the gate. I shuffled forward, lingering back from the larger group as I stood by Hawthorne's side. The organizer listed off the projected weather alerts, recited the rules of the hunt, and the changes to the boundaries. Apparently, the hunt only took place on a small section of the wildlife reserve, but I only half listened to the details, finding myself too distracted by the crowd before us and the shocking lack of firearms.

"Hawthorne," I whispered, keeping my voice so low it was barely audible. He tilted his head toward me, but he kept his gaze locked on the organizer. "Why do so many of them not have rifles?"

"I don't know," he whispered back, and he shifted closer to my side. We both looked at the crowd before us, then Hawthorne turned to look down at me. "Maybe they all use knives?"

My eyes skimmed over the crowd again, and the uneasiness dropped in my stomach like a stone.

"Hawthorne," I whispered, barely breathing the words as I turned to look up at him. "They don't have knives."

I watched his eyes pinch at my words; then, his gaze darted away to survey the crowd for himself.

"They don't need knives," came a low reply near my side, and I jerked at the familiar gravelly sound.

Hakim was standing three feet to my left, and I hadn't even noticed him move there. I thought he had been closer to Vogle when we all shifted forward, and I had no idea how he could have heard my low words over the dull murmur of the crowd and the booming voice of the organizer. He wasn't even looking at me. His gaze was fixed on the front. I gripped the fabric of my pant leg tightly, watching as his head slowly turned and his mismatched gaze met mine.

He was looking at me like I was some sort of idiot.

He lifted his hand, then opened his mouth ever so slightly and tapped his elongated fang with a long, thin index finger. Like Vogle, who only had a knife, Captain Tan, who didn't have a rifle or a knife, and so many of the others, Hakim's fangs were longer than I had ever seen them before.

I stiffened, and I felt Hawthorne shift uncomfortably by my side. I took in all the altered details of my partner's appearance as flashes of the old folktales flooded my mind. Hakim did not look like the Reborn that I knew. His pupils were over-dilated, nearly blown wide. His nails were long, like pointed claws. His ashen skin was tighter, and there was a minute tremor running through his body, as if his muscles were flexing in excitement and couldn't sit still.

There wasn't a doubt in my mind that he and the others had all drained for this, and I wondered if they were the nightmares that Warren and his people had faced.

"These work perfectly fine," Hakim said, and the dark glint in his eyes made my stomach turn over.

Before I could even form a coherent thought, the gates were opened, the crowd moved forward, and several hunters cheered in excitement. Hakim stared at me a moment longer, then slung his hunting rifle over his shoulder and followed the mass of bodies pushing through the gate.

"Better get moving," he said over his shoulder, just loud enough for us to hear. "Or you'll miss out."

The red hunting tag fluttered against my chest in the wind. Rain was starting to fall; it was soaking into my hair and making my skin damp, which was a nice break from the heat typical of this time of year. Hawthorne's arm brushed against mine as we shifted around a large maple tree, but I found I didn't mind. It was oddly comforting having him so close to my side, and given that I wished I was anywhere else in the world right now, I was happy to take any semblance of comfort I could get.

The forest was too quiet.

I had never been afraid of the woods, but right now, I was nervous.

Hawthorne was uneasy too.

I could see it on his face any time I glanced at him, yet neither one of us had spoken a word for the last hour, since following the excited crowd of hunters onto the hunting grounds. It was as if our capacity for speech had been completely lost, which spoke volumes about the level of discomfort, since Hawthorne rarely ever shut up.

My eyes darted to the right at the sound of a creak, but it was just the wind blowing through the trees.

The crowd of hunters, nearly all of which I was now convinced were casual drainers, had rapidly dispersed, some running off alone while others formed small groups. They were regulars. They knew these lands, and it was clear that they each had favourite spots they wanted to get to. Hawthorne and I, on the other hand, had no idea where we were going and had wandered south away from the others. I hadn't seen where Hakim had gone. He had all but vanished into the trees the second we'd passed through the gate, but I knew we were headed in the exact opposite direction as Vogle and Tan—which was precisely what I wanted.

I didn't want to see any humans.

I didn't want to run into anyone from the precinct.

I didn't want to find out what a drained Reborn was capable of or see just how well their fangs worked as a weapon.

I just wanted to get through this night with my sanity intact and never experience this again. If turning up at the gate empty-handed made me look pathetic in the eyes of my fellow officers, so be it. I wasn't going to shoot anyone tonight, and I sure as hell wasn't going to attack someone outright with my hands.

We rounded a thicket of trees, and I stopped.

Every muscle in my body went rigid as the familiar scent of human sweat filled my nose. After spending so much time at the farming facilities and being so close to Warren, it was a smell I would never mistake. Hawthorne froze by my side. I turned my head. I could hear something in the distance. Someone was moving off to the west, and it wasn't a Reborn.

I waited, but the scent only grew stronger.

They were getting closer.

"Gorski." Hawthorne's low voice sounded by my ear. "That smell... is – is that a human?"

"Yes," I whispered, craning my neck and squinting through the trees for any sign of movement. "It's sweat."

Whoever it was obviously didn't know that we were here, but they'd yet to reach my line of sight. I tucked several loose strands of damp hair behind my ear, willing the smell to go away, but still, it only grew stronger. We were downwind. I wasn't sure how well humans could smell, but even if their capabilities rivalled ours, they wouldn't be able to smell us, and they would be here soon. They were coming right at us, and if we didn't move, they would run right into us.

I glanced toward Hawthorne, trying to gauge his expression. I had brought him along because I was hoping he would have no interest in hunting. Everything leading up to this moment had only proved my suspicion correct, but we had yet to outright say it, and I knew that I could still be wrong.

After all, how well did I really know him? How well did I know anyone, for that matter? I didn't even know myself anymore, but I knew if I didn't do something right now, my decision to get involved with humans tonight would be made for me.

"Hawthorne," I said, the words I had been suppressing all night tumbling out in a rapid, blunt whisper. "I don't want to be here. I don't want to hunt. I don't want to kill any humans. Not tonight. Not ever. If you want to think I'm pathetic, that's fine – I don't care. You can judge me all you want, but I can't do it. I won't do it."

"Good," Hawthorne whispered, his breath ghosting across my cheek as he stepped closer. "Because I can't either."

In one swift motion, he grabbed my hand and pulled me away from the thicket of trees. I gripped him tightly, following his lead as he raced away from the scent of sweat. Our feet were soundless as we moved, the weight of my loaned rifle feeling heavy as I ducked beneath a tree branch and then cut across a small clearing. He didn't slow down, but neither did I. We ran full tilt for a solid ten minutes until the smell of rain filled my nose, and the water came down heavy and cold against my skin. It wasn't until the sound of a rushing river rang loudly in my ears that he finally slowed to a stop.

He let go of my hand, running his fingers through his sopping-wet hair before he turned to look down at me with an openly anguished expression.

"Gorski, I can't do this," he said, his breath coming in abnormally rapid pulls. "I can't hunt humans – I can't eat them – I can't. I'd rather die. I got that girl's number from the protest because I wanted to know more, and she's told me so much that I can't. I just can't."

"I know," I breathed, nodding my head and closing my eyes. "I know – I can't either. I'm so sorry, Hawthorne. I'm sorry I asked you to come here with me."

"It's okay."

"No, it isn't." I opened my eyes to look up at him once more. "It wasn't fair. I knew you wouldn't want any part of this, but I pushed you into it anyway."

"Yeah, and I knew you didn't either," he murmured. He looked up into the night, his shoulders collapsing under an invisible weight as he let out a deep sigh. "That's why I agreed to come. I knew if it came down to it, you wouldn't do it. I know you don't want to be here. I know you don't want to hunt. I know you've been thinking about all of this just like I have, and I knew if I didn't come, you'd probably have to tag along with Vogle. And I couldn't do that to you."

I swallowed hard, my throat growing tight as I looked at him through the rain. "Thank you, Hawthorne."

"I cover your ass on a hunting trip so you can look good for your boss, and you still won't call me Theo."

"Hawthorne, I—"

"I'm kidding," he said, dropping his head to look at me once more. "What else are friends for?"

I smiled, a broken laugh cutting from my lips as I ran a hand over my face. "Thank you – I mean it."

"I know." Hawthorne nodded, taking a step toward me and smacking me on the back like he always did before dropping his arm around my shoulders. I let him do it and moved by his side as he started to walk. "But rest assured that my soon-to-be-requested favour is going to be huge."

I laughed again, thankful that he was by my side tonight and that he had taken the position nearest to the river. Being near water made me anxious. It brought back all the horrible memories from the Academy, and I was grateful to have Hawthorne with me since he knew the extent of those fears.

"I would expect nothing less from you."

"I'm going to pretend that isn't an insult."

"And I'm going to pretend that this"—I gestured to his arm, which hung loosely around my neck—"isn't some weird hero tactic you're using to try and get me to sleep with you."

He snorted and shook his head, and I couldn't help but smile once more. We continued walking for a while, moving along the river to the south in silence until the rain got so bad we stopped to stand under some trees. It was difficult to hear anything through the storm. All I could smell was rainwater and dirt, and even though images of Warren still crept through my mind, I found myself relaxing as the night grew later and nothing else happened.

After a few more hours had passed, we decided to head back. We would get to the gate before the night ended, but given the rain, we figured that an early return was reasonable. Hunting in this weather must be difficult. How a Reborn would be able to locate a human in this mess was beyond me, all the scents blurred together, making tracking seem impossible. Besides, I was exhausted, and I figured that our return would go unnoticed by anyone but Vogle and Hakim. And I doubted they would come back until the night was done, so they would never know.

We walked north along the riverbank under the cover of trees, following the bend until the ground started to rise, then we made our way up the rocks. Everything was going smoothly. We were just over an hour away from the gate. At a steady pace, we would be there well before sunrise, and I was starting to look forward to climbing inside Hawthorne's car and wiping this night from my memory banks.

Then I heard a crack like thunder.

And the bushes to my right exploded.

Three rapidly moving figures darted from the foliage and nearly rammed right into us. Voices broke out through the night air. I heard someone screaming. The smell of blood filled my nose. Hawthorne shifted to the right. I darted to the left, avoiding the first three figures and another two that burst through the trees before a sixth collided with my chest.

I barely had time to register what was happening before the sensation of falling dropped in my stomach. Three more bodies poured from the trees, moving swift and quick, hallmarks of a Reborn. They were chasing the six humans—or five now, since one of them was tumbling over the edge of the rocks with me. I saw blonde hair, green eyes, and a terrified expression across her face. Then cold water encased my body, and nails dug into my skin.

My head was being pushed under, and panic surged through my veins.

I'm going to drown.

I'm going to die.

I could feel the terror building like a wave in my chest as my single greatest fear wrapped around my body like a vice, squeezing the air from my lungs and the reason from my mind.

Not water.

Not water.

Not water—not like this.

It was the one thing I could not handle. Not since that day at the Academy…

I managed to grab a breath of air before wet hands pushed me back under. I fought against her, grabbing any part of her that I could as I tried to kick my legs. I couldn't see through the rushing mess of water. I tried to breathe again but only inhaled more liquid as the current tugged us both under. I kicked, against the girl or the river, I didn't know, but it made little difference when my body failed to react properly. A rock collided with my side, and I was forced back under again. We were starting to slow, but I still couldn't swim to the surface because I just couldn't make myself swim.

My lungs started to burn.

My brain started to scream.

I couldn't think.

I couldn't move.

I couldn't breathe.

All my muscles seized as my mind completely shut down.

I felt the girl's motions slow as my feet scraped against a rocky bottom—then something grabbed the back of my jacket. I inhaled sharply as my head was tugged roughly above the surface. Water poured from my mouth and nose, my vision blurring with tears as I coughed and gagged.

Someone was dragging me out of the river.

I could hear a familiar voice.

"H-Hawthorne," I sputtered, puking up water as I was dropped to the ground.

I panted for air, coughing up even more river water before I finally managed to look up. But the dark figure towering above me wasn't Hawthorne, and as I blinked my bleary eyes clear and he came into focus, I suddenly wished I had just drowned in the river.

I stared up at Hakim, barely able to inhale as my entire body shook. The blonde who had gone down the river with me was lying by my side in much worse condition, groaning in pain as the sound of Hawthorne's boots thudding against the earth filled the air.

"Valya! Fuck – Gorski!! Are you okay?!"

"Fine," I grunted, hauling myself up to my knees.

Hakim didn't move and continued to glare down at me with a distinctly dark but unreadable expression as Hawthorne dropped to the ground by my side.

"Don't you know how to swim, Gorski?" Hakim asked, his mismatched eyes watching as Hawthorne helped me up from the ground.

"I-I used to," I sputtered, grimacing as another ripple of painful coughs racked from my burning lungs. I glanced up at him again. He was soaked head to toe just like I was, his short hair a mess from the rushing waters.

"Swimming isn't something that you forget how to do," Hakim said. "You either can or you can't."

"She's terrified of water!" Hawthorne spat as he turned and glared at Hakim. "She was stuck in the test tank for over an hour when the overflow failed and the safety watch couldn't get her out. She nearly drowned!"

Hakim's sharp gaze was dangerous as it darted to Hawthorne, and I felt his body stiffen at my side.

"It's fine," I panted, wiping some of the water from my face and giving Hawthorne's arm a reassuring squeeze before looking at my partner once more. The last thing I needed was Hawthorne getting on Hakim's shit list. "I'm sorry, sir – I'll work on it. Thank you for p-pulling me out."

Hakim stared at Hawthorne for a long, nerve-wracking moment until he finally looked back at me.

"You had better," Hakim said, and I felt Hawthorne's hand curl into my jacket tightly. "We live in a coastal city, Gorski. You're lucky they passed you out of the Academy. Take care of it."

"Yes, sir," I whispered.

I watched him move to the left and pick his rifle up from the ground. I was expecting him to turn and leave in his usual indifferent fashion, but he didn't. Instead, he turned back to face us.

"You're wasting valuable blood."

"What?" Hawthorne asked.

"Franklin and Portner went after the other five. It might not be your shot, but they're not here to claim it, so it's as good as yours," Hakim said, gesturing with his head toward the blonde woman who was lying on the ground to our left. "Though, I doubt there is much left at this point."

Hawthorne froze, and my eyes dropped to the figure on the muddy ground. She was lying in a pool of blood, so much of it she surely wouldn't live for more than a moment longer—maybe another five minutes or so at best, but I doubted it. I watched the dark liquid pour from the bullet hole in her leg as the scent registered in my nose. Someone had shot her. Someone had shot her, but she had kept running. She convulsed once as her eyes fluttered open and a noise that sounded very much like a plea for help whispered from her lips.

"If you're not going to take what's left, then put the thing out of its misery and tag the location," Hakim said as he shouldered his rifle. "Undocumented hunts draw in predators. The organizers need to come to collect the remains."

Hawthorne didn't move.

I didn't breathe.

I could feel every single drop of rain as it hit my face and dripped from my eyelashes. Silence stretched around us, then I heard the shuffle of boots against the soggy ground as Hakim shifted. He paused, turning toward us as he unshouldered his rifle, and I forced myself to look at him. His eyes were cold as stone, disgust radiating in his voice as he looked at us through the rain.

"Pathetic," he said, and the word cut like a knife.

Then he moved forward to stand above the muddy girl, and the blonde's eyes filled with water as she stared up into the darkness at his face.

"P-P-lease," she whispered, and I heard Hawthorne inhale sharply at the sound.

Hakim lifted his rifle, aiming it lazily before he pulled the trigger and the crack cut through the air. The woman went still, her eyes wide and lifeless as she stared up into the night.

"What a waste." Hakim shouldered his rifle once more and turned to walk away. "Tag the location before you head back. Surely, you can at least manage that."

I felt my head nod, but I said nothing as I stared at her lifeless body, and the rain continued to pour down and soak the muddy ground beneath my feet.

Choices

I walked down the hallway in silence, my legs moving robotically. It was Friday. Grace was back from holiday. She had been texting me like crazy since Sunday evening, emailing me pictures from her trip and continuously asking me to meet for coffee so she could tell me all about it.

I had rejected every single invitation.

I blamed it on Hakim. I blamed it on my new position as a temporary detective. I told her I didn't have time, which was true, but the truth was, I just didn't care—which sounds horrible. I was probably hurting her feelings and being a terrible friend, but I couldn't even make myself look at the pictures she had sent. I just emailed back a generic reply saying that the trip looked great. I couldn't even remember the name of the hotel that she had stayed at.

I didn't care.

I couldn't care.

I could barely make myself function.

Every time I closed my eyes, I saw that woman lying on the ground in a pool of her own red blood. I saw Warren glaring at me. I heard his harsh voice in my mind, calling me and my people monsters—*vampires*—a claim I wasn't even sure I could refute anymore after what I'd seen that night on the reserve.

That woman had been so much smaller than me. Maybe only five feet tall and probably less than a hundred pounds, but she had fought so hard. Just like Warren, she'd had so much life. She had been real—a real, living, breathing being that could speak and feel.

And Hakim had shot her like she was an animal.

Like she was nothing.

By the time Hawthorne and I had returned to the gate, it had been nearly dawn. I was drenched. My legs wouldn't stop shaking, and Hawthorne was silent in a way that was concerning. Vogle was already back. He was standing beside his car, completely unbothered by the rain and looking distinctly pleased with himself as he chatted to Captain Tan, Hakim, and some other person I didn't recognize. He greeted us with a wave, asked us how the night was, and I forced myself to smile and lie. I said that it was *fun*. Hawthorne thanked him again for the extra tag. Captain Tan asked if we managed to catch anything, and we feigned regret and said no. They said that was typical for a first hunt, and the weather hadn't helped.

Then they smiled and told us it would be better *next time*.

As I spoke to Vogle, Hakim stared at me—the iciness of his gaze making my skin crawl. I had expected him to make some snide comment about our "pathetic" behaviour and my crippling fear of water, but he didn't. I don't know why. He didn't even mention anything about the river, and no one asked why we were drenched. Then again, we weren't the only ones; a few other hunters were dripping head to toe or covered in mud.

He didn't say anything to me about it during our Monday shift either. We met at our usual time, followed our usual routine, and checked the sensors at the second facility. I think my only saving grace was that the river incident had happened off the clock, so technically, he had no grounds to lodge a complaint. He knew it would never be accepted by Vogle or HR. But I knew that he would be looking even closer for any and every reason to get rid of me going forward, because as he met my gaze first thing Sunday evening, his opinion was painfully clear. He thought I was completely and utterly incompetent, which on any other normal night, would eat me alive. But now, I wasn't sure that I cared anymore. I wasn't even sure what I was doing or why I was doing it. I was simply going through the motions.

I hadn't managed to speak to Hawthorne in detail about what had happened yet. Our ride home had been silent. He had dropped me off Saturday morning, handing me his copies of the studies that his human rights activist friend had given to him before I got out of the car. I read them in my kitchen before going to sleep, though I'm pretty sure I just lay there in bed staring at the wall all day as my mind raced.

Tuesday shift was more of the same. Wednesday was nothing but crawling through security footage and starting a new missing person file for the latest dead body potentially tied to our new and growing Jane Doe collection—a collection that was starting to cause quite a stir on the news.

The Female Advocacy Agency city chapter, or FAA as they liked to call themselves, were pushing for answers and a CPD commitment to a full and open investigation, claiming that these murders correlated to rising crimes against women and that the cases were serial, not the result of randomized gang violence. Formally, the CPD disagreed, and the mayor was determined to deny the possibility of linked serial killings despite Hakim informing Vogle that each body appeared to have similar markings on their necks.

It seemed that neither side was publicly willing to step down, and Hakim and I were getting caught in the crossfire—unable to make any real progress.

Hakim gave me the crime scene photos and medical reports that were available, which were limited given the bureaucratic mess surrounding the murders. Then he gave me several unsolved case files from nearly three decades ago, which he thought might be linked to the new bodies. I wasn't sure if he was supposed to dig those up or how he even knew about those files, since they were handled by another detective, Detective Russo, who'd retired a few years ago, but I didn't doubt his suspicions. The marks on the victims' necks were unmistakably similar—large circular scars on the left-hand side, and each victim had suffered extreme blunt force trauma to the back of the head.

Either way, I didn't say a word about my discomfort when I opened each new folder and saw the new grotesque images. Instead, I worked myself to the bone because I didn't know what else to do. But I could feel something building in my chest as each day went by.

Pressure.

A horrible, haunting pressure that got worse and worse by the minute. I could feel it at the base of my throat, as if I was seconds away from vomiting up my insides and collapsing inwards like a black hole. I managed to make it through Thursday without making any mistakes, but the faint rings beneath my eyes were getting darker. I may have managed to reach the end of the week today, but I was hanging by a thread, and I was starting to dread what might come next.

I sighed as I approached the print room. What the hell was I supposed to do with myself now, after everything? And why couldn't I stop thinking about Warren and wondering about his plans?

"Gorski!"

I stiffened, then turned to look behind me. Hakim was strolling down the hall, gear bag slung over his shoulder. He looked like he was leaving, which didn't make any sense because it was only 2 am.

"Yes, sir?"

"I have to go over to Precinct 10 to meet Officer Das," Hakim said, pausing just a few feet shy of where I stood. "They have a new dead body, and given the details, Vogle thinks it might be tied to our work. If that's the case, it should fall under our jurisdiction, and we'll be taking it over. The detectives at Precinct 7 don't have the resources to manage an investigation like this, and it doesn't make sense to split the file across precinct jurisdictions, especially with the increase in eastside theft."

"Okay," I said, wondering if Vogle was planning to push the CPD to publicly admit that the cases were eerily similar and likely related. "Do you want me to come?"

"No." The response was clipped. "Check with Corban to see if he got anything on those prints from the farm yet, and finish going through the old folders I gave you yesterday. Take them home with you over the long weekend. Just because Monday is a stat holiday doesn't mean you get a break. Things are going to get busier when the farm facilities bring in new stock next month, and we need to be prepared. I'll see you Tuesday shift. Don't be late, and don't forget to lock the boardroom."

With that, he turned and left, and I closed my eyes.

It was the first night I would be working alone, and it wasn't because he trusted me to do things without him here to supervise. It was because he didn't want me with him. The insult stung. I might be having an implosive identity crisis, but I still needed a job.

I let out a breath, then reminded myself that even though I felt like a mess, my actions still reflected back on Mallick, my peers, and my family. So I grabbed my papers from the printer and quickly made my way to our boardroom. I worked the next two hours in silence, rapidly pushing through all the data Hakim had left me to create a master Jane Doe timeline before I headed down to the fifth floor to talk to Corban in the lab. Unsurprisingly, he hadn't found any matches to our print, nor did he make any mention of the print being abnormal, which meant that human fingerprints and Reborn fingerprints were impossible to distinguish.

I swallowed that detail down quietly while trying and failing to keep images of Warren out of my head. He had been popping up all week, polluting my mind like a plague—the heat of his leg between my hands, the sun-kissed tone of his skin, the words he had spoken—all of it tormenting me and burrowing deeper under my skin as I wondered who he was.

He had to be working with other humans.

Was this the first time that he had broken into a farming facility, or had he done this before and gotten away with it? How old was he? How many other humans did he live with, and where were they? Were they all that tall? Where did they sleep? How long did they live? How had he learned to use a firearm? Were they allied with the Reborn human rights groups, or were they working on their own? It seemed unlikely he would accept help from us, but—

I forced the amplifying thoughts aside as I made my way toward the elevator. I didn't have time to get distracted when I had two massive and growing cases to work on.

I pressed the button to call the elevator, then ran through the list of outstanding items I still needed to complete as I waited for it to arrive. When the dim light finally flickered above the door, I had nearly managed to shove all thoughts of Warren and that awful night in the woods into a tiny corner of my mind, convincing myself that it probably wasn't that bad, my captain would never drain, and this would soon become just another faded memory. Then the doors to the elevator opened, and I found myself facing my old captain.

"Captain Mallick," I said, nodding my head in greeting and stepping into the small space.

"Gorski."

Mallick nodded in return, pressing the button to the eleventh floor for me as I scanned my passcard. I glanced at the buttons. He was headed to twelve, so he must be going to another meeting with the chief. It made me wonder how much time he spent up there, and how on earth he had time to monitor the eighth floor as closely as he did.

"It's been a while since I've seen you."

"Yes, sir," I said, then I frowned. "I'm sorry, sir. I should have stopped by to let you know how things were going and—"

"That wasn't meant as a critique on your performance, Gorski," Mallick said, and he shook his head as he turned to look at me. "It was simply an observation. I wasn't expecting you to stop by to visit. I know Hakim and Vogle have been keeping you busy."

"Yes, sir."

He continued to stare at me, an odd but unreadable expression on his face. I swallowed, shuffling in discomfort as I tried not to be concerned. Maybe I looked even more ragged than I realized.

"You've done well to have made it this far, though," he finally said, and I couldn't help but smile.

"Thank you, sir."

"I heard that Vogle brought you along to the summer open season."

I stiffened, my hands clenching at my sides as all the images I had worked so hard to suppress came spinning back up to the forefront of my mind.

"Yes, sir." My voice sounded weak. "It was very kind of him. I had a lot of fun."

Mallick nodded, his pale brown eyes shifting over my face. "I'm sure you did."

The bell for the elevator chimed, and I tore my eyes away from him to take my leave.

"Gorski."

I stopped, turning back to see Mallick gripping the doors to hold them open.

"Yes, sir?"

"I know how badly you want to be a detective," Mallick said, but his voice was carefully low. "But don't do it at the expense of your own principles. It's okay to say no."

I opened my mouth but found my lips lost for words.

"Don't forget my door is always open, Gorski."

With that, he stepped back, letting the door close between us as I stared after him in silence. I wasn't sure what to make of his words. I had always known that Mallick would be in my corner, but I wasn't sure what this meant in regard to anything else. Did he also hate hunting? Was this part of the reason why he had left the Detective Unit and accepted the role of captain for Patrol and Street? Or was he simply trying to look out for me because I had failed to lie well enough to convince him that I had enjoyed the experience?

I would probably never know the answers to those questions, so I shoved it all aside with the rest and returned to the boardroom. I updated my missing persons map with the old files Hakim had given to me, then submitted six more background checks on known human rights activists flagged as potential threats to the farming facilities and started combing through the crime scene photos on the newest Jane Doe. I was just setting out the photos from several of the case files to look for patterns when my cell phone started to ring.

It was Grace, and I hesitated, debating letting it go to voicemail again. I had been ignoring her text messages all shift thus far, but even I knew I was pushing it. Groaning in submission, I grabbed the phone and answered it on the last ring.

"Gorski."

'Valya.' The flat-toned response echoed in my ear. She was pissed. I could tell. *'Why have you been ignoring my texts?'*

"I haven't been ignoring your texts," I said, closing my eyes and dropping my head into my hand. "I've just been busy, Grace."

'Grace?'

"I'm working, Lexie," I sighed, knowing that she had probably taken the night off to get an even longer long weekend. "I always call you Grace at work."

'Whatever,' she said. *'Look, I just wanted to know if you could come by a bit early to help me set up?'*

"Come by early?" My brow creased, and I glanced over to the boardroom door to double-check that it was closed. "For what?"

Silence echoed on the other end, and I felt my skin prickle.

'It's Friday the 24th – my anniversary party, Valya,' Grace said, and her tone made me cringe. *'You promised that you would come before I went on vacation, remember?'*

"Shit," I breathed and closed my eyes again. "Grace, I'm so sorry – I've been completely swamped with these cases, and I—"

'Yeah, I know,' Grace spat. *'Look, I get that you want to be a detective, but is it really worth it if you have to kill yourself over it and never see your friends? What kind of life is that? And don't blame it on Detective Hakim, either – he can't make you work more than the standard approved hours, especially after what happened to his last partner. That's illegal, and you could complain if you wanted to, but you don't. You're choosing to do this. And if you want to choose not to show up, then fine, but—'*

"I'll be there," I cut her off, pinching my eyes shut tighter. "I said I would be there, so I'll be there. You're right. I'm sorry. I've gotten so caught up in everything I haven't even asked you about your trip. Look – I – I've managed to get almost everything done.

I just need to fill out two requests for file transfers, but I can be there at 7 am. Is that okay?"

'Fine,' Grace said after a moment of silence. *'And don't forget the dress is semi-formal.'*

She hung up, and I dropped my phone to the desk in defeat. Beneath it were the pictures of battered-looking women—maps, notes, a scrawled list of unanswered questions, and a small pile of coroner data I had yet to look through. My heart sank as my eyes traced over the victim's faces. I couldn't see the difference at all anymore, between these girls and that woman who'd knocked me into the river—which lifeless eyes were which...

"It all just looks the same," I whispered as my throat started to burn.

"Thank you so much for coming!"

"Oh my goodness, your home is beautiful."

"Thank you. We just had the floors redone."

"Well, they look great! Did you get this catered by Heather?"

"Yes! Isn't she the best?"

"I cannot wait to try the food – everything looks so incredible."

I stared at the woman who had just entered Lexie Grace's home. She was wearing a light red dress. Her long brown hair was flawlessly curled, and her nails were manicured to perfection. Her teeth shone pristine white as she smiled, her well-practiced social laugh ringing out through the room like little wind chimes. She had pale skin, like everyone else in this room, and her eyes were a milky shade of blue. Her husband was placing their blackout helmets on the rack by the door. His hair was brown, as were his eyes—but they felt colourless.

Dull.

Boring.

Nothing like Warren's.

Borderline lifeless looking now that I had seen the vivid shades of green and brown that humans had to offer. Ours looked washed-out in comparison. Like pastel paintings faded in the sun, which was ironic given that we couldn't stand in the sun. My eyes shifted down to my own blue dress, and suddenly, I hated the shade. It was too chalky. Too pale. Too empty. I looked like a bland morning sky, and I wished I was back home in my comfortable standard-issue CPD shirt and black pants.

The clink of glass rang out to my left, and I turned to watch an elegant-looking woman refill her wine glass. The contents were dark. Red. Like the blood that had poured from that woman's body. Red. Like the blood that had coated my hands as I'd opened that foothold trap for Warren. I swallowed, glancing down at the tiny plate of untouched food in my left hand. I had been all but obligated to take it. Grace and her husband had ordered catered appetizers, and each dish was divine, according to the other guests. Yet, when I looked at it, it just made me feel sick.

If this hors d'oeuvre had come from Warren—would I eat it?

The question had haunted me since the moment I'd returned from setting him free. It was the reason I had been consuming nothing but synthetic gelatin cubes all week, even though I had tried to deny it. Humans were not what I had thought they were. They were not stupid, useless animals too weak or incompetent to use tools, and knowing that now, the idea of eating one…

I fought the urge to gag as I stared at the unappealing dish. The small appetite I had gained after a long night of rushing around the boardroom so I could make it here to help Grace set up before the party started was gone, disappearing the instant the thought crossed my mind.

I didn't want to eat it.

But more than that, I didn't want to be here.

My gaze shifted back up to the room, taking in the polite, happy smiles and other washed-out clothing. The fragrances of different shampoos and perfumes mixed and lingered in the air. It felt fake.

How could they be talking so calmly? Discussing movies and weather and home design without a care in the world. My mind was filled with images of dead bodies, blood, and frail human beings curled up against metal bars—meanwhile, their biggest concerns were getting another set of Ridgeback boots and who would be voted off in the next episode of The Matchmaker.

I finally understood.

This was why Hakim was so cold. This was why most detectives had no families or social lives. *This* was what Captain Mallick was trying to warn me about.

The disconnect.

I watched a particularly beautiful woman with blonde hair swallow a small peach pate, and my stomach curled. If not for the paleness of her eyes and the colourless tone of her skin, she would look exactly like the woman who had bled out at my feet during the hunt. My eyes scanned around the room once more, and the pressure in my chest grew.

How could they eat this food and not care?

Did they simply not know any different? Did they not ever think about it? Had they never once wondered where it came from?

I hadn't.

Those two words stopped my questions and sank like a stone in my chest. How could I stay here and talk to these people and pretend as if I cared about the latest trend in furniture upholstery when women were dying on the eastside and humans, who could speak, read, and think critically just like us, were being hunted alive?

These people should know what's happening in the world around them, and they should care. I should tell them. I should tell them that humans are intelligent and make them care—but even considering it filled my mind with doubts and made me sink deeper into the corner of the room.

I watched a group of three make their way over to the food table to refill their plates, my own growing heavier in my hand.

All this week I had been struggling. I still wanted to be a detective. I still wanted to help. I still wanted to make a difference, and yet I was finding it increasingly difficult to reconcile those goals with what I was seeing because everything in my life felt like it was being ripped apart. The law was there to protect people, and I was struggling to see how I could view Warren as anything other than a person.

We should care that they're hunted and killed like animals.

We should care that they're being kept in cages.

We should care that they can speak and think and reason.

My hand started to tremble, and the tight sensation in my chest grew so painful I couldn't breathe. All the chatter around me blurred into a dull thrum. My muscles started to twitch. With each second, the horrible feeling grew, my heart thudding in my ears until the pressure became so unbearable I couldn't stand it— and I felt it snap.

A burning wave of sickness scorched through my body as my eyes started to sting, and I tasted bile at the back of my throat.

I cared.

I cared so much it made me sick and I wanted others to care too, but more than that, I wanted to *do* something about it, because the idea of continuing on like I had been was impossible. I couldn't. Not anymore. Not like this, not knowing what I knew and having seen what I'd seen. A swarm of emotions burned through my veins. My legs moved before my mind could follow, rapidly carrying me across the room. I dropped my plate on the bar top counter, then made my way to the door as I blinked my eyes clear.

"Valya?"

I nearly grimaced at the sound of Grace's voice as she called after me. She was trying to be quiet, probably hoping to avoid the attention of her other guests.

"Where are you going?"

"I'm sorry," I said, fighting to control the waver in my voice. I glanced over my shoulder, seeing her close the distance toward me. "I have to go."

"But the party only just started," Grace said, lowering her voice even further as a smile strained across her lips. She moved closer, watching in confusion as I grabbed my gloves and started putting them on. "You didn't even eat any of the food, and Mark and I haven't opened any gifts yet."

"I know." I nodded but avoided her eyes. I knew she was angry, but this was happening, and I couldn't stop it. "I'm so sorry, but Hakim just texted me, and I need to leave. We can talk next week."

I grabbed my helmet off the rack and jammed it onto my head. I heard her say my name once more, but I didn't stop as I grabbed my jacket and tugged it on, barely getting it zipped up before I made my way through the double doors and out into the early morning sun.

My heart raced as I drove home, a million thoughts muddling my mind, all of them sounding more and more insane than the last. I didn't slow as I made my way up to my apartment. I barely managed to shut the door behind me before I started stripping off my dress and tights and kicking off my heels. I threw the pale blue fabric into my laundry basket, knowing that I never wanted to wear it again, as I stormed my way to my closet and ripped open the doors. I tugged out a pair of old pants. Then I grabbed an old tank top and nondescript long-sleeved shirt before moving to my dresser to fish out a pair of socks.

My hands shook as I pulled everything on, braided my hair into a French braid down the back of my head, and then stormed my way back to the living room. I tugged on my boots, put on my vest, covered it with my long-sleeved shirt, then grabbed my firearm, map, compass, gear bag, helmet, and gloves before marching right back out the door. It took me twenty minutes to drive to the sketchiest end of Carneth, stopping at a bank machine to withdraw more cash before driving another half hour away to the most run-down twenty-four-hour convenience store I could find.

I bought every medical supply they had, and filled my basket with acetaminophen, water, batteries, and alcohol wipes. I bought a small bag, then I drove to the next store and the next, stocking up on any supplies I could get my hands on and any preserved foods that didn't contain blood or human products until I ran out of cash. Then I drove to the highway, my hands gripping the wheel so tightly that by the time the familiar country road came into view and I slowed to a stop I could barely unclamp my fingers.

I parked behind the same thicket of trees I'd used when I'd first come out to help Warren, ensuring that my vehicle was fully hidden from the road before strapping my firearm to my hip and repacking my bag. Then I put on my helmet and gloves and set out into the woods.

Finding the rock formation was easier this time than it had been the first, but tracking Warren's trail was much more difficult. The rain had done a good job of washing away the blood. I could still smell it in the rock cutout where I had tended to his leg, but it was unlikely anyone would notice it unless they crawled inside.

I headed off in the direction he had limped, tracking what I could from his remaining trail and making assumptions based on the land. I walked for hours. Hours and hours until the sun started to go down, and the night crept in. I backtracked twice, stood in silence looking at my map and compass before crawling around on the ground, looking for any hint of a print to point me in the right direction. Then, after several long minutes of debate, I finally decided to head northeast instead of northwest. Hakim's sensor set footage implied that the perpetrator was headed east in his examination of the facility, which would suggest that he had come from the west, which would explain why I had found him in my section to the east, because it was probably at the end of his route and he would then turn around and return home to the west after scoping out the fenceline.

But Warren was smart.

I had learned that the hard way.

Surely he knew we were investigating the damage. So even though he hadn't known about the sensors and cameras, he must have been covering his tracks. The Norhaven Wildlife Reservation was to the west and extended up to the north, and that was far too obvious. East headed into thicker trees and rocky terrain. There were lakes and small rivers up there, plenty of places to hide and plenty of places to camp out in areas most Reborn never ventured. Whatever Warren was doing, whatever his plan of attack was, I doubted he would run it from his home in Norhaven—assuming he came from the reserve at all. He would probably be working as far away from it as possible while keeping close enough that he could manage the surveillance of the facilities by foot and travel home without too many issues.

I knew that when I found him, *if* I found him, it would be out of luck. And I knew that I would never find him if I underestimated him. I had to stop thinking of him as weaker when he clearly wasn't. He had proved that point rather succinctly when he'd pinned me to the ground and completely disarmed me. His mind was easily just as cunning as any Reborn's.

If he was still alive and still in this area, he would be to the northeast. His base of operation would need to be within half a night's walking distance to the facility, and it would be hidden. Far from the city limits of Carneth and thus far from the notice of Reborn.

I knew it would take me longer than half a night to find it, but I knew I couldn't quit until I did.

I stopped searching for the night just shy of 7 pm, marking my location on my map and crossing out the areas that I had already covered before running back to my car. Exhaustion hit my body as I climbed inside. It was unfamiliar and unnerving. I was barely able to breathe as I started the engine and made my way out onto the main roads.

I drove home, forced myself to eat, and slept for my usual three hours. Then I worked at my kitchen table until it was light enough to avoid morning traffic and headed back out again Saturday midmorning. I ignored Grace's text messages, drove into the country, and parked my car in the trees off a side road that was as close to the direction I wanted to go as possible. Then I set out once more and repeated the process to no avail.

When I got back home from searching all day a second time, I crashed before I could even change my clothes. When I woke up six hours later, it was still dim, so I forced myself to send a few emails before choking down more gelatin cubes and packing up once more.

I was running out of time, and I could feel the stress increasing with each passing minute.

I wouldn't be able to search during the day while working this week. It was impossible. Hakim demanded too much of my time, and slacking wasn't an option because I needed to keep my job. My thoughts had continued to circle as I'd searched through the forest in my blackout gear, but the longer I'd spent in the trees, the more clear things had become and the more sure I was in my decision.

I was going to help Warren.

But the only way I could do that was if I remained a detective and maintained my access to the case file. If Hakim kicked me back to Patrol and Street before I found Warren and told him the details of our investigation, he would eventually get caught. I wouldn't be able to give him warnings about our actions or purchase supplies for him, which meant that I had to find a way to convince Hakim that I wasn't completely useless.

I had to perform better.

I clenched my teeth hard as I pulled off onto the familiar exit, determination burning through my veins. I was going to find him. I had to. This might very well have been the stupidest decision I had ever made in my life, but I was going to do it anyway.

I parked my car in the bushes, off a side road next to the northern woods and much closer to my desired location. Then I packed up my bag and headed out into the trees. The terrain was terrible. It took hours to navigate when looking for signs of trails or regular movement. I followed my map, checking out the areas I had flagged in advance as potential hideout locations. It was nearly dusk when I reached my third search area, and my heart caught in my throat when I saw a smear of dried blood against a rock. The rain hadn't reached this far north last weekend, and I found a second smear a few feet away from the first.

His bandages must have come loose after fighting through the underbrush—or maybe his stitches tore. I wasn't sure which it was, but I found my concern starting to grow. What if he had died? What if he didn't make it? Did I care? Would that change anything?

I wasn't sure. After all, he had all but left me for dead a week ago. I might be planning to help him, but that didn't mean he deserved my empathy.

I pushed on to the northeast for another half an hour, slowing as a small river came into view. There were a lot of rock formations here—a lot of places to hide, just as I had suspected. I stilled, my eyes tracing across the landscape as the sun started to set. A flock of birds burst from the trees across the river, and my ears started to ring. I had the distinct feeling of being watched, yet I couldn't see anything among the trees because of the warp in my visor, and there wasn't a trace of sweat in the air.

I stepped silently across the stone, willing my breath to slow as doubts started to form.

Maybe this was stupid. He had almost shot me once. What was I thinking? I should have just asked Hawthorne for that girl's number and signed some of their petitions, or maybe I could have—my thoughts halted as something crunched behind me, and my hand instantly flew to my firearm.

"Don't even think about it."

I froze at the familiar sound of his voice. I heard him shuffle on the stone, but he kept his distance as he carefully circled into view. He looked exactly like I remembered him, with wavy hair just touching his shoulders. Warm, deep brown eyes so vivid they hardly seemed real. He was wearing a different shirt, and he was holding an old rifle, one that had seen better days and had a stock wrapped in worn tape.

"Who are you, and how did you get here?"

"Warren," I said, and I saw him stiffen at my voice as I carefully raised my hands.

He didn't shoot, but he watched my movements warily as I grabbed my helmet and slowly pulled it off my head. It was dim enough now that the sun wouldn't burn, but I still had to squint a little to see his face properly.

"What the hell are you doing here?" His tone was deadly as he raised the weapon higher and pointed it at my face. "I told you I would kill you if you followed me."

"I want to help," I said quickly, carefully shifting my helmet under one arm. I wasn't stupid enough to let go of it, even if it was getting dark. I didn't trust him not to throw it again, and knowing him, he'd probably toss it into the river in the hopes it would wash away. "I brought this for you." I pulled the bag from my shoulder with my free hand; he watched me warily, but said nothing as I held it out to him. "It – it has supplies."

"Put it on the ground," he said after a long pause, then his eyes flicked down to the firearm on my hip. "And take off your holster."

"I can't give you my firearm," I said as I set the bag of supplies down on the rocks and raised my free hand into the air once more. "I need that for work."

"Take it off." He released the safety on his rifle and took a step forward. "I won't ask you again."

"Alright," I conceded, and I slowly reached for my holster. I undid the strap, then set it on the ground by my side.

"Take three steps back," he ordered, and my legs moved in compliance. He shifted forward to grab the bag, looping the strap over his shoulder before quickly stepping back. "Did you put a tracker in here?"

"What? No – of course not."

"I'll know if you're lying."

"I'm not lying. I wouldn't—"

"What do you want?"

I stared at him, at the blatant hostility radiating from his gaze and wondered if I was insane to want to help him. His leg was still braced with the sticks I had used, but the whole of his injury was rewrapped in new bandages, undoubtedly from the bag he had stolen. And suddenly, my face faltered, and my hand dropped back to my side.

"I already told you why I'm here," I said as my eyes narrowed into a glare. "I came here because I want to help you. I just spent three days trekking through the woods to find you. I brought you more supplies."

"And you think that's helping?" His voice was dangerously low. "You think dropping off a bag filled with random stuff will make up for everything you vampires have done to us? That I'm stupid enough to trust you because you *say* you want to help?"

I flinched at the word as a scoff left his lips.

"You're even stupider than I thought you were."

The jab stung, and I felt the pressure that had been simmering in my chest burst.

"And you're an idiot," I whispered, my hand clenching at my side.

His eyes narrowed at my words, but suddenly the fact that he had a rifle pointed at my face didn't seem to matter anymore when I had already come this far. Maybe I was upset because he was right, and I was stupid—stupid for thinking that bringing a supply bag would mean anything in the face of everything else. But he was shortsighted and missing the bigger picture, and it was starting to piss me off.

"I'm a police officer, Warren," I said, holding his hard gaze. "You know that. But what you don't know is that I'm a detective working on the case file for the factory farm break-ins. I know everything about their facilities. I have maps, data about their camera locations and security measures. We're monitoring the perimeter of multiple farms right now, and we caught you on video. Right now, my partner doesn't know that you're a human. He thinks this whole thing is being led by Reborn human rights activists, but he found some of your fingerprints, and they are looking for you. If you linger around here much longer, you're going to get caught, and if that happens, I can't imagine that will go well for you or anyone else involved in this."

Warren had stilled at my words, the anger fading from his face as it shifted into a carefully blank expression.

"So what do you want?" he repeated.

"Nothing," I said, shaking my head in disbelief. "This isn't extortion. I didn't spend three days borderline overheating in blackout gear just to turn around and screw you over. I'm not going to tell anyone about this; I'm offering to help you. I can give you information about our investigation and bring you supplies so you don't get caught."

"Why?"

I stared at him, searching for some kind of indication that he didn't think I was a soulless, heartless being who had trudged through the woods with the sole purpose of ruining his life. But there wasn't any, and my shoulders dropped.

"I don't know," I said, and my voice felt quiet. "I just want to help. Please."

"So you can feel better about yourself?" Warren whispered. "Grew a conscience over the weekend, did you?"

I didn't say anything, because I didn't have anything to say to those words, and I wasn't even sure if I could refute them.

"If you really want to help," he said after a long moment of silence had passed. "Then you'll come back next weekend – new bag, new supplies, and bring me maps of the facilities and any information you have. I want to know where your sensors are, how they work, and what their range is."

"Okay." I nodded. "They're activated by a trip laser that—"

"I can read." Warren cut me off. "Write it down and put it in the bag. Bring batteries, matches, medications, medical supplies, shoes, printed weather reports for the next month, and tape."

"Okay."

"There's a small cave to the east, another five kilometres away. Drop the bag there and leave. If I need anything else, I'll leave a list for you and let you know when I need it by."

"Alright."

"But don't come back here otherwise."

"I won't."

"Good," Warren said, gesturing with his head toward the treeline. "Now leave."

I stared at him, feeling horrible and empty. I don't know what I had been expecting—but it hadn't been this. It wasn't like I thought I was a hero, but a thank you or something other than blatant hatred would have been nice. I swallowed, nodding slowly as I reached up to tuck a loose strand of hair behind my ear.

He tensed at the movement, and I suddenly felt even worse.

"I have to pick up my firearm," I said quietly. "I can't leave without it."

"Carry it by the holster away from your body until you get back into the trees."

Warren didn't leave any room for argument, but I didn't feel like fighting against him anyway. Not when it felt like I had just been gut-punched by his words. So I carefully collected my weapon from the ground and turned and walked away—hoping that he wouldn't change his mind and shoot me point blank.

Jane Doe

"Where's the folder for the latest Jane Doe?"

"On the cabinet to your left."

"We need to run the prints. It's unlikely that anything will show, but—"

"I already did it."

Hakim paused mid-reach and turned to look at me.

"Both federal and provincial record systems, and FIDA?"

"Yes." I nodded, having completed the Federal ID Archive request just a few hours ago. "And I asked our Forensics Department to go over her clothes again – they just arrived with the rest of the evidence for her file. Given where the body was found, I suspect that the initial team from Precinct 9 didn't do an overly thorough job. So I told Louise to recheck everything."

"Have you added her to the map?"

"Yes."

"Placed her approximate TOD on the timeline?"

"Yes."

"Requested security footage from the traffic cameras?"

"Yes."

"Everything in a ten-block radius?"

157

"Fifteen," I said, glancing up to catch him arching a brow. "Three of the bodies were dumped not far from the end of a subway line. Unlikely as it is, it is possible that someone used the subway to dispose of their bodies, and given that we haven't had any luck with missing vehicles or found anything suspicious by the other sites, I thought it was worth a look. The first stop on that line is fifteen blocks away, so I wanted to make sure we got the complete picture."

"Good." He nodded, grabbed the file, and turned away again. "Send a follow-up email to Carl at farm facility one before you go home to see if he's finished implementing all of our recommendations."

"Alright."

It was the nearest thing to a compliment he would ever give me, and I would take it. The report he was referring to was the one that I had drafted. He had barely made any changes to it before sending it out, so that was another compliment in and of itself.

Somehow, despite all odds, I had not only managed to keep my job, but I had also managed to get better at it over the last month. I knew some of it was probably luck, and some was pure resilience on my part toward Hakim's brutal nature, but the biggest factor that had changed and reinvigorated my motivation was Warren.

I worked harder. Smarter. Longer.

I watched Hakim closely, took notes, and started to anticipate his thinking. I filled out forms before he asked for them, followed up on requests, and meticulously combed through our data and kept things organized. It was challenging, especially since I was essentially acting as a double agent and sabotaging our own investigation, which made me feel a little sick, but it was worth it.

It felt right.

As an officer of the law, I had a duty to protect people, and that was exactly what I was doing. Helping him sparked something inside me, and it changed everything.

After walking away from Warren on July 27th while trying not to think about the rifle that was pointed at my head, I'd spent another hour slowly trekking back to my car. Then, I'd driven home in silence and immediately got to work replanning my life. I started making all my purchases with cash, slipping in some of the items that Warren had requested while out on my usual grocery trips. I gathered the rest from several stores all over Carneth in between working with Hakim throughout the week. I wrote up an explanation for how the cameras and sensors worked, then made a copy of my master map, facility details, and other information that might be useful. It was easy to do. I often brought my work home with me, so Hakim didn't bat an eye when I left carrying multiple folders.

When I drove out on the 31st of July to make the first drop, I wondered what I would say if Warren was there. I planned out several questions, trying to think of a way to start up a conversation with him and perhaps decrease some of the tension, only to arrive at the cave and find it completely empty—aside from a hand-written note in the center pinned under a rock. I should have been anticipating that, but I found myself oddly disappointed as I read the note over, then left the bag and made my way back home to plan the next drop of supplies.

Despite being beautifully printed, the note was blunt and to the point. There was absolutely nothing personal about it. There was no thank you either, just a list of items and a drop date of a week later. He requested updated weather reports, refillable water bottles, pens, blankets, and more batteries. He wasn't there for the second drop on August 7th, nor for the third drop the week after that on the 14th, or the fourth drop I'd made two nights ago on Tuesday.

The fifth would be this coming morning. The newest bag, a large, dark canvas material gear bag I had found for fifty percent off, was already packed and stored in the trunk of my car. All I had to do was get through the rest of this shift, and then I'd be heading back out into the woods once more.

Between driving out in that direction with Hakim to check the sensors nearly every other day and my own midmorning jaunts, the trip was so familiar I felt like I could drive it with my eyes closed.

Of course, over the last month, we had found absolutely nothing on the sensor data, and nothing else had happened at the farms. I briefly tried to sell Hakim on the idea that maybe the human rights activists had given up and moved on, but he wasn't convinced. If anything, he just grew curious about the sudden lack of activity, and he became even more determined to figure out what was going on. I would need to leave a note for Warren this drop to ask if he could walk by a sensor to provide some sort of data to mislead Hakim—perhaps at the other facility to really throw him off course. Then again, after giving Warren all the data that I had, including a copy of my report and the recommended upgrades, I myself was starting to wonder what his goal was and if he was planning anything else.

More specifically, if he was planning anything for the "new stock" that the facilities had just imported.

The "stock" were all under sixteen months, and I knew that they were on Warren's radar even if he wasn't leaving me any notes that indicated his plans, which was problematic. Dolan's Agriculture had been implementing the improvement suggestions from our findings report and had installed all new security alarms on the building doors. Thus making their facilities much harder to breach. The only item that they hadn't completed was replacing their old backup generator at the first facility because Carl said it was "too expensive" and he wanted us to "just catch the perps already" so he wouldn't need to spend any more money.

I frowned, letting out a sigh and wondering how long this would drag on until Hakim gave up. I got the impression that he wouldn't, and that if we didn't get results soon he would take action, just like how I knew Carl would probably ignore my newest email and continue to refuse to follow our advice completely.

I pushed the thoughts away, my eyes lingering on the image of the latest Jane Doe, and I felt my heart sink. Our investigation into her death and all the others before her had been delayed multiple times, and we had made zero progress. The entire thing was rife with issues. First, Precincts 38 and 40, which had found the first bodies, had done a terrible job of collecting evidence and had barely filled out the required paperwork. It was clear they didn't view the deaths as worth their time, and the crime scenes had long ago been contaminated, leaving Hakim and I with nothing to go on. Second, Precincts 9 and 10, who had found bodies with similar descriptions, had failed to send over the proper files and evidence when Vogle had tried to take over the cases. Then, in the midst of the mess as new bodies continued to be found, the chief of police from Precinct 24 had tried to make a case that *his* precinct should be the one handling the investigations since their forensics lab, although slightly smaller, was technically newer.

Vogle wasn't having it.

I had seen him come and go from a multitude of meetings over the last few weeks until finally, after extensive pressure from the local FAA chapter, it was publicly acknowledged by the mayor that Carneth had a problem—the string of deaths might indeed be related, and Detective Hakim would be formally leading the investigation from the 33rd Precinct with a small task force.

After the public statement, in which the mayor begrudgingly admitted the murders may be the result of the first serial killer Carneth had seen in over a hundred years, the evidence and files from Precincts 7, 9, and 10 slowly transferred over.

Vogle seemed pleased with the results, thinking it was some sort of victory that would secure our precinct as the main CPD headquarters for the foreseeable future. Hakim was indifferent to the win, and I just felt disappointed. This wasn't a victory. I support having procedures, they're there for a reason, but lost time was lost evidence and leads, which was a loss for these women. Whatever had happened in Vogle's meetings had taken far too long. Frankly, I was astounded it had happened at all, and I assumed someone must be looking into it. The initial investigating officers should be put on leave, and whoever had slowed this down should be reprimanded to ensure this never happened again because we had only *just* gotten all the autopsy reports this week. And I'd yet to hear anything about the additional resources for our alleged task force.

My eyes traced over the photo again.

It was better quality than some of the others we had received. The victim's skin wasn't quite as pale as normal, and her nails, which showed no signs of a struggle, were long. I frowned again, flicking back to the picture of her face as I tried to figure out what was bothering me. I had been staring at her for a while, but I couldn't put my finger on it.

Her cheeks appeared plump, and her eyes were open. Her irises were slightly less dull than what would be considered typical, and the dried blood that covered the side of her head was more mahogany than dark umber. It wasn't necessarily uncommon or suspicious, but I still didn't like it.

My eyes dropped to her mouth for what had to be the hundredth time, to her slightly parted lips. Her fangs were short. Incredibly short. She must have been well nourished and well-off, which was odd given the location where her body was dumped and the fact that she seemed to be unregistered. Her prints hadn't come up in the system, she had no ID on her person, and we hadn't been able to find any record of her existing anywhere, which was only common among the poorest Reborn living on the east side, and they were often ragged in appearance.

It didn't make any sense. You usually only saw this sort of physical description for Reborn who were—

I stilled, my entire thought process coming to a momentary halt as the thought hit—then my mind started to race.

I scrambled through the papers on my desk, grabbing the autopsy reports for her and two other Jane Does. They'd been completed by the coroner from Precinct 7, whose unit was much smaller than ours. They had the oldest lab and equipment within the province as well as substantially fewer resources across the board, and that showed in the shocking lack of details within the initial reports. It was either that or the coroner didn't care about these cases. Regardless of the reason, the paperwork was halfhearted at best. Yet despite this, as I skimmed through the sparse notes and images, I found what I was looking for in the limited bloodwork.

"Hakim," I said, still not taking my eyes off the report. I heard him shift at his desk, but I was too busy flipping through my papers to meet his gaze. "This woman's white blood cell count is much higher than normal."

"And?" His reply was toneless. "All females have higher counts."

"Not like this," I said, shaking my head. I stood from my desk, taking the pages with me as I moved toward him and held them out. "They also don't typically have plump cheeks or long nails with short fangs. This only happens if the woman is pregnant. Hakim, I think all these Jane Does recently gave birth. And given their location—"

"You think they were purposely taken, then dumped after giving birth," Hakim finished, grabbing the papers from my hand and quickly looking them over.

"Yes," I confirmed. "It wouldn't be the first time that pregnant women have been targeted for that reason. Conception isn't easy. A lot of females struggle to get pregnant and never carry to full term. A few decades ago, there were reported incidents of infants being stolen from hospitals. I know because I used it as a case study for one of my courses. But whoever this coroner is from 7, he didn't check. He just ran some minor bloodwork to rule out drugs. The cause of death was rather obvious since their heads were smashed in, so he didn't bother to do a full investigation on any of the bodies he examined."

"Even if their heads weren't bashed in, he wouldn't have done anything else," Hakim said, flipping the page over to look at the second victim. "There were cuts to the CPD because they blew last year's budget, Gorski, and Precincts 1 through 10 always suffer first. Since these women couldn't be identified and nothing came up from their prints, there was no push to dig into it until the FAA started making noise. Vogle may have fought to get these cases, but he's just trying to keep the 33rd as the front runner and shut down 24's push to take over. We only got these cases because the mayor is anxious about the sheer number of bodies showing up on his streets. The news attention isn't exactly helping his platform – twelve bodies in two months is a lot, even for eastside Carneth, and he needs it to look like he's doing something. Otherwise, he'll be screwed in the November election."

"I want to request that our forensic pathologist does a complete autopsy on all the bodies."

"They'll never approve that request," Hakim said, handing the papers back to me. I was about to open my mouth to argue, but he didn't give me a chance. "At best, we get one, so put the request in for Jane Doe number 3; her counts are the most elevated. If your theory is confirmed, then we might have grounds to run the other bodies through our own team, but I doubt it. This is the unfortunate reality of detective work in Carneth, Gorski. No budget. No support. Most of the public won't care. The CPD is chronically understaffed and underfunded. These women are largely from the southeast side – they're not *worth* the effort."

"But you just said that the mayor—"

"Wants it to *look* like he's doing something." Hakim cut me off. "Just until the election is over. He needs to be able to tell the small group of women and FAA lobbyists speaking up and complaining about this that he's doing something. But if he spends money he doesn't have from a budget that is already stretched thinner than pantyhose, he'll be dragged through the coals by his opponents. There's a reason why the precincts located on the eastside did such a poor job with the initial investigations, Gorski. They have even less funding than we do, and those officers won't even get a slap on the wrist for not doing their jobs. There will never be a special task force assigned to a collection of dead bodies when none of them are high-profile or even registered within the Federal ID Archive. We're not getting any additional resources to solve these murders.

"I was assigned simply so that the mayor and CPD chief can tell people that I'm working the case," Hakim said. "The decision was calculated, and Vogle knew that going in. My name is known to the public; it presents a very specific image, but no one within the walls of the CPD is actually expecting these cases to be solved. Come the end of November, provided that nothing happens to change the parameters of the case or the victims targeted, the files will be publicly handed over to a different lead, and then they will be buried. What did you think happened to Detective Russo's files thirty years ago? This is all about optics, Gorski."

I held his cold and indifferent gaze, my heart sinking in my chest.

"I see," I finally said. "Well, that's disappointing."

It was impossible to disguise the disgust that rolled off my tongue. I reached out to take the papers from him, wanting to yank them away and just go back to my desk so I could sit and stew in silence, but he didn't let go, and he stood from his seat as he continued to grip the other end of the reports.

"I didn't say that I was treating this as a temporary case to appease the public, Gorski," Hakim said, his low, gravel voice making me tense. "Put in the autopsy request to Dr. Perez, and confirm your theory. Even if we don't get approval for the additional autopsies or support for additional resources, we'll still get an answer we can use going forward, and we'll know what to look for when more bodies show up. My job is to solve these cases. Bureaucratic power struggles and political optics are not my concern, but I am a part of them, and there is nothing I can do to stop Vogle from taking this case away after the election is over."

He let go of the paper and took a step forward.

"But all that means… is that you and I will just have to work even harder before our time runs out. Understood?"

"Yes." I nodded, swallowing as I took a step back toward my desk. "I'll get the request in before going home."

"Good," Hakim said, then he turned and made for the door. "I'm going to go push Mallick to add extra patrols to the area."

I made my way through the last of the thick trees, letting out a sigh as my boots touched stone and I reached the familiar clearing by the river. There was a strong breeze blowing at my back from the south, and I lamented that my blackout gear kept me from feeling its relief. This supply bag was heavy—filled with matches, oil, paper, batteries, and so many other things that I could hardly even remember all of what I had shoved into it before heading into work—and the summer heat made carrying it tiring.

I had managed to narrow the drive from the precinct down to an hour with carefully selected areas of speeding. The entire way, I did nothing but replay our conversation in my head while wondering who the hell my partner was.

He was such an enigma, and I was struggling to wrap my head around his behaviour. He didn't seem to care about anything or anyone and was perfectly content to kill humans in cold blood without batting an eye. He flicked through each case file and looked at each image with indifference, and yet he was very clearly motivated to try and solve those cases before they were pulled from his hands, going so far as to speak to Mallick directly to push for increased street patrols. Maybe the only thing he cared about was himself, his job, and his reputation. Or maybe he just really liked solving puzzles.

"He doesn't make any damn sense," I muttered as I made my way out of the intense sunlight and into the shadow of the cave. "I don't understand him at all."

"Do vampires always talk to themselves – or is that just you?"

I froze, my head quickly jerking up at the familiar voice as my hand instinctively flew to the firearm on my hip. I didn't draw it, but I didn't let go either. Warren was leaning against the inside wall of the cave, his rifle in hand, brace no longer strapped to his leg. I had missed picking up on his scent, so his injuries were clearly healed, and the wind from the south must have covered any remaining trace of his presence, just like the first time I'd found him out here. It wouldn't even have surprised me if he had planned that, given that he had the weather reports and he was undoubtedly reading them.

"Only sometimes," I said, slowly relaxing my hand. I hesitated a moment before I dropped the new bag of supplies on the ground with a heavy thud and then removed my helmet. He wasn't aiming his rifle at me this time, but he wasn't not aiming it at me either. "I take it you need something else a little more complicated?"

"I do," he answered, his clipped voice sounding nearly as indifferent as Hakim's.

I grimaced at the mental comparison, silently wondering why I felt the need to try to work with and please people who so clearly disliked me.

"Well, this works out well because I need something from you," I said as I tucked my helmet under my arm. "What are you doing?"

"What do you mean?"

"You know exactly what I mean," I said, squinting in the dim light of the cave to see his face. "I mean, what are you doing with the facilities and the information that I gave you. What are you planning? Are you going after the new stock or—"

"Don't call them *stock*," Warren interrupted.

I stiffened at his dangerous tone, and my already squinted eyes narrowed into a glare.

"Then stop calling me and my people *vampires*." The word tasted like acid in my mouth, but I didn't regret saying it in this context. I saw the muscle in his jaw clench, but he didn't say anything else, so I pushed on. "They're all young enough to be helped without needing huge amounts of resources or support. With some decent antibiotics and time, they'll probably adapt to life in the woods, so I know they're on your radar – but they're on my partner's radar too. He's getting suspicious that we haven't found anything yet. Up until I started doing this, everything pointed toward something big happening, and he's still expecting it – hence the security upgrades."

"That's not my problem to manage."

"I didn't say that you had to manage it." I frowned. His terse tone and bad attitude were starting to get on my nerves. "I want to help you, Warren – how many times do I need to say it until you finally believe me? Regardless of what you might think, getting those supplies and trudging out here to deliver them in the middle of the day isn't an easy task.

"I want to know what your plans are – I *need* to know what your plans are. Hakim, my partner, doesn't always give me warning before he implements things. At best, the data you have is three days old. If I don't know what you're going to do and when, and Hakim decides to place a stakeout around the property or move his sensors without telling me, or whatever other new idea he comes up with, then I won't know if I need to try and fight him on it," I explained. "I have no way of warning you. I already tried to convince him the human rights activists must have given up and are focusing their efforts on fighting the ag-gag law directly, but he didn't bite. He's still adamantly convinced something bigger is going on. So if you're planning to break in and take the – the children – then I need to know when and I need to know which facility."

"We don't have a set date yet," Warren said, his voice stiff and reluctant. "That's why I'm here. We're running into issues."

"Okay," I said, happy that he was at least willing to tell me something. "Then what do you need?"

"Your last report noted that the vamp – *man*"—Warren corrected as I glared at him—"running this facility added those new security systems to the doors. I looked over the manufacturer's schematics you provided, but those don't show how he tied them into his existing security system. So shy of cutting a hole through the wall of the building or shorting out power to the entire facility, there's no way around them. I need to know how he tied them in – all the wiring was done inside the building, so I wasn't able to find anything useful when I checked it out. I need a copy of the updated schematics for the entire facility, and revised camera layouts in case he added any inside the building, and I need to know what the response time is."

"The security response time?"

"Yes." Warren nodded, his rifle seeming much looser in his hand now. "And the police. I need to know what happens if the system trips and how much time I would have. Their team on site is small – usually only one – so it's manageable. If they have to call the police themselves, it will buy us a few more minutes, but if the alarm goes straight to the nearest precinct, it makes this a lot harder."

"Alright," I said, knowing the only way I would be able to get those schematics would be to illegally print them as I copied over the facility surveillance footage—assuming Carl left me unsupervised. "Police response times will be easy to calculate. The provincial police will be notified, but it will take them at least an hour and a half to get here unless they have a patrol car nearby. It will be Precinct 15 that will send the first responding units because they're nearest to the site. I have to go out to collect the perimeter camera footage from each facility tomorrow night anyway, so I can dig around and try to get a copy of the schematics. Depending on where Carl is, though, it may take me a week or two to grab them. He doesn't always leave me unattended. Otherwise, I can ask some questions about the system and cameras."

"Don't make it obvious."

"I'm not an idiot," I said, my eyes narrowing into another glare. "I know how to ask questions and be discreet. Their security is my job, remember?"

"Sure." His tone made my skin bristle. "Make sure the schematic you get shows the tie-in to the grid and generator."

"Alright. Anything else?"

"Everything on this list." He pulled a piece of paper from his pocket and then tightened his grip on his rifle as he stepped forward to hand it to me.

I was taken aback by the gesture, as I was half expecting him to drop it on the ground and make me pick it up. But he didn't, so I stepped forward and took it from him, noting that he was indeed an inch or so taller than me. I dropped my gaze to the list, quickly skimming over the familiar items before I paused at the bottom.

"That's a lot of acetaminophen."

"So go to multiple stores," Warren said. "I don't care how many stops you have to make to get it."

My hand crumpled the list, and I clenched my jaw. He watched me intently, as if he was purposely testing my limits to see how long I was going to stick this out while he gripped his rifle in preparation for my inevitable snap.

"Alright," I said, stuffing the list in my pocket. I refused to be the monster he still seemed to think I was or give him any reason to doubt me. If he thought he could push me out of this arrangement now, he was going to be disappointed, though that didn't make me any less annoyed with him and his lack of decency, and it didn't stop my next few words from sounding sarcastic. "I'll get it. Any other drugs you want? Do you need me to steal some narcotics too?"

"Not today."

"Fine," I said, then my eyes dropped down to his leg. "How's the leg?"

"Fine," he answered, but his voice was stiff.

I wondered if he hated knowing that I, a *vampire*, had been the one to patch it up.

"Good," I said, finally stepping back from him.

His hand instantly relaxed against the rifle now that the space had returned, and I fought the urge to frown. He still didn't trust me, not even the tiniest bit. It stung a little, given how much I had sacrificed to help him thus far. But when my mind circled back to the night of the hunt, I wasn't sure I could blame him.

"So." I cleared my throat. "When do you need this by?"

"Monday afternoon."

"Alright." I tried not to think about how difficult it would be to gather all this up in time. "I'll see what I can do, but I can't promise I'll have the schematics. I might need more time, especially if Hakim decides to come with me. He does that sometimes and doesn't always give me warning."

"He doesn't trust you?"

"He doesn't trust anyone, Warren," I said, my voice growing tight. "And it has nothing to do with me. That's just who he is. I got praised by my boss because I've managed to stick it out with him for more than a week – so give me some credit. I know you don't trust me, but just because Hakim doesn't, that doesn't make me an untrustworthy person."

"We'll see."

I stared at him, that same horrible sinking feeling that I had gotten the day I'd left Grace's party shifting through my bones. I hated this, and I hated that he hated me simply for existing. I didn't hate him, even if he was a complete asshole.

I opened my mouth, maybe to say something back in retort, maybe to ask one of the million questions I had about him or his people, but nothing came out. So I just exhaled, clamped my jaw shut, then turned around to leave.

"Wait."

I slowed as I heard him walking toward me.

"What?" I asked, trying and failing not to sound irritated as I forced myself to turn around and face him once more.

He paused a few feet away, reaching into his jacket pocket with his free left hand and pulling out a small and rather battered-looking black flip phone.

"Take this." He held the small phone out to me. "If you can't make it Monday, if you get delayed, or if your plans change – text me. I don't want to walk all the way here only to find out your partner screwed everything up."

"You text?" I stared at him in disbelief. "You're giving me a cell phone?"

"We're not animals," Warren said, his tone taking on an acidic edge. "I know how to use a cell phone – and it's just a burner phone, nothing fancy."

"Burner phone or not, do you have any idea how dangerous this is?" I asked, taking the tiny flip phone from him and looking it over. It must have been at least five years old; it still had a pop-out antenna. I looked back up at him, floored by his stupidity, especially given how clever he liked to make himself out to be. "They can locate you with these. Even with an older phone like this one, they could pin your location down accurately enough based on cell phone towers to know that the messages are being sent from around the northern forest."

"You don't need to worry about that."

"No, you're right – *I* don't," I said, my hand tightening around the tiny little death sentence Warren had pulled from his pocket. "But you do! Do you want to get caught?! I thought you said you weren't an idiot, Warren. But this"—I held the cell phone up between us—"is incredibly stupid."

"Actually, it's just making you look more stupid," Warren said as he leaned back and looked at me assessingly. "Do you seriously think I would be foolish enough to carry around a cell phone and use it if I hadn't found a way to take care of that problem?"

"You can't take care of that problem." I countered as my annoyance at his arrogance grew. I had come to accept that humans were not stupid, that was clear as night, but obviously there were massive gaps in what they thought they knew. "It's impossible – the CPD works with the service providers all the time on cases. Every single signal gets collected up into a massive database, and yes, you might get away with it for a while if they aren't looking for you, but eventually, someone is going to notice that there are texts coming from the middle of the woods! It's not something you can avoid. That data is permanently collected and—"

My voice cut off as my eyes grew wide in realization. I could see the muscles in Warren's shoulders tighten as he stared at me, knowing that he had given away too much.

"You *are* working with other Reborn," I whispered, and his tense silence was the only confirmation that I needed. "Someone who works in telecommunication – someone who can erase your footprint as it happens."

"It's getting late," Warren said, his tone clipped again. "You need to leave."

"How big is this?" I took a step closer, and his hand tightened on his rifle, but he didn't step away. "How many people are involved in this? What else are you working on? Who gave you these phones? Why didn't you tell me there were other Reborn helping you?"

"Because those details are none of your business," Warren snapped, his eyes growing hard as he took a step forward. He stared down at me, his hatred all but burning my skin as his deep brown eyes traced over my face. "This has been going on since before you were born, and it's bigger than you could possibly imagine. You've hardly been in it for a second. You've sacrificed nothing and you're nobody in this story, and yet you think I owe you an explanation? You *vampires* are all the same. Somehow everything has to be about you, and you want to paint yourselves as the hero in our fight even though you're the ones who did this to us – like you're a bloody saviour doing us a favour. Did I make you come here? Did I ask you for your help?"

I stilled, the fingers of my left hand curling into the fabric of my pants as I stared back at him.

"You don't know anything, and you don't need to know anything unless I say so." His voice was cold. "You want to help so you can continue to make yourself feel better? Then keep bringing the stuff I ask for. But don't for a second think that I owe you or any other *vampire* a damn thing. You're here because you chose to be, not because I need you to be. Don't ever forget that."

He held my gaze a moment longer, then stepped back and lifted his rifle, leaning the barrel against his shoulder.

"There's only one number programmed into that phone." He gestured to the device that was now clenched tightly in my right hand. "Don't add any others, and keep it charged and locked. The pin is 2407. Memorize it. If I need anything else before the drop date, I'll message you. If your partner screws anything up, tell me. Otherwise, keep the phone somewhere nearby, but don't use it and don't leave it out. Now get out of here. I have stuff I need to do."

Code Names

The unfamiliar sensation of buzzing vibrated against my leg. I shifted in my seat, glancing at Hakim to make sure that he hadn't noticed. His head was bent over the papers on his desk, his attention completely captured by the results of the autopsy that we had managed to push through first thing Monday's shift. It confirmed my suspicion. Jane Doe number 3 had recently given birth, yet despite it being a blatant red flag given the other bodies and the past cases of child trafficking rings operating within Carneth, my request for additional autopsies on the other victims had been denied two hours ago, just as Hakim had anticipated.

It was disappointing, to say the least.

Yet, true to his word, Hakim wasn't half-assing it or ignoring the information. He was pouring over the notes, and we were now proceeding based on the assumption that all the cases were related and all the victims had recently given birth. I was already combing through security images and trying to find connections between the victims.

I had managed to snag the schematics Warren had requested from the first facility during Friday's shift, and I'd made the drop last morning before coming into work. I had texted him on Sunday evening to let him know everything was good to go, and

I had even managed to gather the ridiculous amount of acetaminophen he had asked for without raising any suspicion.

All I got in return was a one-letter response:

A: K

That was it, and he hadn't been there at the cave when I'd dropped off the bag. I hadn't been expecting him to be, but it still left me feeling dejected. Just another reminder of how little he thought of me and, as I was now coming to understand, how small my actions were. He didn't need me, and he had made that perfectly clear.

I let out a low breath and raised my hands into the air, stretching my back before standing from my seat.

"Do you want a coffee?" I asked, glancing at Hakim as I pushed in my chair. It wasn't an abnormal question; I had started asking him every time I went to grab some of the sludge from the kitchenette, even though his response was always the same.

"No."

"Alright."

I made my way toward the boardroom door, forcing myself to walk normally, even though the phone buzzed against my leg again and sent my curiosity spinning. I kept my pace steady, nodding to some of the other detectives on the floor whose names I had finally begun to learn. Then, I ducked into the bathroom and made my way to the stall farthest from the door. The second it was closed and latched, I pulled out the burner phone and flipped it open.

A: Set of pliers, two 12V lead-acid batteries, gloves (6 pairs), masks (6)...

I had yet to figure out why his number was saved in my phone under the contact name A, or why my own profile seemed to be set up under the letter C, but I didn't dare change it. My eyes quickly skimmed down the remainder of the list until I got to the final message.

A: Drop Wednesday afternoon, 12 pm

I stared at the words in disbelief, then quickly typed back.

C: Wednesday, as in tomorrow?

The reply was nearly instant.

A: Yes

I frowned.

C: I'll see what I can do

He didn't write anything back, so I repocketed the phone and then made my way toward the kitchenette to get the coffee that I didn't want before returning to our boardroom.

Wednesday, August 26
1:26 PM

I clenched my teeth as I pushed my way through the trees toward the familiar clearing. My chest felt tight, burning with so much pent-up frustration I could taste it like acid in my mouth. If I could have removed my helmet to try and spit it out, I would have. But I couldn't. Because it was hot as hell, and the sun was scalding my blackout gear—the rays searching for any crack in my armour so they could reach the pale skin beneath and burn that too.

Grace was angry with me—again.

We hadn't talked much since the evening I'd walked out on her anniversary party. I had texted her, apologized, and made up a plethora of excuses that she wasn't interested in hearing. I had left a coffee on her desk one evening and even invited her over for dinner, but the visit felt stiff and awkward. She complained that I had bought synthetic-based food, then talked about how shopping in the city centre was easier since the city council had ordered the ag-gag protestors to leave after several officers got sun poisoning and three were severely burned. Then she said that she hoped the activists' actions would help to make a difference and improve the conditions at factory farms because humans deserved to be treated better.

I didn't say anything in response, because I wasn't sure how one could treat humans better while still farming them for consumption...

Instead, I pushed through the visit as best I could and blindly agreed to go to the movies with her because I knew she was still unhappy with me. I had hoped that by agreeing, I could repair some more of the damage, but I knew our awkwardness was deeper than just my blowing her off. Things between us were completely off-kilter. I was struggling more and more each day to care about anything she had to say when my mind was consumed with Warren and the two cases I was working. So not only did I genuinely not have time to spend with her, I was struggling to want to make any.

If not for needing to continue to appear normal to all those around me, I wasn't sure that I would have bothered to try and mend our friendship. And I wasn't sure how to feel about that realization.

After driving around all over Carneth yesterday morning to collect the final supplies, I'd barely managed to squeeze in three hours of sleep before getting up to make it to work on time. My night had been no different than any other, up until the point that Grace had called me at the end of her shift to confirm our movie date—having decided on her own that Wednesday morning was the perfect time to go because the tickets were always cheaper.

I had completely forgotten about agreeing.

I was in the middle of crawling through the surveillance footage that Patrol and Street had finally sent over from the fifteen-block radius I had requested and was trying to track a built-looking male with a suspicious duffle bag when my personal cell phone rang and nearly buzzed off my desk. Hoping it was Carl finally agreeing to install the backup generator we had suggested, I answered it without checking the number.

That had been my first mistake.

My second was telling Grace that I wouldn't be able to make it to the movie while I was still sitting in the boardroom with Hakim. I should have stepped out into the hall the second I realized who was on the other end, but I hadn't, and I was promptly reminded by my partner that personal calls were to be made on my own time while Grace yelled at me and hung up. I didn't bother telling Hakim that 11 am *was* personal time, and I didn't text Grace back after the call went dead. I just finished my work, left the boardroom at 11:57 am, and texted Warren to tell him that I would be late before driving out into the sunlight.

Now it was nearly 1:30 pm, I had yet to eat anything decent, and the strap of the latest supply bag was digging into my shoulder as I stalked across the stone toward the cave.

I was tired and starting to feel a little discouraged. I wanted to keep doing this. I needed to keep doing it because I simply could not return to how my life was before. Yet despite being dedicated to my decision to help Warren, I was finding the execution of said "help" wasn't easy, and it felt like everything in my life was working against me and trying to tell me to stop.

I had never been big on talking about how I felt. It didn't come naturally to me, but I desperately wished I didn't feel so entirely alone in this. The only person who might possibly understand was Hawthorne, but he had been put on day shift. I hadn't seen or spoken to him in weeks, and I wasn't stupid enough to text him anything incriminating. He let me know that he had stopped by my apartment a few times, but on each occasion, I wasn't home because I was either still at work or out here cutting through trees, carting supplies like a pack mule.

Even if I had been home, I still probably wouldn't have said anything. What I was doing was dangerous, and it wouldn't have been fair to wrap Hawthorne up in my mess.

I groaned in relief as I stepped into the shade of the cave, thinking about the voicemail I had received from my mother earlier in the night. She had called to remind me about my father's birthday party this Friday and told me to bring a cake. I didn't have the heart to call back and tell her no, so now I needed to figure out if there was a way for me to leave work early so I could join them for dinner.

I dropped the supply bag to the ground with a heavy thump before I ripped off my helmet and gloves and inhaled deeply.

Warren wasn't here, but that was no surprise. I glared at the bag, wondering if he waited in the trees for me to leave or if he simply came by whenever he felt like it and the drop times meant nothing. I could hear the nearby river in the distance, the faint sound of birds chirping as the warm summer breeze echoed across the opening of the cave. I closed my eyes, letting the air out of my lungs, wishing that I could feel the wind on my skin and that I wasn't covered head to toe in UV-proof clothes.

A part of me wondered what it felt like—to be able to stand in the sun without burning. I swallowed, turning my head to look out the cave before my feet started to shift. I walked to the edge of the shadow, far enough out that I could feel the air, and I had to squint my eyes almost shut to see.

Then, I lifted my hand.

I don't know what I was expecting or what possessed me to do it. But I hissed in pain after only a few seconds as the sun burned my skin, and I quickly retracted my fingers from the light. I stared at them, watching as the burnt skin grew angry and red before it quickly began to heal. Then I collapsed to the ground with a thump in the shadow of the cave, setting my helmet by my side and dropping my head into my hands.

I don't know how long I sat there, but some time later, I heard the rustle of movement, then the sound of shoes across the stone. I knew it was him, but I didn't bother to look up as he approached.

"Is there a reason why you're still here?"

He sounded angry.

Always so angry and always at me.

"Everything is a mess," I muttered as his footsteps grew closer.

"What?"

Apparently, their hearing isn't as good as ours.

"Drop the bag and leave – that's how this works," he continued. "Or do you *vampires* have no memory capacity either?"

"Stop calling me that," I whispered.

"What?"

"I said stop calling me that!" I snapped, lifting my head to glare up at him. He was standing four feet before me. His tall frame darkened the shadow of the cave, but I still had to squint to see his face. "I am *not* a *vampire* – and my memory works just fine."

He stared at me, his thoughts unreadable like always. "Why are you still here?"

"Does that even matter?" I asked, startled by the noticeably hurt tone that left my lips. "It's not like you care. My life is a bit of a mess right now, and I just wanted to sit down and feel the wind on my skin, okay? That's all. Or is my presence *so* unbearable that you can't tolerate it long enough to grab the gear bag and go? Can't you just ignore me and do whatever it is that you usually do? I was going to leave soon anyway."

He continued to stare at me, and for a brief moment, I thought he would say something else to push my patience, but he didn't. Instead, he turned away and walked inside the cave. I quickly shut my eyes against the bright light, trying to focus on the feel of the air ghosting along my skin and ruffling the hair that had fallen loose from my braid—and not on the sounds of Warren grabbing the gear bag.

"Here's the next list." His voice sounded to my right a moment later.

I cracked open an eye and squinted up at him even though it stung. The gear bag was slung over his shoulder, and there was a folded slip of paper in his outstretched hand.

"Great." I took the note from him and tucked it into my vest pocket.

I didn't bother to read it. I could already guess what would be on it. Instead, I closed my eyes and ignored him. I expected to hear him leave, and I nearly jumped in surprise when I heard the heavy bag hit the ground off to my right. I turned to look over at him, my eyes creasing against the light as Warren sat down on the ground ten feet away, rifle laid carefully by his side.

"What are you doing?" The words slipped out before I could stop them.

"Enjoying the sun."

I squinted at him a moment longer, trying and failing to make out his exact expression through the glare. I couldn't tell if he was being sarcastic, but when he didn't say anything else, I turned my head away, closed my eyes once more, and attempted to ignore him. He didn't move, and I didn't leave, and we sat there in silence for a while until I grew uncomfortable.

"You don't have to sit with me," I said, turning to look at him despite my best efforts to refrain from doing exactly that.

"I'm not." He sounded irritated. "I'm waiting until you leave – I can't risk you following after me again. I've been screwed over enough times to know better than to trust you."

I snorted, shaking my head and letting out a sigh.

"Of course that's what you're doing," I muttered.

He really didn't like me. Not at all. I closed my eyes again so I didn't have to see his hatred, silence filling the gap between us as I wondered just how long he would stay or if he truly would remain here until I got up to leave. It was impossible to know. It wasn't like he gave out information freely.

I continued to try my best to ignore him, but as each second passed, the pressure of the unanswered questions stewing in my mind became too much, and I found them impossible to keep in.

"Why is my name saved as C in the phone you gave me?" I asked. I heard him shift, so I glanced over in his direction to find him looking at me with a pinched expression.

"It stands for Corvus."

"Corvus," I repeated. "Like the crow?"

"Yes."

"What is it, a code name?"

"Yes," Warren repeated, and he only sounded more irritated as he looked away. "It helps protect the network. The more exposed assets have one."

Exposed asset.

It wasn't the worst thing he had called me, though I still frowned. I wasn't sure if I should be insulted because crows were often considered bad omens or pleased because they were very clever birds.

"So what's yours then?"

"Aries."

"Like the ram?"

"Yes, like the ram." Warren turned to glare at me. "Any other stupid questions?"

"No." I turned away, glaring at my knees until Warren let out an annoyed breath, and I couldn't help but look at him again. "You know, I do have other things I need to do aside from following you around the woods. And I do need to get some sleep today, so if you don't want to sit here, you can just leave."

"I thought sleeping was a rumour," Warren said, and I moved my hand to block the light so I could look at him better.

"Well, it's not," I replied. "We sleep – usually three to five hours a day. But getting three is enough for most Reborn."

He nodded but said nothing.

"Why – how much do you sleep?"

He remained silent, and my shoulders dropped in disappointment. I should have anticipated this. Of course he wasn't going to tell me anything that wasn't absolutely necessary, so I turned away again.

"Eight hours."

I stilled at Warren's quiet reply. I could feel his gaze on my temple, and I did my best not to show my surprise.

"Some people need more, but some people need less."

I nodded, not really sure what to say, then slowly turned to look at him. He was watching me closely, almost curiously, and for the first time ever, there wasn't an underlying sense of disgust in his gaze.

"You really can't see well in the sunlight, can you?" he asked.

"No," I answered. "It's very blurry and bright, and it hurts our eyes."

"If it hurts so much, why don't you put your helmet back on?"

"Because it's considered rude to have a conversation with a helmet on – and because it's hot, and I'm tired of wearing it. They're functional, but it feels like being in a fishbowl."

He stared at me for another moment. "You don't do well in the heat either, do you?"

"Not particularly," I said, bringing my knee up so I could rest my elbow against it. If I hunched and turned my head as I leaned it in my hand, it blocked out more light and made it a bit easier to see. "We do best in the cold. July, August, and September are always the worst months. What about you?"

"The opposite. The cold can be rough," Warren said, hesitating before he continued. "We can withstand it, but we don't heal the way you do. So if we don't have the proper clothes or a heat source, we'll freeze to death."

It was such an odd concept for me. I'd never once had to worry about being too cold.

"We can overheat and die," I replied without thinking. "It doesn't happen often – especially not here, but it's a big risk in the lower latitude cities. It's why we don't settle anywhere near the equator."

He nodded as if he knew this already. "Have you travelled outside of Carneth?"

"No." I shook my head. "I was born here, went to school here, and now I work here. We don't really travel much, and if we do, it's usually not very far. I've never really thought about leaving. Do you – do you travel far into the woods?"

"Far enough," Warren answered vaguely. "Did you always want to be a cop?"

"Yes. Much to the disappointment of my parents," I said, and a tiny smile touched my lips. His brow arched, so I elaborated. "They wanted me to go into academic research or become a lawyer. They never understood, and it's always been a point of contention."

"Do they have much say in what you do?"

"No," I said carefully. "Not exactly, but they don't make it easy. There are a lot of expectations in our society – and my parents fall into a higher bracket than most with a background in scholarly pursuits. I voluntarily chose a *lesser* position in their eyes."

"Why?" he asked. "Why choose to be a cop?"

"Because I wanted to make a difference," I whispered, and suddenly, I felt my throat grow tight.

He stared at me, and we both sat in silence.

"How old are you?" he finally asked, and I couldn't stop the scoff that left my lips. "What?"

"Nothing," I said, shaking my head and letting out a sigh. "My partner asked the same thing when he met me. It's hard to tell because we tend to age in brackets. After twenty, not much changes until you pass fifty. Between fifty and ninety, everyone looks the same, and nothing big changes after that until you hit one hundred and thirty. No one looks old until they have cleared one hundred and fifty, but it's considered rude to ask."

"You live annoyingly long lives."

My eyes narrowed at him.

"The recent average has been about one hundred and seventy years," I said. "But it wasn't always like that, and hardly anyone reaches two hundred. How long do humans live?"

"We used to average between eighty and ninety years," Warren answered, but his tone had gone flat. "But that changed. Now it's hyper-dependent on luck, weather, and supplies. Most of us don't live past seventy, but in rare cases, some still cross over a century."

"I see."

I knew that their lifespans were shorter than ours, but seventy was much higher than the stats recorded by the farming facility.

"I'm thirty-four," I said.

"Thirty-six," he answered before I could ask.

I nodded, wondering what he would look like in thirty years and if he would make it past seventy. I had never really considered our lives long. They were just normal to me, but thinking about dying in under a century made my heart hurt. It wasn't a lot of time. He was going to miss out on so much. Maybe this was part of the reason why he was so focused.

"Is that considered young?" Warren asked.

"Yes," I answered. "We're considered adults at eighteen. We go on to higher education before our twenties. Most Reborn decide to get multiple degrees or doctorates, though, and so many don't graduate until their thirties or forties – and most police officers don't apply to be detectives until they're at least fifteen or twenty years in. I'm one of the few exceptions to that."

"So it's the same as it was before," Warren muttered, more to himself than me. "You just live longer."

"Before as in—"

"As in before you and your people turned us into cattle – yes, that's exactly what I mean."

My face fell, his harsh tone reminding me exactly who and what I was talking to. The tight ball in my chest reappeared, burning up my throat as I watched him look at me with renewed disgust.

It hurt, and I hated it.

I sat up, grabbed my helmet, and stood from the ground.

"Not that it matters," I said as I pulled on my gloves, "or that you'll care, but we don't know about humans – not like this. It isn't taught."

I didn't tell him about the horrible suspicion that was starting to grow in the back of my mind—the one that made my stomach curl each time it popped into my head. That maybe, some Reborn did know, and maybe... it was being intentionally suppressed.

"Most Reborn have never set foot outside of the city, let alone seen a human before," I continued. "We buy our food from stores. They don't know what they're eating. We go to work so we can pay our bills, and a lot of people are just trying to get by."

"Are you expecting me to feel bad for you?"

I stiffened, glaring at him before I tugged my helmet onto my head.

"No," I said, my voice coming out strained. I was glad he couldn't see my face anymore because I knew it had crumpled into a mess. "I don't expect anything from you. I need to leave. I have to go make a cake for my dad's birthday this Friday and figure out how the hell I can get you the stuff on your next list without destroying the lives of those around me or running my bank account dry. If you think of anything else you might need, just text me. Otherwise, I'll follow the drop time you wrote down."

FRIDAY, AUGUST 28
11:00 AM

"You're late."

"I know."

"It's your father's birthday. You couldn't at least try to get here on time? We already finished dinner."

"I know, Mom," I said, forcing myself to smile. "I'm sorry – I got caught up at work."

"Surely they can live without you for a few hours," my mother replied, taking the cake I handed her before looking me over. "You look thinner – are you eating enough? There are leftovers in the fridge; you can make up a plate."

"I'm fine," I replied as I hung up my helmet and kicked off my boots.

It was 11 am; I didn't bother trying to explain to my mother that this *was* me getting off work early as I followed her up the stairs toward the dining room. She would just say something about the police budgets being mismanaged and me wasting my time, and there was no sense in arguing. I had learned a long time ago that our opinions differed, so it was better to just say nothing in these cases.

We cut across the living room toward the large archway. I could hear my brother, along with an unfamiliar voice. It must be his new girlfriend, Sara. I didn't know anything about her, only her name from my mother's voicemail, but I really hoped that she was nice because I wasn't sure that I had the capacity to deal with anything else right now.

"Valya!" My father's voice rang out as I entered the dining room.

"Hi, Dad," I said as I made my way over to give him a quick hug. "Sorry I'm late."

"That's alright." He smiled, looking genuinely happy. "We were only just about to start dessert."

"Well, perfect timing." I gestured to the cake in my mother's hands. "I brought cake."

"Let's hope it's more edible than the last one."

I turned and glared at my brother.

"Really?" I asked, grabbing my usual chair and pulling it out. "I've been here for fifteen seconds. Can you not?"

"Sorry." Dimitri shrugged, but saying the word was a formality, and I doubted he understood the true meaning. He turned toward the beautiful, auburn-haired woman by his side. "Val, this is Sara, my girlfriend. She's a doctor at the University Hospital."

"Nice to meet you," I said, reaching my hand out across the table to shake the one she had extended as my mother brought in plates and a tray of brownies.

"It's nice to meet you." Sara smiled, and the corners of her pale green eyes crinkled. "Dimitri told me a bit about you. He said you work as a cop?"

"Yes." My muscles tensed. This was always a topic we tried to avoid. "A detective, actually."

"Oh, they promoted you? Great," Dimitri said, though his tone conveyed otherwise. "How's that going?"

"Fine," I said stiffly, reaching to help pass around plates and hoping to drop the topic.

"Oh, a detective!" Sara said, and her eyes shone with interest. "That must be challenging. Are you working on a case right now?"

I saw my mother roll her eyes from the corner of my gaze, but I answered Sara anyway. "Yes – I'm working a few."

"Are you allowed to talk about them?"

"A bit." I hesitated, then decided to press on. "I'm working on the Jane Doe cases from the eastside."

"Oh wow," Sara said. "Is it difficult?"

"Yes," I answered, ignoring the not-too-subtle scoffing sound my brother made. "Funding is one issue, but the cases themselves are difficult. The bodies of the victims weren't properly processed, so it's been a challenge to find any leads."

"This is the same case as those women they've been talking about on the news?"

"Yes," I confirmed.

"How did they die?"

"Head trauma – by some sort of blunt object."

"Val." My mother shot me a look as my father frowned in disapproval. "Can you not? We're about to have dessert."

"Yeah, and I really don't want to have it ruined by hearing about dead drainer bodies," my brother said as he turned to give me a look of disgust. "Besides, it's not like your investigation will change anything. The southeast side has always been a mess, and the police budget is already too large. They should be dumping that money into research."

"Exactly," my mother agreed, passing a piece of cake to Sara. "Dimitri, why don't you tell us about your new project?"

My eyes flicked around the table at the blatant distaste across my family's faces before Dimitri set off into an explanation of the work he was doing. It was like they didn't even want to hear what was happening on the other side of the city, let alone acknowledge the problems existed. As if they just thought of it as some completely different world that had no impact on them whatsoever and that the Reborn within it weren't worth the time of night.

I swallowed and dropped my gaze to my plate, staring at the synthetic chocolate cake I had made the evening before. If they didn't care about lower-class Reborn, why the hell would they care about humans? I could feel my grip start to tighten on the fork I was holding, my brother's voice drowning out as a ringing sound filled my ears.

"Valya!"

"Yes?" I lifted my head, looking toward my mother.

She was eyeing me carefully again—judgingly—probably nitpicking my too-casual appearance, the improper crease lines of the plain dress shirt that I shouldn't have worn and the faint rings under my eyes. Probably berating herself for *allowing* her daughter to join the CPD when it was so clearly bad for me. For her. After all, my actions reflected on the family.

"I asked if you wanted a glass of water?"

"Sure," I said, neither wanting nor needing it. "I'll grab it."

I stood from my seat before she could say anything else and quickly made my way to the kitchen as my brother continued to drone on, much to the pleasure of my parents. I grabbed a glass at random from the cupboard before going to the sink to fill it up. Then I stood there, staring out the tinted window, wondering how on earth I had been born into this family.

"I think the work you're doing is important."

The low voice was so quiet I barely heard it. I had been so lost in my own thoughts I hadn't even heard her come into the kitchen with her empty glass. She walked toward me, her movement graceful and silent, and flicked the tap on once more, but as the water ran, she looked down at me and gave me a tentative smile.

"I mean that," Sara whispered. "It matters."

"Well," I said, smiling weakly in return, "at least one other person thinks so."

Rescue

"We're making our move next weekend on September 5th," Warren said as he leaned against the inside wall of the cave. "During the rainstorm. If it doesn't hit per the weather reports you gave me, we postpone."

He had been waiting for me to arrive, and the second I saw him, I knew something was up.

"Okay." I nodded, removing my helmet and resting it on my hip. On the one hand, the rain would make it harder to track them. On the other hand, it would be darker and easier to see during the day, giving us an advantage. Though I figured he must have weighed those odds. "Just the first facility?"

"Yes."

"What do you need me to do?"

"Nothing."

My heart dropped at his quick rejection.

"Are you sure?" I asked, and I hated that it sounded almost desperate. "When the guardhouse makes the call, even though the response won't come from our precinct, Hakim will be informed. Forty minutes isn't a lot of time to get in and get out. How are you planning to execute this?"

"That doesn't matter," Warren said, and I couldn't help but frown.

"If you don't trust me and aren't planning to tell me anything useful, then why tell me anything at all?"

"Because, as you pointed out before, you need to know the date so you can make sure your partner doesn't change anything. All I need you to do is text me the night before and let me know if anything is different from the information you give me today."

"Fine." I let out a sigh. "But there is a possibility that I will get called in to respond. If that happens, and I find you or anyone else near the facility, it's going to be really difficult to let you go and cover it up with other officers in the area. So you had better have a plan to divert them. I think you should go to the second facility this week and get caught on the security cameras a few times to help me misdirect Hakim. On the day of, lay a false trail from the facility off to the main road and make it look like you drove away. They're looking for Reborn human rights activists, remember? They have no reason to go gallivanting through the woods to find you unless you do a really poor job of hiding your trail. I'll text you and do what I can to try to give you a heads up, but I will only be able to do so much."

"I'll keep that in mind."

I shook my head, running my hand over my braided hair to push the loose strands away from my face. I wondered how many people were going to be involved in this. How much he wasn't telling me and what the hell was going to happen when Hakim got the call from Carl.

He was going to be pissed.

"Alright," I said finally, turning to leave once more. "Let me know if you need anything else."

"Not planning to sit and enjoy the wind this time?"

His voice stopped me in my tracks, and I turned back to look at him. "Last time you made it pretty apparent that I was wasting your time. Just like you've made it abundantly clear that you don't need my help and don't plan to tell me anything. I'd hate to make you endure my presence any more than necessary."

He stared at me, but his eyes were fixated on my lips, not my eyes. Then I saw his hand tighten on his rifle.

"When was the last time you ate, Corvus?"

His low tone made my skin bristle.

"Seriously?" I whispered, stepping toward him once more. "You think after everything that I've done – I would be stupid enough to allow myself to become depraved? That I'd put myself at risk of slipping into a bloodlust?! I realize that my efforts mean nothing to you, but they mean something to me, and I'm not going to mess this up by making idiotic mistakes! I had to skip dinner in order to come here on time. It's perfectly normal for our features to fluctuate a bit, you know. It's only a problem if we don't eat for a few days."

"How many days?"

He was eyeing me carefully, but upon catching the hint of curiosity in his voice, the tension in my shoulders lessened. Warren might be well-educated and clever, but he didn't know everything about Reborn—that much was clear based on the exchanges we'd already had. I let out a sigh. Maybe he would be less nervous around me if I explained more.

"We can go forty-eight hours without eating, and it isn't a problem," I said, and my voice grew softer. "During that window, we might feel fatigued—tired, grumpy, we can lose some weight, and our skin becomes a bit paler. After that, we become depraved."

"And what does being depraved mean?"

"It means we're starving to death," I said. "It's an incredibly dangerous state to be in. I've never experienced it myself, but we studied it at the Academy, and we're taught to look for the early symptoms. It puts Reborn in a heightened state. My understanding is that it's like a high. You can sense more, your fangs and nails become longer, and you get a buzzing sensation throughout your body. But it isn't something that Reborn do. It's illegal. If it happens by accident, you get a mark on your permanent record and a fine. But if you're caught draining, you can go to prison."

"Draining," Warren said, his eyes narrowing as his grip on the rifle loosened. "What's draining?"

"Draining is intentional starvation. Purposely not eating to reach a depraved state," I answered, but I felt a bit uncomfortable.

Draining wasn't something that Reborn did or liked to acknowledge. Drainers were degenerates. Addicts. People deemed to be the lowest within our society. Except I was starting to question that stereotype now after having joined my fellow officers for a hunt.

"Some Reborn do it to experience the high. Apparently it's addicting, but it's only really a problem in southeast Carneth, and the CPD takes it seriously. It's a disgusting act, and it can be a federal offence for repeat offenders. It's selfish and dangerous. It puts everyone at risk."

"Why?" Warren pressed. "What makes being depraved so dangerous?"

"It's not actually being depraved that's dangerous," I said, and I could already see the next string of questions shining in his eyes. "It's what comes after."

"What comes after?"

"A bloodlust," I said, fighting through my discomfort and ignoring the urge to look away from his intense gaze. "A fever sets in. It only takes a few hours, and it grows until it feels like a white-hot iron is being shoved down your throat. Then it itches and burns, and suddenly you're not really there anymore. The high goes away like a switch being flicked, as does any of your logic, and you will attack anything with a heartbeat.

"It's a survival mechanism," I said. "A last-ditch effort by our bodies to avoid death in one violent burst of energy. That's why being depraved is so dangerous, why draining is risky and illegal, because the slip into a bloodlust can happen over a matter of minutes, hours, or seconds, depending on the person. There's no way to know how long you'll be depraved before the tipping point is reached. The average is four days, but it's different for everyone. It's dependent on so many things it's impossible to predict with any certainty, which is why it's taken so seriously. It's not something that happens in our world. It's not something that's talked about either. Draining is considered lesser, and I only know what I know about the process because we studied a hunger strike that went wrong as part of the Police Academy training.

"It's not something that I would ever let happen, Warren." I dropped my gaze to the ground. "But I'll make sure to eat before coming here next time, even if it will make me late. I'm sorry – I didn't mean to make you uncomfortable."

"I'm not uncomfortable," Warren said, and I glanced back up at him. "I just don't know much about your kind aside from how to kill you."

"Of course." A small, morbid laugh left my lips like a scoff. "I don't doubt you have that mastered – but if you ever actually want to know something, you can just ask. I'll tell you."

He nodded, his eyes sweeping over my body thoughtfully for a moment before he spoke again.

"Are you considered short?" My shoulders slumped at his words. "Or are the ones that hunt just exceptionally tall?"

"No." I found it impossible to hide the irritation from my voice. "They're probably all average height. I'm considered short – and I've never met anyone who hasn't commented on it."

"Well, you're not short to me," he said. "You're tall for a female – by our standards."

"And you would be considered short by ours," I said, eyeing his frame. "The average male is around seven foot four."

"Do you all have pale grey eyes?" he asked after a moment, and I found it difficult to look away from his warm brown ones.

"No," I answered. "They're different colours—brown, green, blue, grey. Just pale. Dull."

"I see." He paused, then added, "Before you I only ever saw them at night, and they look much different. They shine – almost like they glow in the dark."

"I see," I said, not really sure what to make of his remark. He didn't say anything else for a moment, and I hesitated, wondering if I should leave.

"Did you make your cake?" he asked suddenly, and I found my brow arching.

"Cake?"

"You said it was your dad's birthday." He sounded hesitant.

"Oh," I said, surprised that he even remembered the offhand comment I'd made the last time we'd spoken. I tried not to think too much about why it made me feel strangely happy. "Yes. I – I found some time to make it. It wasn't very good though. I'm not a great cook."

"What are you good at?"

I hesitated, wondering if this was just another baited insult.

"I don't know anymore," I said, barely believing the honest answer as it slipped from my lips. "I thought I was good at my job, but I'm starting to question that. I thought I was good at solving puzzles and fixing things, but – you've made me question that too. I think the only thing I'm good at anymore is working hard. That, and I'm still a good marksman."

"Have lots of experience with that, do you?"

His voice had taken on a cold edge, and I felt my body stiffen.

"On the practice range," I clarified, and I knew he could hear the agitation in my voice. "I don't hunt if that's your real question. I never have. I went one time because my boss invited me and I had to go. It was the worst night of my life, shy of nearly drowning in the Academy, which is really rich given that I nearly drowned that night too. Maybe it's a sign or something that it's destined to happen one day – but I wanted nothing to do with that hunt. And no, before you ask, I didn't kill anyone. I've never killed anyone."

He didn't ask anything else, and I didn't feel like talking anymore, so I left. He texted me early Sunday evening, the buzz of the cell phone next to my pillow waking me from my sleep. He needed a few more supplies, and I agreed to bring them the following Monday afternoon. He was there when I dropped off the bag, and we spoke briefly. He asked about my other case, and I told him I was investigating several Jane Doe deaths, but the conversation remained short and to the point.

Tuesday shift, I collected the sensor data from the second facility with Hakim, and sure enough, Warren had purposely walked by the cameras as I had suggested. He'd kept his face and distinguishing features hidden, but it was convincing enough that Hakim called Jonathan and told him to increase his security staff because they were most likely the next target. I said absolutely nothing to hint otherwise and contributed to the suspicion by noting that their facility would actually be easier to break into given the location of the nursery building—and highlighted that they had more new "stock", which made them a better target choice.

Warren texted me the following day and asked for plastic bags and extra shoes of multiple different sizes. I brought them Wednesday afternoon, and even though he didn't tell me what they were for, I had my suspicions. He was going to make false trails, probably walk a few paths through the woods around the first facility to misdirect the investigation, as I had suggested. He was waiting at the cave when I arrived, and we spoke that afternoon too.

I got the feeling he was feeling me out. Slowly asking more and more questions, gathering information about Reborn and who I was—probably judging my answers and assessing my worth to his cause. Yet each time I saw him, despite his hatred of my very existence, I couldn't help but feel like he was getting increasingly relaxed in my presence. He gripped his rifle less tightly. He didn't stand as far away from me as possible, and he didn't hesitate so much before speaking.

So when I showed up Thursday afternoon to drop off a final bag of supplies, I was surprised to find the cave empty.

THURSDAY, SEPTEMBER 3
2:07 PM

I looked around the large empty space, finding no note. The sky was dim and clouded. The weekend storm was rolling in early, just as I had forewarned Warren, and the light drizzle of cool rain had left the heated woods clouded with mist. I dropped the supply bag I was carrying, then took off my helmet and turned to look out the opening. It was dim enough that I could actually see without squinting, but there was no sign of Warren. I had texted him before I'd left work, and he hadn't replied, which was abnormal per our new frequency of correspondence.

My pulse started to quicken as I pulled out the old flip phone to check for a message, but the inbox was empty. I stared at it for a long moment, then quickly ripped off my gloves and texted him again.

C: At the drop, are you coming?

Rain echoed in the cave. No bird calls. Just the rushing river and wind. I stared at the screen, willing a message to arrive, but the phone remained silent. My eyes darted back out into the dim afternoon light, scanning across the grounds but finding nothing. I hesitated a moment, then tried calling him. It disconnected almost instantly, and when I tried twice more the same thing happened.

Something was wrong.

I moved back toward the mouth of the cave, drawing my firearm and inching out into the rain. I kept my back to the rocks as I scanned the misty treeline. If someone had caught him, it was possible they were coming here today. It was possible this whole operation had been exposed, and Warren might be dead.

My heart beat quicker as I strained my ears against the noise of the wind and rushing river. I took another three cautious steps out into the rain, then I heard the sound of footsteps. They were approaching quickly. Whoever it was was jogging. I stepped out from the pine tree, aiming my firearm and preparing for the worst.

The footsteps grew closer.

I braced my footing.

The rain came down harder as the forest grew even darker. Lightning flashed across the sky. I opened my mouth and shouted a verbal warning. Then the wind shifted, and a familiar scent of sweat caught my nose seconds before Warren came running through the treeline. He skidded to a stop on the stone, nearly slipping and falling backward as he stared at me wide-eyed.

"What the hell are you doing?" he yelled, his hands already reacting to grab the rifle that hung loosely off his shoulder.

"What the hell am I doing?" I yelled back. "You scared the bejesus out of me!"

"I scared you?" He looked at me in disbelief, his rifle pointed at my chest. "You nearly shot me!"

"I didn't nearly shoot you," I said, reholstering my firearm while trying to ignore that I was irrationally comfortable with him pointing his rifle at me. "I realized it was you just before you came through the treeline. I picked up your scent right after I yelled, but even if I hadn't, I wouldn't have shot blindly. Besides, the safety was still on."

"You smelled me," he said, finally lowering his weapon. His hair and jacket were soaked through, water trailing off the end of his nose as it crinkled.

"Yes." I glared at his disturbed expression. "But I don't go around smelling people if that's what you're thinking. Humans just sweat, and it has a specific scent. I recognized the smell from the first day I met you, so I knew it was you."

"What, and you're saying that you don't sweat or smell?"

"No," I said, my tone flat as I crossed my arms over my chest. "Reborn don't sweat. Not unless we're dying, pushing our bodies into extreme circumstances, or slipping into a bloodlust. If you ever see me sweating, you have every right to be deeply concerned, and we only smell if we wear scented products."

He stared at me with an unreadable expression, and then his eyes narrowed.

"Isn't it dangerous for you to be out in the open during the day without your helmet?"

"The sky is dark enough right now that I won't get sun poisoning or burn." I turned away from him to move toward the cave. I could hear him following behind me, so I kept talking. "It makes my skin feel uncomfortable, but I'm fine. I thought something was wrong. I was worried you might have been caught."

"I wasn't," Warren said, pushing his dripping hair back from his face as we entered the cave. "The phone I had died, and I couldn't repair it. It happens – these burner phones are at the end of their lives when we get them. I got a new one, but I didn't have your number on hand to add it back in."

"I see," I said, guessing that Warren had probably never bothered to memorize it. Not only was I disposable, but his connection to me was dangerous. I didn't doubt they had a record of all their contacts' numbers, but not knowing them by heart would be better if he was ever caught and questioned. He probably stored his supplies in multiple places too, always preparing and trying to lessen the blow to his network.

"Did you get the message I sent about the weather before it died?"

"Yes." Warren nodded, reaching out to take the flip phone I had removed from my vest pocket. He unlocked it, then quickly updated the number for his contact profile, then entered my number into his new phone. "Change in plans – we're doing it tomorrow."

"Tomorrow?" I repeated as I took my phone back from him. "Are you ready for that?"

"No," he answered, his honesty catching me off-guard. He let out a sigh and then leaned his rifle against the cave wall so he could remove his jacket. "But we'll figure it out."

I stared at him, unsure of what to make of this. It was the first time he had ever not held a weapon in my presence, and he had dropped his hold on it in favour of wringing out his jacket.

Without it on, I could see his build more clearly because his shirt was wet and sticking to his skin. He was broad-shouldered but lean. He easily had the same muscle mass as a Reborn like Hawthorne, except the muscles sat differently on him. It looked more natural, less forced, like he was literally built to carry it.

"Do you have to work hard to keep that build?" I asked, the words leaving my lips before I could rethink them.

He stiffened, his hands stilling on the wet fabric as if he just now realized what he was doing. Then he glanced up to meet my curious gaze, uncoiling his jacket only to retwist it and wring it out once more.

"Yes and no," he said, his voice far quieter and less condescending than I was expecting. "Life is a lot harder out in the wild than what you're used to. If you're not fit, you're less likely to survive – but most of the work I do is just part of life."

"I see." I nodded as I toyed with the wet fabric of my pants. "Reborn can gain muscle mass, but it isn't easy for us. We're not genetically inclined to build it, so it takes a lot of effort."

"That would explain why the few of you I've seen in person have all been lanky beanpoles," Warren muttered.

I couldn't stop the tiny puff of air that left my lungs, and I turned away so he couldn't see the smile tugging at my lips. I looked out the cave as he finished wringing his jacket. The rain was getting worse, and the low rumble of thunder seemed endless. I found myself wondering what it must be like to live out there in the woods, weathering these storms and the fluctuating temperatures. How much time did they spend just collecting food and trying to get by?

An ear-splitting crack rang out, and lightning cut across the sky as if to cleave it in two, and it felt like an answer to my question. I frowned. It was no wonder he hated us so much. There were just so many reasons to.

"Are you planning to wait this out?"

"What?" I jerked at the question, turning to look back at Warren. He was standing there watching me with another one of his odd and unreadable expressions.

"The storm." He gestured to the rain outside. "You'll be here all day. This won't let up until Saturday."

"I know." I forced my lips into a polite smile even though my heart suddenly felt heavy. "Sorry – I'll leave so you can go. I was just lost in my head."

I moved to grab my helmet, aware that he was watching me closely as I tucked it under my arm and set off through the rain once more, not caring that it was soaking through my hair and pouring down the collar of my vest.

FRIDAY, SEPTEMBER 4
2:13 PM

The rain was coming down hard, pounding against the glass windows of my living room as I paced the floor clutching the tiny flip phone in my hand. I had texted Warren well before the sun came up to confirm that nothing had changed and that Hakim was still following our usual schedule. He'd replied right away in acknowledgment, but since then, I hadn't heard anything, so I had no idea where he was, if he was at the farm now or walking through the woods toward it.

I glanced out the window again, my heart beating abnormally fast as I looked at the darkened sky and tried not to worry.

A million questions were racing through my head. How many were they planning to take? All of them? Half of them? How were they going to transport them? Surely he wasn't going to try and carry more than twenty-five human children under the age of two through the woods, was he?

I was just about to start my pace back toward the kitchen when a crack of thunder rattled the windows, and the electricity flickered. I glanced at the flashing clock on my stove, then my cell phone started to ring.

"Gorski," I said, answering it on the third tone and faking a sleepy voice.

'Wake up and get your gear on,' Hakim's voice echoed in my ear. *'Carl just called me – there's been a power outage at the facility, and the backup generator didn't kick on. He isn't concerned, but I told him to send security out to check the buildings. All of this is too coincidental. I'm heading out there now and can grab you on the way.'*

"Okay." I moved to my closet to grab my jacket. I was already dressed and ready to go, wearing my vest, badge, and firearm. "I live at—"

'I know where you live, Gorski. It's in your personal file. Be ready in five.'

He hung up before I could say anything else, and I rapidly pulled out the phone Warren had given me.

C: Security was just sent to check the buildings. H is suspicious. He's picking me up in five, and we're coming out. You have less than six minutes before the guard gets to you. I probably won't be able to message while in the car, so watch yourself. Remember, police arrival time is forty minutes from when the call is placed.

I pulled my jacket on over my vest, grabbing my helmet and gloves as I left my apartment. I was halfway down the stairwell when my vest buzzed, and I pulled out the tiny flip phone again, skimming Warren's response as I ran the rest of the way down the stairs.

A: We can manage the guard. Planted trail headed NW toward cty rd 76. Get here before the police and direct them that way. We'll be out in 35 min

C: I'll do what I can

I shoved the phone into my inside vest pocket again, then jammed on my helmet and raced out under the building awning. If the guard had placed the call before going out to check the buildings, we wouldn't get there before the other officers, and Warren would still be there. It took roughly fifty-two minutes to get to the farm from my apartment, but if Hakim pushed the limits of our speed, we could make it in forty.

This would be close.

Extremely close.

At the sound of an approaching car, I made my way to the curb, watching the black vehicle slow. It was Hakim; I had memorized his plates. He barely stopped to let me get in. I hadn't even done up my seatbelt yet and he was already driving down the street toward the highway.

"You think the power outage isn't an accident?" I asked as I tugged off my helmet and pushed the shorter bits of hair away from my face.

"No," Hakim answered, but his eyes were focused on the road as he drove through the heavy rain and brought us onto the highway, where he immediately picked up speed. "I told Carl to call it in, but this has happened before in bad rainstorms, so he's convinced it's just the generator. He doesn't think anyone would try anything in this weather."

"If he's wrong, his insurance won't cover this. Our report explicitly told him to replace that generator because it was a risk," I said, glancing at the speedometer. Hakim was driving very fast. "Should we call it in?"

"I already did," Hakim said, and my hopes of causing more delays plummeted. "But there was a small pile-up on the Highway 78 off-ramp – debris from the storm on the road – so responding officers from Precinct 15 will be delayed. We might get there before them."

"Alright." I nodded, hoping that was indeed the case.

I watched the trees whip by the window, wondering how the hell Warren was transporting kids in this weather. I felt the faint buzz of the flip phone against my chest but forced myself to ignore it. Then I jumped ten minutes later when Hakim's cell phone started to ring.

"Answer it," Hakim said, pulling the device from his vest pocket and handing it out to me, not once removing his eyes from the road.

I hesitated a second, then grabbed the phone and answered the call.

"Detective Hakim's pho—"

'Gorski?' Carl's familiar voice rang in my ear. *'Where the hell is Hakim?!'*

"He's driving," I answered, glancing over to my left. "We're on our way out. What do you need?"

'Raymond hasn't come back from his rounds,' Carl said, his voice ringing with panic. *'Should I go out there? Or have Dennis go try to restart the generator or what?'*

"Security didn't come back yet," I said to Hakim, and his expression grew dark. "What do you want Carl to do – go out there, or—"

"No," Hakim answered, cutting me off as he shook his head. "We'll be there in twenty minutes. Tell him to stay in his office and place another call to dispatch; there's nothing he can do now. The facility is already going to take a financial hit today, I don't need a potential second dead body on top of it."

"Alright," I said, then relayed the message to Carl.

'Then you had better get here as quickly as you can!' Carl yelled, his voice so loud I had to hold the phone away from my ear. *'I thought you said Jonathan's facility was the target? How incompetent are you two! If I lose even one of my stock today, your captain is going to be hearing from our lawyers!'*

He hung up, and I grimaced. "He's pissed."

"He's incompetent," Hakim said, his tone cold as he increased our speed once more. "I called him last night and told him to increase his staff as well – he chose not to. His insurance followed up with us to double-check that our recommendations were necessary, and I told them they were. His facility might operate under the same parent umbrella as Jonathan's, but he has less funding because his farm is older. Carl is on thin ice, and he knows it. He has no grounds to sue for anything because he didn't comply with our directions. If Raymond was injured on duty and they lose all their new stock today, this investigation and our precinct will be the least of his worries."

I nodded, handing Hakim his phone back as we started to make our way down the old country roads. By the time we reached the familiar-looking gatehouse, it was raining so hard it was nearly impossible to see. The car skidded through the gate. Hakim didn't bother to stop; we both knew no one was manning the booth, and every second mattered. I tightened the straps on my vest as he sped down the center lane toward the nursery building along the far northern fenceline. If Warren was still here and he saw me, he would shoot me—he had to. So I needed to be careful because there was no way to know what type of ammunition he had in his rifle.

I stuffed my helmet on, my heart racing as Hakim slammed on the brakes. I exited the vehicle seconds before him, both of us drawing our firearms as the faint sounds of sirens echoed in the distance and Hakim's radio buzzed. Officers from 15 would be here any minute, and two nearby provincial cruisers were en route.

Hakim took point, and I raced along behind him through the mud toward the building, silently cursing the fishbowl effect of my visor. Another fifteen steps, and I saw the cut in the fence. The door to the building was busted open, there was a body in the mud along the wall, and Hakim was on his radio faster than I could blink.

"Dispatch, this is Randall Hakim," he said, not bothering to give his badge number and quickly kneeling by Raymond's body to check for a pulse. "Facility security guard is down – confirm first responders en route. Gorski – check the building!"

'Hakim, this is dispatch, confirmed. First responders ETA two minutes. Officers are less than sixty seconds out.'

I could already hear the sirens getting closer. I moved ahead, letting out a sigh of relief when I found the building empty.

"Clear!" I called before rapidly moving toward the fence.

I carefully scanned the ground, looking for anything that Warren might have left behind. Everything was so waterlogged it was difficult to make anything out, which was exactly what I had been hoping, but I purposely stepped in something that looked a little bit like a footprint and smeared it with my boot before calling back to Hakim.

"Is he okay?"

"He'll live," Hakim said. He stood from the ground and moved toward me. "Let's go – they couldn't have gotten far."

I nodded, manoeuvring through the cut fence and intentionally stepping in and ruining two other suspiciously treadless smudges that lead east. Then I directed my attention to the much more obvious trail that headed west.

"Hakim!" I said, faking urgency and pointing to the tracks as he cut through the fence behind me. I knew the rain would take care of the rest of Warren's real prints if I could buy him a little more time, so I leaned into my desperation to sound as convincing as possible. "Tracks! They're fading – but they're here! Heading west!"

Flashes of red and blue filled the facility grounds as officers from Precinct 15 flooded the site. I rushed eagerly after the fake trail, only to stop abruptly when Hakim grabbed my shoulder.

"I don't need you getting shot today, too, Gorski," Hakim said, tugging me behind him. "I'll take point."

"Yes, sir."

I didn't bother arguing with him and instead took the radio he handed me, letting the others know that the suspects had fled west. I requested assistance, then tacked the radio on my belt and ran along behind my partner into the trees. The wind ripped at my jacket as we sprinted. Rain flooded over my visor in thick sheets of water as I panted and struggled to keep up. He moved faster than I ever could have anticipated. So silent it was eerie as he cut through the brush and followed the trail that Warren had set.

"This is leading toward County Road 76," Hakim called, speeding up. He reached out behind him, and I handed him his radio, instinctively knowing what he wanted. "Dispatch – this is Hakim. Suspects proceeded west to County Road 76. Tell Provincial to send out additional highway patrol. Look for unmarked vans, trucks, tractors, transports – anything that could move twenty-five-plus bodies. Start monitoring camera feeds on the overpass by Line 29 and—"

Hakim droned on, calling out more orders as we sprinted through the trees after nothing with half a dozen more officers trailing along behind us. When we reached the highway, all we found was a smear of mud and debris that scattered out onto the road and the faint remains of indents, which could have been tire tracks destroyed by the rain.

The detail was a nice touch—I'd have to tell Warren that later.

Only Reborn would have been able to sprint this far with over twenty-five human children. Only Reborn could drive, as far as other Reborn were concerned, and only Reborn would be bold enough to venture out in this weather to pull off a stunt like this.

I stood there, my heart pounding so hard I thought it might explode as Hakim handed me his ringing cell phone once more and told me to "deal with it" while he moved toward the approaching officers from 15 to direct the investigation and get the road roped off. I answered the call, finding an extraordinarily pissed-off Carl on the other end, while our backup began canvassing the area for evidence.

But as the rain soaked my jacket and thunder rumbled across the sky, all I could do was smile.

Probation

SATURDAY, SEPTEMBER 19
4:02 PM

"Hello?" I answered the phone, my eyes still closed and my words sounding groggy.

'Gorski.' Hakim's voice filled the silence of my bedroom. *'Congratulations, your probation has been extended another three months, so you're now officially working this weekend. Get up, and get your gear on. I need you on the west side in fifteen minutes.'*

"Wha—" I sat up, prying my eyes open as I struggled to pull my mind from the deep sleep I had been in seconds ago. "But my probation doesn't end until October 3rd."

'I extended it early,' came the clipped response. *'Are you awake or not? Or should I just revoke the extension now?'*

"No – I'm awake," I said, stumbling off my bed and across the floor toward my door. "I'm up. I'm ready. I'll be in my car in ten."

'Good. I'll text you the address,' he said. Then his voice rang out once more. *'And don't eat anything.'*

He hung up before I could ask him to explain, but I figured that wasn't a good sign. I forced my brain to wake, running to the shower and jumping under a cold stream of water to help shake off the last of the sleep. I was dressed, with my hair twisted into a braid and my teeth brushed, within four minutes. I raced to my hall closet to grab my gear and strapped on my vest, badge, and firearm before grabbing my gloves and helmet. Another three minutes later and I was racing down the staircase to the underground garage—not trusting the elevator to be quick enough—as I wondered what the hell was going on.

After Warren had escaped two weeks ago and texted me to confirm that he and the rescued children were safe, I had dived headfirst into "helping" with the farm facility investigation—doing everything that I could to derail it.

I ruined more footprints. I tucked a strand of hair I found inside the nursery building into my pocket before forensics from Precinct 15 got there and purposely ran my gloved fingers over any surface Warren may have touched while inside to smear any lingering fingerprints. He had likely worn the gloves I'd provided, but I wasn't taking any chances, and I touched everything that I could when no one was looking.

I poured through useless traffic footage, reporting two suspicious-looking vans that were headed west on the 29, then wasted time and effort running the plates and coordinating with the Provincial Police to locate the vehicles while Hakim dealt with the responding officers from Precinct 15 and worked to coordinate our investigation efforts with their Detective Unit, who tried to argue they should be involved because it was Precinct 15 officers who had responded to the scene.

It was a bit of a jurisdictional mess, but Vogle said he would work it out.

I went to the hospital with another officer to visit Raymond and take his statement, and I was happy to find out he hadn't seen anything before being hit over the head and shot multiple times in the chest and neck with standard animal-grade rounds. He was lucky to be alive. Had Warren and his people used Reborn-grade ammunition, Raymond would have died before we could reach him. One Reborn-grade round was deadly enough, but six, that would be a guaranteed death sentence.

Those cartridges were designed to kill.

Unlike animal-grade ammunition, which was mandated as a first line of defence because the rounds were non-toxic and lighter grain, designed to temporarily maim and slow down targets,

Reborn-grade ammunition was composed of toxic radioactive materials. They were heavy, designed to hit hard and expand over twice their diameter, leaving a large wound channel and maximizing internal damage. The resulting injury would drain a Reborn of their limited blood while the radiation from the bullet slowed their ability to heal. Immediate professional medical attention was required if you wanted any chance of surviving.

It was why Reborn-grade magazines were never initially loaded in our firearms and were only ever to be used as a last resort. The rounds were carefully controlled, and usage tracked and monitored. An officer could lose their job and go to jail if they were found to have used the ammunition without there being just cause or a threat to public safety.

Carl called nearly every hour for the first two nights until Hakim and Captain Vogle met with the director of Dolan's Agriculture and forwarded them a copy of our recommendations report and email correspondence with Carl. After which Carl was promptly fired. The backup generator was replaced three days later, and Jonathan from the second farm was brought on to temporarily manage both facilities until Dolan's could find a replacement.

I worked nearly night and day that first week, twice falling asleep at my desk, only to wake up two hours later and use the locker rooms within the precinct to shower. Both times, Hakim didn't say a word, and each time I woke up, he was still working at his desk ten feet away—looking as if he had not moved an inch.

Perhaps that was why he had extended my probation, because even though I was ruining our investigation and pointing us in the wrong direction any time I could, I appeared entirely dedicated and willing to sacrifice my personal life for the case.

I had dropped off a supply pack at the cave last Monday morning. Warren wasn't there, and I didn't stick around because I had to get home to do more work, but I texted him to make sure that he got the bag. Then I blew off Grace's coffee invite and texted Warren again before heading into work that night to ask if he needed anything else. He sent me a list early the following morning. It was blunt and to the point, like usual. But, to my surprise, he didn't give me a drop time, and ten minutes later, he texted me again and asked how the investigation was going.

I smiled when I read the note from the bathroom stall at work.

I couldn't help myself.

I told him I was working my ass off night and day to track down a sketchy-looking white van that had taken the off-ramp at the 29 and gone west. Then I complimented his work on setting the false trail. He told me all twenty-eight kids were safe and relatively healthy—though six had high fevers. I volunteered to bring him more first aid supplies, but he told me they still had lots. I told him I would get some to add to the next drop anyway, then let him know Precinct 15 was going to be assisting the Provincial Police with patrolling the area for the next few weeks. He said it wouldn't be an issue because they didn't have the resources to pull any other jobs right now, and he wouldn't be anywhere near the facilities for a while.

He asked if the security guard had made it, and I told him that he had. He didn't say anything else after that, but he texted me the following morning and told me to let him know when I could drop off the next bag. I had stared at the tiny phone in disbelief, blown away that he would let me dictate the time of our next drop, until I realized he was only doing it because he couldn't afford me raising any suspicions, what with me working around the clock and needing to dodge the new highway patrols.

Still, though, it was nice and far more considerate than any of our other interactions to date.

I told him I would let him know the drop date soon. The bag was packed and stowed in my trunk, but still, I had yet to find the time to bring it out. I had only gotten home from work three hours ago, and I desperately needed sleep. Now, as I ran across the parking garage toward my car, I wasn't sure when I would even have a minute to breathe, let alone find time to drive back out to make another drop.

It took me less than a minute to find the address Hakim had texted me on the map I kept in my car, and I was off driving across Carneth toward the richest neighbourhood in the city. I had never been there myself. I lived on the north side of the city center, and while my parents and family were from the west side, we weren't "from the west side". I came from the northwest, which, while well off, was not grotesquely wealthy like the southwest was.

I did my best not to gawk at the size of the mansions as I made my way down a long, winding drive. Most of them had gates. Two I passed had little security booths, and all of them were so lavish it felt absurd.

I rounded the next corner, immediately spotting the red and blue lights flashing at the end of a three-car-wide driveway that climbed up a small hill. The house atop it was white brick with stone accents, and huge floor-to-ceiling windows on the front with dark tinted glass. I spotted Hakim's car on the road and parked behind it, then quickly stuffed my helmet on and made my way toward the other officers.

"Officer Gorski," I said, holding up my badge as I approached. I still hadn't taken to calling myself a detective. It felt wrong given that my position was temporary. "Hakim called me and—"

"He's already inside," the tallest officer replied, stepping toward me to glance at my badge. I didn't recognize his name, but his uniform confirmed he was from my precinct. "Go on in."

He gestured over his shoulder, and I nodded, glancing at the other officers and noting the mixed badges. Several of the officers were from the 24th Precinct, which meant that this case was quickly going to turn into another administrative mess.

This street sat right on the boundary between Precincts 21–30 and Precincts 31–40. Precinct 24, which had a Detective Unit and supported the other smaller precincts within the 21 through 30 group, would probably want this case. Dispatch would have called in whatever patrol officers were nearest, and it looked like our cars had gotten here first. I wasn't sure why Hakim had been called to the scene. I could only imagine it was because Vogle had his number on speed dial, and the man never stopped working.

That, or maybe he lived around here—I really didn't know very much about my partner outside of his working habits.

Either way, it wasn't my issue to resolve. Captain Vogle was probably awake and on the phone with Captain Constance from

24 battling this out. They would decide who would run the show. In the meantime, I had a job to do.

I jogged my way up the driveway, cutting across the grass toward the front doors. Another set of officers checked my badge before they let me inside and pointed me down a wide hall. I could hear them arguing behind me as I took off my helmet and left it by the door with the others, then made my way toward the back of the insanely massive home. It wasn't until I caught the stark scent of bleach and faint hints of blood that I slowed, then I saw the red smeared across the cream-coloured walls and marble floor.

"Gorski." Hakim's voice rang out the second I turned the corner. I stopped, my eyes raked over the scene, and my stomach twisted. "I've got this room covered – I need you to go downstairs. The door there."

Hakim pointed to a set of stairs off to his left.

"And take statements from the remaining girls," he continued, his tone completely indifferent despite the blood on the floor by his feet and the two motionless bodies to his right. "Forensics will be here in a few minutes. There are two officers from 24 down there already. They just got here – ignore them and take your own notes. Until Vogle and Constance make a call, we're both proceeding per protocol. Go do your job."

I stared at my partner, completely lost for words. There was a young man sitting on the couch near another officer. Blood covered the front of his white V-neck T-shirt. His jaw was clenched tight, and I suspected that he was refusing to speak until his lawyers showed up, but there was something distinctly smug about his expression. The two bodies on the ground were both females. One looked like she'd had her neck ripped out, and the other was covered in so much blood I couldn't tell what had happened. There was a cordless phone smeared with blood streaks just a few feet away from them, an overturned coffee table by their legs, and a broken vase near the massive floor-to-ceiling window that overlooked a well-kempt lawn, pool, and patio.

The tinted glass window was streaked with blood too. Handprints—as if someone had been banging their fist against it...

I felt sick.

I had seen pictures of gorier things at the Academy, but this was the first time that I had ever seen something like this in person, and it was so much worse.

"Gorski." My eyes snapped back to Hakim. He was looking at me intently, his cold gaze hard. "Don't touch anything on your way down."

"Yes, sir." I forced the words out, then turned and made for the door he had pointed to.

The basement wasn't nearly as fancy as the rest of the home. In fact, it had a distinctly uncomfortable vibe to it that I didn't like. The air was cold and smelled strongly sanitized. When I reached the bottom of the steps, I pulled out my notepad and made my way across the large room. It looked almost like a living space, but the furniture and decor appeared cheap, old, and far less maintained than anything I'd seen upstairs. I jotted down a few notes, mapping out a quick sketch of the space. There were four doors along the right-hand side of the wall, and a quick glance inside suggested that three of them might be bedrooms, windowless—which was illegal—and the last room was a small bathroom.

I fought the urge to frown as I turned to face the others in the far corner of the room. There were two girls sitting on a couch along the left wall. The officers from 24 were speaking to them. Three more women were sitting on the floor along the back wall, shins tucked up to their chests, faces hidden because their foreheads were pressed against their knees. All of them were wearing simple clothes, long-sleeved shirts and pants.

One of the two officers turned and glared at me. It was obvious they thought this case was theirs, and they didn't want me here. The 33rd might be the main precinct in Carneth, which supported all the other Detective Units in the city, but that didn't mean that they liked us. Precinct 24 had a newer building, and their chief of police had been pushing to expand. It made me wonder what sort of political games Vogle might be playing and if that was why Hakim was here today—because he was the best and Vogle was trying to make a statement about our capabilities.

I pushed the questions aside and jotted down some more notes. I had a job to do. My only focus was helping these people; the power struggle between precincts wasn't my concern. So I ignored the glares and cautiously approached the group of three.

"Excuse me, miss," I said, keeping my voice low. Unlike the officers from 24, who remained standing as they questioned the two on the couch, I lowered myself down into a crouch on the ground. "Can you please tell me your name?"

Two of the girls didn't move. Their arms just wrapped tighter around their legs, and they kept their faces pressed firmly to their knees. But the one in the middle cautiously raised her head. She appeared uninjured, at least physically—there was no sign or scent of blood down here—but it was clear that she hadn't been eating well, given how thin and small she was.

I watched in silence as she let out a low breath, then slowly opened her eyes. She stared at me, but her gaze looked unfocused. Almost like her brown eyes couldn't see properly, then she squinted, and as her eyes trailed over my face, I stilled.

Her eyes were not pale.

They weren't nearly as warm or deep as Warren's, and they weren't as dull as the "stock" kept at the farms either, but they were not normal. They were faded, probably from years of being kept indoors mostly in the dark while being improperly fed, because what the hell would a rich Reborn know about her dietary requirements. He clearly didn't view them as people if this was where they were living, but he knew, just like I knew the second she met my gaze and struggled to see me through the dark, *exactly* what she was.

"We don't have names," she finally whispered, and a sharp jolt of pain shot through my heart. "We were never allowed them."

My eyes trailed down her face to her neck, and sure enough, there were faint marks. They were on her wrists and ankles too. I could see the faint scars of teeth marks on any bit of skin not covered by her clothes, and I knew that her arms and legs were probably littered with them. The only place that wasn't marked was her face.

My chest grew tight, and I glanced at the officers to my left.

How could they not have noticed?

How could they not know?

It was obvious. Clear as crystal that these girls were human, and yet no one seemed to note the difference because they were so pale. Because they were speaking. Because they were *people* right now—Reborn women who had likely been trafficked. The thought probably hadn't even crossed the other officers' minds, and I knew in my heart that I wouldn't have noticed it either had I not been working on the Dolan case with Hakim. I would have just assumed that these girls were really young, and that's why they were so small.

"How long have you been here?" I whispered, dropping my voice as my mind started to race. What would happen when the officers from 24 found out? What would happen when Hakim found out?

"Twelve years."

"How old are you?"

"Nineteen."

Sickness curled in the pit of my stomach. I opened my mouth to ask another question but was immediately cut off as Hakim's voice rang out.

"Gorski!"

I heard his feet on the steps, and I turned in time to see him coming down the stairs, phone pressed to his ear. His voice dropped low as he answered something else on the call. I knew whatever was happening must be serious, and for a moment, my heart fluttered with hope that he, too, had figured out these girls were human and this would become a federal case with hefty charges.

"Yes, sir," he said, to the phone, not to me. He rapidly made his way across the living space, nodding once at whatever the person on the other end of the conversation said. "Understood."

He abruptly ended the call, pocketing his phone before he reached me and outstretched a hand.

"Notebook."

His tone was clipped, and I immediately stood and handed him my notebook.

"Sir? What's going on?"

He glanced at the sketch I'd made and the notes beneath it. Then, to my horror, he ripped the pages out, crumpled them, and stuffed them into his pocket.

"We're done," he said, handing the notebook back and turning to look at the other two officers. "Get upstairs—*now*."

His tone left no room for argument, and the officers from 24 quickly pocketed their pens and made their way toward the stairs.

"Sir?" I stared at my notebook, positively dumbfounded. "Wha—"

"Upstairs," Hakim said, grabbing my shoulder and rapidly steering me back across the room.

He all but forced me up the steps, pushing me back into the room bathed with blood and past the other officers who were also rapidly leaving. The man who had been seated on the couch was standing now, his arms crossed lazily over his chest, wrists free of cuffs as another officer from Precinct 24 confiscated the notebooks from the officers who had been downstairs with me. I stumbled as Hakim pushed me down the hall, my head buzzing with the commotion.

"Hakim?" I said, finally tearing myself out of his hold as we reached the shelf by the door. He grabbed his helmet, then grabbed mine and thrust it into my chest. "What the hell is going on?"

"Put your helmet on."

"No." I shook my head, clutching my helmet tight as some of the officers pushed past us to leave the house. They glanced at me warily, and Hakim's eyes narrowed. "What are—"

"Put. Your. Helmet. On," Hakim repeated, his voice dropping so low it nearly came out as a growl. He took a step toward me, and I couldn't stop myself from taking a step back. "Or I will drag you outside without it."

My eyes pinched, my jaw clenching tight before I shoved the helmet on my head and marched outside. I didn't want to, but I knew whatever was happening was important, and I knew he hadn't been lying.

I made it nearly halfway down the massive driveway before he grabbed my shoulder again and steered me toward his car. I jerked out of his grip ten feet away but went to the passenger side of his vehicle anyway and climbed inside. The second the door slammed shut, I ripped off my helmet, and suddenly my voice flooded the small space.

"What the hell is going on? You took my notes! That's illegal! Those are part of this investigation, and they have to be filed with the case report – and why are the officers from 24 leaving?"

"There is no case report—"

"*No* case report?!" I cut him off, turning to glare at him as my gloved fingers dug into my helmet with a crunch. "THERE ARE TWO DEAD BODIES IN THAT HOUSE AND FIVE GIRLS IN THE BASEMENT!"

I hadn't intended to scream those words, and the heavy silence that followed made the air thick. I stiffened as he turned to look at me, all of the air in my lungs seizing at the dark expression on his face.

"There. Is. No. Case."

Each word was punctuated just like inside. I could see some of the other cruisers pulling away in my peripherals, but I held his hard gaze.

"The details of why don't matter," he said, his voice taking on a dangerous edge. "When I tell you to leave – you leave. When I tell you to put your helmet on – you put your helmet on. When I tell you to do anything – you do it, understand?"

I stared at him, shaking my head in refusal and swallowing hard, and feeling like any last hope I had of him being a decent person was fading away.

"Those were humans in that basement," I whispered, and I could hear my voice shaking. "It's illegal to own humans. These are federal charges, Hakim. This *has* to be reported. I can't stand by and—"

"Then I suggest you go back to the precinct and turn in your badge right now." Hakim cut me off. "These orders came from the top, Gorski, and while I'm sure Vogle would admire your moral fortitude, he has bigger issues to deal with than your ethical problems. The dead bodies of a few illegal humans in the home of Scott Beckette"—I stiffened at the name—"is more trouble than you're worth. But if you feel strongly about this, go ahead."

He pulled out his cell phone and held it out freely.

"Call Vogle." He held my gaze. "Tell him you want to file charges and see what happens."

I didn't move. My grip on my helmet tightened, and I stared at him in silence as the last of the other patrol cars left, leaving Hakim and me alone on the street.

"This is wrong," I whispered, but his face remained completely emotionless. I watched him for a long moment, willing him to say something—anything. But he didn't. "How do you live with this?"

He stared at me, his eyes cold as stone.

"I spend my time on things that actually matter."

It hit like a kick to the gut. Images of him shooting that woman during the hunting trip flooded my mind as bile filled my mouth. He didn't care. He didn't care because they were human. That's what had happened. That's what had changed. Either he or someone else from 24 had realized the women upstairs were human and called it in—then they'd been told to pack up and leave because no one cared. Vogle wasn't going to charge Chief Justice Beckette's son for owning humans when no other judge would dare prosecute it.

I watched Hakim repocket his phone.

"Go home, Gorski," he said, his tone dropping to a low growl once more. "Mull it over. Figure out whether or not you want to come in on Sunday night. I don't care what you decide to do, but if you do come in, don't *ever* question me again."

His gaze was deadly, his mismatched eyes all but burning into my own as the air around us grew tight.

"You pull something like that again, question my orders or refuse to leave a scene when directed, being handed back to Mallick in Patrol and Street will be the least of your career concerns. You follow my direction when I give it, understood?"

I didn't want to answer. I wanted to throw up, but my reflexes betrayed me and the word left my lips.

"Understood."

"Good," Hakim said, then he pulled out his keys and started the engine. "Now get out of my car."

I swallowed, nodded, then shoved my helmet back on my head. I ripped open the door and clambered out of the car, then slammed it shut behind me. My legs shook as I made my way back to my vehicle and got inside—only to rip off my helmet once more and throw it on the passenger side floor.

I couldn't breathe. I couldn't think. Before I even realized what I was doing, I reached inside my vest and pulled out the tiny flip phone I kept plastered to my person.

I texted Warren, telling him I was coming to drop off the bag now, then added a second message asking if he could meet me. I didn't wait for his reply. I had no idea where he was or how long it took him to reach the cave. I just started my car and drove away from Scott Beckette's house as quickly as I could. By the time I reached the familiar road where I always hid my car, the afternoon was nearly gone, and soon evening would be setting in. Warren had messaged back and said that he would try to make it, so I grabbed the supply bag from my trunk and set off through the trees.

I cut along the familiar trail to the cave, my teeth clenched tight as my heart continued to race. I couldn't stop replaying what had happened. The blood. The bodies. The girls sitting there against the wall. The hollow look in her nameless eyes. Hakim's words and the crushing realization that this sort of thing must happen all the time. I picked up my pace, but the gut-wrenching feeling only continued to grow.

I was going to be sick.

I burst into the clearing, making it there faster than ever before. The sun was still too high for me to be exposed, but I didn't care. I was suffocating in my blackout gear. I ripped off my helmet, running blindly across the stone toward the cave like it was the only sanctuary I had left. I winced in pain as the late evening sunlight burnt my face. I could feel myself hyperventilating as my skin blistered and my breath came in quicker and quicker rasps. Then I dropped the bag before the mouth of the cave and crumpled over, and retched.

"Corvus?"

I groaned, turning away from the sun's rays and throwing up again as my eyes stung from pain. Even if I hadn't recognized his voice, I would have known who it was by the name. I could hear his feet getting quicker as he ran toward me.

"What the hell – Corvus, what's going on?"

If I didn't know any better, I might be stupid enough to think that it was concern that laced his voice and that he might actually care. But I did know better. I knew a lot better now.

I forced my eyes open, barely able to see my helmet on the ground, only inches away from my mess. I guess I'd dropped that too. I inhaled, the air burning my lungs as I straightened once more and hissed in pain as the sun burned my face yet again.

"What are you doing?!" He grabbed my shoulder, just like Hakim had, then pushed me inside the shadow of the cave. "Are you trying to kill yourself?! You realize that your face is burning, right?"

"I couldn't breathe," I said, swatting his hands away from me and turning around to glare at him.

"What happened?" His eyes were trailing over my face in confusion, and I knew it was probably red and blistered. "Are you okay?"

"No, I'm not okay!" I yelled, acid burning my throat as I gagged again. He quickly unshouldered his rifle and then grabbed the supply bag and my helmet from outside the cave. "Nothing is okay! Nothing about any of this is okay, Warren!"

I let out a breath, pinching my eyes closed tight as my face started to heal. I could feel the skin reforming, and it itched with discomfort—but it felt like nothing in comparison to the pain that was radiating from my chest. I forced my eyes back open, moving toward the supply bag that Warren had just dropped on the ground, grabbing one of the water bottles inside, and rapidly downing half of it. Yet it did nothing to quench the boiling rage that bubbled up from my chest, and there was no hope of stopping it as it started to pour out in an angry, unfiltered rant.

"My partner called me in today, extended my probation, and asked me to meet him at a crime scene. I got there, and it was a bloodbath! Two dead women in the middle of some rich guy's living room! He sent me downstairs to go get statements from the remaining women. Five. Five of them, Warren!" I said, turning to look at him as I crumpled the half-full bottle in my hand. "I figured it was another trafficking incident. Some guy with too much money and no moral compass—and Hakim and I would get to bust him and lay down a bunch of charges. So I went downstairs and found all these rooms. He was keeping them down there. They were living in his basement, but it turns out that they weren't Reborn at all!

"They were humans, Warren!" I yelled, and he stood there in silence, watching me explode. "And the other officers didn't even notice! They had no clue that they were interviewing humans! But the second the leads upstairs figured it out, the precinct chiefs called the whole thing off! My partner ripped pages out of my notebook! He forced me to leave! Owning humans is a federal offence, but they're burying the case because the rich guy is Scott Beckette – the son of Joseph Beckette – our provincial chief justice!"

I exhaled hard, dropping the water bottle and threading my fingers into my braided hair.

"And if I report it, if I push this – I'll lose my job. My partner doesn't care. He'd rather spend his time on things 'that actually matter'. The idiots from 24 probably still don't even know – the only reason I knew is because I know you!" I said, gesturing toward him as I started to pace in the small cave. "And no one cares! Not a single person! They didn't even have names! They weren't *allowed* to have names, and she's been there since she was seven. SEVEN! She was covered in bite marks! Just – all over – and I had to leave her, and it was – I just—"

My voice cut out as I struggled to inhale, and I finally stopped pacing.

"There are Reborn women going missing in the eastside, and my family doesn't care," I whispered. "The mayor doesn't care. My department doesn't care. The case is going to be taken away from us at the end of November when the election is over, and then they'll bury that too."

I stared at the stone wall of the cave as the red glow of evening started to filter across the opening.

"It's wrong," I whispered. "All of this is wrong – and I'm sorry."

I swallowed hard, my fingers curling into the fabric of my pants as I turned to face him. He was staring at me with a strange expression, but he didn't say a word.

"I'm sorry," I said again, wanting him to know that I meant it. I wished he would accept it, but knew that he never would as he remained there, motionless. "I'm sorry for all of this."

Silence rang through the cave for a long moment, then Warren's voice finally filled the air.

"So what are you going to do about it?"

His gaze was hard, but somehow the words came out soft and unlike any he had spoken to me before. I stared at him, my eyes trailing over his broad shoulders and messy locks of hair, across the stubble that covered his jaw and the cheekbones that made him look strong. I knew his face, but I knew nothing about him. I knew nothing about his people. I knew nothing about what they were working on or the broader aspects of their plan. I was but a tiny little thread attached to the edge of a massive needlepoint picture, and I wanted that to change.

"I want in," I whispered, stepping toward him. He didn't move as I approached, and his hands remained unarmed and loose at his sides as I stopped a foot away and looked up to meet his gaze. And this time, he didn't appear nervous by how close I was. "I want to know everything. All of it. I want to help. I want to be a part of this – whatever it takes. No matter the cost. No matter the risks. I'm in."

He stared at me quietly, his eyes trailing over my face in the fading light as my heart continued to race.

"Alright," Warren said, his deep voice flooding my body with relief. "You can meet Orion."

Orion

Without another word or explanation, Warren stepped away, shouldering his rifle before gesturing to my helmet. "Are you coming or not?"

"Now?" I asked, watching as he pulled out his phone and rapidly sent a message. He waited a moment, eyes locked on the device's screen until it buzzed with a reply.

"Yes." He looked up to meet my gaze. "Unless you have somewhere else to be?"

I stared at him, then glanced outside the cave at the slowly setting sun. It was almost Sunday, but I had the distinct impression that Hakim and Vogle would not be contacting me tonight after what had happened. They would wait to see if I would come into work for Monday's shift, which meant that I had just under twenty-four hours of uninterrupted time until anyone would be looking for me. If there was ever a moment to go gallivanting through the woods with a human, this was it.

"No," I said, turning back to look at him. "This is where I need to be."

"Alright." He nodded, lifting the supply bag. "Then let's go."

I grabbed my helmet from the ground, stuffed it on my newly healed head and followed him out into the sunset. We headed north toward the river, then shifted east along the shore for twenty minutes at a brisk pace. When the sun finally fell beneath the top of the trees, I took my helmet off and breathed a quiet sigh of relief. I hesitated when Warren slowed, and I realized that he was leading us to a collection of large stones that crossed the rushing waters.

"Are – are we crossing that?" I asked, breaking the silence as Warren moved toward the first rock.

"Yes." He glanced back at me as he stepped onto the second stone. "Is that a problem?"

"No, it's okay."

I tried to say it confidently, but even I could hear the waver in my voice as I squinted through the dim evening light and cautiously approached the first stone. Warren waited on the second rock, watching me in silence, and as I carefully stepped onto the stone, my legs began to tremble.

"Do Reborn not like water?" he asked, and a halfhearted laugh left my lungs.

"No." I forced myself to inch across the slick surface. "Reborn are fine with water."

He moved to the third rock and stopped again, watching as I stood there paralyzed. I wanted to move to the second rock. I told my legs to do it, but my CPD-issued black laced boots remained firmly planted beneath me as the sound of rushing water filled my ears.

"But *you're* afraid of it," Warren said, and I couldn't help but let out a sigh.

"Gee, what gave it away?" I asked.

It was just another thing for him to turn into a string of stinging insults. I forced myself to meet his gaze, to face whatever brutal commentary he planned to dish out next, but to my surprise, he was smiling. It was small, more like a tiny tilt to his lips as opposed to a full-blown grin, and he looked like he was trying to hide it.

"Here—" He stepped back onto the second rock and extended his hand.

I stared at it like it was a foreign object, absolutely stunned that he would offer to help and allow me to touch him voluntarily.

Yes, I had touched him before, but that was different. This was not at all the same thing.

"I won't push you in," he said after a moment of silence had passed. "Probably."

I looked back up to his face again, intending to glare at him, but I found my lips twitching into a tentative smile instead when I saw the open amusement shining in his eyes.

"Alright." I reached out and took his hand, and even through my glove, I could feel his warmth. Despite having touched his skin before when I'd healed his leg, I found the heat surprising. I hadn't realized just how cold my own body was in comparison. "Thank you."

He nodded but didn't say a word as I stepped onto the rock by his side, even though I was definitely gripping him way harder than necessary. I tried not to think about how incredibly close we were. I could tell he was a bit uncomfortable, but he tolerated it and helped me across the rest of the rocks in the same fashion, never once commenting on the tremble that shook through my hand. When we got to the northern side of the river, he set off at a jog, weaving his way into the sparse trees along the bank and continuing in an easterly direction. It wasn't until another ten minutes had passed that I spoke.

"So, this Orion," I said, easily keeping up with his pace and wondering if I should offer to carry the supply bag. I could smell the sweat on his skin from the effort of hauling it. "Is that – is he your boss? Is he the person in charge of your group?"

"Yes," Warren said, nodding his head. "He's our leader."

"Did he recruit you?" I asked. "Is – is he—"

"Yes, he's human," Warren answered when I struggled to ask the question.

"So, does he lead all of you? Or – how did you meet him?" I asked, glancing at him again and noting the odd expression on his face. I couldn't tell if he was apprehensive or just thinking. Then I noticed the faint gleam of sweat across his forehead. "Do you want me to carry that? It's a little bit heavy compared to some of the other bags I've brought."

Warren scoffed, the sound almost like a laugh as he glanced over at me.

"I can manage it," he said, then he looked away again. "Orion is my father."

I faltered, slowing for a moment before I sped up to jog by his side again.

"Wait – so you're the son of the leader of your people?" I asked, unsure of what that meant or if that title came with any importance. "Are you – are you like the heir to—"

"It's not like that," Warren cut me off, preventing whatever ignorant comment I was surely about to make.

"Then what's it like?" I asked, genuinely wanting to understand. "What does that mean?"

"It doesn't mean anything," Warren answered. "He isn't a king if that's what you're thinking, and I don't get special treatment for being his son. People choose to follow him. He leads our group, but there are multiple groups of humans across the country."

"How many?" I asked it without thinking, and Warren shot me a look that suggested it was an answer I would never get. "But you help him? And he's the one in charge of the stuff going on around here?"

"Yes."

I could tell he was growing uncomfortable again, so I tried to keep my remaining questions at bay for a while as we slowly moved away from the river and made our way north through the trees.

Then I caved.

"How long has he been leading?"

I couldn't help it. There was so much that I wanted to know, and for the first time ever, it felt like Warren was speaking to me like a real person, without the usual hatred that laced his voice, and it was a nice change. It felt... normal, and I liked it.

"Since before I was born," he answered.

"I see."

I glanced at Warren, wondering if he looked like his father. Or did he look more like his mother? I wondered if I would ever meet her too. Did he have other siblings? What would they think of him bringing me back to wherever it was we were going?

Would they be angry? Would they glare at me and look at me with hatred, too?

I tore my eyes away from him, uneasiness starting to form in the back of my mind. I had gotten used to being around Warren, and slowly over time, his blatant distaste for me had faded some. That said, I knew he still fundamentally hated me, and I accepted that. But I wasn't sure if I could manage being around a crowd of humans glaring at me like I was the devil incarnate.

"He, uh – he knows I'm coming with you, right?" I asked as I glanced over at him again. "He said this is okay? That's who you texted? I'm not – this isn't going to be a problem, me showing up?"

Warren slowed, coming to a stop near a thick pine as he looked down at me with a strange expression. The trees had started to thin, and the birds were getting quiet. And I was suddenly aware of just how alone we were.

"Are you changing your mind?"

"No," I answered, my voice firm as I looked up at him. "I said I was in, and I'm in. I just—"

"You're afraid," he said, disbelief in his voice.

His eyes swept over my face in the low light, looking at me again—really looking this time. I didn't say anything. There was no point in refuting him because he wasn't wrong; I just wasn't afraid in the way he thought I was. I knew I was physically safe, probably. I just wasn't sure if I could mentally bear their collective hatred, but I didn't want him to know that.

"Imagine that," Warren muttered, his eyes meeting mine once more. "A Reborn afraid of a small group of humans. Never thought I'd live to see the day."

"I just don't think I'm the sort of surprise guest you should bring home unannounced," I said, looking away from his warm gaze to stare at the massive pine. "Regardless of whether or not you're willing to accept help from me, I can't imagine that your people would appreciate that."

"Well, I'm not bringing you to my home," Warren said, his low voice drawing my eyes back to him. He was looking at me differently again, like I might actually be a living, breathing being with feelings for the first time in his eyes. "I'm bringing you to another hideout we have, and yes, he knows you're coming."

"Alright."

He looked at me for another moment, then pulled out a small plastic light from his pocket and turned away. "And if I was going to kill you, I'd have done it already. I wouldn't waste my time walking you into the woods, so relax. I'm not bringing you to my dad just so I can stab you through the heart."

"Thanks," I muttered, following along behind him while I avoided looking at the light he shone across the ground. I would never be able to understand how humans could see anything through it. "Though if you really wanted to kill me, you'd have more luck cutting off my head. Blows to the heart are fatal, but they're not guaranteed kills. We can heal from those."

"I'll keep that in mind."

We walked for another ten minutes, shifting east again until the ground grew rockier, and Warren stopped to send another quick message on his phone.

"Give me your helmet," Warren said, turning back to me and holding out his hand. "And your gun."

"My helmet?" I handed it over and reached for my holster. I had completely forgotten that I was wearing it, but I took it off, knowing that this was not up for debate. "Why?"

"It would be better if your hands were free and you weren't armed," Warren answered, tucking my helmet under his arm. He looped my holster over his other shoulder with his rifle, then shone his light over my body and gazed at me assessingly. "Any other weapons?"

"No." I shook my head, squinting in the glow of the bright light. "Officers don't carry knives or mace anymore. That law was changed fifteen years ago."

"Alright." Warren nodded, dropping the light back to the ground. "Just keep your hands visible by your sides."

"Okay." I followed him as he moved east once more, eyeing him from the corner of my gaze as we cut through the trees. "Warren"—I swallowed—"I would never hurt your dad. Or you, for that matter. I hope he doesn't think—"

"It won't be my dad that thinks you're dangerous," Warren said as he stepped out into a small clearing. "He isn't afraid of your people, and I'm not afraid of you – it's the others."

"I see."

I didn't ask anything else. Whatever thoughts or questions I had fell away as my nervousness grew, and I followed him across the clearing toward a cave. It was much larger than the one we met at, and I could smell smoke. The dull flicker of firelight which emanated from the mouth grew brighter as we got closer, and Warren flicked off his light.

I could hear low voices. I couldn't make out the words over the distortion from the cave, but there had to be at least four other people in there.

Warren slowed a few feet away, motioning me to his side. The light from the fire was warm as we cleared the entrance, but it didn't burn like the sun, and even though it made it a little more difficult for me to see, I didn't mind it. If anything, it probably evened the playing field between us. I blinked twice to adjust my eyes, then instantly stiffened as I squinted at my new surroundings.

I was right. There were four people. Three were young like Warren and must be around his age. Their skin tones varied in colour, but all of them were sunkissed to some degree and shorter in height. They looked strong, though—and every single one of them had their rifles aimed at my face.

I could see the disgust in their eyes as my own flicked between them. It felt exactly like the first time I had met Warren, except this time, it hurt worse.

I understood now exactly why they hated me, and it made me feel sick. I swallowed, not moving an inch until something touched my shoulder and nudged me forward. It was Warren, and his warm hand pushed me inside another few steps, but I didn't look at him. I couldn't, because I couldn't look away from the hatred that was burning in my direction.

"I thought you said you were bringing a *vampire* back," the shortest human on the left said with a scoff.

I cringed at the word, knowing and hating that Warren would have felt it before he dropped his hold on my shoulder. The woman's eyes darted between the two of us, a frown forming on her thin lips. Her skin was just as tanned as Warren's, but her hair and eyes were lighter. Almost sandy. In fact, her features all seemed to blend together, leaving her with a rather monotonous appearance compared to the other humans that stood by her side and exhibited stark contrasts within their appearances.

"What is she?" the woman continued. "A defect? Or are they really getting smaller?"

I bristled, my eyes narrowing before another voice rang out.

"That's enough."

My eyes darted to the right to the tallest man in the cave, who was unquestionably Warren's father. Even through the firelight, I could see the resemblance. He had the same deep brown eyes and wavy hair, except his had streaks of grey that caught the flicker of the fire.

He looked strong. His leather jacket was worn and faded from time. There was a serious glint to his eyes, perceptive and wise, hard, yet wrapped in a blanket of deep, brown warmth that made me wonder just how much this man had seen as his gaze trailed over my frame.

"And lower your weapons," he said, his voice firm with command. "She's unarmed."

The girl he had told off let out a huff and rolled her eyes. But she and the other two males dropped their rifles, slinging them over their shoulders as Orion stepped toward me.

"I'm Orion," the man said, outstretching his arm. "It's nice to meet you, Corvus."

I stared at his open hand. It looked so much like Warren's, except for the two incomplete fingers. His pinky was nothing but a stub, and his ring finger had been severed just below the middle knuckle. From the glint of white skin across both nubs, it was clear the loss was due to injury, and I wondered when it had happened. I tore my eyes away and forced myself to meet his gaze once more as I took a small step closer.

"It's nice to meet you, sir," I said, taking his hand in mine and returning his firm shake.

I heard one of the humans behind him scoff, but Orion ignored it, gesturing with his head toward the fire as Warren unslung the supply bag.

"Here," Warren said, handing the bag to the nearest human, a male with dark eyes and long black hair that was tied back in a single braid. "This has the new batteries."

The man nodded, taking the bag without question and moving toward the opposite side of the cave to sit down. He pulled something from his pocket. I couldn't tell what it was as I glanced at him while I followed Orion over to the small fire, but he started going through the supply bag while the unpleasant monotoned-looking woman and the other male, who had a lengthy red scar running along the length of his neck, remained stiff and unmoving.

"So," Orion said, sitting on the largest rock before the flames and motioning for me to take the one across from him. "Warren says you want to help?"

I sat down awkwardly, trying to ignore the discomfort crawling across my skin from the heat of the fire as Warren moved forward and took a seat on the rock to my left. I briefly wondered if this was another tactic to see how serious I was— would I tolerate the discomfort of the heat, or would I snap and turn on them? I glanced at Warren, hoping to get a better read on the situation, but he didn't look at me. He simply placed my helmet and firearm on the ground by his feet before unslinging his rifle and laying it across his lap.

Clearly, I would not be getting my gear back any time soon— probably not until this meeting was over and he escorted me away. I could feel the others watching me, and I knew that the woman was outright glaring because her gaze was like daggers stabbing into my temple, but I refused to react to it or give them any reason to doubt my intentions. I could manage discomfort for a few minutes.

"Yes, sir," I answered, returning my attention to Orion. "I want to help. I want to do more."

I hesitated, fingers curling into the fabric of my pants before I continued.

"I don't know what your plans are or what you need, but I know you're working with other Reborn, and I want to join. I have access to a lot of data through the CPD. I work as a detective at Precinct 33, so I can access the national criminal databases and feed you information. I can continue to bring supplies. I can help you on missions – like the one at the Dolan's factory farm two weeks ago. I have a pretty good idea of what's happening in Carneth and can keep you up to date on whatever you need."

I held Orion's gaze, wondering what he saw as he looked at me. Did he think I was a defect too? Did he believe me? I had assumed that I was in because Warren had brought me here, but maybe I was wrong. Maybe this was an interview. Maybe Orion was assessing my worth and my being here meant nothing.

"I know that I'm small by Reborn standards," I said, ignoring the monotoned woman as she scoffed. "Most of my peers doubt my capabilities too. But they're wrong to do so. Being smaller has never once prevented me from doing anything, but it does keep me off everyone's radar. I am more than capable of doing whatever is needed to help, and I'm in this until the end. No matter the risk. Even if you say no, I'm never going to stop helping. I'll find another way."

Orion stared at me thoughtfully, the crackle of the flames filling the air around us as everyone waited in silence.

"Alright," he finally said, and I let out a breath. "You're in."

"Thank you, sir," I breathed, and relief flooded my body. "I won't let you down."

I heard a snort from one of the other humans, probably the woman again because she seemed to hate me most, but it didn't bother me. I was too relieved—I could feel the weight that had been crushing down on my shoulders since the moment I'd met Warren beginning to lift, and I couldn't stop the hesitant smile that crept across my lips.

"So," I said, gripping my legs with my gloved hands and leaning forward intently. "What do you need me to do?"

"Right now, what we need is more information."

"What kind of information?"

"Information on a man that you have apparently already met," Orion answered, and I glanced over at Warren, who was watching me intently. "Scott Beckette."

I stiffened, my jaw clenching tight as bile burned up my throat. The reaction was so quick and visceral, I had to swallow to stop myself from throwing up once more.

"What information?" I asked, my words coming out far darker than I intended it.

"Everything," Orion said, and his voice took on a more serious tone. "I need to know when he sleeps, what he eats, where he goes, what he does. I want copies of his records, his credit card statements, his taxes, his fingerprints – his entire personal file. Anything and everything that you can get from the system, and then I need your assistance with surveillance."

"Okay," I breathed out, nodding my head. "Why? What did he do? Is this about those girls?"

"It's not what he *did*," Warren said. "It's what he's *doing*, and it's bigger than you realize."

"We have contacts in multiple places within your society," Orion explained. "They help us get resources. They're allies in this fight, and they want to change the world with us. We've been chipping away at it slowly for years, but we only really made substantial progress in the last few decades with the invention of RealTECH."

"Wait—" My eyes widened. "You helped create synthetic blood?"

"Not directly," Orion said as he sat back on his stone and crossed his arms over his chest. "But I helped, and some of our supporters in your world invested in the technology to make it possible. Without them, it never would have made it to market. In the last decade, we have taken huge steps, but for each movement forward, there are those that aim to stop us and keep us 'in our place'. This ag-gag law is a problem. It conflicts with some of our future plans, but it isn't the only problem – and that itself is the problem.

"There are a lot of moving pieces in this fight, Corvus," Orion said, his voice low as he eyed me across the flame. "And the second we resolve one problem, something else pops up, each new item landing a blow, weakening our stance, and delaying our progress. There's the factory farms. The ag-gag laws. The political parties and agricultural unions that aggressively lobby against the RealTECH industry. There are the recent advancements in your technology like GPS tracking that put us at a disadvantage. Then there are the hunts, the raids, and the human trafficking that decimate our populations. The only positive that persists is that it's difficult for your people to reproduce, so thankfully, your populations remain low.

"We're working on all of these pieces simultaneously, and while some of our allies are powerful, well-positioned people, they can't always get us what we need without drawing unwanted attention. We are constantly facing setbacks and struggling to stay on target. It's difficult to prioritize missions and decide where our efforts are best focused, because the reality is every item on the list is critical, and they all impact us negatively in one way or another. On top of that, it's challenging to keep my people motivated that things will ever change when Reborn culture is inherently elitist and horrendously classist. Despite the recent shift we've seen in your kind, most of you don't even care about your own people of 'lower standards', so it is incredibly difficult to believe that any of you will care about us."

I nodded, a familiar sinking feeling reforming in my stomach at his words.

"That is the reality of our situation," Orion said. "This isn't an easy fight, and it isn't a quick one. This battle consumes our existence and dictates our future, but with more help, we can tackle more things at once and dismantle this quicker. Make no mistake, we *are* making progress. We have several significant irons in the fire right now, but the one you can help with, the one related to Scott Beckette, is human trafficking."

"Okay." I nodded in agreement. "I'll do whatever you need. Just tell me where to start."

"I have a contact named Eridanus," Orion said as he leaned toward me. "They're well-positioned within your world. They act as my main point of contact and link me to our other Reborn allies. Together, we're making a plan to take Scott Beckette out of the equation. He is the east coast king for trafficking. He controls everything on this side of the country, and his exports have been increasing each year to the point that it is becoming a serious threat to our survival. Our allies in the Wildlife Preservation Programs are doing what they can to combat poaching, but it isn't enough.

"Eridanus has been funnelling us information tied to poaching and exports for the last two years, but usually, everything we find comes after the fact. It wasn't until recently that we finally caught a break and were able to link the Beckette family to the operation and confirm that our people were being exported directly out of Carneth ports. For the longest time, we thought everything was based out of Holton, but it isn't," Orion said. "And now we know the Beckettes are involved. We know there's a massive shipment of people being moved down from the north this month, and we know that they're being exported out of the Carneth ports in October.

"What we don't know is the exact date, which port, and how many people," Orion continued. "We're working on it, but the Beckettes are exceptionally good at covering their tracks, and I can't risk exposing Eridanus by having them gather any other information. They're too valuable, so that's where you come in. We need more feet on the ground; allies who can move around unnoticed, as you said you can. I need you to pull up everything that you can about Scott Beckette from your networks and government databases without drawing unexplainable attention to yourself, copy it onto CDs, and drop it off to Aries. He'll continue to give you supply lists. Gather the items and drop them per your usual routine. We'll keep in close contact over the next few weeks as you monitor Beckette's movements and collect data.

"Track him as best you can. Watch the docks and see if you can figure out which buildings they might be operating out of. I have some other people working on this as well, so you're not alone in it, and you don't need to trail him every day, but the more data we can collect, the better. And once we know what their plan is, we'll take them out."

"Take them out," I repeated, my eyes creasing as I looked at him. Aside from asking me to break every information security law imaginable and abuse my access to confidential government systems, he was also asking me to take part in what? Murder? I swallowed, hoping that I was wrong in my assumption. "Take them out how?"

"Permanently," Orion answered, and I felt my shoulders sink. "Once we know the date they plan to move our people, we'll plan a counter-attack. We stop the export. We expose the circle. We remove the Beckette family from the equation completely if the opportunity presents itself and force law enforcement's hand. The second Beckette's contacts realize he and his operation have been exposed, the raids will stop. At least temporarily, and that buys us time to recover and implement other strategic moves.

"Reborn have been changing," Orion said slowly, his strong voice carrying a hint of hope. "In the last few decades, we've noticed a difference in your younger generations. There's a split happening – a divide between your people, but it isn't just cultural. Eridanus and their contacts believe it's genetic. Some Reborn are continuing to grow more cruel, violent, detached, and selfish. They're the Reborn we have always known. The monsters that view us and the lessers of their own kind as nothing more than cattle and waste. But others have calmed and developed a conscience, and they've become naturally empathetic."

I straightened on my rock, leaning forward as I hung onto his every word.

"Reborn might not traditionally care about anything other than themselves, officers may turn and look the other way on a daily basis, but if this story is exposed globally, they will be forced to respond, and they will be forced to care. At least for appearance's sake, if nothing else," Orion said. "They have to, because a decent portion of your population will force their hand, or they'll be faced with more protests and civil unrest. Things are already coming to a head between your people, and we want to capitalize on that. Eridanus has a contact looking into it. The study isn't complete yet, but they're estimating that at least a third of the population is expressing variants of the mutated genes, which you yourself probably have, Corvus.

"We've had some luck in other countries," Orion said, his voice lower now as he watched me intently. "Human rights groups are growing in the West. They're pushing for protective legislation and mandated minimum synthetic productions. If we expose this before year-end, we will be taking a huge step toward a much brighter and very different future. With the internet having come into play, we think it will be a lot harder for them to silence things. We're not there yet – but Eridanus has confirmed that the web is growing, information is being uploaded, and it's accessible globally. This new network is a double-edged sword, and many Reborn political figures are starting to figure that out, which is why we need to move quickly before they find a way to censor that too.

"But those are details for another time. All I need to know from you tonight," Orion said as he sat back once more and fixed me with a firm stare, "is, once we find out what port is going to be used, if I ask you to help lead the raid – will you help us? Will you pick up a weapon? Will you, should the need call for it, sacrifice some of your own in the hopes of making a better future for all of us?"

I heard the humans off to the side shift. They were watching me. Dead silent and tense. I heard one of them unshoulder their rifle, and my stomach rolled over.

I could feel my nails digging into my knees through my gloves as I stared at the man across from me. I understood what he was asking of me and why, but I didn't like it. The idea of breaking the law made me uncomfortable, and I hated that he might ask me to hurt someone.

That he might ask me to *kill* someone.

I genuinely didn't know if I could. How could anyone be expected to answer that question? I had no doubts that some of my fellow Reborn were horrible people, but killing someone wasn't something that I ever wanted to do. It wasn't something I thought myself capable of. But when I looked over at Warren, meeting his warm brown eyes through the flicker of the firelight, I felt the bite of my nails lessen. He was looking at me intently, his hands balled into fists on his thighs as he waited in anticipation—as he waited to see if he'd made a mistake by bringing me here…

I swallowed.

I hated what Orion was asking of me, but I hated what was happening to his people more. So despite my doubts, and without really knowing if I would be able to do it or not, I answered with the only response I could give.

"Yes," I whispered, and I saw Warren's whole body relax as he let out a silent breath. I turned my eyes back to Orion's stern gaze, ignoring the bile that burned up the back of my throat as I uttered the next words. "I'll do whatever it takes."

Gloria

The loose strap of my gear bag tapped gently upon my leg as I walked down the hall with my head held high. I smiled at two detectives, greeting them with a nod while I silently wondered what case they were working on. It wasn't uncommon for detectives to come in early. Over the last three months, I had come to realize that nearly every single desk chair on the eleventh floor was occupied and the bullpens were bustling by 8:00 pm, a full hour before the clock technically started. But Hakim and I were part of a much smaller crew that arrived even earlier, usually by 7:00 pm or 7:30 pm, and we didn't leave until well into the morning.

I assumed they must be working other high-profile cases and that they were probably some of the most senior detectives within Carneth. I had yet to learn all their names, as there had to be well over a hundred people working on this floor alone, but I was getting better at recognizing them.

I made my way around the outer edge of the building, taking the same path that Mallick had led me three months ago when he'd brought me up here to meet Vogle and my new partner.

That was, unquestioningly, the night that forever changed the path of my life.

Of course I didn't know that then. Three months ago, I had been naive. I'd thought that this precinct and its officers had integrity. I'd thought that being a detective was the perfect way to make the city a better place and help people. I'd thought that Captain Vogle looked like a nice guy and that my partner, although rough around the edges and unwelcoming in his nature, would stick to the letter of the law, and I would get to help him put away bad people.

I'd had no idea how wrong I was, but none of that mattered now.

My life as I had known it was over. I'd made my choice last night, though in truth, I had made it the second I'd let Warren go free, and now, everything that was happening was so much bigger than just myself or the risk to my family. I was stuck on a boat that I certainly wasn't steering, but even I couldn't deny that I'd had the opportunity to abandon ship several times and had chosen not to. No one had forced me to go searching for Warren. No one had forced me to help him, and no one had made me come back here.

Had I decided that I was out, I could have walked away with no questions asked and gone back to school to start over in a brand-new career. A career that would make my family happy, that wouldn't go anywhere near the woods, and that would keep me from the terrible truths I'd failed to see.

I nearly snorted at the thought.

No—this was my choice. I wanted to be on this boat. I couldn't not be after everything that I knew and everything that had happened. So regardless of whatever else came my way, I knew I would push on to the end because, for the first time ever, I genuinely felt like I had a purpose, and that naive little dream of making a difference was actually starting to feel real. It was just coming to fruition in a way I could have never anticipated.

I straightened my shoulders as I turned at the end of the hall, making my way toward the familiar boardroom. I knew Hakim would be there. I knew he wouldn't be expecting me after the explosion in his car Saturday afternoon, and I knew that I had to keep any and all distaste to myself if I was hoping to stay on board so I could help Warren and his people. I gripped the strap on my bag tighter, taking a deep breath before I reached for the handle.

"Good evening," I said, opening the door and making my way over to my desk as I smiled at Hakim.

He was seated in his usual chair—back rigid, notebook opened before him, and an empty coffee mug on the corner of his desk. The porcelain was white and nondescript, and it was always empty when I came in. The tiny ring of dark brown liquid at the bottom of it was the only evidence of it having been used. I suspected that he must arrive sometime between 5:30 pm and 6 pm, and he never had coffee throughout the rest of the shift. How he could manage to work the hours that he did on a single cup of coffee was beyond me, but I pushed the thought aside as I dropped my gear bag onto the floor by my desk and pulled out my chair.

"Are we still going out to farm one tonight? Or were you wanting to go through more footage for the Jane Doe case?" I asked, turning to look at him as I sat down and started up my computer.

He was staring at me, his mismatched eyes trailing slowly over my body as if looking for some unseen detail. I forced myself to keep my face impassive. I knew he wouldn't mention this past weekend or my behaviour. I knew he wouldn't say a word about it, but it was clear from his piercing gaze and silence that he was expecting me to.

"We'll head to farm one to grab the latest security footage and then swing by the suspects' homes to question them," Hakim finally answered, though his eyes continued to bore into me with an unsettling intensity. "After that, we can head down to Patrol and Street. Mallick mentioned he put cars in the areas we flagged, and one of the officers said they saw someone with a large duffle bag getting on the subway. We need to see if it matches the description of the guy you saw on the security footage."

"Alright." I nodded, glancing down at my keyboard before I typed in my password by touch memory. "Leave at the usual time? 7:30 pm?"

"Yes," Hakim said, his eyes taking one last slow pass over my face before he turned back to his desk. "7:30 pm."

"Perfect," I said, then I opened up my email inbox and looked for a reply from Corban to see if he had found anything useful on the most recent dead body. "I'll print some screen captures of the guy I saw on the subway line so the officer from Patrol and Street can compare them to the person they saw."

Hakim didn't say anything, so I got to work, clipping out the best images possible and sending them to the printer. Then I made my way down the hall to collect them before we got ready to head out.

Each step I took was quick. I didn't want to give any illusion of slacking or any opportunity for Hakim to change his mind and kick me out, but I slowed the second I saw Captain Vogle turn into the hallway and immediately make his way toward me.

"Gorski," Vogle said, and I could hear the surprise in his voice. His eyes swept over my body as he approached as if he too was scanning for any signs of Saturday, and I didn't miss the quick side glance he took to make sure the hallway was empty before he slowed to stop just a few feet away. "I'm glad to see you here."

"I'm happy to be here, sir," I said, a genuine smile forming across my face. I meant those words, just not in the way that Vogle would interpret them. "It feels like we're finally making some progress. We've got a potential lead on the Jane Doe case, and we're headed to farm one today to gather the latest data. Hopefully, the additional alarms Jonathan ordered will arrive tonight and then we'll be able to relieve the officers from 15 who have been helping to patrol around the facility. It should prevent any future attacks since the rest of our suggestions have already been implemented. This is above and beyond what we suggested."

"That's great news," Vogle said. "Any luck with those vans?"

"No, not yet," I answered, shaking my head. "But one of them hasn't been returned to the rental agency yet. It was last seen somewhere near Holton City, so Hakim has requested help from a local precinct there with locating it. Right now, it's our only lead, but we're going to question some potential suspects about it."

"Good." Vogle nodded. "Well, tell Hakim to keep me posted and to pop by my office before he goes home. I need to speak with him."

"Okay," I answered, and a small smile pulled at the corner of Vogle's lips.

"And Gorski," Vogle said, his voice dropping low. He took a step forward so there were only a few inches between us, and I had to tilt my head to meet his gaze. "I knew bringing you on was a good idea. You made the right choice."

"Thank you, sir," I whispered, and my stomach curled as he placed his hand on my shoulder and gave it a squeeze. "I appreciate the opportunity to prove myself."

"You already have," he said. "And it's Vogle, Gorski. No need to be so formal."

"Right." I nodded. "Thank you, Vogle."

I watched his eyes crinkle as he nodded, then he patted my shoulder and turned and made his way back down the hall.

FRIDAY, SEPTEMBER 25
3:28 AM

"If he invites us inside, don't touch anything."

"I won't."

"Is your microphone ready?"

"Yes."

"Make sure you don't obstruct it. Keep your hands at your side and, if possible, try to get a clear view of everything in his apartment and make a mental note of it so you can record it later."

"Alright."

I followed Hakim up the stairs, glancing down once to make sure that the tiny microphone I was wearing was still properly attached to the collar of my vest. The last thing I wanted to do was mess this up—it was the first legitimate lead we'd gotten on the Jane Doe case since taking over the files.

It turned out the officer from Patrol and Street that had told Mallick she had seen a man carrying a duffle bag toward the subway entrance matched the ID of the individual to the images I had pulled. The quality of the image wasn't the best, but Officer

Beaulieu was insistent that it was the same person. So Hakim and I grabbed the timestamp from the footage, then ran through the passcard data the city metro had handed over to us last week to compile a list of all passengers who used a swipe card to gain access to the subway. Then we ruled out the possibility of any attendants seeing the suspect because no one staffed the booth at that hour.

At first, I figured the suspect couldn't possibly be stupid enough to use a subway passcard for access, given that it would be trackable, but Hakim wasn't so sure. Using a pass didn't guarantee traceability. It could have been purchased under a fake name, and if it was a thirty-day pass, not a yearly card that needed an address and photo ID, no identification would be required at all, thus providing the man quicker access and less visibility on the platform. The one-time ticket machines at this stop were notoriously broken, as I learned on Tuesday's shift when Hakim and I went to check it out, and fighting with them to gain entrance would only draw more unwanted attention. Besides, based on the time the man with the duffle bag entered the underground stairwell, he only had a minute at best to get in the car, assuming the subway arrived on time, thus making it even more likely that he used a passcard.

We ran all the names from the yearly passcards through the city resident database, and sure enough, two of the names were unregistered. Our stroke of luck came when the surveillance photo, which I had run through the Federal ID Archive on Tuesday morning, finally came back last night with three potential matches, and one of them had a prior arrest for minor drug possession in the same area of Carneth ten years ago.

His name was Andrew Morin. He had an outstanding offence on his record for skipping his parole meeting, and his last known address was 368 Forsyth Street, Apartment 4E.

We hit the street first thing, dressing in our full uniform blackout gear to make it to the subway station right as the attendant arrived for his shift. We spoke to him for twenty minutes, showing him the photo of the suspect and confirming that he had never seen the individual before. Knowing the station was a dead end, we traced the suspect's steps as far back as we could based on security footage Patrol and Street had been able to provide, and the path the man had taken headed in the direction of Andrew Morin's last known address.

So we decided to operate under the assumption that Morin was indeed our suspect, at least for now, until we were proven to be wrong.

As we made our way toward Morin's address, Hakim stopped twice. First, to speak to a homeless man living four blocks away from our destination, and second, to talk to a group of young teens skateboarding along the railings of an old motel. At first, I thought that the kids were going to run away from us when we approached. It wasn't outright illegal to skateboard on the sidewalks, but it was frowned upon, and cops weren't exactly well-liked in this area.

To my surprise, they spoke to us, though that was only after Hakim called out one of the kids by name, freezing him on the spot and halting the others before they ran. The kid, who Hakim seemed to know, confirmed that he had seen the man in the photo around the area, but when I went to ask additional questions, Hakim cut me off, dismissed the group, and then led me away.

I followed his direction without complaint. After all, that was essentially a condition of my continued employment. So I kept my mouth shut, keeping my questions to myself as he rapidly led the way to the old, run-down four-storey walk-up on the corner of Forsyth Street.

Now, taking the last few steps up to the fourth floor, I wondered if we would have any luck.

"Change the magazine in your firearm."

I stilled on the landing, turning to look at my partner, thankful that the visor of my helmet would hide my shock.

"Sir?"

"Now," Hakim said, taking out his own firearm and quickly switching the standard black magazine to the red Reborn-grade ammunition that we were absolutely not supposed to use as the first line of defence. "You might not get the chance to do it later if things go poorly."

I hesitated only a moment, then grabbed my firearm and made the switch.

"And take your helmet off," Hakim said, his voice low as he reached up to remove his own. "Our gear isn't designed to stop Reborn-grade bullets at close range anyway, and we don't want him to think we're here to cause problems."

"Yes, sir."

I removed my helmet, tucking it under my arm as we approached the door at the end of the hall. When we reached 4E, Hakim motioned for me to start recording, so I switched on my mic, then stood off to the side as Hakim raised his hand to knock.

The dark green paint that covered the door was so old it was discoloured and pieces had completely peeled off to reveal streaks of black, blue, and red beneath—remnants of a past when this building was at the heart of the city center. More flakes dislodged and fell to the floor as Hakim's hand made contact. He hadn't knocked hard, but the door rattled against the frame anyway, and I found myself frowning. There couldn't possibly be extra locks on the inside, at least none that were useful, so I doubted that Morin still lived here, let alone conducted illegal activity.

"Andrew Morin," Hakim said, knocking against the faded paint once more. "Mr. Morin, we'd like to ask you a few questions about a parole no-show three weeks ago."

Silence rang through the hall, and I glanced around to make sure we were still alone.

"Mr. Morin."

Hakim knocked again, louder this time, but still, no one answered. He shifted, and dust rose from the disgusting carpet that covered the hallway floor as he leaned in to listen. I held my breath, waiting for something to happen, until I nearly jumped at the sound of a lock turning behind me.

"He's not here."

The voice was silky, and as I turned to face the apartment opposite us, I was surprised to find the owner was a scrawny-looking woman with greying hair.

"Haven't seen him in a few nights," she said as her eyes trailed over us. "But that's pretty normal round these parts."

"Do you recall what night you saw him last?" Hakim asked as he stepped toward her.

The woman hesitated for a moment, then opened the door a little wider. "You CPD?"

"Yes," Hakim answered, but he didn't give any other information.

"We only have a few questions for him," I added, giving the woman a small, tentative smile. "We're just trying to get in touch with him to sort out his parole conditions."

"Well, I doubt he'd help you with that," the woman muttered. Her eyes traced over my frame, lingering on my badge before she let out a sigh and glanced down the hall. "Wearin' that badge round here is more likely to get you killed than not – you'd best come in before someone else sees you, but turn off your mic if you're wired. Otherwise, you two are on your own."

I glanced up at Hakim, who nodded his head without a word, his mismatched eyes daring me to argue.

I didn't. Instead, I lifted my right hand to my belt and switched off the tape. Records of interviews were extremely important per the CPD rulebook. This woman had the legal right to request an unmonitored conversation since this wasn't a formal interrogation, but per protocol, we were supposed to advise against it—both for her protection and our own. Two weeks ago, I might have argued with Hakim and questioned his call, but I wasn't about to ruin our chances of getting information on our lead, and I knew better than to expect any integrity from this man.

The second I switched off the tape, the woman opened the door, gesturing for us to move inside. I followed Hakim as he stepped into the woman's home, and I did my best not to crinkle my nose at the smell. The air in here was stale and musty, layered with the thick scent of cigarettes and old wet fur, but a quick glance around the large one-room unit gave no evidence of any other life within the shabby apartment.

My guess was she had owned some sort of pet a long time ago, despite it being illegal, and she probably hadn't opened the windows in a decade.

"We appreciate the help," Hakim said, his voice not sounding the least bit appreciative, as I shut the door behind us. "Do you remember what day you saw your neighbour last?"

"No," the woman said, reaching into her silk housecoat pocket and pulling out a pack of cigarettes. She fetched a lighter from the opposite pocket and quickly lit the stick without a second glance in our direction. "Probably not since last weekend, maybe the weekend before. He comes and goes, and I'm not always home. Never stays long and dresses too good to be from round this part. I figure this is his old place, and he's just not got to sellin' it yet. But there're always people comin' and goin' when he is here."

"A lot of different people? Or have you seen him with the same people regularly?" I asked as I eyed the woman's appearance. She took a long drag of the thin stick between her slender fingers, and I fought the urge to frown.

Both her nails and her teeth were long... too long.

"Hard to say," the woman answered vaguely. "I try not to listen to them if they get too loud – I've been round a long time, girl, and I'm not stupid enough to get caught up in other people's messes."

"What mess?" Hakim asked, but the woman ignored his question and continued to stare at my face.

"I used to be just as young as you. Just as *fresh*," she whispered, her pale blue eyes glazing over as her gaze trailed down to my neck. "But that was a long time ago."

"What did you hear them say?" I swallowed in discomfort and tried to ignore the uneasiness I felt at the way her pupils dilated with hunger. She was a drainer. There wasn't a doubt in my mind, and she was pushing the limits of her high.

"A few things," she whispered. "Nothin' of substance – just a few names."

"What names?" Hakim pressed as he took another step closer, clearly unbothered by her state and having no plans of saying anything about it.

The woman's eyes refocused, his movement seeming to pull her from whatever memory she had been lost in.

"Tremblay," the woman replied, her pale eyes shifting to Hakim. "Someone named Lucas and a woman named Sophia. I remember her name because her voice is unique, rough, deeper than I would have thought it would be from the glimpse I caught of her."

"You saw her?" I asked, quickly pulling out my notebook and pen to jot down her words. "Is she here often?"

"Often enough – the others not so much," the woman said, taking another long drag from her cigarette and slowly letting out the smoke. "The others are more so just names I've heard. There have been other people that've come by, but I couldn't say if they go by the names that I've heard. They could be talkin' about different people."

"Roughly how many different people have you seen go by his place?" Hakim asked as I began scribbling notes.

"I couldn't say," the woman replied, her thin housecoat slipping to show more pale white skin as she shrugged her shoulders. "Maybe five – maybe ten. I don't usually go look."

"Can you describe any of them?" Hakim asked. "The woman, Sophia – what about her?"

"Hmmm," the woman mused as she pursed her lips. "Can't describe any of the men, but the woman – she's average height, average weight, average build."

Hakim's eyes narrowed, and the woman's lips twisted into a smile.

"You might not like the description, officer, but it is accurate," she said as she crossed her arms over her chest and gave us an amused smile. "She had dark auburn hair if I recall correctly – cut short – and a tattoo."

"Where?" I asked.

"On her leg – left calf just above the ankle. And before you ask – I have no idea what the symbol was. Didn't get a clean look, so I can't describe it."

"Was it black, greyscale, coloured – how large was it?" Hakim asked.

"About the size of my fist," the woman answered, raising her left hand and clenching it tight. "And there was no colour. I saw it only because of how stark black it looked against her skin."

"What did you hear them talk about?" Hakim asked.

"I told you I didn't listen."

"But you heard them say something," I pressed. "Other names? Dates? Anything you heard, no matter how insignificant it might seem, could be incredibly helpful."

"I really can't recall," the woman said, slipping the cigarette between her lips once more. "I just remember the names – and the woman mentioned somethin' about a loss. About it bein' a waste and Lucas gettin' pissed. She said this next one had better make it, or they weren't goin' to get paid, and Tremblay was gonna put his boot down her throat. It sounded like they were workin' together, but obviously their latest endeavour didn't go so well from the sounds of it. Sophia – the woman I saw him talk to – she said they should change jobs, but Morin refused. Said she would draw too much attention.

"And that's it," the woman concluded, pulling her housecoat back up to cover her shoulder. The fabric instantly slipped down when she shrugged again and toyed with the cigarette between her fingers. "That's all I heard – and I didn't even want to hear that. I lived here long before he came round and long before this area went downhill. I know Morin had drug charges against him a decade ago, because the CPD came round then, too, but he really isn't here all that often anymore. Last I heard anything at this end of the hall was maybe a week or two ago. He's never here long either – so I doubt you'll run into him. Especially if you're dressed in uniform."

"Noted," Hakim said as I finished jotting down the information. "Anything else you know that might help us locate him?"

"Nope," the woman said, her pale blue eyes now trailing over Hakim's wiry frame. They lingered momentarily on his neck, then slowly shifted back up to his face. "But is there anything else you might need, officer?"

My nose crinkled at the near purr that escaped her lips.

"Just a name," Hakim said. "Then we'll be on our way."

"Hmm, shame." The woman inhaled the last of her cigarette, then put it out on her forearm, the white skin sizzling into a red burn before it rapidly healed once more. "The name's Gloria."

"Gloria what?" Hakim pushed when she failed to elaborate.

"Gilbert," Gloria said, giving Hakim another sickening smile. "Gloria Gilbert. I work just round the corner in case you ever have any other questions."

Hakim didn't say anything. He simply turned and moved back to the door.

"Thank you, Ms. Gilbert," I said, tucking away my notebook and quickly following behind my partner. "We appreciate the help. I'll be in touch if we need anything else."

"Sure."

I could feel her eyes on my back as we exited into the hall, and I quickly yanked the door shut behind me.

"Should we remove our badges?" I whispered as I caught up to Hakim and glanced at the other apartment doors near the stairwell.

"No," Hakim answered as we started down the stairs. "Even without a badge, you look like a cop. If anyone sees us here, they'll know we're CPD. Morin knows there's an outstanding parole offence on his record – he'll be expecting someone to stop by eventually, so coming in as cops was the best option. The next step is to get in touch with the Parole Department, file some paperwork, and send a formal letter. Our presence as regular CPD officers won't disrupt his pattern, and it won't stop him from doing whatever it is he's doing. Otherwise, he would have shown up to his meeting. Had we come undercover, though, and had he seen us, he'd have known we were on to him for something else. We'd have lost him and lost our lead."

"Right," I said, following him out the main door and back out onto the street.

We cut across the road, weaving between a few cars and ignoring two angry honks before heading west toward our parked cruiser. A part of me was surprised to find it unharmed, but then again, we hadn't been gone all that long, and usually, most vandalism occurred during the day while people were inside asleep. Who knows, maybe Hakim knowing that skateboard kid did us a favour.

I glanced at Hakim as he pulled out the car keys and unlocked the doors.

"How did you know that kid from earlier?" I asked, slipping into my seat and shutting the door. I glanced at him as I tossed my helmet in the back, watching for a reaction, but there wasn't one.

"From a previous case."

It was clipped but not cold, meaning there was room for a follow-up if I asked carefully.

"What case?" I prodded, keeping my voice calm and void of the interest that was burning in my chest. "Was he arrested?"

"No," Hakim answered, starting the car and swiftly ending the conversation with his next words. "I want you to run the names that Ms. Gilbert gave us when we get back to the precinct while I go speak to Vogle about getting an undercover officer in this area."

"We're not going to stake it out ourselves?"

"We might," Hakim said as he pulled away from the curb and into traffic. "But that would be inefficient. If we can bring on an additional officer until November, things will go a lot more smoothly. Besides, you don't have any stakeout experience, and this isn't the type of case to learn it on."

I nodded, but my heart sank. I knew what he meant even though he didn't outright say it. This case was too high profile. Vogle, the chief, the mayor, and Hakim were not going to risk me messing this up before the election. I would probably get put back on security footage duty and research while someone more experienced worked the surveillance.

"You will be following up on those names and taking more of a lead on the Dolan case until it closes," Hakim continued. "You can manage collecting the sensor data on your own and the security footage at both sites going forward."

"Yes, sir."

I didn't say anything else as we made our way back to the precinct, but I felt like I was starting to get a better understanding of how things worked and what was about to happen. Low-life drainers were not our priority. The pressure on the Jane Doe case was rising. Hakim would need to spend more time on it, and we weren't getting anywhere on the Dolan case.

Each potential suspect we had questioned this week about the farm break-in had credible alibis—they were all either at work, caught on camera entering their apartments for the day, or lingering around the city center downtown despite the protests having been broken up weeks ago. Several people and CPD officers had seen them there. We even followed up on two less enthusiastic human rights activists, and they, too, had credible references for their whereabouts on the afternoon of September 5th.

Jonathan, who was still running both facilities and doing a fine job of it, seemed to believe that the threat of attack had lessened after their stock was stolen, since it was clear the stock was the target all along, and Hakim agreed.

As of yesterday, it was beginning to look like the case might get wrapped up—at least in terms of our daily and weekly involvement.

The sensors would soon be pulled from the woods because nothing had shown up on them in three weeks. There were no footprints around the facility and no suspicious vehicles lurking in the area. Jonathan had hired another security guard at each site and installed the additional cameras he ordered around the most vulnerable buildings. The doors were all protected with new alarms, and with the backup generator replaced, the risk of another attack was incredibly low.

Increased patrols by 15 were still ongoing. The case file would remain open, and the suspicious vehicle description would stay on the radar for the officers in Holton, but there was no need for Hakim and me to go out and collect data every few days. I suspected that over the next few weeks, the Dolan case would formally be handed over to Precinct 15, who would maintain the files and continue to search for the missing stock, but as time went on, the case would be shelved and likely forgotten about until the next time Warren and his people raided a farm.

As annoyed as I was to be relegated to data collection and cleanup on a dead case, it did present an opportunity. I would be able to meet up with Warren during my shift to drop off more supplies and information, thus lessening the odds of getting caught driving out there in the middle of the day.

The Docks

When we arrived back at Precinct 33, I followed Hakim up to the eleventh floor and got to work. I submitted the names Ms. Gilbert had given us to the Federal ID Archive and limited the results to southeast Carneth. I knew it would take some time to get the results back, so I got to work checking through our arrest database and compiled a list of over thirty-five possible people. It would take a long time to vet, but it was the best I could do with first names.

True to his word, Hakim immediately went to speak to Vogle to ask about adding an officer to the team. He returned an hour later, working the rest of the night in silence at his desk until 11 am when he finally called it quits. I slowly made my way down to my car and waited for Hakim to leave the parking garage first before carefully driving toward the riverfront.

The docks that ran along the river on the southeast side of Carneth were hardly a place for people to hang out or spend time. The area was heavily industrialized, and while it wasn't technically illegal for civilians to be down there, lingering would inevitably result in a call to the CPD or dock security.

To combat this, I had decided to avoid going directly to the docks altogether. Instead, I took advantage of a small wooded area that ran along the river, north of the docks, separating them from the nearest residential housing. I parked at the tail end of a hiking trail that ran through the woods, changed into blackout running gear, and brought my badge. Then I ran a kilometre along the trail, ensuring I was deep into the trees and completely hidden from view before I darted into the bushes and cut south, down toward the docks.

It wasn't ideal. It was unbearably hot inside my blackout gear, even with the tall trees and breeze coming off the water, but I forced myself to do it anyway because I needed to collect my sensor data.

This was my third trip.

I had come up with the idea during Monday's shift when Hakim and I had gone out to the factory farms to collect the latest sensor data. I had wiped the data from the last sensor set in my area, making sure it was one of the devices provided by the CPD, and slipped it into my bag. Then I'd scuffed up the area, digging up the dirt and making a mess with my boots before running back to our usual meeting point.

I told Hakim the device was missing, faking anger and frustration as I explained that my late return was a result of having scoured the woods looking for the thing. Hakim wasn't pleased with the loss, but he believed me, and when our shift ended, I made my way down to the dockside trail with the stolen piece of equipment to implement my plan.

I had run this hiking trail during my Academy days, so I was familiar with the area, and since I couldn't come up with any other way to scope out the docks without raising suspicions, I figured it was worth a shot. I had taken the same route I was on now that first day, cutting through the forest, down the hill to the south until I neared the edge of the woods. Then creeping through the brush and bushes until I reached the large stormwater ditch at the bottom.

From there, it was just a matter of sneaking up to the main road that ran along the docks and setting up the sensor so I could monitor the incoming traffic and record licence plates.

It wasn't easy, and any time I darted out across the road to move the sensor on the opposite side, I put myself at risk of being caught. But so far, it had worked, and that was the best I could hope for—because the alternative was collecting zero information.

I had come out on Wednesday to collect the first set of data and spent the rest of my afternoon crawling through the footage at my apartment. I was able to make out all of the vehicles that went through, and sorted them by type, company, and size. I wasn't yet sure what I was going to do with the data, but I planned to tell Warren about it this afternoon and discuss the best way to give him copies of the large files.

Now, I was about to get my second set of data, and I could already feel a nervous tremble creeping through my body as I approached the edge of the woods.

I slowed, ducking into a crouch, half crawling and half sliding down into the large ditch. There was more water this time, and it smelled like sewage because of the heat. I grimaced as I cut through it, then carefully made my way up the opposite side of the ditch, crawling through the tall grass that bordered the road toward the sensor I had hidden just out of view. It didn't take me long to swap out the hard drive, and as I clipped the new one into place and reset the device, I felt the small phone inside my vest buzz.

It was probably Warren confirming our meeting, which I was currently running late to.

I inched forward on my stomach, pushing aside the curtain of reeds and grass to see the road. My eyes scanned over the empty asphalt and across the lifeless-looking buildings on the other side. There were so many warehouses down here, and finding which dock Scott Beckette was using would be like locating a needle in a haystack. My only hope was to monitor the road here, nearer to the main gate, until I could determine something that would help me narrow down the search. If I could tie one of these vehicles to Scott or his people and track it down the road, I could determine which warehouse they were using, then plant the sensors nearby to gather more data to determine Beckette's routine.

Warren would need to know how many people came and went and when and how often if he was going to make a plan to stop the shipment and put an end to the operation. Yet despite being determined to get him that information, I found myself doubting. It was possible that Beckette and his people never came down here until the nights they brought in their cargo.

It was possible that they just rented space from someone else when they needed it. I had no idea if the Beckette family owned any of these warehouses, but I doubted that they would be stupid enough to use a warehouse registered under their own name. Then again, maybe Scott Beckette didn't worry about those sorts of things because he knew that no one would do anything about it. Perhaps, just like how he had sat smugly on his couch while dead humans littered his living room floor, he truly was that arrogant.

Maybe he wasn't hiding anything.

I felt the phone in my pocket buzz again, and I stilled. Warren and I texted frequently throughout the day, and I often found myself counting the seconds until his replies came in, but he didn't usually send multiple messages in a row, so something must be up. I pocketed the hard drive I had just collected, then retreated from the edge of the road, making my way back across the ditch and up to the bushes as I made a mental note to try to find a way to check the titles on the properties down here.

The phone buzzed again and again as I sprinted up the hill and into the shade of the trees. I quickly reached into my vest, only to realize it wasn't Warren's phone that was ringing.

It was mine.

"Hello?" I answered as I huddled into a particularly dark shadow so I could flick my visor up to speak into the phone properly.

'Valya?'

"Oh," I grimaced, mentally kicking myself for not checking the caller ID first. I had just assumed that it would be Hakim wanting something. "Hey, Hawthorne."

There was a pause, then his voice filled my ear.

'Why do you sound out of breath?'

"I'm not," I lied. "Just tired – it's been a long week."

'*Tell me about it,*' Hawthorne groaned, and my shoulders sagged in relief. I really didn't like lying to Hawthorne, and I was glad he let it go without pushing. '*So, wanna hang out?*'

"Now?" I asked, squinting down at my watch.

'*Yeah, now.*'

"It's after noon – I'm already in bed."

'*And why on earth would you think that would be a deterrent?*'

"Don't be gross."

'*Aww, come on. We can have some tea? I promise I won't make fun of your pajamas.*'

"As much as I would love some tea, maybe another time, okay?" I said as I reached into my pocket and pulled out the small phone Warren had given me. "It's just been an awful week, Hawthorne, and I really want to go to sleep. Maybe next weekend?"

There was silence on the other end of the phone again, and for a moment, I wondered if he was annoyed.

'*Alright, fine,*' Hawthorne conceded, though his tone lacked some of its usual warmth. '*Next weekend. If I'm even free next weekend – things with this ag-gag law have been making patrol shifts crazy. The mass of protestors may be gone, but they increased patrols in the city center because of some vandalism, so even if I can get days off, I'm still going to be stuck in this mess.*'

"That's unfortunate," I said as I leaned against the tree. "Hopefully it doesn't last too long."

'*I hope so too, but I doubt it,*' Hawthorne sighed. '*I think it'll get worse before it gets better. There's this underlying tension you can just feel in the air when you're out on patrol – but I won't keep you up with my ranting. I'll let you get some sleep. Don't let Hakim work you too hard this week! But hey – if you're too tired for tea next weekend, we can always just take a nap together and—*'

"Ugh." I rolled my eyes. "No – I'd rather just work the whole weekend."

'*I'm so hurt,*' Hawthorne said, the mock indignation in his voice hardly believable when it was followed by a barely covered-up laugh. '*I can't believe you would reject my offer of a platonic nap.*'

I shook my head, and a small smile touched my lips. "I think that might be the lamest pass you've ever tried to make."

He sighed again. *'You always doubt me so, but alright. Night night, Gorski! I'll see you next weekend!'*

I ended the call, shaking my head again as I tucked the phone away. I didn't bother to answer the texts he had sent me before calling, and instead quickly texted Warren to let him know I was late and that I would meet him at the cave in two hours. Then I raced back through the thick bush and trees, slowing as I neared the edge of the running trail and lingering out of sight in the branches until I was sure the coast was clear. Then I darted out onto the gravel and ran back to my car.

By the time I made it out of Carneth and parked in the trees, it was well after 1 pm. I could feel a heavy fatigue sitting deep within my bones, a sensation I had not felt since the night I'd almost died in the test tank, yet I found myself smiling as I pushed through the trees and made my way toward the familiar clearing. My heart felt lighter here, and I couldn't wait to get inside the cave and rip off my helmet.

My steps began to quicken, and soon, despite my exhaustion, I found myself running through the last of the trees and across the small rocky clearing toward the cave. I was all but sprinting as I crossed the threshold, ripped off my helmet, and inhaled deeply—the tension in my shoulders completely falling away as I let out a sigh of relief.

"What's the rush, Corvus? Are you melting?"

My smile widened, and I turned to squint at Warren, who was jogging toward the cave behind me, rifle strung casually across his back.

"You try wearing military-grade blackout gear on a day like today and tell me how you like it," I said, placing my helmet on the ground before dropping my small supply bag next to it. "It's positively sweltering."

He smiled and unslung his rifle, leaning it against the cave wall.

"Lucky for you, the weather will break soon. There's going to be a cold front coming in next week, and then the rainy season will start when we hit October."

"Which will be a welcomed change," I said brightly, then I glanced down at my outfit and frowned. "Though really they need to find a way to make these suits more breathable."

"So if not for the sun burning your skin," Warren said as he crossed his arms over his chest and looked at me assessingly, "what would you normally wear in weather like this? You said that you don't have to worry about getting too cold, so what, do you wear shorts in the snow?"

"Sometimes," I said, grinning at him in amusement. "Though I'm not really the shorts type. Most Reborn just wear the same sort of attire year-round – lightweight long sleeves and pants. We do have winter jackets, but they aren't overly thick. They're really just for style since we don't need to worry about frostbite or anything, and snow doesn't bother us. Do you have to wear a lot of layers in the winter?"

"Yes." Warren nodded, leaning back against the cave wall next to his rifle, looking completely relaxed. "A lot of wool, fur, and, if we can get it, polyester or nylon outer layers to keep dry."

"I don't think any of our clothes are made out of wool," I said thoughtfully. I let my eyes trail over his well-built frame as I tried to imagine him being cold. It seemed impossible, given how much warmth I knew he radiated. "That's got to be stressful – trying to plan for the varying temperatures to make sure you have the right gear."

"It can be," he agreed. "Especially for the kids – they don't keep warm as well, but we've found ways to make things easier. It's not as bad as it used to be. We have heaters now, so we don't have to rely on fire, and several specially designed camps that we use when things get really cold. The supplies you bring help with that."

"Oh," I said as a strange sensation tightened across my chest. It was the nearest he had ever come to thanking me, and he seemed to realize it as his deep brown eyes flicked between my own. We both stood there in silence, unsure of what to say until I finally forced something out. "Well – I'm glad it helps."

"So—" Warren cleared his throat, his gaze breaking from mine to drop to the supply bag. "What did you bring?"

I swallowed, shaking my head to chase away the strange feeling before I launched into a dissertation on my findings from the last week. I told him about the Dolan case slowing down, how the insurance company was content now that all of the suggested upgrades had been implemented, and how Jonathan and Hakim did not anticipate any other attacks this year. I let him know that we had the opportunity to meet on any of the nights that I had to go out to collect the sensor data on my own, if he could make it, until Vogle decided to pull the plug completely and pass the maintenance of the case to Precinct 15.

He said there wouldn't be an issue meeting by the facility so long as I gave him a day's notice.

I told him about the sensor I had stolen and placed by the docks on Monday and that I was checking it every two days and planned to move it along the road. He said he would speak to his father and figure out the best way to get the surveillance footage from me, but in the meantime, to continue what I was doing with watching the traffic and trying to find patterns.

I gave him copies of Scott Beckette's information—a printout of his ID, phone numbers, licence plates, date of birth—everything that I was able to easily get from my computer without searching in any databases that would draw attention. Then I told him about my plan to try to find a way to complete a title check on the warehouses down by the dock to see if the Beckettes owned any of the property.

He told me that his father's contact, Eridanus, was already chasing that down. He wasn't sure how, if Eridanus was doing it themselves or if it was being completed by another member of the network that Orion had built, perhaps someone working in real estate, but he assured me that once he had the information, he would share it. I thanked him and told him I would focus my time on the Federal Coast Guard Register instead. As far as I knew, no special access privileges or warrants were required to download the base schedule that documented arrival times at specific docks. The river was incredibly busy, and the basic traffic information had been made available to the CPD several decades ago in an effort to coordinate safety measures between the Coast Guard and us. But additional details, such as those revealing what goods were to be shipped out, what items were coming in, crew counts, boat sizes, weights, and corresponding companies, would be difficult to get.

Then I told him I had started a simple background check on Scott Beckette this week to see if he had any expunged criminal records from his past. I suspected that he did, and while I doubted that they would be linked to his current involvement in human trafficking, I wanted to see if he had any collaborators that he still kept in touch with, because tracking them would be easier and would draw much less attention than tracing Beckette directly.

At some point during the conversation, Warren removed his jacket, and I unzipped my vest. We both sat down near the mouth of the cave, the gentle breeze ghosting our skin as the conversation danced between the issue at hand and questions we had for one another.

I learned that the children they had rescued were doing well. Only two had died, which he said was a massive improvement compared to the last time they'd done this. He asked me more about Reborn, what typical civilians did, and if I could get him some updated maps of the city, our current overall population, and a headcount at each precinct in Carneth.

I said that I would, then I asked to know more about the other humans who had been present the night I'd met Orion. He told me they were his friends, people he had known since childhood, and they were all around the same age. He didn't tell me their names, but I hadn't been expecting him to, and I doubted it was information I would ever learn. I was just happy that he seemed willing to share the tiny bit that he had. Then he told me that his father had been working with Eridanus for decades. He wasn't sure how they'd met, Orion never spoke of it, and as far as Warren knew, no one else from his group had ever met the contact in person.

"I was thinking about that," I said, turning to squint at Warren through the afternoon light. "About Eridanus – are all the code names named after constellations? Or is that just a coincidence?"

"Ah, so you noticed." He grinned as he turned to look at me. "My dad thinks they're easier to remember than making up random names. He assigns them all."

"I see," I said, wondering how he had decided to pick mine or if it was just random. I stared at Warren as I thought, then a slow smile crept across my lips. "I see why he picked Aries for you – seems fitting, given how difficult you are."

I half expected him to react poorly to my words, and a part of me couldn't even believe that I had said them out loud. But to my surprise, he didn't, and he rolled his eyes instead.

"At least I'm not a crow," he muttered, but I caught a glimpse of the grin he wasn't able to hide as he leaned back on his hands and looked up at the sky.

A small laugh left my lungs, and he shot me a halfhearted dirty look. I leaned back on my hands, a smile playing across my lips as I closed my eyes and imagined that I was looking up at the sky too.

Lies

"So, what have you brought me this time, Corvus?"

"Less than I wanted to bring," I said, taking off my helmet and setting it on the ground.

I slipped the small canvas bag that I had been using to cart supplies off my shoulder and handed it to Warren. After my meeting with Orion, Warren had stopped stealing my delivery bags and started to bring his own, so I'd been able to continue using the lightweight black one I'd bought from a second-hand store. I wasn't sure if it was because his father had directed him to stop or simply because they didn't need any more bags, but either way, I didn't ask. I was just happy that I didn't need to constantly buy new ones, especially now that I was coming out twice a week to update Warren and bring supplies.

I dropped to the cool cave floor, stretching my legs out past the mouth and watching as Warren began to empty the contents of my bag into his own. He was getting quicker at it, each time taking less than the last, though our meetings had not grown any shorter.

"As suspected, Scott Beckette and his father don't go anywhere near the docks from what I can tell," I said as I watched Warren work. "I did find his school records – he was either incredibly smart or his father paid for his good grades. I know your dad asked for his credit card statements, but I can't get those without a warrant, and the files I found from his youth are sealed. I can see them in the system database, so he was definitely arrested for something, but there's no way I can get into them without proper access authority or by submitting a request to our Computer Security Department, and that's out of the question – unless Eridanus or your father happens to have an ally there somewhere in the CPD?"

"I doubt it," Warren sighed, stuffing the last of the supplies into his pack and straightening from his hunched position to walk toward me. He handed me the empty canvas bag, then dropped onto the ground near my side as he ran a hand through his hair. "Otherwise, he wouldn't have asked you if you could do it."

I nodded, turning away from him to look out at the slow drizzle that poured from the dark grey sky. It was one of those annoying rains, where everything's wet and yet it's hardly raining at all, so the whole night feels like a bit of a waste. The only good thing about the weather was that the heat had finally broken, the rain would wash away any of my lingering tracks to this area, and I didn't have to squint so hard to see Warren.

"Did you bring the hard drive?"

"Yes," I said, unzipping my wet vest and reaching inside to pull out the sealed plastic bag I had used to transport the sensor hard drive. "Do you have the other one?"

"Yeah." He reached into his jacket pocket and pulled out the third hard drive we had been using to exchange the dock surveillance footage.

So far, Hakim hadn't pulled the sensors from the farming facilities. After some internal debate, the insurance company Dolan's was using decided they wanted to send out a third-party inspector to visually confirm everything was in compliance with our recommendations. Jonathan had argued that it wasn't necessary since he had submitted proof of purchase for the new equipment and modified facility drawings, but Hakim had agreed that it was a good idea and convinced him that it would be in his best interest to go along with it.

The third-party inspector had yet to schedule a date, so our monitoring continued, and I was able to sneak a third hard drive from our inventory.

The resulting rotation worked seamlessly. One hard drive in the sensor, one spare with me to swap with the sensor, and one with Warren containing the latest data. After taking the hard drive from the sensor and replacing it with my spare, I would bring it home to copy the data onto my computer, then bring it out to Warren, where he would return the last one that I had given him so I'd have a new spare.

"It was wiped, so it's ready to go," Warren said as we exchanged the drives, and I tried to ignore the way it felt when his fingers brushed mine. "Anything else?"

"Nothing useful," I said, stuffing the hard drive inside my vest and rezipping it before I turned to look at him again. "I haven't been able to properly surveil his place. A lot of those mansions have guard shacks and cameras, and they would notice if I went by more than once or twice. I did find a set of traffic cameras near his home, though, so I could use those to track his movement, but I don't have access to the traffic camera database anymore. I lost the permission after Hakim extended my probation because detectives just submit requests to Patrol and Street when they need it – so I need to find a way around that."

Warren nodded.

"Did anything come back on the title search yet?"

"No, not yet." Warren shook his head. "But my dad said Eridanus should have something this weekend. As soon as I get it, I'll let you know."

"Alright."

We sat there in silence for a long while. Neither of us moved as the lazy rain continued to fall, and I had to fight against the urge to turn and look at him. Staring would be rude. So instead, I found myself talking—talking as if we could actually be friends... not two beings brought together by chance while a dark and disturbing history loomed between us.

"Was it hard growing up with your dad in charge?" I asked, my voice coming out low as I cracked my right eye open and stole a glance in his direction.

He wasn't looking at me. His eyes were fixed on the hard drive that he was turning over in his hands.

"Sometimes," Warren said, flipping the drive over once more and staring at it thoughtfully. "When I was younger, I didn't understand the significance of what he did or what was going on. From a young age we know about your kind, but we don't *know* about it in the way I do now. He would be gone for weeks at a time on occasion. People constantly needed his time, so even when he was home, he wasn't really there."

If he knew I was staring at him now, he didn't seem to mind. Or, at the very least, he didn't say anything. I watched him turn the hard drive over again, realizing only then just how close he was.

I could have reached out and touched him if I wanted to.

I wouldn't, but I could have, because he was only three feet away. I watched the damp air rustle his hair, and a million more questions fluttered through my mind. Then, before I could stop myself, the next words came out.

"Is your mother part of—"

"She's dead," Warren answered before I could even finish my words.

"Oh," I whispered. My heart dropped, but his face remained impassive. "I'm sorry."

"It was a long time ago," Warren said, flipping the hard drive once more before he finally stuffed it into his jacket pocket.

I half expected him to leave. It wouldn't be the first time that one of our conversations was ended abruptly by an uncomfortable topic or impassable hurdle—of which there were a lot, given that I had grown up eating his people—but to my surprise, he didn't go. Instead, he leaned back on his hands and stared out into the rain.

"So—" I wondered if I should drop the topic completely or try to talk it through. I opted for what I hoped was a middle-ground option. "Is – is it just you and your dad?"

"No." I watched him swallow, his shoulders dropping with a silent breath as he dropped his gaze to his boots and hesitated before continuing in a lower voice. "My sister is still alive."

"You have a sister?"

"Yes."

He didn't offer any other information, so I decided it was best not to ask. After all, details could be damning if this plan fell apart. Genuinely not knowing too much about his family or their whereabouts would be helpful if I was ever questioned, so I dropped my gaze to my boots and watched the rain wash off the mud.

"Do you have any siblings?"

"Yes," I answered, a little surprised that he cared to ask. Maybe he was just being polite, but polite and being Warren didn't really fit in the same box. I glanced over at him again and found he was looking at me now. "I have a brother. His name is Dimitri."

"What's he like?"

"He's an ass," I said without thinking, and Warren's lips twisted into a small smile. I grinned in return, then felt my face falter. "He's an engineer – smart, calculating, focused – working hard to keep himself in the upper-west side. He – he's probably a lot more like how you expect us to be."

"Do you get along?"

"Not really." I dropped my eyes back to my boots. "But we don't not get along either. My relationship with him is the same as it is with my parents. They're content not to question things and happiest when I don't mention my work. I never really fit in within my family."

"Even as a kid?"

"Especially as a kid," I answered, my lips twitching into a bitter smile. "I was told I was wasting my life away more than once. They didn't understand me and what I wanted. I pestered my parents into letting me take self-defence lessons and constantly read books about detective stories. They hated that. So in some ways, I'm glad that Dimitri is there so he can be the child that they wanted. Without him, I might not have ended up here. I think he's the only reason they didn't push me too hard."

Silence rang between us, and I wondered why the hell I had just told him all that information.

"Well," Warren said, and I glanced up to see him still watching me. "Your parents should really get a refund for those self-defence lessons. You're pretty terrible at it."

I laughed, the unexpected sound breaking from my lungs as a smile touched his lips.

"You caught me off guard," I argued, narrowing my eyes at him. "Had I not underestimated you, you wouldn't be smiling right now."

"Sure," he said, but the doubt in his voice was obvious as he continued to grin.

I watched him as he turned to look back out at the treeline, noting how free he looked when he smiled. He had a handsome face regardless of the expression that splayed across it, but when he smiled, his eyes shone, and it was by far the most attractive expression to grace his features. It was like a physical weight was lifted from his shoulders, and I was seeing a completely different side of him, a stark contrast to the stoic demeanour he usually held.

It made me wonder what he was like with his family. Was he just as serious at home with his dad and sister, or did he ever get a moment to breathe?

I swallowed and dropped my gaze back to my boots. The thought of him rarely having moments to relax and drop his guard made me sad, and an uncomfortable knot formed in the pit of my stomach as I realized I had just admitted that I found Warren handsome. That was a thought that was better left alone, left out here in the cave where the real world faded away and our two worlds could collide for just a moment.

I let out a breath and tried not to think about it. I knew I should push it away, and yet it felt impossible to ignore, and I couldn't even make myself deny it even though I knew it was fundamentally wrong.

I liked spending time with Warren.

I couldn't deny that either. I wanted to know more about him. I wanted to ask him so many things, and yet despite the pull I felt to try and get closer, I knew that was an impossibility because that would put everything at risk. Not to mention that the basic principle of being a human's friend was absolutely insane.

I closed my eyes as the rain started to get heavier and tried to ignore the dull ache forming in my chest.

"Did you find any leads on the Jane Doe cases?"

Warren's voice tugged me out of my thoughts, and I found myself meeting his warm brown gaze once more.

"Sort of," I said as I pulled my boots in from the rain and crossed my legs. "I've pretty much confirmed that whoever was disposing of the bodies was using the subway line. I have over a dozen images pulled from the security feeds, and we managed to get the name of the guy we think is doing it, but I don't think he's the only one. Autopsies confirmed that Jane Doe number 3 recently gave birth, so it's safe to assume that the others have too."

"Is this related to your people having difficulties conceiving?" Warren asked, twisting to face me fully.

"Yes," I answered, my voice taking on a serious tone. "It's clear that these are not random murders, and this isn't some serial killer MO either. It's an operation – it's organized. And Hakim and I are proceeding under the assumption that these victims were either captured because they were pregnant or they're part of a trafficking ring. Either way, the people running it are trying to pass it off as gang-related violence by dumping the bodies in the worst areas of Carneth. It doesn't help that none of the girls are registered in any database in the country, so we don't even know where they came from.

"There have been issues of missing women in the past, stolen infants linked to child trafficking rings – but I think this is worse," I said, swallowing hard as I told him the horrible truth I had been starting to suspect. "I think someone, or some group, is using these women simply for the purpose of obtaining a child, then they dispose of the bodies after they're done with them. Or maybe they're just getting rid of the women who can't bear any more children. I'm not sure, but having kids is incredibly difficult for Reborn. They would easily be able to sell the infants to rich families who can't have children on their own without notice, especially since Reborn are very private about their pregnancies. They keep it quiet for as long as possible. Many manage it right until the baby is born because they don't want to disappoint their families with continuous false alarms."

I dropped my gaze to stare at his chest, because I could no longer look him in the eye.

"Besides, it isn't like adoption is really a thing," I said almost absently, slowly trailing my eyes along the lines of his damp jacket as I thought. "The wait lists for it are long, extensively so. There are procedures and medications women can take to try and help with fertility, but they don't always work, and some of them are exhausting – not to mention expensive. Most women struggle to have one kid. Having two is a rarity. My mother was very lucky, and I'm extremely lucky to be here, and that's the worst part of all of this. I'm not even shocked it's happening. It's probably been happening for a long time, and the more I think about it, people probably know."

I swallowed hard, sickness curling in my gut as my eyes trailed up the tanned skin of his neck, and I forced myself to meet his warm gaze once more.

"I almost wonder if that's the real reason why the mayor and the chief of police plan to pull the case from us in November," I whispered. "Because they know, and because they allow it to happen because the women they use are viewed as disposable. Because they don't care or because someone more powerful than them paid them off to look the other way. Or maybe they benefit from it. I don't know the reason, but the longer I'm in this, the more I start to doubt everything and everyone around me."

Warren didn't say anything in response.

He simply held my gaze as we both sat in silence. The rain continued to fall as my eyes traced his face, memorizing every detail I could make out in the dull light. And as each second ticked by, I found myself wishing more and more that I could just stay here all weekend.

TUESDAY, OCTOBER 6
12:11 AM

"Gorski! It's been too long – how have you been?"

"Hernandez," I said, smiling at the man as I made my way into my old bullpen and tried to ignore the slight shake in my hands. I hadn't expected him to be here. I'd thought he was still on days, and his presence would completely ruin my plan. "Things are going well – busy, but I can't complain. How about you?"

"Oh, you know how it is down here," Hernandez said as he pushed his chair out from his desk and turned to face me fully. "Signed up for the OT patrol duties for Halloween weekend and trying to see if I can sucker Hawthorne into doing more paperwork for me."

"Classic." I crossed my arms over my chest to try to hide the tremble.

"So what brings you down here? Don't tell me they sent you back already – because if they did, they made a huge mistake."

"No – no, they didn't send me back." I shook my head. "I just popped in to see Grace, but I must have just missed her."

"Yeah, she usually leaves right on time for lunch."

I knew this, which was exactly why I'd come late on purpose.

"I got delayed on the elevator." I lied, and Hernandez rolled his eyes in understanding. "Did she say if she was going far? I can always leave a note and come back."

"I think she was just running down to the cafe to grab something quick – mentioned something about needing to push some reports off this afternoon, so I don't think she'll be gone long. I was actually thinking of heading down there myself to grab something – wanna come?"

"Oh, no, that's okay. I honestly really don't have that much time. I was headed down to see Corban, so I thought I would sneak in a quick visit."

"Still working through lunch, huh?" Hernandez grinned. "Alright – well, I'm going to head down there. The initial rush should be thinned out by now. I can tell Grace you stopped by the pen."

"Thanks." I waited as he stood from his desk and stretched. "I'll leave her a note too."

"She'll like that," Hernandez said, grabbing his wallet off the desk and moving across the pen. "I know she misses you."

"I know," I replied, but my voice had dropped low as I watched him leave the pen. "I miss her too."

It was true, kind of. What I really missed was the simplicity of how things were before. I sighed, pushing the thoughts aside. Grace would be back soon, so I needed to hurry.

Without hesitating, I marched over to the corner of her desk, grabbed the tissue I had stuffed in my pocket and used it to open the top drawer. Then, as I watched the entrance to the bullpen to make sure no one caught me, I slipped my hand inside, twisting it until my fingers brushed the sticky note she'd hidden on the underside of her desk. I carefully took it out, then pulled out my notebook and pen and rapidly copied down her login password.

I wasn't proud of what I was doing.

In fact, I hadn't slept at all since deciding to go through with this.

After I'd talked to Warren on Saturday, Hawthorne had texted me and cancelled the tentative plans we had made for Friday to hang out and catch up. It was for the best. My apartment was a mess, and I ended up spending the entire rest of the weekend working and wondering how I could regain access to the Patrol and Street network. I needed to be able to view street cameras, but there was no way in hell I could justify submitting a request for surveillance near Scott Beckette's house, especially after what had happened with Hakim on the 19th.

This was the only solution I could come up with that wouldn't raise suspicion. I knew Grace kept her login details written down on this sticky note because I'd seen her do it three years ago and had lectured her about breaking the rules. It was basic computer safety 101—they had covered it in orientation and had hammered home that we were not to write down our login details or store them at our desks.

My heart sank as I tucked my notebook back into my pocket and then carefully returned the sticky note to its home. I almost couldn't believe what I was doing, but I didn't have time to think about it because I could hear footsteps approaching, so I quickly shoved the drawer closed and stepped away from the desk.

"Valya?"

"Hey!" I said, my voice a little too loud as Grace froze in the bullpen entrance.

"What are you doing down here?"

She was looking at me like she couldn't believe I was here, and I realized that this was the first time I had set foot in the bullpen since I'd left July 3rd, three months prior.

"I just wanted to pop in to say hi." I felt a pang of guilt through my chest at the disbelieving look on her face. "I was headed down to talk to Corban in evidence – I haven't been back to the pen in a while, so I thought I would drop in."

"Ahh." Grace nodded, a bitter smile crossing her lips. "Yes, that makes sense. Only reason to come down here anymore is because it's on the way to evidence. More nameless drainer bodies wasting our tax dollars, I bet."

I closed my eyes as she walked by, resisting the urge to retort because it would be a wasted effort. It was impossible to win arguments with Grace, and besides, she wasn't wrong about my lack of availability. I hadn't exactly been a great friend lately.

And I had just stolen her login information so I could illegally access traffic camera footage and bypass the proper channels.

"I see Mallick hasn't given away my old desk yet," I said instead, opting for something I hoped was neutral as I turned to face Grace.

"Of course he hasn't," Grace said as she pulled out her chair and took a seat. "He likes you."

I let out a small laugh, but it sounded awkward. Things had unquestionably gotten worse between us. I'd thought the dinner date had been awkward and uncomfortable, but this was even lousier. Lexie Grace had moved beyond expressing her annoyance toward me in blatant words and had turned to the cold, bitter, and resentful tactics I had only ever seen her use with other people.

"He likes everyone in here." I forced myself to push through the tension that hung in the small pen. "But you're right, I do need to make a better effort to get down here. I'll try to stop by more. I just missed you and wanted to drop in and say hi."

I saw the anger in her eyes soften, and she let out a sigh as she placed her coffee on her desk.

"I miss you too," she said, sitting back in her chair and giving me a small smile. "It's not the same without you, and patrol duty with Tilson sucks."

I gave her a sympathetic smile, even though I completely disagreed with her about Tilson.

"You could always come and join me in the Detective Unit."

"Ha! I don't think so," Grace laughed, a full smile finally breaking across her beautiful features. "I like my life as it is, thank you."

"You're missing out."

"I doubt that. You look horrible, and it's been, what, only three months?" She took a sip from her paper cup, then seemed to remember something. "Oh! We're having a Halloween party again!"

"I thought you said Mark didn't want to do that again after last year?"

"He changed his mind," Grace said, waving her hand dismissively. "It's going to be on Saturday – think you can make it?"

"Sure." I nodded, even though I didn't want to go. "I'll come."

"Great." Grace smiled. "I'll text you the details."

"Alright, well—" I hesitated, glancing back at the bullpen entrance. "I should probably get down to the fifth floor before Corban thinks the elevators legitimately broke."

"Okay." Grace nodded. "And let me know if you get a free night. I want to show you the curtains I got for my dining room."

"I will."

I turned to leave the bullpen, nearly making it out before a familiar voice split the air.

"Gorski!"

My eyes widened. How could my timing be so horribly wrong? I slowed to a stop just past the entrance to the pen as Hawthorne came into view.

"Hawthorne," I said, and his face split into a wide grin at my obvious surprise. "I thought you were still on days?"

"Nope!" Hawthorne announced, his eyes crinkling at the corners as he looked down at me. "That's why I had to cancel last weekend – I worked a double, then helped Jefferson complete two reports so he would trade days off with me. Finally back on nights. I think my internal clock might be a bit messed up, but it's totally worth it. So, we still good for this weekend? Or are you going to be crawling through the woods again looking for clues?"

"Actually, the Dolan case seems to be slowing down. But I'm sure Hakim will keep me busy just the same."

"Yeah, I don't doubt that," Hawthorne sighed. "Alright, well, let me know – but I'll try to swing by this week sometime anyway because I want to show you something."

"Alright." I agreed because I didn't know what else to say. "Just message me before you come by, or I might not be home, but I should go – Corban is waiting for me."

"Okay," Hawthorne said. His eyes lingered on my face a moment, then his eyes narrowed as he took a small step forward and lowered his voice. "Gorski – you feeling okay? You look pale."

"Yes, I'm fine," I lied.

"Is this about the case?" he whispered, and my body stiffened as his voice dropped so low I could barely hear it. "About the humans on the farm?"

"No." I shook my head, forcing myself to hold his concerned gaze. "Just tired from working so much – but I really need to go, or I'll be back here permanently when Hakim fires me."

I stepped around him, glancing back over my shoulder as I cut across the next bullpen. He was watching me, his face just as deadly serious as it had been when we'd spoken at my dining table. He looked apprehensive, but more concerning than that was the dangerously blank expression on Grace's face as her eyes flicked between us.

Thursday, October 8

11:24 AM

"Valya!"

I turned around, Hakim slowing by my side as he glanced over his shoulder. Grace had just gotten off the second elevator and was quickly making her way toward me.

"Grace." I found it impossible to hide the surprise from my voice. "You're here late."

"Mallick made me stay to get a report done," Grace replied, rolling her eyes before she glanced up at Hakim. "Ah, Detective Hakim. We haven't met yet – I'm Lexie Grace, Valya's old patrol partner. I've heard a lot about you."

Hakim's mismatched eyes dropped to the hand Grace had extended, and he stared at it for a moment as I clenched my teeth. The way Grace had chosen to say those words suggested that I was telling her about Hakim and possibly even our cases, which I knew Hakim would not appreciate.

"Do you need me for something, Officer Grace?" Hakim asked, his eyes flicking back up to her face while his hand remained unmoving at his side.

"No," Grace said.

Her eyes creased, and a tight smile curled across her lips. She dropped her hand and adjusted the strap of her gear bag. I knew the rejection stung worse than she was showing. Grace had always been very proud, like most Reborn.

"I just wanted to say hello and see if Valya might be free one of these nights. It's been hard to find time to hang out – she's been exceptionally busy lately."

"Grace," I warned.

"Maybe next weekend?" she pressed innocently as her eyes flicked between us. "We could go catch a movie or maybe get some dinner at that new restaurant that opened up on Fourth? I heard the food is incredible – and it's organic."

"Alright, maybe." I agreed with a tight smile, wishing that she would just leave. "I'll text you about it later, okay?"

"Alright." Grace nodded, and this time her smile was genuine. Then her eyes shifted back to Hakim. "I'll cross my fingers you don't need her next weekend then."

I grimaced, and Hakim stared at Grace. His expression was unreadable, but I could feel the air in the underground parking garage getting tighter as silence rang in my ears. Then his body turned, and his piercing gaze shifted to meet my own.

He didn't say anything, but he didn't have to.

I swallowed hard as he stared at me. One more nail in the coffin. One more X next to my name. I had managed to repair some of the damage I'd inflicted when I'd screamed at him in his car, but this had just cut a brand-new gash in the ever-tenuous relationship that was our partnership.

He turned away after an unbearable moment of silence, walking toward the area of the parking garage where he regularly parked his car, and I felt my shoulders sag as anger began to burn in my chest.

"What the hell was that?" Grace asked, her voice ringing out to my left as I stood there and watched my partner walk away. "He's even more unwelcoming than the rumours, isn't he?"

"What the hell was that?" I repeated, turning to look at my old patrol partner as my fingers dug into the strap of my bag. "What do you mean 'what the hell was that' – what the hell were you thinking? Why would you do that?"

"Do what?" Grace asked. "Stand up for you?"

"Stand up for me?" I said in disbelief. "Are you serious?"

"Why are you mad?" Her tone grew defensive. "He's been working you to the bone, running you into the ground like his dead ex-partner and you haven't said anything about it."

"Because I don't want to!" The words came out far louder than I had intended. "I like my job, Lexie! I need my job – I have to keep my job! You have no idea what you're toying with."

"You make it sound like your life depends on it," Grace scoffed. "Your family is well off – you'll be fine. You know he's probably a drainer too, right? Just like his degenerate partner. How else could he manage so much work?"

"He isn't a drainer, Lexie," I said, even though I had my own doubts about Hakim's eating habits and no idea why I felt the need to defend him. "You can't just go around calling people that! And I don't need you coming to my defence and making it sound like I complain about him off-shift and talk to you about our cases. You could seriously get me in trouble."

"Him texting you all the time and making you work all these hours is ridiculous, and you know it!" Grace spat as she crossed her arms over her chest and glared at me. "I'm sorry for caring about you and your well-being. Frankly, I'm shocked he has the nerve to call you in as much as he does. He could get in trouble if they ever looked at his phone logs. He can't fire you for wanting to have a life outside of work."

"I *do* have a life outside of work."

The words slipped out before I could even think them through, and Grace's eyes narrowed as she adjusted the strap of her bag once more.

"Right, I'm sure you do. Look, I'm just trying to be a good friend and help you out – make sure that Hakim knows people are aware of how he's treating you. Standing up to him isn't going to get you in trouble, but it might get him to stop drowning you in case files, so you could be a little more grateful," Grace said as she ran her hand over her hair to smooth it out. "I'm just trying to make sure you don't kill yourself over this job – it's not worth it. You need a night off, and you need to relax a little. I'll see if I can get us a reservation at that restaurant for next week. We'll go, we'll have fun, it will be just like before you transferred into this stupid job, and when the meal is over, you'll thank me."

I watched her walk away in silence, keeping my angry reply tightly locked up as I wondered how the hell I was going to manage everything without just completely cutting her out of my life. Then I turned and made my way in the opposite direction toward my car, briefly considering if I could just tell her what was going on and have her join me as an ally. I outright laughed at the thought as I tossed my gear bag onto the bag seat and got into my car.

Grace didn't strike me as the type to be sympathetic to much of anything, let alone humans and their struggles. If I was going to trust anyone with this, it would be Hawthorne—but that was out of the question. It wouldn't be fair to drag anyone else into my mess. I let out a sigh as I reached into my vest and pulled out the tiny flip phone I used to contact Warren, then sent him a message.

> C: Got off work early. Heading out now to drop off the supplies.
>
> Should be there in two hours.

I didn't wait to see if he answered, because I wasn't expecting him to be there when I showed up. I had told him earlier that I would try to come by this morning, but he said he might not be able to make it because he was working on something else. So I was taken by surprise when I arrived at the cave to find him standing there waiting for me.

"Warren," I said as I stripped off my helmet and removed the gear bag from my shoulder. He had yet to correct me in using his real name, though I assumed the circumstances would be different if others were around. "I didn't think you'd be here. Is everything okay?"

"Everything's fine," he said, accepting the bag from me and setting it on the ground by his own empty one. He didn't appear to be in a rush to exchange goods, and I tried to ignore the jolt of happiness that sparked in my chest. "I just finished what I was working on early, so I thought I'd come out here to meet you. Besides, it was a nice day for a walk."

I couldn't help the smile that formed across my face as I looked at him, the tension from my confrontation in the parking garage with Grace fading from my mind.

"Well, I'm glad you're here," I said, not thinking about the words as they left my lips. He smiled, and we stared at each other in silence for a moment before I cleared my throat. "So – any word on that title search?"

"Got it right here." He pulled a sealed manila envelope from his pocket and came to join me near the mouth of the cave.

We both sat down on the ground, and I gladly took the envelope from his hands, not commenting on the way his fingers gently brushed mine.

"Excellent," I said, turning the envelope over to see that both sides were blank. "Did Eridanus have any issues getting it?"

"I don't think so," Warren answered. "I think it just took some time to do it without raising any suspicion. There's a lot of property down there from what I understand."

"There is." I nodded. "This should help narrow it down, though. Have you found anything else out about when it might happen?"

"Nothing definitive." Warren shook his head and let out a sigh. I watched as he leaned back on his hands and stared out at the treeline. "But everything right now is suggesting the end of the month. We have allies up north who have flagged the compound where they're keeping some of our people. It's in Sherridon, but we don't have the resources to take action there or the time to bring them in. It's too remote and too secure, not a good option for success. Especially with the rain and colder weather coming. We're hoping they'll catch the loading and be able to identify the trucks so we can track them as they head south, but all we know for certain is that they've not left yet."

"If it is them, it will take them at least four days to get here, assuming they don't run into any problems. I can't imagine that they'd want to keep the captives at the warehouses for too long after they arrive," I said, and Warren nodded at my words. "Even if they've paid off the dock gate security to look the other way, it's a risk. Most of the buildings have independent cameras that will capture them driving by. And they can't risk any of your people escaping, so they're not going to let them out once they get here. But they'll need to eat eventually, so the window's going to be small."

"It will be," Warren said as he turned to look at me. "But we'll be ready."

"We will," I agreed, and we both smiled again.

His eyes circled over my face, and I fought not to squirm. He didn't stare often, but whenever he did look at me closely, it always made my stomach knot.

"So," I said, pulling my eyes away from him and dropping my gaze to my lap. "What were you working on this morning?"

"I was actually helping my sister," Warren said, and his honest answer surprised me.

"Really?" I asked and immediately turned to look at him again. "Doing what?"

"Fixing her oil stove," Warren said, and his eyes shone as they creased. "She uses it for everything, and it stopped working four days ago. So – it was clearly an emergency."

"Of course it was." I grinned as he smiled. "Does she cook a lot?"

"Yes." Warren nodded. "But she prefers baking, even though it can be difficult. She got pretty creative last week, making fruit cake in the stone oven. It doesn't always turn out the best, but it's a great way to preserve our leftover fruit from the summer and fall harvests."

"I've never had fruit cake. Most of our cakes are desserts – like chocolate or vanilla – and they're covered in icing."

"Icing." He arched a brow. "What's that?"

"It's a coating on the cake," I answered, trying to think of how best to describe it. "It's mostly made from sugar, so it's sweet. Usually they add dye to it to make it colourful – and really, it's just a decoration. Sometimes they make it out of chocolate, too, and some people put way too much of it on."

"I see," he said, then snorted. "Well, not really. I've never had it, so I've got no idea what you're talking about."

I laughed at that, shaking my head as I turned to squint back out at the treeline for a moment.

"Well, you'll have to try it sometime," I said quietly. "It's pretty good."

"I'll keep that in mind."

I sat there by his side in silence, wondering what it must be like to live out in the woods with nothing but an oil stove and stone oven to prepare meals. He didn't have gelatin cubes, grocery stores, or takeout food for days when he was tired and didn't feel like cooking. If he or his sister didn't cook, they likely didn't eat, and it must be exhausting to try to manage their supplies. I tried to imagine what his home looked like for the hundredth time, but no matter how hard I tried to picture it, I couldn't, and instead, I found myself wondering if I would ever get to see it.

Secrets

"I narrowed it down to a section of twenty or so warehouses," I announced as I stripped off my damp vest and gloves and threw them on the ground next to my supply bag before collapsing on the ground beside it.

"Twenty?" Warren repeated as he pushed away from the wall and made his way toward me. He had been leaning against it waiting for me, but, like he always did now, he came to join me on the ground. "How big of an area is that?"

"Still big," I admitted. "But it's better than hundreds."

"True," he agreed. "They're all at the eastmost side?"

"Yes. They're part of the section that the Beckettes own. You'll need to tell your dad to thank this Eridanus person. Without that title search, I wouldn't have known what I was looking for."

"It was a joint effort – you're the one who found the company name."

"I suppose so," I murmured, closing my eyes and letting my shoulders slump.

The previous eight days had been utter chaos. I couldn't remember the last time I had gotten a solid three hours of sleep, and my feet were starting to hurt from walking so much. It wasn't a feeling I was comfortable with. Reborn didn't get tired—or sore. Not unless they were nearly killing themselves… so perhaps that was what I was slowly doing.

On Tuesday, Jonathan had confirmed the date of the insurance company's inspection. It would be happening next week, and as I had anticipated, Hakim would pass the case over to Precinct 15 shortly after. In the meantime, the Dolan case rested entirely on my shoulders. I was responsible for driving out to both facilities to collect the security footage from the guard houses and swap out the hard drives from the sensors in the woods, which took a decent amount of time, given that I had to walk both sensor routes.

It remained a useless task, but I completed it without complaint because I needed to avoid pissing off Hakim any further. He was still displeased about the run-in with Grace last week, and he seemed happy to partially remove me from the Jane Doe case and stick me in a temporary corner. So, I used my unmonitored farm facility check-ins to drop supply packs for Warren by the rock formation where I had first found him.

He met me there some nights, and we would swap dock surveillance hard drives as I updated him on my findings. More often than not, he would end up walking alongside me as I made my way through the woods to collect the sensor data and then we would part ways just before sunrise when I reached my car.

Each time Warren left, I felt the pressure in my chest grow, and each time I saw him waiting for me in the trees, my heart would flutter. As we walked, I learned more about him and his people, and each new detail only made me want to know even more, and I found myself wishing that the nights could go on forever.

The second benefit of being left alone to manage the Dolan case was the progress I had been able to make on Scott Beckette, which had jumped substantially.

I had used Grace's login to download traffic camera footage from the intersection by Scott Beckette's house and had run the plates of the cars I'd seen going down his street. Most of them belonged to neighbours. A few belonged to him, but I never saw any of those vehicles get anywhere near the docks, so I determined that the traffic cameras were a dead end, best abandoned for the time being.

It was Eridanus, who I still knew very little about, that had been extremely useful in my efforts to determine which warehouses they might be using. Without the title search results for all the docks and surrounding buildings, I'd have gotten nowhere the previous week. That said, the task hadn't been easy.

It had taken me nearly two days to shift through the data and compile a comprehensive list of all the companies and their owners. None of them were owned by Scott Beckette, Scott Beckette's family, or any of their known associates. Instead, most of the property was registered to large, global corporations and several small companies, and trying to make heads or tails of it felt like a lost cause.

I'd evaded Hawthorne's request to hang out last weekend in favour of spending more time snooping around the docks and digging deeper into the list of businesses I had compiled. Then, on Monday, October 12th, Warren had given me an envelope filled with cash along with another list of supplies. He said the money was from Eridanus, and when I opened the envelope to look inside, I nearly gagged. Either Orion's contact was loaded, or his allies had pooled their funds—either way, it made me a bit uncomfortable taking it home. For all I knew, this money could be dirty, and keeping such a large quantity of it hidden in my bedroom made me feel like I was a criminal.

Which, technically, I suppose I was if anyone were to find out what I had been doing with my CPD access.

By the 13th, I was starting to lose confidence in my ability to find the warehouse or tie anything useful back to Scott Beckette. I abandoned my efforts of crawling through dock surveillance footage entirely and instead started digging into Scott Beckette's family. We already knew they were smart enough not to link anything back to their name directly—so they had to be using someone else's facilities or using a different name.

I doubted that even they could get away with purchasing warehouses under a fake name since industrial properties required a federal approval process, in which verification of registered identity was required. So I knew the name had to be tied to them in some legitimate way. Judge Joseph Beckette might have had pull in our province, but the very fact that his "goods" were being captured out of province and shipped through these ports hinted that he did not have pull at a federal level.

Maybe.

Or these docks were just the best way to move humans because the channel connected directly with the Atlantic and the other provinces to the west were landlocked. Either way, it was the only rock I had yet to overturn that was still within my grasp. So I spent my days crawling through the Beckette family tree, looking for anything that might mean something.

Then I had found it.

Natasha Lionetti.

Scott Beckette's aunt—via marriage to Joseph Beckette's brother Christopher. She had changed her surname to Beckette after getting married, which wasn't all that uncommon, but it wasn't the norm for well-off families. What was particularly strange about it was how the names Lionetti and Beckette never existed anywhere together. Ever. It was as if the two families had never met despite having married into one another, and after Christopher Beckette had died two decades ago, Natasha had never changed her name back. Yet she didn't seem to have any current involvement in the Beckette family.

Which was very strange.

Typically, Reborn without children retook their maiden names after their spouse passed. They would remarry and move on. If they didn't, it was because they remained closely tied to the family of their deceased partner, either personally or professionally, and those ties were typically obvious and visible in richer families.

Everyone knew who the Beckette family was. It wasn't uncommon to see their name splattered across the cover of the newspaper—usually in regard to charity donations, marriages, births, or successful business ventures. They were easily one of the wealthiest and best-known families in the city. Yet I couldn't find anything that mentioned Natasha except the obituary for her deceased husband, which was the only reason why I found her maiden name at all, but the second I saw it, I felt an itch in the back of my mind, and I knew I had seen it before.

In a matter of minutes, I found the connection within the list I had compiled from the title search.

Docks 57c through 62d, owned by a company called Illumination Enterprises, registered to a Ms. N. A. Lionetti. Once I had that connection, I immediately made my way down to the docks and moved my sensors, narrowing the search down to a section of twenty or so warehouses which belonged to the docks Ms. Lionetti owned. I still couldn't confirm with one hundred percent certainty that these were the docks that would be used to ship out Warren's people, but it was the best lead we had, so I was running with it.

"There's still a long way to go, though," I said, opening my eyes a sliver to look at Warren.

He was less than two feet away. I could feel the warmth radiating off his body as I sat there by his side. It was such a contrast to the pleasantly cool air, but I found I didn't mind it. His shoulders were relaxed. His eyes were warm and thoughtful. There wasn't a hint of the hatred that I had seen the night I had first met him, and as I stared at him, I realized I couldn't remember the last time I'd seen it. I couldn't remember the last time things between us had felt stiff and laced with the unbearable tension that I now felt every time I left this cave.

My world had completely flipped.

At home, my life had become a lie. I felt isolated, terrified, and utterly lost as to how I was ever supposed to look at my people the same again. And now, somehow, despite the insanity of it all, Warren had become the person that I felt the most comfortable around.

I swallowed, dropping my eyes to the unbuttoned collar of his shirt. I could see his tanned skin in the dim afternoon light, and I found myself wondering what it would be like to—

I quickly closed my eyes again, squeezing them tight for a moment before I shoved the thought away and forced my brain to refocus.

"But I'll keep working on it," I said, giving him a small smile before I remembered what I had originally wanted to tell him.

"Oh! Also, I remembered what you said about your sister and how she likes cooking and baking. Here."

I reached for my bag, pulling out a smaller bag I had packed separately and handing it over to him.

"The baking soda should last for a while so long as the container is sealed properly, and the wooden spoons are all new. I tossed in a few other things, but this," I said, reaching back to my bag and pulling out a small thin bar, "is for you."

He took it and turned it over in his hands, his eyebrow arching as he read the words.

"Chocolate," he said, looking up at me in disbelief. "You bought me chocolate?"

"Well, you said you've never tried it." I shrugged my shoulders. "If you don't like it, I'm sure your sister would be interested in trying it. She hasn't had it either, has she?"

"She hasn't," he said, and I struggled to place the strange expression on his face as he looked at me.

Then it hit.

"Oh!" A hint of the awkwardness I'd not felt in nights slid through my bones. "I bought it from a small chocolate shop near my place, and I double-checked the ingredients. It – it's just chocolate. And they only deal with chocolate there, so there's no cross contamination."

"I know." He nodded. "I didn't think you would give me something without checking it. I just wasn't expecting it."

He dropped his eyes back to the bar in his hand.

"What does it taste like?"

"Like chocolate." I laughed as he rolled his eyes at me and, to my surprise, leaned over and nudged me with his shoulder. "I have no idea how to describe it – just try it."

"Alright, Corvus," he said as the low rumble of distant thunder echoed in the cave. "Fine, I'll try it."

I watched quietly by his side as he opened the packaging and broke off not one, but two small pieces, and turned to hand me one.

"You don't have to give me any. I can have chocolate any time."

"It feels weird just eating it by myself," Warren said, reaching out to take my hand when I refused to accept his offer. I fought to suppress a shiver as his fingers touched my skin, and the warmth felt like an electric current jolting through my body. "We share everything at home – you don't just eat things on your own."

"I see," I whispered, dropping my gaze away from his face to stare at the thin, dark square sitting in my open palm. I swallowed, desperately trying to ignore the lingering feeling of his touch against my skin. "Alright then, thank you."

"You bought it."

"Yes, but not for myself."

"Just eat the damn square."

He grinned as he brought the piece of chocolate up to his mouth and bit off the corner. I blatantly stared as he did it— barely breathing as his even teeth cut through the thin square. I watched his face, the way his brow furrowed at the taste and his jaw moved as he chewed. He chewed it a few times, then swallowed, and looked back down at the rest of it.

"So?" I asked, leaning toward him in anticipation.

"It's sweet," he answered. "This is bad for you, isn't it?"

"It certainly isn't good if you eat a lot of it."

I took a bite of my own piece, and he watched me much the way I had watched him. His eyes flicked to my fangs as I opened my mouth, circling my face briefly before returning to my lips to watch me chew.

"Seems to be the way the world works," he said as he turned back to his own chocolate, and I couldn't help but feel like we were somehow sitting even closer than when we'd first sat down. "Anything that tastes good is bound to kill you."

"I'm glad you like it."

"I'm glad you brought it."

We both ate the rest of our pieces, then Warren carefully wrapped up the bar to take home to his sister.

"So, how's the Jane Doe case going?"

"Not great," I admitted as I let out a heavy breath. "Hakim managed to get another resource approved for surveillance. The officer has been staking out the apartment of our only lead, but nothing's come of it. There haven't been any more dead bodies, which on the one hand is good, but on the other, our prime suspect might be on to us and might have moved the operation, which lessens the chances of us catching the people involved. Especially since the case is going to be ripped away in November after the election. On top of that, Hakim's trust in me is shaken. My old patrol partner made a comment suggesting that I'm upset at the ridiculous hours I'm working – and she hinted that I'm talking about the case outside of work too."

"She said that to your partner?"

"In front of him," I sighed, my body sagging as I pushed some of the loose strands of hair that had broken free of my braid away from my face. "He hasn't kicked me to the curb yet or cut back my working hours, but he's been keeping me at arm's length since it happened. Honestly, I think he's dragging this Dolan case out on purpose. Jonathan probably could have booked the insurance inspection sooner, but I guess Hakim mentioned that monitoring for a few days more would be worth it, even though we all know the data is useless. But it keeps me busy while he runs the Jane Doe case largely by himself. I still help a little, but mostly just paper-pushing and grunt work.

"I think I'm just going to have to find some more time to spend with her," I said, my voice growing quiet. "Even though I don't have the time with everything else going on – let alone the fact that I don't want to. But cutting Grace out of my life would probably cause me more problems, so I'm just going to have to find a way to manage all this."

"How much sleep are you getting?"

His voice was low, and it almost looked like there was concern in his eyes as I turned to face him.

"Two hours," I said. "One and a half some nights."

"Is that maintainable?"

"No," I answered honestly, giving him a tired smile. "Not long term, but I'm alright for now. I promise – I'm not going to go depraved on you. I can handle it."

"I know."

Even though our relationship had crossed into strange new territory over the last few days, I hadn't been expecting him to blatantly voice any confidence in my abilities. He'd always maintained a level of distrust toward me, and while it hurt, I tried not to take it too personally. I knew it was simply because I was a Reborn. So hearing his words now, hearing him outwardly express that confidence, it was like someone had lifted a giant weight from my shoulders, and I felt my heart flutter.

I stared at him in silence as the slow drizzle of rain that had been falling all day started to grow. His eyes were skimming over my face again, and I could feel my chest growing tight as I tried and failed to think of something to say. I could hear the thunder getting louder as the rainstorm grew closer, the heat radiating from him getting warmer as my brain hyper-fixated on just how close he was. My eyes dropped to his mouth, tracing over his lips and all the dangerous thoughts that I had been pushing from my mind began to creep in once more as my hands began to tremble.

Then something buzzed, and the moment was instantly broken. Warren dropped his gaze to his right as he fished his phone from his pocket.

"Is everything alright?"

"Yeah." He nodded, quickly typing something in reply. "Just an update from my dad – nothing to worry about."

"Okay."

"But I should head back," Warren said, and I felt my heart sink. "It's supposed to get worse, and the river might flood if this doesn't let up."

I nodded, carefully pulling myself from the ground and avoiding his gaze as I fought to steady the tremble of my hands so I could pull on my wet gloves. But no matter how hard I tried, I couldn't seem to stop shaking.

Did he look forward to seeing me the same way I looked forward to seeing him? Did he wish the days were endless so we could stay here forever, talking as the sun was frozen just above the treeline? Did he feel this strange pull too?

I finally got my gloves on and then knelt down to help Warren transfer the supplies. Twice more our fingers touched, and each time it just made the tightness in my chest worse until I finally shouldered my empty bag and grabbed my helmet from the ground.

"Corvus."

I turned, forcing myself to meet his warm brown eyes again. "Yes?"

He stepped closer, and I stilled. He was looking at me carefully, but I couldn't decipher the expression on his face.

"Let me know if you need anything," he finally said. "If you need a day off, we can always skip a supply drop so you can sleep. It isn't a problem."

"Okay." I nodded, my voice much quieter than usual. "I will – but I'm alright, really."

"Alright."

I stared at him a moment longer, until another rumble of thunder rolled across the sky. Then I turned away, pulling my helmet over my head as I set out through the rain.

SATURDAY, OCTOBER 17
5:53 PM

I wiped away the streams of water that poured down my visor as I darted down the sopping wet hiking trail toward the parking lot. It was nearly impossible to see, and I was tired of wearing it, so I ripped it off as I ran and let out a sigh of relief. The sun was nearly set. The woods were getting darker. Even though I doubted anyone would be venturing out for an evening stroll during a rainstorm, I needed to leave as quickly as possible. Traffic along the dock roads and surrounding area would soon be increasing, and I wanted to avoid being seen as much as possible. Besides, my boots and pants were covered in mud, my vest and jacket were drenched, and I was excited to get home and take a shower.

I was just glad that I had taken the time to store my phones in plastic bags before heading out.

After speaking with Warren yesterday afternoon, I'd returned home and immediately got to work. I'd spent hours digging into Natasha Lionetti and slipped into work to download traffic camera footage near her home on the lower west side. Thankfully,

Hakim wasn't there when I showed up, so I spent a few extra minutes in the boardroom looking up her records and saving copies onto disks. I ignored Grace's mid-night phone call, allowing it to go to voicemail instead. I listened to it when I got home and learned that Grace had apparently gotten us onto the reservation waitlist at that new restaurant.

I crashed just before dawn, falling asleep on my table until nearly noon, only waking because my pen fell to the floor. At which point, I found I had two missed calls from Hawthorne, one from my mother, and three unread texts from Grace, but looking at the notifications just made my stomach churn, so I ignored them all. I scarfed down more cubes, making a mental note to eat something more substantial when I got back home, then I ran around my small apartment, preparing to venture out into the rain.

It didn't matter that I was still tired; I knew I couldn't miss the opportunity that the horrible weather presented.

The docks were always less busy during the day, even less so on the weekends, and with the heavy rain, I knew my tracks would be washed away and there would be no one around. I would be able to get closer than ever before, so I planned to use the opportunity to move my sensors, swap hard drives, and investigate the Lionetti docks as much as possible.

Now, as I tossed my bag into the backseat of my car and pushed the loose strands of wet hair away from my face, I knew my efforts had been worth it. Five of the roughly twenty warehouses I was investigating seemed to be abandoned. The doors on all four sides were boarded and bolted shut, and I doubted anyone would be using them any time soon—even to illegally transport humans. There were no security cameras on the buildings, several of the windows were broken, and they were much too visible from the main road.

That left just over fifteen more warehouses to vet between now and the end of the month.

I sighed as I climbed into my car. It wasn't a lot of time to figure this out, especially since we still didn't know what night the humans would be arriving at the warehouse or leaving the docks. It could be October 31st, or it could be the 22nd—or any day in between or before. "The end of the month" was vague and I didn't like it. I would need to come back here tomorrow, spend the day crawling through the next section of ditch and see if I could spare a few of the days this upcoming week to continue my efforts. I didn't like the idea of poking around during the work week, but I didn't have many other options. I just had to hope that Hakim didn't call me in for anything over the next little while.

I made it into my apartment parking garage before my phone started to ring. I groaned as I quickly backed into my space and yanked the plastic bag from my drenched vest.

"Hello?" I said, trying to make my voice sound tired.

'Hey,' came Hawthorne's reply. *'Where have you been?'*

"I haven't been anywhere." I faked a yawn as I got out of my car and quietly gathered my gear from the backseat. "I just woke up."

There was silence on the other end of the phone, and I checked to make sure the call hadn't dropped as I made my way into the stairwell.

'I see.'

His voice sounded flat, and uneasiness inched its way down my spine. It was bad enough that Grace was annoyed and interfering and making comments in front of Hakim. I didn't need Hawthorne getting upset with me, too, or becoming any more suspicious.

"I saw you called." I said. "Did you want to hang out?"

I didn't have time to, but maybe if I set a date, Hawthorne would let some of my odd behaviours and neglect of our friendship go.

'Actually, I wanted to talk to you about last week,' Hawthorne said, and my heart faltered. *'And Grace said she couldn't get a hold of you last night.'*

"Yes," I said, my brain racing to come up with an excuse as I took two steps at a time and ran the rest of the way up to the seventh floor. "I know. I'll call her tonight to explain – Hakim asked me to come in, and I was swamped all night. He kept me there until nearly noon, then I passed out when I got home."

I stopped at the door to my floor, juggling my gear bag, helmet, and phone so I could reach for the handle.

"I think Grace was right. I need a night off," I said, an awkward laugh leaving my lips as I tried to downplay my continued unreliability. But he didn't laugh. He didn't say anything, and at his silence, I decided to change tactics. "I'm sorry for being so flakey. Things have just been crazy with these Jane Doe cases. But once the Dolan case closes out, things should get a bit easier. I'll have more time, and maybe I'll have the energy to hang out after work."

I finally shoved the stairwell door open and made my way onto my floor.

'Sure.'

Hawthorne's voice seemed to echo as I raced down the hall, then turned the corner and immediately came to a stop.

My throat went dry. My heart dropped like a stone in my chest. I could feel water dripping down the back of my shirt as two trails slid from my hair and ran along the side of my face.

"Or maybe," Hawthorne said as he ended the call and lowered the phone to his side. "You'll keep spending your days sneaking around and lying to your friends about where you are."

I swallowed, my arm dropping to my side as I stared at Hawthorne. He was standing in front of my apartment door, holding a cardboard tray with two paper cups.

"Hawthorne, I—"

I didn't know what I was planning to say, but whatever it was, it didn't come out. My voice cut off, and I could feel a dull tremble starting to shake through my bones. My eyes darted to my apartment door, then to each side as I tried to find a rational response. I knew he wasn't going to leave no matter what I said, and he would want an explanation that I just couldn't give him. I heard the familiar rattle of the elevator down the hall, and my panic grew. It might still be early evening by civilian Reborn standards, but it was late enough that people were up and moving around, and whatever conversation was about to happen, I didn't want to have it in the hallway.

I swallowed hard once more, then forced my legs to move toward the door as I juggled everything I was holding into one arm so I could pull out my keys. Hawthorne didn't say a word as I moved past him, and I tried to ignore the water dripping into my eyes as my heart started to beat dangerously fast. I unlocked the door, willing my brain to come up with something— anything—any reasonable excuse for me to be covered in mud and drenched head to toe as I shoved the door open and stepped inside.

"I went for a run."

It was weak; even I knew that.

"Yeah – and I just got promoted to captain," Hawthorne said, shutting the door behind him with a heavy thud. "Gorski, what the hell is going on?"

"Nothing."

I dropped my bag and helmet on the floor, but I didn't even get the chance to reach down to unlace my boots because Hawthorne grabbed my shoulder and spun me around.

"Nothing?" he said, disbelief tugging hard on each accentuated syllable. "Are you kidding me?"

"I don't know what you want me to say, Hawthorne." I pulled his hand from my shoulder and stepped back. "It's true."

"Bullshit." He dropped the tray of teas on the small table near the door. "Don't lie to me."

"I'm not lying."

"Yes, you are!" Hawthorne yelled, and his indignation only seemed to make my own grow. "If you were out for a run, you would have just told me! Why the hell would you lie to me about just waking up?"

"That's none of your business!" I snapped. "I don't owe you an explanation for what I do in my spare time!"

Hawthorne stiffened, and I could see the hurt forming across his face as the crease between his brows grew deeper.

"I know that," Hawthorne said, and the low tone of his voice made my heart falter. "I know that you don't owe me anything, Valya, but you are my friend, and I do care about you. I called you because I was here knocking on your door and you didn't answer. Just like how you didn't answer the last time I stopped by or the time before that. I know Hakim is working you to the bone – so I wanted to make sure you were alright and that you're not spinning yourself down into a depraved state, just like you did for me three months ago."

I swallowed, my shoulders dropping as his gaze trailed over my face.

"I don't know what's going on," Hawthorne said as he took a small step forward. "I don't know why you're never home, why you're always tired, and why you're out crawling through mud in the middle of the day. I don't know why you're avoiding Lexie, why you're avoiding me, or why you won't talk about the farms or what happened the night we went hunting. I don't know why you lied about being called into work this weekend—"

"I didn't lie abo—"

"Yes, you did." Hawthorne cut me off. "I know you did because I had to go in to complete my firearms testing, and you weren't there. You've parked in the same space for years, Valya, and your car wasn't there."

A million excuses tumbled through my mind, each one more pathetic than the last. I opened my mouth, closed it, then opened it again as the pressure that constantly seemed to be sitting on my chest swelled and ignited like a ball of fire.

I couldn't do this.

There was nothing I could say to make this right. Nothing I could do to make him let it go. The only tangible option I had to resolve this was continual denial backed with cutting and nasty remarks to get him to leave—and I couldn't do it. He didn't deserve that, and more importantly, I didn't want to.

Hawthorne was my friend.

Likely my only real friend in this messed-up world.

He had saved my life in the Academy. He was the only person in Carneth I felt I could remotely relate to, and I didn't want to lose him. Yet I knew there was no way I could keep him in my life without hurting him or ruining his life.

My head started to shake as I stared up at him, a dull thudding pain making its way through my chest.

"Valya," Hawthorne said, his voice getting softer. "What's going on?"

I shook my head harder, my hands trembling at my side.

"Hawthorne—" My voice came out broken, and to my horror, my eyes started to sting. "I – I can't."

"Are you in trouble?"

"No."

"Is someone hurting you?" His voice grew serious. "Is someone blackmailing you?"

Of course he would think that. Those were known problems for detectives in Carneth but making him believe that wouldn't help me either. Hawthorne would just try to help and pressure me to talk to Mallick.

"No."

"Why are you covered in mud?"

"I went for a run."

"Please don't lie to me," he pleaded as he took one final step closer.

"I can't tell you," I whispered, and my jaw clenched shut as the fire burning in my chest began to scorch the back of my throat. I was going to be sick. Just like when I had puked outside the cave and Warren had dragged me into the shelter of the shade.

"Valya." I watched his hand lift from his side, then felt it grip my shoulder once more. "Please."

I knew he could feel me trembling. I knew he was worried. It was written all over his face as he looked down at me, his pale green eyes circling mine in concern, searching for an answer that might make sense in all this madness.

"You don't owe me an explanation," Hawthorne said. "But you don't have to do this alone. Whatever it is – I can help you. You can tell me."

"I can't," I whispered. "It's dangerous. I don't want you to get involved."

"Let me decide that for myself."

"You could lose your job. You could lose everything."

"I don't care," Hawthorne whispered. "You can tell me, and I can help you. I promise you, Valya. Whatever it is, it's okay."

His voice was gentle, the cold pressure of his hand against my shoulder like an anchor, steadying me from the storm that raged within my chest. And even though my hands wouldn't stop shaking, and my throat burned as if it had been drenched with acid, I found the unspeakable words falling from my lips as my body made the decision for me—reaching for the safety line he had extended and offloading some of the weight that had been crushing me alive.

"I met a human," I whispered, Hawthorne's body stilling at my words. "And I've been helping him."

Allies

"How long has this been going on?"

I stared at the paper cup gripped between my hands. I could see the dull tremble that still lingered in each finger. My heart was still beating much too quickly, and my head felt like it had just been stuffed underwater. Hawthorne's voice was distorted, and he looked blurry in my peripherals, yet I knew he was staring at me. Waiting. Still looking for the explanation that I didn't know how to give.

I had just exposed myself—cracked under pressure—and told Hawthorne that I was helping humans because I was more exhausted and desperate than I wanted to admit. Yet as each minute ticked by, I just felt sicker than ever.

My eyes dropped to the worn surface of my table, and I swallowed back the bile that kept creeping up my throat.

I was putting Warren at risk. Anything I told Hawthorne could be used against Warren and his family and completely ruin everything that we had worked for. And yet, as my eyes slowly drifted up to meet Hawthorne's gaze, a part of me couldn't help but wonder if this had been inevitable. After all, it was Hawthorne that had led me down this path. It was his words that had stilled my hand the day I'd met Warren, and if there was ever another Reborn to understand, it might be him.

He hadn't run when I'd whispered the truth. He hadn't called Mallick and reported me, and he hadn't berated me or immediately started asking why. Instead, he'd just stood there, gripping my shoulder tight as he looked down at me with an unreadable expression, then let out a heavy sigh. He'd led me toward the table, pulled out my chair, and told me to sit before moving back to the door to grab the tray of teas that he had brought with him.

That had been ten minutes ago. Now, after it was clear I wasn't going to say anything else, he was prodding. I dropped my eyes back to the table, the shake in my hands getting worse as I gripped the cup tighter.

"July," I whispered.

"Before we went hunting?"

"Yes."

Silence followed, and I tried not to fidget in my seat as I anticipated the blow of his anger.

"Valya." The soft tone of his voice startled me, and when I glanced up, I found not frustration across his face but a deep look of sadness instead. "Why didn't you tell me?"

"What was I supposed to say?"

"You could have started with, 'guess what, I met a human'. It would have at least opened up the conversation."

"It isn't that simple."

"Then explain it to me. I promise I can keep up."

"I can't," I said, leaning back in my seat and letting out a sigh. "Anything I tell you puts him at risk. It puts you at risk, and it—"

"You don't trust me," Hawthorne said, a small scoff leaving his lips as he shook his head. "After everything we've been through and what I told you back in July?"

"I'm saying it's dangerous."

"And I'm saying I don't care," Hawthorne said as he leaned forward and fixed me with a serious stare. "I told you three months ago that I was doubting everything. I told you I was in touch with that human rights activist, and I told you I didn't want to kill any humans when you begged me to go on that hunting trip. Did it not once in the last three months cross your mind that I might be on the same page as you?"

Hawthorne let out a frustrated groan, dropping his head into his hands and threading his fingers through his hair as his entire body sagged under an invisible weight.

"I haven't eaten a single human product since I spoke to that young woman at the protests," Hawthorne whispered, and the tremble in my hands stilled. "I can't. I can't even look at the stuff after what she told me. I signed the petition they had against the ag-gag law, and I've had to back out of three dinners at my parents' just to avoid this thing entirely – not to mention avoiding the meals that were ordered in for day shift OT. Do you have any idea how difficult it is to dodge around that without anyone noticing? Then again, you probably do. You know what some of the officers in our precinct are like."

I watched him let out a sigh as he straightened and met my gaze.

"Whatever it is that you've gotten involved in, I want in – because I'm already in it, Valya," Hawthorne said, and his voice sounded agonized. "I can't go back to how things were. I need to know – I need to know what they're like. If they really are as clever and intelligent as that girl told me they are."

He held my gaze, his eyes willing me to speak.

"Please," he whispered. "I have to know."

The silence between us stretched. I felt like I could hear time slowing down, as if I could see the world coming to a head—two different roads mapped out before me.

One where I was alone, exhausted, terrified, and struggling.

And one where Hawthorne stood by my side, helping to share the weight.

Before I could even rethink it, my body made the decision for me for the second time. My mouth opened, and the words tumbled out.

"The wild humans who live in the woods are nothing like the stock kept at the farms," I murmured, and Hawthorne immediately leaned forward, hanging on my every word. "Wild humans are larger. Stronger. Clever and articulate. The first time

I met one, I found him stuck in a foothold trap while I was collecting sensor data by the Dolan farm. I freed him instead of turning him in. Then I went back out into the woods a few hours later to help him. I stitched his leg closed and gave him some supplies.

"In a matter of ten seconds, he disarmed me, pinned me to the ground, disassembled my firearm, stole my helmet, and tossed all my gear out into the woods. Leaving me stuck in the shade of a small rock cutout with no way of leaving," I said. "That was the first time I met Aries."

"What happened the second time you met him?" Hawthorne asked, his words nearly breathless.

"He pointed a rifle at my head and nearly shot me." A small smile touched my lips. It almost felt like a fond memory now. "But a lot has changed since then."

"Tell me." Hawthorne leaned even further across the table. "What are things like now?"

I let out a quiet breath, wondering what the hell I was doing and if I was about to make the biggest mistake of my life. But as I stared at my friend, at the blatant and almost desperate curiosity burning in his eyes, I knew in my heart that it was honest, and he would never turn me in.

So I told him.

I told Hawthorne everything.

He sat there quietly, barely breathing as I recalled the night that I had found Warren trapped, my hectic coverup of his existence, and my decision to go back and help him. I described how warm he was, how hot his blood had been when it had covered my hands, and how the entire ordeal had left me terrified. I told him how I'd tracked him down. How after the hunt in the woods with Vogle, seeing my partner kill that human woman in cold blood, and going to Grace's party and listening to people talk about upholstery, I'd known I had to find him again.

I'd known I had to help.

I told him about our meetings, but I didn't tell him everything that Warren had said to me. I left out large pockets of conversation. At first I thought I was censoring my words because I wanted to show Warren in the best light possible as I tried my hardest to explain his anger and frustration toward our people. But the more I talked, the more I realized that wasn't the only reason why I was editing my words. I was censoring them because they felt private.

Warren had shared details of his life with me and information about his village, just as I had done with him. We had talked for hours, sometimes about things completely unrelated to our task, and sharing those words with Hawthorne not only felt like a violation of Warren's privacy, but it also made me feel uneasy and awkward. I didn't know what Hawthorne would think. This whole situation was difficult enough as it was, so I wasn't about to tell him that Warren had become something much more to me than an acquaintance.

Something more to me than just a casual friend.

More than even I had realized until this moment.

So I skipped all of those details, telling him only the information pertinent to our main interactions and the things we had been working on. I told him about the code names, never once using Warren's real name and telling him I was always addressed as Corvus. I told him that I helped Warren plan the break into the Dolan farm facility and that humans under a certain age could be rehabilitated to join the groups that lived in the woods. I told him how I had misdirected Hakim's investigation, destroyed evidence, and sent Precinct 15 on a wild goose chase after a sketchy white van.

I told him about Scott Beckette and the human trafficking. How it was my latest mission with Warren and how it was consuming all my time. I told him about the stolen sensors, how I was using Grace's login information to download traffic camera footage, and that I was constantly driving out to the woods to drop off supplies and information. Then I explained that I had been down by the dock warehouses all day, crawling through the ditch as I desperately tried to narrow them down—that was why I was never home and why I was in such a dishevelled state.

By the time I finished talking, the mud caking my boots and pants had dried into a stiff layer that cracked and fell apart anytime I moved my legs. My hair was no longer dripping, and small, damp tendrils were now glued to the sides of my face. My voice sounded hoarse, and my eyes felt dry, but for the first time in weeks, I actually felt like I could breathe outside of the woods. As if the weight on my shoulders had lessened just a fraction, and it no longer felt like I was being ripped in two.

"So that's it," I said, letting out an exhausted breath and staring at the blank expression on Hawthorne's face. "That's what I've been doing. That's why I haven't been home when you've stopped by. That's why I've been blowing off Grace. That's why I'm covered in mud, and that's why I didn't want to tell you. Because it's dangerous. It could cost you your job, land you in jail, or worse, get you killed.

"It was never about me not trusting you," I said, my voice growing quieter as the tension in my shoulders finally started to fall away. "I just couldn't risk getting you involved. I couldn't do that to you. You're my friend, Hawthorne, and I didn't want to get you tangled up in my mess."

Hawthorne stared at me for a moment, then his eyes creased, and he let out a heavy sigh.

"You're such an idiot sometimes, Gorski," he said, shaking his head.

"How am I an idiot?"

"I want in."

My mouth fell open, and I stared at him in disbelief.

"Did you not listen to a word of anything I just said? Hawthorne—"

"I heard everything that you said." He cut me off. "And you're an idiot, and I want in."

"You could lose your job!" I immediately shook my head in rejection. "This is dangerous – you could die!"

"All the more reason why you could use some help."

"Theo," I said, all but glaring at him from across the table. "I'm not joking."

"Clearly," he laughed. "What is that, like the fourth time you've ever addressed me by my given name?"

"Hawthorne," I stressed. "I'm serious."

"And so am I," he said, his pale green eyes growing hard as his deep voice took on a hint of annoyance. "I know you helped me through some aspects of the Academy, Valya, but it isn't your job to take care of me or keep me out of dangerous situations. I want in because I want in – because I give a shit – and as I already told you, I can't go back to pretending like I don't know what's happening. It isn't right, and I want to help.

"And from the sounds of things, you and your human friend could use another set of eyes and ears. You're walking a thin line. I can see it, and it won't take long before Hakim or Vogle or someone else at the precinct starts to notice it too. You need to get more sleep. You need to make sure that you're still eating. Synthetic foods aren't directly comparable to the real thing, which means you need to eat more of it to make up the difference, and I doubt you've been doing that because it's a rough adjustment to make, and you don't have the time for proper meals with all the running around you're doing.

"I can help with that," Hawthorne said, his voice taking on an almost pleading tone as he leaned forward and reached across the table. My eyes dropped down to my hands, to the long, thin fingers that were now clutching my own, and all I could think about was how cold they were in comparison to Warren's. "We can take shifts down by the docks. That way, you can monitor what's going on every day. And I can help you gather supplies. You can show me the route through the ditch and how to get to your drop points. I can use my access to get more traffic footage, and I can swap my patrol route to the southeast side so I can scope things out at night too.

"I won't tell anyone, and you know that," Hawthorne said as he squeezed my hands tight. "You know I'm good at my job. You know people talk to me and tell me what's going on. I can be your ears in Patrol. I can be your second set of eyes."

"Hawthorne, I—"

"I'm not asking because I feel obligated or because I think you need my help. I know you, and I know you can manage this," Hawthorne said, a small, almost sad smile touching his lips. "I'm offering because I want to, and it has nothing to do with you. Had I been out there and met that human – I would have done exactly the same thing you did. So, please, Valya. Please let me help you. You don't have to do this on your own. I want to help."

I stared at him, my heart beating much too quickly again as a million more thoughts fluttered through my mind.

Could I really let him help? Let him sacrifice his career and life for people he didn't even know?

Telling him was one thing, but allowing him in was another. It seemed like too much. It didn't seem fair, and yet the more I considered it, it didn't seem fair for me to have told him everything that I had and then to tell him he wasn't allowed to be a part of it either. Really, had my top priority been keeping Hawthorne safe, I would have refused to allow him in my apartment after he'd caught me in a lie, and I would have ended the friendship right then and there for his own benefit.

But I hadn't.

I'd let him in because I had selfishly wanted to keep him in my life. Then, I'd gone another step further and unveiled a plethora of secrets that could ruin his life if he was found to be participating in my illegal activities. The second he'd crossed the threshold of my apartment, he was involved, and there was no going back. I had officially ruined his life and changed the course of his future. Refusing him any say or involvement going forward would be not only insulting to his integrity but also to his autonomy.

I let out a heavy sigh, gripping his hands in return as I all but slumped down against the table.

"Fine," I whispered, and his eyes brightened as a huge smile split across his face. "But I have to okay it with Aries first."

"Alright." He nodded easily, agreeing instantly without complaint. "How – how do you do that?"

"I text him," I said, pulling my hands from his and bringing them up to my vest.

"He texts?"

I nodded, unsurprised by the surprise in his voice as I unzipped my vest and pulled out the plastic bag housing my tiny black flip phone. Hawthorne watched in tense silence, almost as if he was expecting something extraordinary to happen when I pulled out the old phone and flipped it open. Of course nothing did. I simply punched in the lock pin, opened the messages, and began drafting a note to Warren.

It took me a bit to decide where to start. I hadn't messaged him in hours, and I didn't think that explaining what had just happened over text was appropriate, so I went with something more normal.

> C: Staked out the docks today.
>
> Made some progress narrowing it down.

I sent the message, counting in my head as I stared at the screen, and Hawthorne waited patiently across the table. Twenty seconds later, Warren's reply came in, and the way Hawthorne abruptly sat up straight as a rod in his seat, you would think the buzz of my phone was an interview.

> A: Good. What's it down to now?
>
> C: Just over fifteen.
>
> Still lots more to go.
>
> A: True, but it's progress.
>
> C: I guess so.
>
> Any word from up north?
>
> A: Nothing yet. Still no movement.
>
> C: Well, at least there's that.
>
> A: My sister loved the chocolate by the way.

My lips twitched, and I had to fight to keep the smile off my face.

> C: I'm glad! I'll have to bring more.
>
> A: Alright, but not too much.
>
> Don't want to spoil her more than she already is.

I cleared my throat, trying to hide the second smile as I hesitated. A huge part of me didn't want to say what I needed to say. I liked it the way that it was with just Warren and I working together, and I didn't want it to change. But Hawthorne wasn't wrong. His help would be invaluable, and it would increase our chances of being successful. I had no control over the workload Hakim gave me, and without Hawthorne, I might fail at finding the warehouse in time.

Objectively speaking, not accepting Hawthorne's help would be incredibly foolish. And I was fairly certain that if Orion found out he had the opportunity to gain another resource and I had turned it down on his behalf without even offering it up to him as an option first, he wouldn't be happy. Orion was a logical man, and this, even though it worried me, was logical. We needed all the reliable help we could get, and Hawthorne was reliable. We could trust him.

Or maybe I was just trying to convince myself.

I let out a breath, shoving the thoughts away. They weren't helping, and what was done was done. I had to tell Warren.

C: I'll make sure to bring some for you, too.

So you don't feel left out or steal your sister's.

A: Ha ha.

So thoughtful of you.

C: There's something I wanted to run by you.

A: New stakeout plans?

C: No, actually I think it's something that will better our chances.

A: Alright, I'm game.

What's the idea?

C: I have a friend who could be used as a potential resource.

They're trustworthy. I would trust them with my life.

CPD officer, too, so they have access to stuff.

And they can get on night-shift patrols by the dock.

It would better our chances of finding the warehouse.

And they would help with the counter-mission.

Would you and Orion be interested in meeting/vetting them?

Silence rang in my ears. I stared at my screen as I counted the seconds and waited for him to respond. Thirty seconds went by, then fifty. I tried to convince myself it was because Warren was probably speaking with his father and deciding what to do, but when a minute with no reply hit, I started to fidget.

I scrunched my toes in my boots, suddenly realizing I was still wearing them and how damp and stiff and uncomfortable I was in these clothes as Hawthorne remained deathly silent across from me. I struggled not to fidget as I waited, gripping the phone tight between my thin fingers until it finally buzzed. A full three minutes after my last message.

> A: Bring them to the cave tonight.
>
> 10 pm.
>
> No weapons, and blindfold them on the way out.

My shoulders dropped, and my eyes fell closed as I let out an audible sigh of relief.

> C: Alright.
>
> Need me to bring anything?
>
> A: No.

He didn't write anything after, and even though I was relieved that he and Orion were willing to meet Hawthorne, I couldn't help but feel a bit uneasy at the abrupt end of the conversation. Usually, Warren and I would keep texting until much later into the night, but I supposed he probably had things to do before trekking to our cave.

"So?" Hawthorne asked, his eyes brimming with hesitant optimism as I finally looked up to meet his gaze. "What's the news, Corvus? What did he say?"

"He said you can meet Orion tonight at 10 pm," I said, and Hawthorne's face split into a wide grin.

"I promise you won't regret this," he said, looking more alive and animated than he had in months. "I'm going to help – they're going to say yes – and we're going to find that warehouse."

"I hope so," I said, looking down at my phone and finding it impossible not to frown.

Everything about this was surreal and uncomfortable, and I didn't like it. I glanced at the clock; there wasn't much more than an hour before we would need to head out.

"Alright," I said, pushing back my chair. "I need to shower. I'm disgusting."

"A bit, yeah."

I turned and gave him a halfhearted glare as I stood, then pushed in my chair and made my way back to the door to take off my boots.

"Don't touch anything while I'm in the bathroom," I said as I unlaced both boots. "If anyone knocks on my door, don't answer it, and don't call me Corvus outside of this apartment or during recon by the docks, and never on the phone or anything traceable back to you."

"Got it." He nodded, his expression becoming serious again. "But have you eaten?"

"Uh—" I thought back, trying to recall the last time I'd had anything substantial.

"I'll take that as a no," Hawthorne said, standing and pulling his keys from his pocket. "And I doubt you have anything here to make."

I frowned but didn't bother denying what we both knew was true.

"I'll run out and grab something quick." He made his way toward me. "Go shower – do you have any spare keys?"

"Uh, yes." I hesitated, and he gave me a look.

"I'm not going to keep them," Hawthorne said. "And I won't make a copy of them either."

My eyes darted to the door.

"And I'm coming back," Hawthorne said as if he knew exactly what I was thinking. He took a step toward me, meeting my gaze with another serious expression. "Valya – I'm not going to tell anyone. I'm not leaving so that I can go turn you in. I would call and order food here, but it's Saturday, and ordering takeout will take too long, and you need to eat something."

I sighed, nodding my head in defeat because he was right.

"I know."

I stepped around him, not worrying about leaving more mud on my floors because they were already a mess, and made my way into the kitchen. I opened the first cupboard, fishing out the second set of keys I had on a small hook.

"Here." I tossed him the keys. "Don't forget to lock the door behind you."

"I won't."

He smiled, hesitating a moment before rapidly walking toward me and pulling me into a tight hug. I stiffened in surprise, my body awkwardly pressed against his, my arms sticking out at odd angles, until I finally remembered I was supposed to do something in return and clumsily patted him on the back.

"You're bad at hugging," he said, and my gentle pat turned into a thump that made him grunt. "But thank you."

He pulled back, hands gripping my shoulders as he looked down at me with a strange expression.

"Thank you for letting me in," he said. "I promise you won't regret it. Now go shower – you smell horrible."

"You're such an ass," I said, but I couldn't help the smile that touched my lips as he gave me a lopsided grin.

Then I kicked off my boots and made my way to the bathroom.

SATURDAY, OCTOBER 17
9:40 PM

"So, did you really text your human accomplice and set up a meeting, or are you just leading me out into the woods so you can have your way with me?"

I groaned, pushing Hawthorne forward and resisting the urge to smack him.

"You know, if you have a blindfold kink, Gorski, you could have just told me, and we could have gone down the hall to your – OW, hey! I can't see, remember?"

"Then don't be gross," I said, grabbing his vest to steady him after having shoved him forward another three feet.

"In all seriousness, though, I feel a bit sick," Hawthorne said, his lips twisting into a frown below the scarf that was wrapped around his eyes. "Riding in the car with this on was awful."

"I know." I directed him around a small divot in the ground. "Sorry about that, but it's just a precaution for their safety."

"It's alright. I just feel really weird with it on. I know you're there and everything, but it feels like I'm alone, and I don't know. It's just unsettling."

I nodded in understanding, then realized he couldn't see me and verbally agreed.

Everything about this was unsettling.

While I had never truly feared for my life in Warren's presence or felt threatened by the woods, it was the first time that I was making my way out here without my badge, firearm, or my gear bag stuffed to the brim, and I didn't like it. All I had was my vest, strapped securely on top of my thin, long-sleeved shirt, and the sensor hard drive in my otherwise empty bag. I didn't even have my helmet on because it was well past sunset. I carried it in my free hand, just as Hawthorne carried his—except his nails were cutting marks into the black carbon fibre.

It was the most nervous I had ever seen him outside of the two times I'd nearly died in front of him and that night back in July when he'd told me about his fears. It felt strange to see him like this, but then again, it had also felt weird to come out of my bedroom and find him sweeping my kitchen floor.

"I know you said not to touch anything," he had said almost sheepishly. "But I got back before you were out of the shower, so I went looking for a broom. I swear I only looked in the kitchen closet – I didn't go snooping around."

I had thanked him for cleaning up most of the mud, then eaten the food he had picked up. He'd already eaten his, so he paced back and forth in my kitchen as he waited, watching me eat. Then we quickly packed up and got ready to head out. I told him to grab his vest from the gear bag in his car but made him leave his firearm and badge at my apartment in my lockbox. He didn't question me when I pulled out the scarf and wrapped it around his head before leaving the parking garage, and the ride out into the country had been mostly silent.

Now it seemed he couldn't stop talking.

"So," Hawthorne said, turning his head in my direction, "what are they like?"

"They're remarkably like us," I said, thinking of how best to describe Warren and his people. "Just a little shorter, and they don't burn in the sunlight."

"Convenient," Hawthorne mused, then a small smile crossed his lips. "Shorter than you?"

I groaned, shoving him again. "Can you please take this seriously?"

"I am." Hawthorne slowed to a stop, turning to face me completely. "I'm sorry – I'm just nervous."

"It's fine," I sighed, dropping my hold on him to push some loose tendrils of hair away from my face. "I was nervous the first time I met Aries and even more nervous when I met Orion. But it's going to be okay. Just – keep in mind what I said."

"About them not liking us?"

"It's more than that," I said. "Some of them *hate* us, Hawthorne, and the way they will look at you, it – it isn't always easy, but you just have to remember it isn't personal. It's not about you."

"Right." Hawthorne nodded. "But you and Aries are on good terms now?"

"Yes," I answered, smiling because I didn't have to worry about Hawthorne seeing it. "We get along pretty well now."

"Okay." He nodded again, but I could hear the nervousness lingering in his voice. "Is there anything I should do – or not do, for that matter?"

"Keep your hands open and down by your sides," I said, thinking back to what Warren had told me the night I'd met Orion. "We didn't bring weapons, but some of them will view you as a threat regardless. Orion won't be afraid of you, and neither will Aries."

"How many of them will be there?"

"I'm not sure. When I met Orion, there were three others there."

"Okay," Hawthorne said, taking a deep breath. "It will be fine."

"It will," I agreed. "Just don't insult their intelligence by assuming they don't know things or that they don't understand what you're saying. Don't treat them any differently than how you would treat a fellow officer – and speak to Orion as you would to Mallick."

"Got it. Anything else?"

"Just be you," I said, then I smiled at him and shook my head. "But I mean the real you – the serious you that's underneath the crap you show to most of the world."

He snorted and grinned at me.

"I can do that," he said, extending his hand toward me. "Lead on."

"Nice try." I swatted his hand away and grabbed the rough fabric of his vest once more.

I gave him a shove, and a small chuckle left his lungs as he staggered forward. We walked mostly in silence for another fifteen minutes, only speaking when I needed to give Hawthorne directions to step over something or duck under low-hanging tree branches. The entire time I tried to remain calm, but by the time we broke out into the rocky clearing, my heart was thudding in my chest.

I led him another twenty feet across the rocks toward the small cave, then slowed. I could already see the flicker of fire from the opening, and my discomfort grew. Warren had never set a fire in our cave before, and the idea of there being a bunch of people in our space felt weird.

"Wait here," I said, tugging Hawthorne to a stop.

"Are we there?" he asked as I set my helmet down so I could reach up to remove the scarf.

"Yes." I untied the knot behind his head, hearing the familiar movement of feet across the stone. I glanced over my shoulder. I could see Warren making his way toward us, and suddenly my throat went dry. I turned back to Hawthorne, rapidly unwrapping the scarf and dropping my voice to a whisper. "Remember what I said – treat them with respect."

"Of course I'll treat them with respect," Hawthorne muttered back. He blinked his eyes, running his hand through his hair before he looked around. Then his eyes settled on Warren's approaching figure, and he seemed to falter. "Is – is that him? Your friend?"

"Yes." I turned away, stuffing the scarf into my pocket. "Stay here."

"Okay."

Hawthorne didn't argue as I quickly grabbed my helmet off the ground and moved toward Warren.

"Warren," I said, unable to stop the smile that split across my face or the reflexive way I called him by name as I closed the distance between us, only to come to an abrupt stop when he raised his rifle.

My smile faltered.

"Aries," he corrected.

His voice was cold as he pulled a light from his pocket and clicked it on. I squinted as he shone the beam over my face and down my body. He looked tense, irritation shining in his eyes. Then his expression darkened as his eyes shifted to Hawthorne, and I felt my shoulders drop.

"Go stand with him and put your helmet on the ground," Warren said, then his hard gaze shifted back to me. "Both of you. Did you bring any weapons?"

"No," I answered, stepping back toward Hawthorne and putting my helmet on the ground beside his. I desperately tried to ignore the sinking feeling in my chest as Warren swept the light over Hawthorne's body, then my own again as if he didn't believe me. "We didn't bring anything. I just have the hard drive."

"I'll take it now," Warren said, but he kept his feet planted firmly where they were and his rifle trained on Hawthorne.

I nodded, removing my small gear bag and fishing out the hard drive. He took it when I stepped forward to hand it to him— no thank you, no brush of fingers, and no acknowledgement of any kind. Then he secured the drive into his jacket pocket before returning the spare to me. The exchange was reminiscent of some of our first interactions, and that realization hurt far worse than I had anticipated.

"Alright, let's go," Warren said, gesturing with the rifle.

I nodded again, moving ahead of him with Hawthorne so he could continue to keep us at gunpoint.

"His name is Warren?" Hawthorne whispered, but I scowled and shook my head, thankful his words wouldn't be overheard. "I thought you two were friendly."

"Be quiet," I muttered.

We walked in complete silence, nothing but the sound of the river and the crackling fire filling the air as we approached the small cave. I squinted as we stepped into the warm light, and Hawthorne's arm brushed against mine as he came to a stop by my side. My eyes darted around the cramped space, taking in three familiar figures to the right, each with their own rifle pointed in our direction.

Orion was standing in the middle next to the fire. His expression was unreadable, but his eyes were warm and deep. Warren shifted around us, face tense with visible agitation as he leaned against the left side of the cave.

He didn't lower his rifle.

"Thank you for agreeing to meet with me again, sir," I said when it became apparent that no one was going to say anything.

"Well," Orion said, "it isn't every day we receive offers for new recruits."

"This is Hawthorne," I said, gesturing to my left. "He works in the Patrol and Street department at my precinct. We went to the Academy together – I've known him for years, and he's a good man. He wants to help, and I think he would be a great asset. He can assist me with locating the warehouse and collecting supplies. He has access to the street cameras, and he's another set of eyes and ears in the CPD."

"And another potential leak," a human on the right growled.

I ignored the snide remark, it came from the same monotone-looking female who had been rude to me, so it was hardly surprising, but I felt Hawthorne tense at my side.

"He's reliable," I said, my voice firm as I held Orion's gaze. "He won't let you down."

"And how can you be so sure of that?" Orion asked, though his words didn't hold any malice, and it seemed to be a genuine question.

"Because he saved my life," I said, glancing over at Warren to find him staring at me. I swallowed, forcing my eyes back to Orion. "And I would trust him with it again."

Orion's gaze shifted to Hawthorne, trailing over his frame before finally locking to his face.

"Has Corvus told you what's involved with this operation?" Orion asked.

"Yes," Hawthorne answered. "But only in broad terms – she hasn't given me any details."

"But she's told you the risks, I assume."

"Yes, sir." Hawthorne nodded.

"Then you understand how important this is," Orion said. "And how dangerous."

"Yes, sir," Hawthorne repeated.

"And you're willing to accept that?" Orion asked, taking a step forward and arching a brow. "Willing to risk your job, your status, your life? Willing to lose everything? Willing to pick up a weapon and fight – to kill your own kind?"

"Yes," Hawthorne answered, his deep voice echoing through the small cave. "I'm willing to do whatever it takes. I can't go back to how things were – that life is already over for me. I want to help. This is something I'm meant to do, I know it. And if you give me the chance, I will prove it to you."

Orion stared at Hawthorne, the long, tense silence growing unbearable as my eyes flicked between the two of them.

"Alright," Orion said, and I exhaled in relief. "Then I accept your offer."

Orion stepped forward with his hand outstretched, and I couldn't help but smile. I turned to glance at Warren, I'm not sure why or what I was expecting, but my face fell the second I saw his expression. His warm eyes were dark with disapproval, and his jaw was clenched shut so tightly I could see the muscles twitching beneath his skin. He looked angry, but worse than that, he looked hateful.

His eyes flicked toward me, and I felt my stomach lurch.

It was the same burning gaze of hatred he had pierced me with the day I'd met him. Except this time, it felt so much worse. As if he had physically struck me, punched me straight through the chest with a burning fist of fury.

My throat started to burn, and I could feel something strange happening in the center of my chest. I forced my eyes away, turning them back to Hawthorne and Orion, who were now shaking hands, and it was at that moment I realized why humans were so afraid of us. Why that rude woman and the others hadn't taken me seriously when Warren had brought me in, but now they gripped their weapons like death. Why the tension radiating from their bodies made the air in the cave so thick I felt like I couldn't breathe. And why Warren had spat words of venom at me when he'd first met me.

Reborn were massive in comparison to humans.

I hadn't fully realized or appreciated the extent of the gap because I was an inch shorter than Warren, so while the few humans I had met were definitely notably smaller than my fellow Reborn, I hadn't seen the comparison as I was seeing it now. Hawthorne was a typical Reborn male, and he towered over Orion and the others like something from a different world. His pale skin looked solid, like porcelain, reflecting the glow of the flames in an uneven and unnerving pattern, and his eyes appeared so pale they nearly looked entirely white.

I had never seen a fellow Reborn in so much light before, and I wasn't sure what to make of it.

He was too tall. Too broad. Too strong. The difference between our two worlds was blatant and massive, and it unsettled even me.

"Have him help you locate the warehouse," Orion said, his words shaking me from my thoughts.

"Yes, sir," I responded.

"You will continue to make the supply drops to Aries as needed, but he can help you gather items."

"Yes, sir."

"And you will be the main point of contact. If anything changes or we get new information, Aries will let you know," Orion said.

I nodded, shaking Orion's outstretched hand and thanking him again for meeting us. I assured him that we would do everything that we could to find the warehouse. Then, as we turned to leave, I took one last look over my shoulder and felt a sharp stab of pain cut through my heart.

Warren was staring at me with a bitter look of hatred etched upon his face.

Problems

"This is awful."

"I know."

"How have you been crawling through this for so long?"

"I'm a lot smaller than you," I said, inching forward on my elbows until I reached the sensor. "It's easier for me, and some of the other sections aren't as bad because they're deeper, and you can crouch."

"Ugh," Hawthorne groaned as the mud from the bottom of the ditch we had just crawled through soaked into his jacket. He inched forward another two feet, dropping flat on his stomach with a small grunt. "Well, it's no wonder you smelled. The storm sewer that drains into this ditch is from the oldest southeast system, you know. I bet all kinds of shit gets dumped into it."

"Probably," I agreed as I tried to ignore the smell from the stagnant water behind us and wondered why someone hadn't invented a filter for our helmets yet while tugging the new hard drive from the small bag on my back. "But complaining won't make it any better. Just be thankful it's not hot out anymore."

"You're really not bothered by this, are you?"

"Nope." I propped myself up on one elbow so I could change out the hard drive.

"You're a champ," Hawthorne sighed, slapping me on the shoulder as he moved closer to watch what I was doing. "Now show me how it's done so we can get out of this stink pit."

I snorted, shaking my head. "We're not leaving the 'stink pit', Hawthorne. Once I change this out, we're going to make our way down another 300 metres and scope out the next set of warehouses."

"Right."

"Are you regretting your decision to help?" I asked, turning to look at him.

"No," he said firmly, and even though I couldn't see his face through the tint of his visor, I knew he was scowling. "Absolutely not. There isn't enough stink in the world to make me change my mind. Though I am a bit bummed out that I didn't get a cool code name yet."

"I'm sure you will," I said. "And pay attention because you might need to do this without me. Another body was found last night, and the Dolan insurance inspection is tonight. Hakim told me I'll be closing out the case this week and getting back to work on the Jane Does."

"Well that's good," Hawthorne said, and I nodded. "So is he happy about that? Or is he still pissed about what happened with Grace?"

"I'm not sure that Hakim has ever been happy," I muttered. "Or that he's capable of it. He seemed annoyed when he told me, but I think his hands are tied. Technically, he has no legitimate reason to dismiss me, and Vogle seems to like me – so it's probably not worth the hassle to get rid of me right now when he can use me to push papers and do his grunt work. Apparently, I'm better than no partner at all."

"Such a compliment," Hawthorne muttered.

"It's the most I'll ever get from him," I said. "But that doesn't matter – I'll do whatever he asks because I need to keep this job. Besides, it's still helping those girls, and that case needs as much help as it can get if there's to be any chance of solving it before Vogle yanks it back. But that just means that I'll be at Hakim's beck and call again twenty-four hours a night and working well into the day. I'm not sure how much time I'll have to come out here with you while doing that and making the supply runs, so you need to know how to change these."

Not that the supply runs were taking as long as they usually did…

I frowned behind my visor, trying to convince myself that Warren not showing up to the drop I'd made yesterday wasn't indicative of a bigger problem and that his short, blunt text messages meant nothing. He had every right not to trust Hawthorne immediately, and it was fair for him to be skeptical. He was also busy. We were running out of days to figure this out, and he probably didn't have time to talk and meet me at the cave.

My frown deepened as I detached the current hard drive and showed Hawthorne how to reconnect the new one and reset the sensor.

I desperately hoped that was the case, but I couldn't help but worry about the uncomfortable shift in dynamic. We had been busy before, but he had found time to meet me. Whereas yesterday, he hadn't even responded when I'd told him I was headed out to make the drop. I'd arrived to find the cave empty and reluctantly left the bag after texting Warren again to ask him if he was coming. He had responded with two simple letters:

A: No.

I'd thought about asking him why, but in the end, I'd just decided to leave. I genuinely didn't have time to linger and wait. Hawthorne was coming by so I could give him a full rundown of the mission, and I needed to stop and grab some groceries. Otherwise, I was going to wind up in serious trouble.

I let out a quiet sigh, securing the hard drive in the plastic bag to prevent it from getting covered in mud before tucking it into my small gear bag. Then I led Hawthorne back to the ditch and deeper into the mud. The crawl was long, and about ten minutes into it, the sky darkened and it began to rain. It wasn't ideal, but at least it would wash away our tracks and possibly some of the mud from our clothes before we got back to my car.

I tried not to think about Warren as Hawthorne and I spent the rest of the day in the "stink pit" and surrounding tall grass surveying the warehouses, but it was a struggle. I wondered if he would be there on Wednesday when I made the next drop. I wondered if he would write me back this evening when I texted him to tell him our findings. I wondered if his sister had tried any of her new baking supplies or if his allies in the north had found anything useful that could help us pin down a precise date. Then I wondered if we would talk again, properly, like we had before, and if the horrible mounting pressure in my chest would ever go away.

But as my clothes soaked through and grew heavier by the hour, my heart felt like it was sinking into the mud beneath me, and I found myself wondering if I had made a huge mistake that would jeopardize everything.

THURSDAY, OCTOBER 22
3:40 PM

Warren wasn't there on Wednesday when I dropped off the supplies. His texts had remained short, blunt, and bordering on rude. I felt like I had fallen back in time, starting at the beginning with our slate wiped clean and all of our progress lost.

And I didn't understand why.

I'd thought we had genuinely taken steps. That he trusted me now, trusted my judgement, and believed that I was on his side. That I would never do anything to threaten the success of our mission or his people, and that I took what we were doing seriously. I thought of him as my friend because things between us had changed.

They had become... different.

I knew Warren inherently didn't trust Reborns, but I thought he had trusted me. I knew bringing Hawthorne on board could be a mistake, but it didn't feel like it. He had already covered my surveillance two days in a row while I worked to close out the Dolan case and hand it over to Precinct 15. He helped me comb through more surveillance footage from the docks, switched his patrol route over to one on the southeast end, where he spent most of his shift circling as close to the warehouses as possible from city streets, and he had gained us valuable insight into the regular night traffic. Not to mention that he'd caught wind of another protest being organized—a big one—and he was planning to meet up with his contact from the human rights group to ask her about it so we could make sure that it didn't interfere with our work.

His help was invaluable.

We were covering twice as much ground, and I didn't understand how any of that could be a bad thing or how Warren could be so angry about it, especially since I had asked Warren if his involvement was okay. Orion had *met* Hawthorne and approved it. If they didn't want more help from Reborn or didn't trust Hawthorne to be loyal, why had they agreed to accept it?

I let out a quiet sigh.

Maybe Warren hadn't liked the idea, but his father had overruled him...

"Did you ever manage to find out who's running Natasha Lionetti's business on the night-to-night?"

I glanced up at Hawthorne. He was sitting at the other end of the table, a mess of papers sprawled out between us. It was becoming an increasingly common sight, and I wasn't sure how I felt about it. On the one hand, it was a bit too familiar and personal for my liking, having him at my apartment nearly every day this past week, touching my stuff and using my bathroom. But on the other hand, it was nice. I felt less alone, and when we worked here at the table, it reminded me of our time back in the Academy when we used to study together at the library. Back when things were much simpler.

"From what I can tell, she's the one running it," I said, dropping my head into my hand.

Looking back on how busy this week had been, I knew I wouldn't have made it this far without Hawthorne's help. He had already ruled out another two warehouses because they seemed to be getting regular shipments from Cypher, a legitimate electronics company, and from what Hawthorne could tell, the buildings were packed.

"I ran a few plates from the cars I see most often down near her docks," I continued. "One I tracked headed to her house. The name Sokolov came up, but I haven't been able to narrow it down any further than that."

"No first name?"

"No." I shook my head. "Which, if this were real CPD work, would be grounds enough to pull the cars over, bring the drivers in for questioning, and open an investigation. But that's not our situation, so despite it being illegal to register cars without an address or first name, I can't do anything with it."

"Right," Hawthorne sighed and sat back in his seat. "I feel like my hands are tied behind my back here."

"Tell me about it," I groaned. "And it's just more of the same at her warehouses – regular security dock patrols, Crosswell Transport trucks shipping products from multiple reputable companies, fork trucks coming and going, the cars of the employees working in the offices, and vans from Jensen's Janitorial, Andy's Repair Services, and Proctor Delivery – none of which tie back to her."

I let out a sigh, dropping my eyes back to the map of the docks I had been staring at for the last several minutes while trying and failing to find some sort of answer.

We still had over ten warehouses to examine, and I was doing my best to be strategic about selecting the next two to look at. I was trying to find a pattern, something to hint that one warehouse might be more likely than the other, because every time we went down there, we put ourselves at risk of being caught. We were running out of time, and the faster we narrowed this down the better.

But for every advantage I thought I saw, there were disadvantages for each warehouse based on their location, security, and the traffic data from the sensor, and I had no idea where to look next. If these were smaller warehouses, it wouldn't be such a problem. If we could get closer to them or access them via the main road without crawling through a ditch after running kilometres down a nature path and clambering down a hill, it would be easier.

But we couldn't, and some of these warehouses were the size of several small city blocks.

"I wish I could consult Hakim," I muttered, and Hawthorne snorted at my words. "He always sees patterns that I don't."

"Yeah, I'm sure that would go over swimmingly," Hawthorne said, standing from his seat to stretch as I glowered at his choice words. "How have things been going with him this week?"

"Fine," I sighed, leaning back in my seat to look at him. "So far, at least, but I'm still not back to working with him on the Jane Doe files fully. The Dolan case is set to close tomorrow. I already cleared the sensors at the second site and handed the files over to 15. I just have to go collect the equipment at the first farm tonight and bring it back. He had me scour through a few hours of traffic footage the other night to try to find something to tie Andrew Morin to the latest body and run some new plates while he canvassed the areas where previous bodies were found to see if any locals saw anything, but nothing came of it. We'll see how things go next week when I'm back to shadowing him one hundred percent."

"That sounds exhausting already."

"It is," I agreed. "But it's worth it."

"How are you going to handle the missing gear?" Hawthorne asked. "Or do you need me to pull the sensor by the docks so you can return it?"

"I already handled it," I said. "Told Hakim it was missing and blamed it on some non-existent animal."

"Perfect. What about the extra hard drive Aries has?"

I tried my best not to physically react to Warren's name, but I could feel my body tense. Hawthorne had questioned me about what had happened the night they'd met, and I had dodged answering it the best I could. I'd blamed Warren's cold, detached behaviour on the apprehension from the others in the cave, but I wasn't sure if he'd bought it.

"I'll say it went missing tomorrow when I turn in the gear."

"Won't he be mad?"

"Maybe," I said. "But we need it."

FRIDAY, OCTOBER 23
7:15 AM

Water trailed down the back of my neck under the collar of my standard-issue shirt. It didn't matter that I had worn my waterproof jacket on top of my vest. Downpours like that, the ones Carneth got during the rainy season, soak you to the bone regardless of what you're wearing. They eat through your clothing like moths, finding even the tiniest seam in your armour, then slithering in through the cracks, saturating everything, leaving it soggy, heavy, and cold.

The wind hadn't helped much, and neither had the trees. The downpour had pierced through the branches, sheets of water blasting me from all sides as I ran through the woods collecting sensors. It had taken me all night. Warren had ignored my message about meeting up while I collected them, but honestly, it was probably for the best. He might have gotten lost or washed away in the rain. The only good thing that had come of it was that I'd stolen another sensor set because I knew I would easily be able to blame the missing equipment on the weather. It was currently in the trunk of my car, carefully tucked beneath the felt fabric that lined the interior and covered the spare tire.

I wasn't expecting anyone to search my vehicle, but I figured it was better to be safe than sorry.

I readjusted the strap of the equipment bag Hakim had given me, the sensors shuffling inside the black canvas, as my eyes watched the dim glow above the elevator door. I had returned Dolan's equipment directly to Jonathan before leaving, so after dropping off these, I could head back to the boardroom and spend another few hours assisting Hakim and crawling through more footage.

I wasn't looking forward to it. I was tired and worried about the warehouse and Warren's detached and unwelcoming behaviour.

I let out a quiet sigh as the impossibly slow elevator finally stopped and the doors opened with a groan. Night shift was still out, so the second floor wasn't very busy as I made my way down the hall toward the cage. I got a few looks from bypassers and even a "damn, Gorski, you look like a drowned rat" from Officer Franklin, who remembered me from hunting.

I smiled at him as I walked by, letting out a fake laugh and saying something about it being a great night to go swimming. Then I opened the door to the equipment room and went inside.

"Name and number?" the officer sitting at the desk behind the cage asked robotically as I approached, leaving a trail of water droplets on the floor behind me.

"Valentyna Gorski, Officer 71287."

"It says here you're a detective," the officer said, glancing up from her computer screen and frowning at my drenched appearance.

"Right." I still wasn't comfortable addressing myself as one. "That's correct."

"What have you got?"

"I'm returning the sensors that Detective Randall Hakim signed out."

She straightened at his name.

"All thirty-three of them and the corresponding batteries, cords, and hard drives."

"No." I shrugged off the bag and dropped it on the counter between us. "I'm missing two sensors, two batteries, and three hard drives."

Her frown deepened.

"Where are they?"

"I don't know. We were using them in the woods and lost them in the process."

"Did you even bother to look for them?"

"Yes." I fought to keep my exhausted irritation at bay as a puddle formed around my feet. "I assume one was washed away tonight in the storm. The other went missing a while ago, dragged off by an animal."

"And does Detective Hakim know they're missing?" she asked, her tone so laced with condescension I felt like a new recruit.

"Yes." I folded my arms as I looked at her. "He's aware of the first one. I'll let him know about the second as soon as I get upstairs."

"Make sure that you do." She stood from her seat, grabbed the wet bag off the counter and moved it to the table behind her. Then she took a yellow form out of a plastic bin on the wall. "Fill this out – Detective Hakim will need to sign it."

"Sure." I took the paper from her, ignoring the unimpressed glare she gave me.

"And Captain Vogle will need to initial it," she added as I turned to leave. "To acknowledge that *you* lost the equipment."

"Got it." I shoved my way out of the room before she could say anything else.

"Gorski?"

I paused, closing my eyes and letting out a breath before I turned around to face the familiar voice.

"Captain Tan." I forced myself to smile up at the man as I continued to leak water all over the floor. "It's nice to see you again, sir."

His eyes trailed over my body from head to toe, then slowly made their way to my face as his brow arched.

"What the hell happened to you, Gorski? You look half-drowned. Did Hakim send you out in this shit?"

"I had to collect the sensors from the Dolan facility so we can get the case wrapped up this week," I said. "Unfortunately, I wasn't quick enough." I held up the yellow form. "Lost another sensor in the woods."

"It happens." Captain Tan nodded. "Did Vogle talk to you about the next hunt?"

My irritation instantly evaporated as dread curled in the pit of my stomach.

"The next hunt?" My voice was weak. "No, sir, he didn't."

"He will." Captain Tan smiled. "He managed to get a spare tag for the fall event. Knowing him, he's probably saving it so he can surprise you with it, so if he calls you into his office to tell you – act surprised. Hopefully this time you'll catch something."

I felt my right eye twitch as I faked another smile.

"Yes, hopefully so."

The words made me want to puke.

"Anyway, you should get back to work before Hakim comes looking for you," Captain Tan said, smacking me on the shoulder as he moved away. "See ya, Gorski."

"See you later, sir."

I stood there, breathing hard as I watched him walk away and memories from that night started to circle my mind. I had forgotten about the autumn hunt. With everything that had been happening, it had completely slipped my mind, as had the prospect of me being invited to yet another nightmare event. And now, all I could see was that girl lying on the ground, covered in blood and mud, staring at me with her green eyes. I could feel her nails clawing at my skin as she fought against the river. I could hear her voice as the thick smell of iron and water flooded my nose.

Did Warren know her? Had she been part of his group?

I closed my eyes again, taking a deep breath as I curled my free hand into a tight ball.

Don't throw up.

Acid burned my throat.

Don't throw up, don't throw up, don't throw up!

I nearly gagged.

I'm going to throw up.

I let out the breath, tore my eyes open, and then forced my feet to move. I could feel the bile burning higher as I slammed my way into the stairwell. Knowing the elevator would never be fast enough, I ran up to the eleventh floor and fumbled with my passcard to get the door open. I all but fell through it, stumbling into the wall before racing to the bathroom near the boardroom. I didn't bother to check if it was empty. I just shoved open the first stall and vomited into the toilet as my eyes started to sting.

I took a deep breath, then threw up once more.

Then I stood there in silence, staring down at the bowl as my eyes burned with tears.

I have no idea how long I remained that way, staring blankly as water from my still-drenched hair dripped down my face. I didn't move until my phone buzzed, but the sensation only made me feel worse because I knew it wouldn't be Warren. My eyes pinched as my heart started to ache, but I made my body straighten, flushing the toilet before pulling out my phone.

It was Grace, and she was letting me know she had snagged a reservation for a late lunch tomorrow.

I scoffed, shoving the phone back into my pocket and finally leaving the stall. I had no idea how I was going to get out of this one, given that I had already agreed to it. I doubted the place served synth. It was located on Fourth, and that was prime fine dining territory. I would probably have to go, then just find some way to not eat the food, or piss Grace off beyond repair and completely back out. I rinsed my mouth out at the sink, then used a few paper towels to remove the excess water from my hair.

I frowned at my reflection. I did look remarkably like a drowned rat.

A drowned rat who would smell like vomit, which was yet another problem to deal with. Suppressing a groan, I made my way toward the boardroom, hoping I could get to my makeshift desk and grab a mint before Hakim asked me any questions.

"Did you return Dolan's equipment to Jonathan?" Hakim asked the second I stepped into the room. He glanced up at me, his eyes lingering a fraction longer than they normally would as he took in my ragged appearance. "Did it go okay?"

"Yes," I said, trying not to breathe out too much as I rapidly walked by him to my desk. I pulled open the top drawer, trying to make it look like I was putting things away as I pulled out my mints and popped two into my mouth before continuing. "But I lost another sensor from our set."

I held up the yellow form.

"After I fill this out, you and Captain Vogle will need to sign it," I said. "I'm sorry, sir. I looked everywhere for it but—"

"It's fine," he cut me off. "I don't care about a missing sensor. Just fill out the form and make sure that Vogle initials the right spot when you're done. I need you to finish going through the footage from 44 and check with Corban to see what he got back from the labs."

"Yes, sir."

I placed the slightly damp yellow form on the corner of my desk so I wouldn't forget to bring it home, knowing that if I started to fill it out now, Hakim would not be pleased. Instead, I got to work on what he had asked. I started the download on the next batch of footage from the network, then called Corban, who reluctantly agreed to give me a copy of his preliminary findings at the end of his shift so long as I promised to get my ass down there to grab it at precisely 9 am before he went home.

I crawled through the footage that had downloaded as I waited for Corban to finish his report, ignoring the prickle I felt along the back of my neck each time Hakim glanced in my direction. He was looking at me more frequently than normal, but if it was because he thought I was behaving strangely or knew that I had thrown up, he didn't say anything. So I ignored it, ate two more mints and a gelatin cube, then promptly left my desk at 8:50 am to go get the preliminary report from Corban.

By the time 11 am rolled around, I had completely forgotten about the impending reservation with Grace. That was, at least, until my desk phone rang, and I answered it to find her on the other end of the line.

"Grace?" I questioned, glancing over at Hakim's empty desk and wondering how long it would be before he came back from Vogle's office. "Why are you calling my office phone?"

'Because you didn't read my text,' Grace said, her irritation clear. *'You never do – so obviously the only way to get a hold of you is by making you think it's work-related. I made the reservation for tomorrow.'*

"Yes, I saw." I pinched the bridge of my nose as I lowered my voice. "Look, now really isn't a good time to discuss this. Can I call you back from my cell phone later? I'm still working and—"

'You're always still working,' Grace countered, but the inflection on "working" made me bristle.

"Yes, because I'm trying to help solve murders, and it isn't an easy task."

'Whatever,' Grace said. *'Look, the reservation is at 4 am. I know it's late for lunch, but it was the best I could do, and it will totally be worth it. Mark's coworker went the other night, and they said it was amazing! The dress code is—'*

"Grace—" I cut her off, my voice much harsher than I meant it to be. "Look, I don't think I can go."

Silence rang heavy from the other end of the phone.

'What do you mean you can't go?'

"I can't go," I said, lowering my voice again and wishing the cord was long enough that I could get up and kick the door to the boardroom the rest of the way closed. "I'm sorry, I can't. I just—"

My cell phone buzzed, and my eyes dropped down to the screen to see the incoming message from Hawthorne. I quickly unlocked the device and scanned his text.

> H: Thinking of going for a swim.
>
> Want in?

Hawthorne was heading out to the docks. I groaned, quickly typing out a reply and attempting to manage both conversations at once.

"I can't go, Grace. I'm so sorry—"

> V: Still working.
>
> Go without me.

"I know how much it means to you, and I'm sorry I said I would go, but—"

> H: Np.
>
> I'll bring you back a snack.

"But I just can't afford it," I blurted.

The words sounded as desperate and torn as I felt. It was a bit of a weak excuse, but the sad thing was, it wasn't even a lie. I didn't have the money to afford a fancy lunch when I was spending most of my cash on gas and supplies.

"I don't have any money right now," I said, leaning into the lie as I let my voice waver. "I didn't want to say anything about it. I'm not trying to be difficult. I just – I don't have the cash to eat out or go to movies."

Silence stretched, then I heard her let out a tight breath.

'You could have just told me.' She didn't sound mad, but I struggled to place the underlying tone in her voice. *'Instead of making plans and backing out. Getting that reservation wasn't easy, you know?'*

"I know." I glanced back to the door as I heard voices in the hall. It was Vogle. I couldn't make out what he was saying, but I knew the tone, and it meant Hakim would be coming back any second—possibly with our captain in tow. "I'm sorry – I just didn't want you to worry."

Well, it's hard not to!' Grace let out an exasperated sigh. *'You've been acting bizarre these last few weeks, and you look ragged. It's not like you to have money problems. What the hell happened? Did you get yourself caught up in some gang trouble or something because of your work on the south side? Did Hakim put you up to something? Is he still pushing you like crazy?'*

The door to the boardroom opened fully, and I looked up to see Hakim enter the room. His eyes darted to the phone in my hand, and I fought to suppress a grimace as I quickly tucked my cell phone away.

"I'd really rather not talk about it." I dropped my eyes to my desk while silently hoping Hakim wouldn't remark about how I wasn't to be making personal calls during working hours even though it *was* my personal time. "I need to get back to work."

'Fine,' Grace said, but I knew the conversation wasn't over. *'I'll cancel the reservation. I'll just come over to visit instead, and we can grab some takeout. Does 4 am still work for you?'*

"Yes," I agreed, hoping to wrap this up as quickly as possible. "I'll see you at 4 am."

'Good,' Grace said, though she still didn't sound happy. *'See you then.'*

"Personal calls should be made on your own time, Gorski."

I hadn't even put the receiver back on the hook. There was a pretty decent chance that Grace had heard that, which would surely only make things worse.

"Yes, sir," I said as I hung up the phone. "I apologize, sir. The number didn't come up. I didn't realize it was a personal call until I answered. I'll do my best to ensure it doesn't happen again."

He didn't say anything else, so neither did I. I just got back to work, wading through endless haystacks of footage, looking for a needle as I wondered how the hell I was going to manage all these problems.

Pressure

I glanced down at my watch, wishing that Grace would just get up and leave. She had only been here for twenty-five minutes, and things were already headed toward disaster. Part of me wanted to outright ask her to go, while the other half just hoped that she would finally snap at me and storm out on her own. Honestly, I didn't really care what caused it at this point. Every minute that dragged on since she'd arrived felt like an eternity, and it was laced with nothing but tension and unspoken hostility.

I didn't see how this was going to end well, so I just wanted it to be over.

By the time I'd left work on Friday and collected stuff for the next round of supplies, it was past 3 pm. The weather was still horrendous, and Hawthorne was busy at the docks scoping out the next set of warehouses. I didn't go out to join him. We'd agreed it would be suspicious to park both of our cars by the trail in a rainstorm on the off chance anyone saw them, so I set up shop at my small table and started crawling through more security camera footage. He showed up at my apartment a few hours later, dragging along what must have been half the mud from the ditch with him, as well as a few leaves and broken twigs.

335

Thankfully I was able to buzz him in without anyone seeing his dishevelled state, but I didn't want to risk it happening again when I knew there would be other days like this, so I gave him my spare set of keys, telling him to use the building side door and eastern stairwell—threatening that if he ever came over unannounced or used the keys for indecent purposes, I would break his neck. He promised he wouldn't. Then, after a moment of silent debate as I stared at his horrid state, I caved, let out a heavy sigh, and got a rag to wipe off his muddy gear bag before shoving him down the hall to go take a shower.

I tried not to think about him using my towels, or being in my shower and touching my stuff, but I couldn't exactly leave him covered in mud, and we needed to get back to work and discuss his findings. So while he showered and did whatever it was that Hawthorne did in the bathroom for twenty-five minutes, I cleaned the floors, put his boots on the shoe rack, and got back to work. I was already downloading the sensor data he had retrieved when he came into the room wearing a fresh set of clothes from his bag, hair still damp.

I agreed that he could leave his small surveillance gear bag here since he was planning to come back tomorrow anyway so we could go back out to the docks together. Then we both sat down at the table, and my discomfort with him being so at home in my apartment was forgotten as he debriefed me on his surveillance efforts. He noted that the warehouses he'd observed today had working cameras, new locks, and motion sensor security lights that were going crazy in the storm. The buildings were far enough back from the road that they weren't easy to see, and one actually had a rear loading zone and upper office unit that faced the water. He'd seen a truck from Jensen's Janitorial service show up just before he'd left, so it was safe to assume the office was in use.

Both buildings were good potential options for temporarily storing humans prior to shipping them out through the docks, but until we reviewed the sensor data or saw something to confirm it was our target, we agreed that our ditch-creeping efforts would have to continue.

There were still eight more warehouses to examine, and we couldn't afford to get this wrong. Warren and his people were depending on us. They didn't have the time or resources to cover more than one warehouse the night the humans arrived. We couldn't wait for the truck to show up and then surround the building. Coordinating that would be impossible—the area was simply too large, and we had no idea how long the window between arrival and departure would be or what sort of security Scott Beckette would be using.

Would they unload their cargo in one of the buildings or simply pull the trucks inside and then load the entire vehicle on the boats a few hours later?

Eridanus and their network hadn't been able to confirm the plan, so right now, we were grasping at straws and making educated guesses based on the typical boat traffic and dock activity because we knew we had to be ready and waiting for them. Warren and his people needed time to prep their extraction team, develop an exit plan, get down to the docks, surround the building, and have their own trucks ready to go—assuming they even planned to use vehicles. I had no idea if humans could drive or what the hell the plan was. The logistics of this mission were a nightmare, especially since Warren still wasn't talking to me, and I was seriously starting to get concerned.

While Hawthorne and I had sat at the table working through the rest of the day, Warren had messaged me another small list of supplies, but still, he'd given me no drop time. No good afternoon greeting. No update on his progress or request about mine. No indication that he viewed me as anything other than a pack mule to be used for dropping off goods or that he ever wanted to speak to me or see me again. And as I read the words, I felt something inside me crack. Like a tiny little fissure had formed between my ribs, leaking the buried anger and frustration that had been building in my chest since the whole mess had started.

Texting him was like texting a wall.

It was a problem, and enough was enough.

I had no idea what was going on with him, but I knew we wouldn't be successful if we didn't sort this out. Whether I had done something to upset him or there was something else happening behind the scenes, it didn't matter. We had to talk, and we had to fix this. So I texted him just after Hawthorne left, telling him I would gather the remaining supplies and drop them off early Sunday afternoon before heading into work for my Monday shift, but that we had new information and I needed to see him so we could discuss it.

I had asked him to meet me at the cave, but I still hadn't heard back.

I was hoping that was only because I'd messaged him at 10:21 pm and not because he was planning to ignore me, and that he would message me when he woke up so I wouldn't have to stake out the cave all Sunday afternoon and ambush him when I dropped off his requested supplies.

After giving up on waiting for his reply, I had headed out into the night, this time driving to the north end of Carneth to gather the requested items. Everything Warren had listed could be passed off as regular everyday things, so I stopped at three stores, bought everything without my helmet on using the cash from Eridanus, and headed home to pack up my gear bag.

I ended up passing out on my couch for two hours, waking up with barely enough time to cram all my research into my bedroom, hide the overstuffed supply bag in my closet, stuff Hawthorne's in next to it, and complete a once-over of my apartment to make sure there was nothing obvious sitting out before Grace arrived and I buzzed her into the building.

I had been planning to order us lunch from Albert's; it was quick, easy, cheap, and of course, synthetic. It went along with my lie—which wasn't really a lie—that I didn't have the money to get anything decent to eat. But to my horror, she had shown up with food despite me specifically asking her not to, and that was when this night had begun to completely fall off the rails.

She'd brought takeout from her favourite place in the Westchester Mall near her home. The gesture, while kind in nature and completely unlike Grace, was entirely problematic given that it was made from real blood, and I had zero intentions of ever eating it. I hadn't eaten in a while, and the smell of it was both intoxicating and revolting, and that only made me feel worse.

I told her it was too much, that she should keep the dish and take it home for Mark, and I would just order something cheap for myself from Albert's because I couldn't afford to pay her back.

She told me it was her treat, that she was doing me a favour. I *deserved* to have something nice every once in a while, and it was a pre-thank you for helping to set up her Halloween party—which I had not agreed to previously. I had smiled at her, the muscles in my face stiff and the expression surely looking more like a grimace of pain than anything else, as I'd reluctantly accepted the container and brought it to the table.

That had been ten minutes ago. Now I was beginning to run out of reasonable excuses not to eat it, and Grace was starting to push.

"I don't understand why you're so hung up on this," Grace said as she took another bite of her food and eyed me from across the table. "It's no big deal. I've bought you lunch before."

"I know."

I felt my small flip phone vibrate in my pants pocket, and I had to resist the urge to pull it out.

"It's your favourite dish from Lotus."

"I know," I said again, stirring the stir-fry mix with my fork but refusing to take a bite.

"Then what's the problem?" I could hear the agitation growing in her voice. "Why the hell are you being so difficult?"

"I'm not being difficult."

The phone vibrated again, and the constant pressure in my chest started to grow as my mind began listing off all the reasons why Warren might be texting me before five in the morning after days of silence. Had something gone wrong? Had they missed the truck departure? Had we already failed? Or was he simply answering my request to meet? Did he agree? Or was he blowing me off again?

"Yes, you are!"

Her words came out much angrier than I'd expected. I knew Grace was losing the little patience she had, but so was I, and after her confrontation with Hakim in the parking garage two weeks ago, I was seriously starting to question how we had ever become friends. Had I just never noticed how vainglorious and selfish she could be? Or had I been that way, too, and changed over the last few months?

"You're being ridiculous, Valya," Grace continued, her contemptuous tone grating on my last nerve. "I came back from vacation, and it's like you became a completely different person! Stop lying to me! What the hell is going on with you?"

"Nothing's going on!" I snapped, stuffing the fork deep into the takeout container as I sat back in my seat and latched to the first lame excuse I could muster. "I'm just pissed you brought this over when I specifically asked you not to."

"You're pissed at me for bringing you food?" Grace looked at me in disbelief. "Are you kidding me?"

"No." I let out a frustrated sigh as I tried to figure out what the hell I should do. "I just – I appreciate the gesture, Lexie, but I'm just not comfortable accepting it. I told you I can't afford this."

"Yeah? And why the hell not?" Grace spat as she stuffed her fork into her own takeout box so forcefully I heard it puncture the bottom. I could see sauce leaking out across my table. It was red, and I had to fight the urge to gag as my mouth started to water. "Your pathetic evasive tactics are really starting to piss me off. You're not yourself. What the hell have you gotten yourself into?"

"Gotten myself into?" I tore my eyes away from the mess on the table. I didn't need to fake the confusion in my voice because I couldn't wrap my head around how she could be this angry about me allegedly not having money or not wanting to accept charity meals from her.

"Seriously?" Grace leaned forward. "You're going to play stupid?"

"I'm not playing stupid," I insisted. "Look, can you please just drop this? We've been friends for years, and I'm telling you I'm fine. I just don't want to talk about my financial situation. That doesn't mean something's wrong – it just means it's personal, and I don't want it spread around."

She scoffed and rolled her eyes. "So you don't trust me, then. You think I'd spread it around at the precinct that you're broke? When have I ever spread anything about you?"

"You told the entire eighth floor I was promoted to Detective before I actually was."

The second the words were out, I knew it was a mistake. The room went eerily silent, and Grace's eyes narrowed into a glare. The phone in my pocket had one more untimely buzz—and this time, her eyes narrowed further.

"Which I'm not mad about." I tried to backtrack and divert her attention. "It's just not something that I want to—"

"Fine." Grace closed her takeout container, her lips pursing into a tight line. "Look, I think I'm just going to head out. Mind if I use your bathroom before I go."

"Sure."

I watched as she stood from her chair and made her way down the hall, waiting until I heard the click of the door shutting. Then I immediately stood from my seat, grabbing my own takeout container as I went. In less than two seconds, I had the garbage can open, container poised above it to throw it out when the door to the bathroom burst open, and Grace's voice flooded my apartment.

"You know what I hate more than liars," Grace said, her words dangerously low. She paused, holding up a towel she had taken with her from the bathroom. "Drainers."

I stiffened.

"Lexie, what the hell are you talking about?"

"It's one thing for you to choose to ruin your own life," Grace said as she moved toward me, each step punctuating her words. "And I was almost going to let it go. I thought – hey, you know what, if Valya wants to go become Hakim's next drainer partner and end up dead in a sewer drain, then fine. If she wants to get caught up in all that shit that goes on on the eastside of town, ruin her life, work herself to death, pretend like nothing is wrong, and lie to everyone around her as her life crumbles apart – fine. You're an adult, and if you want to make stupid choices and wreck everything that you have then I guess that's on you."

She paused, her fingers curling deeper into the fabric clenched tightly in her fist as her beautiful features darkened into a violent glare.

"But it's a completely different thing," Grace whispered, a disgusted tremor creeping into her voice, "to drag another person into it and ruin their life too."

I straightened, not bothering to hide the fact that I had been about to throw out the food she'd brought me because that damage was done, and she could clearly see the open garbage bin beneath my hovering hands—but I put the container on the counter instead of dropping it.

"Lexie," I said slowly, turning to face her as my personal phone buzzed on the table. It was likely Hawthorne, checking in to confirm our meeting time. "I don't know what you think is going on, but—"

"I don't *think* anything," Grace sneered as she thrust the towel out and her voice grew louder. "I *know* Hawthorne used this towel. I thought I smelled traces of him in your apartment, but I can smell his shampoo! I *know* he's been staying here! Just like I know you've been purposely not eating and draining these last few months!"

My mouth fell open, the blunt accusation hitting harder than I could have anticipated, as I struggled to find my words.

"You think I'm draining," I said, my voice coming out hoarse.

"Of course I do!" Grace yelled, throwing the towel on the couch and glaring at me from across the room. "And now you're dragging Hawthorne into your mess!"

"Why on earth would you think—"

"Look at yourself!" Grace spat, cutting me off as her eyes trailed over me in disgust. "Everything about you screams it! Your fangs are longer, your pupils are dilated – everything about the way you've been behaving! Refusing to eat? Never taking breaks? Avoiding your friends and family?"

"I haven't been avoiding you, Lexie. I've been working! I told you I've been busy with Hakim and—"

"Bullshit!" Grace nearly screamed. "Don't think I haven't noticed how close you and Hawthorne have gotten these past few months or that you seem to find the time to spend with him. I figured that you two were just screwing around, but now he looks nearly as bad as you do! And don't think I didn't hear that buzz from your pocket a second ago! Is that how he contacts you?

Hakim gave you another phone so he doesn't get in trouble for overworking you and running you into the ground? What else did he drag you into? Is that why you have money problems?

"The only reason why I haven't reported you to Mallick yet is because I thought I might be able to talk some sense into you!" Grace yelled. "That's why I stood up for you in front of Hakim! I was trying to help you! But you don't want help, do you? You're already addicted!"

"I'm not a drainer," I whispered as the crushing pressure in my chest began to compound.

"Right," Grace scoffed as she crossed her long arms over her chest. Then her pale eyes narrowed, and she stilled. "No, actually you're right. You're not just a casual drainer anymore. You're a full-blown addict on your way to becoming a fucking degenerate *vampire.*"

Every muscle tensed as a flinch jolted through my body at the word.

The smell of blood from the sauce leaking across my table seemed to thicken in the air, suffocating me as I stared at Lexie Grace and fought the urge to vomit. Acid was burning up my throat. Pain was radiating from the center of my chest. A wave was building. It was getting harder to breathe. All the unspoken things I'd wanted to scream at her, at myself, at the world, for months on end, nearly reaching the tip of my tongue before I crushed them all back down and shut them back into the tiny hole where I'd been stuffing them.

"Get out."

The words were barely a whisper, and yet somehow, they sounded like the most dangerous and deadly syllables I'd ever spoken.

"Now."

She glared at me, unmoving, her eyes flashing with unspoken rage before she finally shifted. She didn't bother to grab the container off the table. Instead, she went straight for the door, grabbing her keys and raincoat along the way. I felt the shudder of the walls as the door slammed shut, then silence rang in my ears.

I tried to breathe as my fingers curled into the fabric of my pants.

But I could barely inhale.

How had I not noticed the scent of Hawthorne's shampoo on my towels? Had I really gotten used to him being around my place so quickly, or was this an inevitable mistake because I was genuinely starting to slip? Grace wasn't wrong. I didn't look entirely well by Reborn standards, and I did need to eat and sleep more, but my appearance wasn't *that* bad either.

How had it come to this?

Grace saw me as a *vampire*, yet I was spending nearly every second of my life trying to be the exact opposite—trying to help humans and undo the endless damage we had done to their people. If she'd known what I was doing, she wouldn't have dared. Then again, maybe she would have. I felt like I didn't even know her anymore. Or maybe I'd just always made excuses for her behaviour, ignoring her harsher traits and turning a blind eye to it. Or maybe this was my fault. Maybe I should have just told her what was going on. Maybe she would have understood, but I doubted it.

Calling someone a vampire was the most cruel and insulting thing you could do—it didn't matter how angry you were, you just didn't do it.

I swallowed, doing my best to shove the pain aside as my personal phone buzzed on the table again. How I felt about Grace or her words was the least of my concerns right now. I had much bigger problems.

I grabbed the paper towels off the counter, then cleaned up the mess on my table, throwing out Grace's half-eaten takeout container along with my own untouched one before I disinfected the entire surface. I tied up the garbage bag, ignoring the way my stomach rolled in disgust and my mouth watered in hunger at the smell as I carried it out to the trash shoot in the hallway. Then I returned to my apartment, washed my hands, and pulled out the tiny flip phone from my pocket to read the messages from Warren.

They were short and to the point. He said he could spare a few minutes to meet with me Sunday afternoon at 1 pm if the information was critical. I reiterated that it was, agreed to his time, and told him I would see him there. Then I choked down six gelatin cubes and grabbed my phone from the table.

'Valya?' Hawthorne's voice answered after the first ring.

"Can you meet me early?" I asked as I made my way toward my room.

'Yeah, I can do that. Do you want me to come pick you up or—'

"No," I said. "I'll bring your bag for you. I think it would be best if you didn't come here, for tonight at least."

Silence echoed on the other end of the phone.

'What happened?'

"I'll explain when I see you." I ripped my closet door open and yanked out our two small gear bags. "See you in thirty minutes?"

'I'll meet you there.'

I disconnected the call, then ripped off my shirt and reached for an old, worn, long-sleeve that I didn't mind getting covered in mud. Five minutes later, I was suited up in my gear, helmet dangling from my fingertips, two small gear bags slung over my shoulder as I raced down the stairwell to my car. It took me another thirty-two minutes to drive down to the docks through the rain because I took a new route, checking my mirrors every few blocks.

I was probably just paranoid. I doubted that Grace was following me. She was probably at home, raging, yelling, possibly drafting a letter of concern to submit to Mallick first thing Monday shift—but I couldn't afford to make any more mistakes. It felt like everything was completely falling apart around me, and it was my fault, yet we were so close to the finish line that I was desperate to hold on and see this through.

My grip tightened on the wheel as the already existing dread that filled my heart grew.

I would need to make sure to eat something substantial before going to see Warren, and I would have to leave Hawthorne at the docks alone tomorrow to complete our surveillance so I could meet Warren on time. I pulled off the quiet side road, taking the narrow entrance to the hiking trail parking lot. Hawthorne's car was already there, so I parked a few spaces down.

"What happened?" Hawthorne's voice sounded as I shut the door to my car and made my way to the trunk. He jogged across the space between our vehicles, helmet in his hand.

"We have a serious problem," I said as I grabbed the two small bags.

"Clearly." He reached me as I shut the trunk and took his bag. "Why couldn't I come by your place?"

"Grace," I said, slinging my own bag over my shoulders. "She came by for a late lunch I couldn't get out of, and we got into it."

"What do you mean you got into it?" Hawthorne asked as we both quickly made our way toward the easterly trail.

"She brought over food from Lotus," I said, and he scrunched his nose in disgust. "Obviously, I couldn't eat it, but she wouldn't let it go."

I told him what had happened, how Grace had been on my case about working with Hakim, and how she suspected I was draining. I told him the details about the confrontation in the parking lot, and how she thought I was dragging him into this and ruining his life too. I didn't tell him that I agreed with her on that front because I didn't want to hear him deny it. I debated leaving out the part where she called me a vampire but decided against it. Hawthorne was in this mess with me for better or worse, and the more he knew, the better odds we had at being successful.

"I told her to get out," I said as we cut our way through the trees and down the hill toward our newest targets. "I didn't know what else to say, but now she's probably going to report us to Mallick, and we could be under investigation this week before we locate the warehouse."

"She's not going to report us to Mallick."

"Hawthorne, you weren't there. She was really pissed. She suspects I'm involved in something more than just draining – and you know how much she hates drainers."

"Yeah, I know," Hawthorne agreed as he lifted a branch and held it up for me. "But she's too proud."

"To turn in her friend?" I nearly snorted as I shook my head. "She turned Pam in for cheating and reported Robinson for suspected draining back in the Academy, remember?"

"I remember." Hawthorne nodded. "But she won't do it without proof."

"Because she doesn't want to be caught being wrong," I concluded, letting out a sigh as I nodded in agreement. "Then we've got to be careful. We'll need to split these surveillance nights up because it's too risky for us to be down here together – but maybe coming to my place actually isn't a bad idea. It will look like we're hanging out. Vogle and Captain Tan already suspect there's something going on between us, so that helps, but you'll just need to come at decent hours and not show up covered in mud."

"I can do that." Hawthorne nodded, but then he stopped and turned to look at me. "But you need to eat more."

"Yes, I know." The words came out far more clipped than they should have. "I'm trying."

"Hey."

I stopped as Hawthorne grabbed my arm, turning to look up at him through the rain as the first traces of morning light split the sky. He was looking at me in concern, droplets of water falling from his rain-soaked hair.

"I know what Grace said was horrible, but it's not true, and she isn't going to report us."

I forced myself to nod, but I still felt like I was being eaten alive with worry. Not just about Grace, about everything. All the uncomfortable thoughts that had been festering in my mind over the last few months were pushing their way up to the surface as I simultaneously dreaded and wished that my conversation with Warren would come sooner.

"It's going to be alright," Hawthorne said, giving me a not-quite-so-confident smile as he patted me on the back. "Or it won't – either way, we keep going, right?"

I snorted, shaking my head as I started moving again.

"That about sums it up. I have to make a supply drop and talk to Aries on Sunday – 1 pm. Do you mind finishing the surveillance on your own so I can leave early?"

"Not at all," he said, then hesitated for a moment. "Are things okay with him?"

"With Aries?" I fought to keep my voice nonchalant.

"Yes."

I could feel his eyes on me.

"They're fine," I said, but it didn't sound convincing.

"Really?" he asked, but I refused to look at him. "Because any time his name comes up, you get really tense."

"Things are fine," I repeated. "We just need to resolve a small issue, but I'm taking care of that."

"Alright."

He accepted my answer without any more prying, but I could feel his gaze lingering on my face as we made our way toward the ditch. I had no idea what he was thinking, if he was suspicious of my relationship with Warren or just curious what the hell was going on between us given his horrible demeanour last weekend, but I pushed the thoughts aside. I couldn't allow myself to get distracted.

Instead, I pulled on my helmet and followed Hawthorne into the muddy ditch. With any luck, in twenty-four hours, I would fix my issues with Warren, our relationship would go back to normal—if I could call whatever was between us normal— Hawthorne would successfully rule out some warehouses, and Grace wouldn't report me for draining. Then we could rescue the humans and move on to the next mission.

I just wished I actually believed it could be so easy.

Rupture

I tugged the helmet off my head, the dark grey skies that were protecting my skin weren't going anywhere anytime soon, and I hoped that removing it might somehow lessen the claustrophobic feeling that was encasing my body.

It didn't.

Even the wind and the rain didn't help. Instead, my already damp hair just got wetter, and the loose strands tangled in the air around my face as the rainstorm blew them in circles. I was quickly reminded why I never wore my hair down and always contained it within a braid. Loose hair was a nuisance, but I hadn't had time to do anything with it before heading out to meet Warren.

I had left Hawthorne down at the docks to finish our surveillance as planned. Then I'd sped home through the sheets of rain, barely having enough time to scarf down more food and take a shower. I'd been so rushed I had resorted to eating my food as I gathered up the final supplies from around my apartment and even chewed the last large bite while I jumped under the showerhead to wash off the mud from our ditch-crawling escapades.

Normally, I would have forgone eating, but that was out of the question now. I needed to pack in as much food as I could to mitigate any rumours of draining that Grace might start. So by the time I'd scrubbed away the last of the mud, I barely managed to run a towel over my hair before changing into a fresh set of clothes, throwing on my gear, grabbing my bags, and racing back down the stairs to my car. Then I headed north through Carneth, carefully checking my mirrors to ensure no one was following me before making my way into the country.

I parked my car in a different spot this time, a few kilometres west of where I usually left it and then sprinted through the trees to make up the ground. Now I was only moments away from the cave, and my heart was beating much too quickly. But it had nothing to do with my sprint. I was nervous to see Warren. I had no idea what to expect when I arrived. I had texted him to tell him I was on the way, but he had yet to write back, and a part of me was beginning to doubt that he would even show up.

I adjusted the strap of the overloaded gear bag on my shoulder, pushing away the stray locks of hair sticking to my cheeks. I could feel water dripping down the collar of my shirt beneath my jacket, but the idea of putting my helmet back on made it hard to breathe. I already felt like I was choking, so I reached up and tugged the neckline of my jacket higher.

The only good thing about the weather was the cold. With each passing day of the rainy season, the temperature continued to drop, and I knew that soon the snow would come—which would bring its own difficulties. I frowned at the thought. The colder temperatures made blackout gear bearable. I wouldn't have to worry about overheating and dying, but the snow and corresponding tracks would make coming out here much more difficult. I would need to rethink my travel methods and come up with another plan, but that was a problem for another night. Those thoughts were simply distractions from the bigger issue at hand, the one I had no idea how to resolve.

I jogged along the ground for another few minutes, dodging the familiar divot and ducking beneath a few branches as my anxious anticipation grew.

Would he be there waiting? Would I arrive first? What should I say?

I burst out into the clearing, the sound of the river barely audible over the continuous rumble of thunder that rolled through the clouds. I squinted through the flickers of light that dashed across the sky, making my way along the slick stone, helmet tucked securely under my left arm as the rain continued to battle the integrity of my waterproof jacket.

I could see a dull glow coming from the cave, which meant that Warren was here. All that remained was what would come of our impending conversation.

I slowed as the cave grew closer, my eyes rapidly scanning the area as my ears strained against the storm. I couldn't hear or smell anything outside to suggest he had brought any other humans along with him, so it looked like he'd come on his own, and I let out a breath of relief. I hadn't even considered that he might come with others until I got here, and that would have completely ruined my plan to fix this.

Gripping the strap of the gear bag tighter, I made my way across the final stretch of ground and ducked into the small cave. The warmth from the fire immediately touched my exposed skin, sending a tiny shudder through my body as I blinked and looked around, then stiffened. Warren was standing by the fire. He wasn't wearing his jacket. It was spread across a rock to dry, and his hands lingered above the flames. They dropped the second he saw me, flexing uncomfortably by his sides as we both stared at each other in silence.

My eyes darted to his rifle, which was leaning against the wall a foot away, and I felt my uneasiness grow. He had purposely positioned himself to be as far away from me as possible, the flames almost between us and his firearm readily accessible.

"Hi," I said, forcing the word out after several long and painful seconds had ticked by.

"What did you find?"

His voice was detached and cold, and it lacked any of the familiarity and warmth we had gained over the last few months. As did his blunt question, making it clear he had no intention of chatting with me.

"We found a possible location," I answered.

My voice came out much more quiet than I meant it to. It nearly sounded like a whisper in the face of the wind whipping across the cave, so I cleared my throat, projecting my next words more loudly as I unshouldered the gear bag.

"Warehouse 236A," I said. "We think that they'll use a building associated with the middle section of docks that Lionetti owns, probably those tied to piers 59, 60, and 61 since they have the most coverage. It wouldn't make sense for them to ship anything out of 57 or 62 since those neighbour other owners, and we don't think they'll use any of the warehouses by pier 58 because they're either boarded up, in use by legitimate companies, or too close to the road. Warehouse 236A is on pier 59. We're still checking the rest of the buildings to be sure, but right now, it's the most promising."

Warren stared at me in silence, then his eyes narrowed. "Is that it?"

"Yes."

He frowned, his lips pressed tight as if he was biting back a thousand unsaid words before a few slipped out.

"You could have just texted me that."

"I know but—"

"But instead you told me it was critical, then wasted both of our time coming out here, to what?" He arched a brow as he gestured to the mouth of the cave and the heavy rain that poured over the opening. "Take a nice afternoon stroll?"

I stiffened, my gloved fingers digging into the canvas material of my gear bag.

"Get some fresh air?" he said, his voice now dripping with sarcasm. "Are you really that bored, Corvus? Or just that stupid?"

He was starting to sound angry, and I was starting to feel done with whatever the hell was going on. I dropped the gear bag on the ground, the thud it made echoing through the small cave before I let my helmet fall after it.

"Alright, that's enough," I said, taking a step forward as I tugged off my wet gloves. I couldn't do this. I couldn't stand here in this tiny cave cocooned up in blackout gear while I felt like I was being roasted by his anger. "What the hell is your problem?"

"My problem?" The scoff that broke from his lungs was bitter as he stepped away from the flames, facing me without an ounce of fear but glaring at me with a burning hatred that made my stomach curl. "You just risked my life by asking me to come here, only to tell me bullshit information that you could have just texted to me!"

"Bullshit information?" My mouth fell open in disbelief as I threw my gloves to the ground. "It's the best lead we have!"

"And you could have relayed that through your phone!" Warren spat. "That's why I gave it to you!"

"I know!" I snapped, startled by how loud my words came out. "But I wanted to see you!"

He stiffened, and the cave went momentarily silent as we both stared at each other. I searched his face, trying to understand how we had gotten here as the rain outside grew worse and a cold breeze ghosted over my skin.

"I needed to talk to you," I said, taking another step forward. "I needed to see you."

He didn't move away, but his grim expression only darkened.

"Every time we meet here, it puts all of this at risk," he said as he sidestepped around me to go grab the gear bag.

"I know that!" The words sounded nearly as exasperated as I felt, and I followed behind him. "But there's clearly a problem, and I want to fix it!"

"The only problem I have is you not taking this seriously and wasting my time."

"Warren, stop!"

I grabbed his arm without thinking, easily jerking him back as lightning flickered across the opening of the cave. My fingers tingled. I could feel his warmth through his shirt, but it was quickly replaced with a gust of cold air as Warren pried his arm from my grip and turned around to glare at me. I hesitated, briefly wondering if I had just bruised his arm before I processed the look of disgust on his face, and I felt my lungs grow weak.

"I don't understand." The words were a whisper as all the nauseating thoughts I'd been having for weeks bubbled up once more. "I thought that we – we had become friends and that maybe we—"

"There is no *we*."

I stiffened at the cold, dark tone.

It hurt.

A lot.

Like he had just physically stuck a knife through my heart, cutting deep into the tissue and twisting it for good measure. A week ago, we'd sat in this cave side by side, laughing. I had made him smile. We had talked for hours, his eyes warm, bright, and full of life. Now they were glaring at me so intently that I wanted to throw up.

"I—" I shook my head as my throat started to burn. "I thought that you trusted me."

His eye twitched at my words, as if they'd hit a nerve and cracked something lingering just beneath the surface of his hateful exterior.

"I did trust you!" he spat, anger breaking across his face more clearly than ever before. "And I can't believe I was stupid enough to actually believe you gave a shit when in reality, you've just been lying to me about keeping our information safe, and you can't keep your mouth shut!"

I took a step back as the angry words poured from his mouth. I had never seen him this livid. Not even on the day that I'd first met him or followed his trail into the woods.

"How many other vampires have you told?" he asked, stepping forward to fill the space I had left as I flinched at his word.

"I didn't, I—"

"How long did it take for you to spill everything?" He cut me off, his voice taking on a cruel tone. "Or was it just that you couldn't bear the thought of keeping something from him?"

"I *asked* you if it was okay!" I glared up at him. "*You* agreed to let him help."

"No, my father agreed to it," Warren said, his voice dropping like a stone. "I'm not okay with it."

I felt my heart sink. Everything I had worked toward seemed to be completely falling apart before my eyes. This was exactly what I had feared. That bringing Hawthorne into this mess was a mistake that not only put him at risk but also ruined everything with Warren and his people. Did his friends not trust me now either? Not that they had ever trusted me before, but had this made it worse? Did Orion feel like I had forced his hand?

Surely by now they knew I would never ask to bring someone in unless I trusted them absolutely—but did that even matter if they didn't trust me?

"But we need him," I said, my voice sounding almost desperate. "He has access to the Patrol and Street database and cameras. He's really good at surveillance – he always knows what's going on at the precinct, and he can cover things that I can't when Hakim is on my ass. Without him, I wouldn't be able to check out all the warehouses!"

"Yeah, I heard your sales pitch to my father." Warren shook his head as he looked at me. "I can't believe how stupid I am – how much I told you. I actually thought that after everything you'd risked, everything you've done, you truly cared, that you were capable of feeling something and wouldn't threaten the success of what we're doing just because you can't keep a secret from your boyfriend. God forbid you have to lie to him or experience mild inconvenience in your life."

"My boyfriend?"

Confusion laced my voice.

"Hawthorne isn't my boyfriend, Warren," I said slowly, my brow creasing. "I didn't tell him because there was some conflict of trust or because I felt like I owed it to him. I did it because he's an asset that can help us. He's just a friend. He's my co-worker."

"Right," Warren scoffed, and acid laced his next words. "Of course not. The way you people use each other without a care in the world is ridiculous. Just a guy conveniently game to ruin his entire life for you? Willing to give up everything? Do you seriously think I believe that? Does he know he's just a friend, or is he hoping that tagging along will finally change that? Or maybe it's just that you don't have the capacity to feel anything about it, and he's just a means to an end?"

I stilled, staring at him in silence as the pre-existing crack in my chest seemed to widen.

"Is that what you think of us Reborn?" I asked, my voice coming out like a low, hoarse whisper. "Or is that just what you think of me?"

He didn't say anything, but even if he had, I'm not sure I would have heard it. Something was ringing in my ears, like a dull thrumming beat, as my body grew numb.

"That I'm the type of person who leads people around and uses them?" I whispered as my hands started to shake at my sides. "That I would use Hawthorne? Put his entire career and life and family at risk without telling him how dangerous this is going to be? Without trying to convince him that getting involved is a bad idea? Without trying to deter him in every way possible? That I would lie to you about him? About anything? That I've just been using you, manipulating you in all of our conversations because that's what Reborn do, isn't it? We're just monsters after all – heartless, soulless beings without a conscience."

His gaze hardened, and he shifted uncomfortably. "That's not what I said."

"But it's what you meant," I said, my voice sharp as I took a step toward him.

He didn't deny it, and his long silence was like another hit to the massive wound that was tearing open across my chest and inching toward my heart.

"I can't believe this," I whispered, shaking my head. "I can't believe I actually thought there was something here between us – that we were friends, and you might see me for who I am, not what you fear me to be."

"I just think it's a bit risky to drag along some guy at the last minute!" Warren snapped. "My father might trust him because he has this ridiculous notion that we need to risk trusting more of you because we can't do this alone – but every time he does it, he puts us at risk! I recognize that we need your help. I'm not an idiot. I know we can't do this entirely alone. I just think it's irresponsible to bring in some random *vampire* who is your supposed friend at the last second after *everything* that we have already done!"

I flinched at his words.

"Right," I whispered, my shoulders dropping under the weight of his angry gaze. I could feel the pressure that had been mounting in my center creeping up my neck, scalding my insides as it flowed like lava to the back of my throat until my voice started to shake. "Because no matter what I do, I'm still a *vampire* to you. Incapable of feelings, so I couldn't possibly have morals, could I? And Hawthorne – well, he obviously must be even worse than I am, right?"

He stared at me, motionless, and I felt something deep inside my soul break as the fissure in my chest finally cracked wide open, splitting my heart in two.

"Well, you're wrong," I whispered, my voice taking on a vicious tone. "For your information, *Warren*, that random *vampire* is the reason you're still alive. If not for him, you would be dead. Despite what you might think, out of the two of us, he's the better person. So if there's anyone you should want on your side, it's him, not me!

"I'm the ignorant asshole who never bothered to think for myself!" I yelled, my nails cutting into the palms of my hand as they balled into fists and all the words I had kept locked up exploding out.

Everything, all of it, all of my self-hatred and disgust, was pouring up and out my throat like a wave, and I simply could not stop it.

"I'm the one who never asked questions! I'm the one who never thought about where my food came from! I'm the one who had the ridiculous notion that good and bad were tangible concepts represented by law when in reality, they're not!

"Without Hawthorne, I probably would have turned you in without a second thought. Hawthorne was the one who made me think. Hawthorne was the one who planted the idea in my head that humans are people, too, and Hawthorne was the one who saved your life that morning!" I bellowed as my eyes started to burn with tears. "If not for him, I never would have known you! And looking back on my life now, I don't even know what to think anymore because meeting you has shattered my world! You've *broken* me and made me hate every aspect of myself on a level I didn't even know was possible!

"I am *exactly* the monster you think I am!" My voice broke, and I could feel tears pouring down my face, but to my horror, I still couldn't seem to stop. "I've eaten your people, Warren! I did it for years without thinking or caring where my meals came from. It never even crossed my mind – not *once*! Not one fucking time! Do you have any idea how sick that makes me when all I have *EVER* wanted to do with my life is help people? After meeting you and your people?! After realizing that everything I ever thought I knew was wrong?!

"Do you have any idea how much I hate myself? How much I hate what I am? How painful it is to go into work every night and pretend to be normal? How sick it makes me to see other Reborn eating food without a care in the world while my captain drones on and on about how great hunting is, and my friends and family are more concerned about new curtains than the welfare of living, breathing beings?!"

I swallowed, my voice growing quieter as the broken pieces of my heart began to shrivel and die in my chest.

"It makes me sick," I whispered, blinking the tears from my eyes as my entire body began to tremble, and my voice rose once more. "But it's *NOTHING* in comparison to what you have been through! To what your people have been through. To what they continue to go through. And I know that nothing I do will ever be enough! No matter how hard I try, no matter how hard I fight to help fix this – I can't change what I am! I can't take back the last thirty-four years of my life, and I will *never* be able to undo the damage that I have done to you and your people.

"I'll never forgive myself! And at the end of the night, I don't even think that I should. No one should, because I was part of this problem. And while I would give anything to take it back, I can't." I raised a shaking hand, wiping away the tears from my face as I dropped my gaze to his chest. To the tanned skin that I could see at the collar of his damp shirt. "And what will haunt me until the night that I die is never truly knowing what I would have done that morning – how seeing the farm would have affected me if I hadn't spoken to Hawthorne first. If I really would have turned you in, or if I would have stopped and thought on my own. I'll never know. So I'll never know if I'm truly the heartless monster you think I am, if I chose to be blind to the things around me in favour of simplicity, or if I was just an ignorant bystander of my own people's creation."

A small breath left my lips like a scoff as I slowly raised my eyes to meet his gaze once more.

"At this point, it doesn't matter. It's so tangled I don't think I can be one without the other, and I will remain a monster no matter what I do because I can't change what I am, and I can't undo what I've done." The words sunk heavily in my chest as I held his bright brown gaze. "And I can't take it back. There is nothing I can do. Nothing I can give you. Nothing I can ever say to apologize and make this right or make up for what I've done. As much as I desperately want it, I'll never ask or expect you to forgive me.

"I accept my role in this," I said, my body sagging under the invisible weight of the burden I knew I would forever carry. "Both the part I played and the one I plan to from now on. All I can do is push forward. Try to find some way to live with this even though I know I never truly can while I do everything possible to support you. It will never be enough, but that's okay, because this isn't about me."

Warren stared at me in silence, as if he had no idea where to go from here, and the truth was, neither did I.

"I should go," I said, taking a step back.

I didn't want to leave, but I knew there was nothing left for me here. I wanted to go back in time and change the entirety of my life, but I'd have to settle for curling up in a ball on my bed as the painful ache in my chest consumed me whole.

"I'm sorry, for everything, and I'm sorry for bringing Hawthorne into this." I meant those words with every fibre of my being, both for his sake and Hawthorne's. "I didn't mean to force your hand or cause any tension between you and your father. I just wanted to help, but I should have come out here and asked you in person how you felt about it first. Not that it means anything, but I would never have brought him to meet you if I didn't trust him with my life or if I thought he was a risk. So please don't hate him. He doesn't deserve that. You can put it all on me — I'm the one who deserves it."

"Corvus—"

"It's okay." I smiled. It was weak and halfhearted, broken like the rest of me, and I shrugged my shoulders in defeat. "It is what it is. I shouldn't have asked you to come here just to talk. You're right. It was stupid. I put you at risk, and I'm sorry. I don't know what I was thinking. I'm just tired. I was worried this would mess up the mission, and I really wanted to see you – but that's stupid, too, because we'll always be worlds apart."

I let my gaze trail over his familiar face once more, but it only made the throbbing ache in my heart worse. Then I unclenched my hands to wipe away the last traces of tears that tracked my face.

"I'll see you later."

I forced myself to turn away, even though it hurt. Even though my chest was being squeezed so tightly, I could barely breathe. Even though I wanted to tell him how sorry I was, again, over and over, until he somehow believed me—and how I would give anything to be different. To be human. To be like him. To walk by his side in the sun. Yet I knew it was pointless. Coming here had been a mistake.

He didn't owe me anything; he never would.

"Corvus."

I ignored his voice, abandoning my gear bag on the ground and grabbing only my helmet and gloves as an endless stream of questions circled my head.

How had I ever thought we were friends? Why had I thought this would work? How stupid could a person be? Why would he ever trust me? Why had I thought our relationship was anything other than what it was? Where the hell had I thought this was going, and how could I have thought it would end any other way?

I was a tool and resource to him, nothing more, as I should be.

"Corvus, wait."

I stuffed my damp gloves inside my helmet and made my way toward the storm. I wasn't going to wear it on the walk back. I didn't care how wet I got or if the sun came out. A painful burn would be a good distraction from the agony in my heart. Maybe I would just wander the trees for a few hours and go straight to work. Did it really matter anymore? For all I knew, Grace had already reported me to Mallick for draining, and I was about to be investigated.

"Wait!"

Cold air ripped across my face as I reached the mouth of the cave, then something grabbed my arm.

"Valya!"

I turned to look back, my pale gaze quickly sweeping over the agonized expression on Warren's face.

"It's not like that," he said, pulling me back from the mouth of the cave. "It's just – all of this is a mess, and I – I don't—"

"You don't have to explain," I cut him off as I tried to ignore the fact that my eyes were shining with tears again. "I get it, Warren. It's fine. I don't know what I was thinking. Obviously we're just allies, and I thought we were closer than we are. It's my mistake. You have every right to doubt my actions and be wary of me, and I—"

"I'm not wary of you." He let out a heavy sigh, dropping his hold on my arm and running his hand through his damp hair. "Or at least I wasn't before. I just – I didn't know all of that about Hawthorne."

He closed his eyes, seeming to struggle internally, before he looked at me once more and took a step forward.

"I didn't realize how critical he was to all this," Warren said, his eyes searching my face as if he was trying to find something. "He came out of nowhere. You'd never mentioned him or wanting to bring anyone else in before, so I panicked. I don't trust people easily, let alone your people, and then I realized how much I've told you, and I – I'm just having a hard time with all this. I didn't realize how close I'd let you get until last weekend, and I just – I don't know what I'm doing anymore."

He looked at me desperately as he took another step forward. I could smell the sweat on his skin; it was mixing with the rainwater that saturated his clothes. I could see the tiny flecks of gold that circled his irises.

"I like spending time with you," he said, and the air in my lungs seemed to seize. "I like talking to you. I look forward to seeing you, and none of that makes any fucking sense."

He took another step forward, but this time it was slow, almost cautious. His eyes darted over my face, showing not an ounce of the hate that had been there moments before. He was so close now that I could feel the heat from his body radiating into my own. I could see all the tiny details of his skin, the way the scar that cut through his eyebrow twisted outward at the bottom, and that his nose actually had a faint scar across it.

"I don't understand it," he murmured, his warm breath ghosting across my face. "It goes against everything – but you're not – I don't see you like that, and I – I don't understand why."

I swallowed hard, the tremble in my hands returning as he took a final step toward me.

"You're not a monster, Valya," he whispered, and I shuddered as his warm hand found the side of my face.

I could feel his thumb brushing over my cheek, smearing the last of the tears from my skin. His eyes dropped to my lips, and I unconsciously wet them before he met my gaze once more. His expression was anguished. I could feel the tension in his frame as he waged his internal battle, then dropped his shoulders in defeat.

"And I don't hate you."

He exhaled the words like they weighed an unholy ton. He shifted, his head ducking closer. The space between us narrowed, and then all the air left my lungs as his warm lips pressed against mine. My entire body stiffened. My brain seemed to stall. His touch was so hesitant and light I could barely believe it was happening as my heart faltered in my chest.

Then his lips moved, and a jolt like an electric current raced down my spine. All thought momentarily vanished from my mind as my eyes closed, and I kissed him back for a breathless second; until our brains caught up to our bodies, and we both froze.

His fingers were threaded in my hair. My hand was touching his chest, knotted into the fabric of his damp shirt. I could feel the heat of him through the material, and I had no idea how it had gotten there or when he had put his hand on my hip. Each point of contact seemed to burn—the sensation digging into my skin and sparking something to life that I had never felt before.

He tasted delicious, and that thought startled me.

I flinched, and he pulled his head back, a dull tremble tracing through my bones as he lingered only inches from my face. His eyes were wide. I could feel his breath on my lips and his heart pounding beneath the fingers that still gripped his shirt as I stared at him through the glow of flickering firelight.

"I—" His eyes traced over my face as his head began to shake. "Valya, I – I don't—"

I couldn't breathe. It felt as if all the air between us had vanished, and my heart was hanging in the balance. I waited for him to pull away completely. For him to recoil in disgust. For reality to set in and the hammer to crash down on my head, determined to crush me under the weight of my biological makeup, but it didn't, and we both just stood there staring at one another until my hip vibrated and a loud beeping filled the cave.

"Shit!" I dropped my helmet in surprise as I all but stumbled back from him.

The beeping went off again as a cold gust of wind moved over my body. It pulled all the heat of his touch from my skin and sent a shiver down my spine. I blinked, rational thought seeming like an impossible task as I reached for my phone with trembling hands.

"Hello," I answered, the single word uneven and breathless.

'Gorski?' Hakim's voice filled my ear, and I cringed.

"Yes," I said, closing my eyes and running a hand through my hair as I fought to steady my breath.

There was silence on the other end for a moment, then he spoke again.

'Is everything okay?'

"Yes, sir." I cleared my throat. On any other night, I may have found it thoughtful of him to ask, but right now, it was just concerning. "Sorry. You got me while I was asleep, but I'm awake now."

'Good,' Hakim said, his tone returning to its usual harsh indifference. *'Because I need you to come in. I'll text you the address – double homicide in the southeast end. Looks drug-related, likely unrelated to our work, but Detective Clive is out on vacation, so Vogle needs us to pick this up just to get the initial work done and confirm with certainty that the*

deaths are unrelated to the Jane Does. You can stop by the precinct to grab a spare camera and meet me at the scene in forty—'

"Uhh—" I interrupted him before he could fire off the rest of his instructions and hang up, wincing preemptively at what I knew was about to come. "Is an hour and a half okay? I – I'm not actually at my place, and I'll nee—"

'I don't care what you do on the weekend, Gorski,' came the sharp reply. *'I'll let it go this time because you're not technically on call, but don't let it become a habit. Detectives in the 33rd are always working, and you'll never last if they can't count on you to show up. Don't bother going to the precinct – I'll grab the camera. Meet me at the scene in an hour.'*

"Yes, sir. Tha—"

He hung up before I could finish the sentence, and I was left with nothing but a dial tone ringing empty in my ear. I let out a deep sigh, my hands still shaking as I ended the call and turned to look at Warren, who was staring at me with a strange expression.

"I – I have to go," I said, holding up the phone in my hand as if he didn't already know. "There was a double homicide, and my partner just called me in."

"I heard," Warren said, looking just as lost as I felt. He cleared his throat, shaking his head as if to clear it. "Will you be able to get back in time?"

"If I sprint." I pocketed my phone. "And speed most of the way back to Carneth. I have a change of clothes in my car, so I'll be fine, but I'll have to come back for the gear bag."

"I'll unload it and leave it here for you," he said, then added, "or let me know if you want me to bring it to the farm if that's easier."

"Okay."

"Okay." He looked like he wanted to say something more. "But you should get going."

"Right." I nodded, an uneasy feeling creeping through my bones as the weight of what had just happened slowly started to sink in. "I uh – let me know if you need anything else this week. I – I'll have my phone, so you can just text me."

"Alright."

We stared at each other for another three seconds, then my phone buzzed with Hakim's text.

"Alright," I swallowed, stepping back and collecting my helmet and gloves from the ground. "I'll – I'll see you later."

I turned and raced from the cave, my heart beating much too quickly. I sprinted across the rocks toward the trees, lightning streaking across the sky above me as the wind whipped my hair. The rain drenched my jacket, and I could feel it running down my face. But as I licked my lips, I could still taste him, and I doubted that any amount of rain would ever be able to wash that away or make me forget how it'd felt when he'd kissed me.

Gathering

"When you finish that write-up, drop it off to Vogle. Tell him to throw Isaacs on the case until Clive gets back. We don't have time to follow up on leads for the bodies of two addicts no one is going to miss."

"Yes, sir."

"I need to go see Corban – and Mallick. The officer he leant us for surveillance hasn't seen Morin yet, so I'm moving him to nights and taking over day shifts before he tanks this case. We'll be in the car all day Wednesday. If you had any post-work plans with your fellow officers, cancel them – you can start making the swing over to days now."

"Yes, sir."

"Don't forget to lock the boardroom when you leave."

"Yes, sir."

"And Gorski," Hakim said, turning to face me from the door, his wet jacket dripping puddles on the floor and his damp fingers gripping a stack of folders. "Get some sleep – you look terrible."

"Yes, sir."

I watched him leave, waiting for him to tug the door closed behind him before I sank into my seat, much like a wounded animal waiting to die, then let out a heavy breath.

How the hell was I supposed to get sleep when he was constantly keeping me at work and calling me in? It felt rather contradictory and insincere coming from him.

I dropped my head into my hands, closing my eyes as I took several long, deep breaths. Even if it was a ridiculous comment for him to make, he wasn't wrong. I did need sleep. I had been up for well over twenty-four hours, and I was starting to fade. I waited another two minutes, ensuring Hakim would be well on his way to the fifth-floor evidence labs, before I pulled out the tiny flip phone securely tucked inside my vest.

It had buzzed shortly after I'd made it into Carneth, but I hadn't had time to check it. I'd been too busy rapidly changing clothes in my car so I didn't look like a drowned rat before I'd tugged on my helmet, gloves, and badge and darted across the street to the address Hakim had sent me. The scene had been a mess. Forensics was already there, as was Hakim, who greeted me with an unimpressed nod before shoving a camera in my hands and telling me to go take my own photos as he moved across the bloody room to go speak to the officer who was first to arrive on site.

We were there for hours, talking to witnesses, gathering statements, reviewing the scene with forensics, and taking down notes. When Hakim finally decided we were done, we headed to the precinct so I could park my car, but we didn't stay. Instead, we headed back out to drop by Andrew Morin's place.

He wasn't home, and his neighbour, Gloria Gilbert, who seemed a little too happy to see Hakim again, informed us that she had heard the man in the hall twice since our last visit. We left a few minutes later, circling by three of the past Jane Doe sites before finally calling it quits and returning to the precinct.

Hawthorne had texted me twice while we were out, but I hadn't had a chance to respond to him either, and I knew he was probably worried. We had tentatively planned to meet up after my conversation with Warren before heading into work, but that had fallen off the table the second Hakim had called my phone, the second my conversation with Warren had turned into something else—something I could hardly believe as I opened the tiny black flip phone with shaking hands and nervously licked my lips.

It didn't feel real.

Surely, it was a dream or some tear in reality.

Yet as I flicked the phone open and pushed the loose strands of damp hair from my face, I knew it had happened, and I knew that the world had once again been ripped from beneath my feet. It would never be the same. *I* would never be the same. I would never look at Warren the way I had before, and I would never, ever, stop replaying that moment in my mind.

> A: Did you make it back in time?

It was the first of several messages that he had sent, and the fact that he had sent anything at all made my heart flutter.

> A: Also, let me know when you can meet.
>
> I think we should talk.

My pulse quickened. He wasn't wrong. We needed to talk, but that conversation somehow seemed more terrifying than anything I had done to date.

> A: I told Orion about the warehouse.

This message was the newest, and it had been sent just before midnight.

> A: He said he is expecting an update from the north soon.
>
> I'll keep you posted.

I drafted up my replies, focusing on the mission instead of our personal mess.

> C: Made it in. The scene was a mess, but everything's fine.
>
> Looks like I'll be on day shift stakeout duty for JD cases.
>
> I'll confirm as soon as I know exact times, but it starts Wednesday.
>
> Yes, we should talk.
>
> I should be out in a few hours, then heading to the docks.
>
> I'll let you know if we find anything.

I slid the phone back into the safety of its plastic bag, tucking it inside my vest before pulling out my personal cell to message Hawthorne. I told him Hakim had called me in, then asked if he wanted to come hang out later. His reply was quick, so I knew he must be back at the precinct already, probably writing up a report of his patrol. He agreed to meet me at my place, and I got to work on my own report. It took over an hour for me to type up my notes and capture all the details that I knew Hakim would want documented. Then I printed off a copy and brought it down the hall.

I had been hoping Vogle wouldn't be in his office, that I could leave the papers on his desk along with my prewritten sticky note telling him that Hakim wanted this case passed to Isaacs, but I wasn't so lucky. He was there, and he happily invited me in after I knocked on the door.

"Gorski," Vogle said, smiling at me as he got up from his chair, apparently incapable of sitting whenever people dropped by. "How was the scene?"

"A bit of a mess," I said honestly, handing him the report as he perched on the edge of his desk. "Hakim asked me to give you my write-up – forensics wrapped everything up at the site. Their report should be filed in a few days, along with their photos. Mine are already uploaded to the network."

"Of course they are." Vogle smiled again as he glimpsed over the report. "You know I never doubted Mallick's claims about your work ethic, but I think he may still have undersold you. You keep this up, and you're going to be a formidable detective. The fact you've lasted this long has caught a lot of people by surprise. Captain Tan and I made a bet – he thought Hakim would toss you back in two weeks after I told him my plan."

"I see." I wasn't really sure what to make of my captain betting on my career. "And what did you bet, sir?"

"Vogle," he corrected, but he didn't look bothered by my continued formality. If anything, it just seemed to amuse him. "I told him you were going to be the youngest detective the 33rd had ever successfully recruited, and so far, it looks like I'm going to be right. If you make it past December, I'm going to formally transfer you. If Hakim hasn't ditched you yet, he isn't going to, so keep doing whatever you're doing because it's working."

"Thank you." I forced myself to smile, then dropped my eyes back to the report in his hands. "Hakim asked me to tell you to pass that off to Isaacs until Clive gets back. He said we don't have time to follow up on the leads."

Vogle snorted, eyeing me knowingly. "I'm sure you're filtering his words, but fine, tell him it's done."

"Thank you, sir." I turned to leave.

"Oh, and Gorski," he said, pausing me mid-step. "Take this with you."

He leaned back, reaching to open his top drawer, then pulled out a single red plastic tag. My heart faltered, my stomach knotting as he turned back to face me.

"You'll have to apologize to your boyfriend on my behalf," Vogle said, holding out the bright red tag as if it were a gift, not the token of violence and death I saw it to be. "I was only able to get one spare tag."

I had known that this was coming, and yet it still hit me like a ton of bricks. I swallowed hard, fighting back against the bile that flooded my mouth. I could see that woman's eyes. Hear her terrified screams as she clawed at my body. So much red—blood pooling across the ground as she stared up into the night, taking one last ragged breath before Hakim's rifle went off.

I clenched my hand to stop the tremble, tearing my eyes away from the red death tag to meet my captain's gaze. I forced myself to smile. It felt empty, detached, my motions robotic as I reached out to take the plastic tag and uttered the words I knew he wanted to hear.

"That's too bad for him." I fought to keep my hand steady and tried to ignore the unpleasant curl in my stomach as my fingers accidentally brushed his. "He'll have to find something else to do that night."

"I'm sure you can make it up to him." Vogle winked, and I stuffed the tag in my pants pocket, keeping my hand there with it. "Alright, you better get back to work before Hakim thinks you're slacking. Same place, same time, November 7th for the hunt. Tell Hakim to pop by before he leaves. I need to talk to him."

"Thank you, sir. I'll let him know."

I left before he could say anything else, before the vomit that was threatening to crawl up my throat could make it another inch. I marched past the bathroom, resisting the urge to go throw up, and beelined to the boardroom so I could get back to work.

Hakim returned around 7:30 am to confirm that I would be spending Wednesday and Thursday in the car with him staking out Morin's place because the officer who had been on duty had no records of Morin ever showing up at the apartment building on the days Gloria Gilbert recalled hearing our lead. Either Gloria had lied, which I doubted, the officer completing our surveillance wasn't paying attention because he didn't care about the case, which was probable, or Morin had an unseen way in and out of the apartment, which was possible.

Either way, Hakim seemed determined to sort it out. He put in a transfer request to Mallick for a new night shift support officer and an additional day car to cover the front of the building while we watched the rear.

I worked for another hour in silence, filling out a warrant request to tap Andrew Morin's phone line and put up cameras around the building, which we both knew would be denied. Aside from catching him boarding the subway with a duffle bag the night before a body was found, we had absolutely no evidence tying him to the Jane Doe case, and a no-show for his parole could hardly be considered insidious. Still, I filled the requests in as Hakim had directed, then submitted the forms to Vogle for review before settling in to watch another chunk of subway security footage.

I called it quits at 10:30 am. Late enough that Hakim wouldn't get suspicious but earlier than usual because I "needed to get some sleep". Which I did, but I had no intention of going to bed, at least not right away. Instead, I rushed home, unlocking my apartment to find Hawthorne seated at my kitchen table waiting for me. He had already mapped out the next set of warehouses, copied over traffic camera footage he'd illegally downloaded from work, and picked up food, which he made me eat in its entirety before we headed back down to my car. We both agreed that leaving his in the covered visitor lot out back was best, so if Grace did come snooping around, it would just look like Hawthorne was over at my place.

"Did you manage to get any sleep before Hakim called you?" Hawthorne asked as he shut the passenger door and buckled his seatbelt.

"No." I shook my head, pulling out from my spot and weaving through the underground garage. "I had to go straight in. I was lucky Hakim didn't fire me for taking so long to get there."

"Seriously? Does he time how long it takes you to get places?"

"Sort of." I double-checked the road was clear before I turned south. "He knows where I live, so he just times it out relative to that. I'm going to need to figure out how to work around it, though, because I can't always be at home."

"No kidding. You should head back early today and make sure you sleep. Eating enough food won't help if you're not getting any rest. I can always finish checking out the docks and jog home."

"Thanks," I said, giving him a tired smile. "And you're going to be on your own Wednesday and Thursday. Hakim wasn't happy with the lack of results from our additional support officer, so he's taken over day surveillance. Starting Wednesday, he's going to be staking out Morin's place, and I'm required to be there."

"Oh, great." I could all but hear the roll of his eyes. His opinion of Hakim had completely flipped after the night we'd gone hunting, and any respect he'd had for the man based on reputation was gone. "I can only imagine how enlightening that experience will be. Do you think he'll say anything or just sit there in unbearable silence the whole day?"

"Likely the latter."

"Rough," Hawthorne said, and I found myself nodding. "That's fine, though – don't worry about the docks. I can take care of it."

"Thanks."

"Oh!" He twisted to face me. "I got in touch with that girl from the rally before I headed into work last night. I didn't think meeting up was a good idea after what happened with Grace, so I just called her and spoke to her in vague terms. She confirmed the next protest – it's starting on Friday and running over the weekend."

"This weekend?" I asked, glancing at him as I slowed for a red light.

"Yeah."

"But that's going to be insane. Downtown is always crazy for Halloween – what the hell are they thinking?"

"I think that's probably the point." Hawthorne shrugged. "She said they lost a lot of traction after the city council ordered us to clear the city center, and they're worried the law is going to slip through because everyone is focusing on the upcoming municipal election and budget debates. They need more signatures and more visibility – what better way to do it than on Halloween weekend when the core is packed. It's going to make a huge scene, and I doubt the extra OT shifts are going to be enough to cover it."

"No kidding," I muttered.

We drove in silence for a few minutes, but I could feel Hawthorne's gaze lingering on the side of my face as faint rays of sunlight started to break through the clouds covering the sky.

"So how did it go?"

"How did what go?"

"Your conversation with Aries," he clarified, and my fingers involuntarily tightened on the wheel. "Did it go okay?"

"Yeah."

I said it much too quickly, and the nodding motion of my head felt awkward. How many times did I normally nod? Three times? Four times? Did I always adjust my hands this much? Or should I blink more? And why did I say "yeah"—I never say that.

"Yes," I corrected, as if that made any difference at all. "It went fine – all sorted."

"Okay."

Everything about how he said that single word suggested he didn't believe any of the ones I had just spoken, but he didn't push. He remained silent, though I could feel his eyes burning into my temple as I drove us the rest of the way to the docks. I avoided his gaze as I parked, quickly tugging my helmet on so he couldn't see my face before we got out, grabbed our gear bags, and then headed down the muddy trail.

The rain wasn't nearly as bad, which would have been a nice break from the recent onslaught of raging thunderstorms, except that the sun finally started to come out and, despite the colder air, heated up our blackout gear.

We crawled through the ditch, having to clamber over broken branches that had washed down the hill in the previous storm. We spent thirty minutes scoping out the first warehouse for pier 61 before we both agreed it would never be used. It was much too small, much too close to the road, and had a secondary branding on the side of the building I had never seen before.

It was probably legitimate, space being rented by another company or dedicated to their products for shipping. I drew a quick sketch of the logo as Hawthorne changed out the sensor hard drives, and then we pushed on. We had just reset the sensors across the road and darted through a series of small bushes to the next two buildings when my phone started to buzz.

I ignored it at first. I knew it was Warren based on the location of the vibration, but I would write him back after we had finished up and gotten back to the car. Then, as we were just figuring out what would be the best way to circle the next building, the phone buzzed again. And again. And three more times.

"Hold on," I said as I moved toward a cluster of tall grass and bushes so I could safely take out my phone.

"What's wrong?"

"I don't know." I unzipped my jacket and vest, huddling in the shade as I fished out the small device. "But Aries just messaged me six times in a row, and he never does that."

I squinted through my visor, crouching even more so I could make out the screen and unlock the phone.

"Is he okay?" Hawthorne asked, popping up to a crouch by my side so he could keep a lookout. "Did something happen?"

"I don't know." My eyes skimmed over the words. "But we need to go – now."

"Go?" Hawthorne turned to look at me. "Where?"

"The cave," I said, rapidly typing out a return message before shoving the phone back into my vest. "He didn't give me any details. He just pinged me a bunch to get my attention. He said to come out right away – so something must have happened."

"Shit," Hawthorne breathed as he sank back down in the mud. "Alright – then let's go."

We crawled back to the ditch, through the disgusting water, and up the other side until we hit the nearest section of brush and grass tall enough to cover our exit. Then we darted into the trees at a run. We didn't stop as the sky clouded over, the quiet drizzle of rain getting heavier as we sprinted up the hill back to the trail and then raced through the mud toward my car. I tried not to think about how quickly my heart was racing or the uncomfortable mix of excitement and dread coursing through my body. I tried not to worry, but it was difficult not to.

Either Eridanus and Orion had found something critical, or something terrible had happened. Warren wouldn't have asked us to drop everything and come out otherwise. I just hoped it was the former of the two options.

I popped the trunk to my car as we approached, tossing Hawthorne my gear bag as I made for the front seat. Then the engine was alive, our seatbelts were fastened, and I was driving through Carneth toward the nearest highway onramp. The entire way, my mind raced; the only calming thought I had was knowing that Warren himself was alright.

Hawthorne and I didn't speak until we reached the countryside road and pulled off into the bushes. I asked him to grab our bags while I ran back out to the road, filling in the muddy tire tracks as best I could with my boot before we headed into the woods. I knew it wouldn't be enough to completely hide our presence from passing cars, but there wasn't much else I could do. The trees were starting to thin, the grass was starting to die, and most of the shoulders along the road were covered in mud.

I would just have to hope that the rain washed away what was left of the marks or that people driving by didn't notice—but soon, very soon, Warren and I would have to come up with an alternative way to meet.

I darted between the trees, Hawthorne hot on my heels. We didn't stop or slow until we reached the clearing and burst out onto the stones. The river was rushing, overflowing with water from all the rain, covering the roots of the trees that grew near its banks and even sinking a few of the rocks that typically protruded through the rapids. I darted to the right, leading Hawthorne toward the large cave, only for my feet to falter momentarily when I saw a familiar figure approaching through the rain.

My heart stuttered in my chest, my breath catching in my throat when I saw him—then my feet quickened, and I rapidly closed the distance between us, easily leaving Hawthorne behind.

What would he say? Assuming that he said anything at all. What was the news? Had something gone wrong? Would he even tell me if it had, or would he simply tell me the new change in plans? My worry grew with every step, the strain across my chest so crushing I found my hand reaching for my helmet despite the faint streams of light that broke through the clouds ahead.

"Warren!"

His name was on my lips before I could form a rational thought, then my helmet was tugged free, my eyes squinting through the dim light as my face scrunched in discomfort. There wasn't enough sunlight for my skin to burn, at least not outright in blistering bubbles or angry red patches, but it still stung like being slapped repeatedly.

"Valya!" he called, and his use of my name rolled through my body like a warm electric wave. "What are you doing?! Put your helmet on!"

We reached each other in less than a second, both of us skidding to a stop on the slick stones.

"I'm fine," I said, waving my hand as if to dismiss his concern, though it was valid, and I couldn't quite remove the slight grimace from my face. It felt like my skin was being stretched across my skull, much like one would do with a thin piece of fabric before stitching in an elegant pattern. "What happened? Is everything okay? Are you okay?"

"I'm okay." Warren nodded as he took a step toward me.

His hand twitched as if to reach for me, but he froze as his eyes shifted to Hawthorne, who was quickly closing the distance toward us, and for a brief moment, I couldn't breathe. My heart seemed to stop. I waited in painful agony, wondering if that familiar look of disgust and hatred would return to his face. If maybe, that moment, those brief seconds of insanity when his lips had touched mine, had changed everything—made things worse and driven the wedge between us so impossibly deep we could never repair the damage.

I waited to feel my heart shatter once more as I stared at Warren through the rain.

I watched as he swallowed, his shoulders tensing momentarily as Hawthorne came to a stop by my side. Silence rang out, our tiny portion of the world grinding to a halt as they both stared at each other. Then, Warren let out a breath and nodded to Hawthorne.

"Come on," Warren said, gesturing with his head. "Everyone's here, and you should get out of the sun."

Deadlines

Warren turned, motioning for Hawthorne and me to follow, and the three of us darted across the rocks until we reached the mouth of the cave. I blinked as we crossed the threshold, waiting for my eyes to adjust to the dull glow from a smouldering fire as Hawthorne removed his helmet and Warren lingered just a few feet from my side.

"I appreciate you both coming out here so quickly." Orion's familiar voice filled the hollow space.

"It wasn't a problem," I said, my eyes finally having adjusted enough so I could take in Orion's appearance.

He looked the same as the last time I had seen him, except there was a tear in his jacket along the sleeve and a stain of blood had dried into the material. I glanced at Warren, but he didn't seem concerned about his father, and I couldn't smell the blood, so I decided I would ask about it later.

"So what's going on?" I asked, looking around the cave and taking in the other familiar human faces.

It was the usual crew, the rude monotonous female, the male with the long black hair tied into a braid, and the extremely silent one with the scar on his neck, but this time their rifles were simply gripped tightly and not directly aimed at our faces. It wasn't a huge change, but it meant the world to me and made my heart flutter with hope.

"Did something happen?"

"Yes." Orion nodded as he took a step forward. "They're on the move."

I stiffened as a rush of different emotions surged through my veins. It was happening. The moment we had been working toward—the one I could hardly wait for while simultaneously dreading.

"As of when?"

"Yesterday," Warren answered, and both Hawthorne and I turned to look at him. "We got the confirmation a few hours ago, and our team was able to flag the trucks. All three of them."

"Three of them," Hawthorne repeated, and Warren confirmed with a nod. "Is that – were you expecting that many? Can we handle that amount?"

"We're working on it," Orion said. "It's more than we were expecting, but it's not something you need to worry about."

"Then what do you need from us?" I asked.

"A contact of Eridanus got a lead through a potential buyer. Eridanus interrogated him this morning. We couldn't verify the warehouse or the dock, but we've confirmed the times and the company. The trucks are stamped with a logo for Sante Lumen Limited. Are you familiar with them?" Orion looked at me, but I shook my head in response. "We need you to dig into them as quickly as possible to determine if this is a one-time thing or if they're tied deeper into this mess. When we cut the head off the snake, I'm not interested in six more popping up, so we need a full list of anyone involved in the business and ties to other companies that might have their hand in the pot."

"Okay." I nodded. "Hawthorne and I can do that, but we're not going to have much time."

"You're right," Orion agreed. "Eridanus confirmed the arrival – the trucks are slotted to arrive this Friday, late evening before the sun goes down, and they're leaving the following day."

"What time?"

"Boat arrives at 3:00 pm Saturday," Orion said. "That gives us a window of fifteen hours to get in, find our people, and get out before they start loading the boat. I can take care of organizing our end, but that means you have to confirm the warehouse."

"3:00 pm," Hawthorne repeated as he ran a hand through his hair. "Boats are scheduled. They can't just show up unannounced. You're sure it's 3:00 pm on Saturday?"

"Positive," Orion confirmed. "Eridanus was very thorough during questioning."

"Okay." Hawthorne passed me his helmet, then slid off his gear bag. "I have a copy of the boat routes for this week."

"I pulled them from the Federal Coast Guard Register, and we looked at them before," I said, setting both our helmets on the ground as Hawthorne opened his notebook. "But without knowing the date, the shipping company, or anything else, the information was pretty much useless to us."

Warren moved closer, all but leaning over my shoulder, as Hawthorne began flipping until he found the page where he had written down the weekly arrival times for Lionetti's docks. I watched him scan down the page until he reached Saturday, then his finger paused by a cluster of entries.

"Dock 57d – 12:30 pm arrival, dock 62b – 1:45 pm, dock 59b – 2:55 pm, dock 58c – 3:15 pm, and dock 60d – 4:45 pm arrival," Hawthorne read out. "There's nothing else on the piers Lionetti owns until 8:00 pm."

"Then it has to be dock 59b," I said. "Which means warehouse 236A."

"Wait." Warren turned, lowering his voice as he glanced between his father and me. "We have to be certain – you're sure Eridanus's contact is reliable? That the information is sound?"

"It's sound," Orion said quietly, nodding to his son. "Eridanus is reliable – I would trust them with my life."

Warren frowned, a brief moment of unspoken communication passing between the two before he finally nodded in submission.

"It aligns with everything we've already established, Aries," I said quietly as I removed my own gear bag. "Piers 57 and 62 are shared docks. They're way too close to uninvolved parties. Even if the boat times did align, it would be an unnecessary risk to load anything illegal there. They have no control over the other owner's security or dock presence. Too many things that could go wrong – it wouldn't make any sense for Beckette to use them."

I dropped my bag to the ground, kneeling before it as I rapidly unzipped the smallest compartment.

"We can eliminate 57 and 62 based on that alone," I said as I pulled out a copy of our map and unrolled it across the ground. "And 61 is out because there are no scheduled arrivals that day. The only other pier with a boat arrival near the time Eridanus gave is 58, but the warehouses associated with it aren't a good fit."

"Most of them are too visible from the road," Hawthorne explained as he crouched down on my left and helped me hold the map flat. The others in the cave moved closer, their curiosity seeming to outweigh their caution. "The ones closer to the dock are boarded up and don't look like they've been used in decades. Warehouse 236A is ideal. It's perfectly located – not visible from the main road, close to the pier, access door facing south, and it looks to have new cameras on the building exterior."

"And the boat time confirms it." I looked up, meeting Warren's warm brown gaze. I thought about everything I had learned back at the Academy, all the training I'd done to become a detective, my partner and the way he seemed to see things that I couldn't—and I found myself nodding in reassurance. "If I wanted to conduct illegal activity, this is the warehouse I would pick."

The others remained silent as Warren looked down at me, then he let out a breath.

"Alright," Warren sighed, and he kneeled by my side, much closer than I would have expected. "So how best would we get into it?"

"The best place to enter would be the northeast corner," I replied as I tried not to think about how close his face was when I turned to look at him. I swallowed, my gaze dropping to his lips before I forced my eyes back to our map. "It's tucked behind warehouse 235, and from what we can tell, there's a gap in the cameras and no security on the roof. We can climb the fire escape on the northeast side and make our way across it."

"Across the roof to where?"

"To the southeast side," Hawthorne answered. "Here."

He tapped the map, and Orion crouched down beside his son, his eyes darting across the paper and intently consuming all the notes that I had scrawled along the edges.

"There's a door to the office unit on the roof," Hawthorne explained. "They would likely bring the trucks in the south bay doors facing the pier. They're just below the office unit, which will make a roof entry ideal. I can't see that they would leave the trucks outside. Fifteen hours is too long, and even with these warehouses being sheltered from the road, it's too risky. They'll pull them inside and wait, then drive them right down the dock and load them on the boat."

"It's possible they may even change vehicles inside or load them into a shipping container," I said. "Pier 59 has a crane. It's one of the bigger docks along the river. They might not be driving them onto the boat at all."

"True." Hawthorne nodded. "Another layer of changing hands to make it more difficult to track the shipment. They could put anything on the side of those containers and load them with a hundred others. We'd never find them."

"Which is exactly why we have to get to them before they leave the warehouse," Orion said. "And if possible, get to them before the trucks are unloaded."

"That might be difficult." I frowned, looking up to meet Orion's gaze. "You said the trucks are scheduled to arrive Friday right before sunset, which is right before traffic will hit and business hours resume. We won't have time to go in. Those docks are busy at night. The roads will be crawling with trucks, security, staff – Carneth is a main port. A lot of boats swap crews here and take up port for several days. It will be impossible to get in without someone seeing us.

"We'll have to wait until sunrise, go in after the regular shift has ended, and get them out before 3:00 pm. The best way to get to the warehouse would be cutting in from the road between warehouses 235 and 234, where the camera gap is, then making our way south between 236A and 236B," I said, tracing my finger along the narrow road that ran between the two massive buildings. "I'm not sure how you're planning to get them out, but there are some cameras between 236A and 236B – and I'm sure there will be even more still by the bay doors on the south. We can probably disable a few just before we make our move, but there's security at the main entrance to all the docks. You can't just drive back out. They'll want papers, IDs, and dockets."

"If it's so difficult to get down there, how do you know so much about the warehouse and dock activity?" the monotone-looking woman asked as she stepped forward and glared down at me. "How did you get down there without being seen?"

"We crawled through the ditch," I said, ignoring her tone and simply answering the question. I moved my finger, pointing to the thick line along the left side of the map to the north. "This ditch catches runoff from the hillside here, prevents the docks from flooding with mud and debris during the rainy season, and it's a storm sewer for part of Carneth. The forest that borders the docks is protected land – part of the Federal Forestry Reserve. There're hiking trails that run through it. We park our car in the lot here, a few kilometres from the main dock entrance, and pretend to go for a run, cutting through the trees, down the hill, and into the ditch that runs along the docks. We use it for cover as we crawl our way along the main road and investigate the warehouses. Then, when the weather is particularly bad, we sneak across the road, keeping to the bushes to scope out the buildings as closely as possible."

"But that only works because it's just the two of us," Hawthorne said. "It's not difficult for us to avoid being seen, but we'd never be able to get your people out that way. Even if we manage to pull this off without drawing attention to ourselves at the warehouse, you can't get that many people across the road and up the hill unnoticed. They have regular security patrols."

"Do you have those documented?" Orion asked.

"Yes." I reached for my bag, digging out my own notebook. "They're not always on time, but this is the rough pattern that they follow."

I ripped the page out, knowing Hawthorne had a copy of the guard schedule in his book too.

"Thank you," Orion said as he took the paper. "I'll speak to Eridanus about the patrols and cameras. We already have a few different evac plans, but we were waiting on this break to set anything definitive. Our biggest issue is timing. We don't have room for mistakes – we have to make sure we get our people out before anyone calls for backup. The Beckette family has allies and clients in the CPD, among other places within the city, so there's a good chance they've already stacked the patrol routes in the area. We'll need you there to help us get inside the warehouse, but you'll have to get out just as quickly if anything goes wrong."

"Understood," I said, wondering how many of my colleagues might actually be bought-and-paid-for cops. "We'll be there, and Hawthorne and I can move pretty quick if we need to. There are a bunch of routes we could take after we cross the ditch into the woods, so I'm not worried about that. The bigger issue is my partner. If he calls me in, I have to answer."

"Can't you just take the day off?" the monotone-looking woman asked, but I shook my head.

"It doesn't work like that," I answered, turning to look at Orion. "I'm on call indefinitely, twenty-four hours a day it seems. If something happens and he calls me in, I have to pick up and go. Even if the execution is flawless and people don't find out what happened at the docks until after it's done, they'll know the window that it occurred in, and my partner will know that I was missing. This is exactly the sort of case my captain would assign him to, and that will just cause problems. The last thing I need is for him to become suspicious – he already doesn't like me and is holding me at arm's length. I can't give him any excuse to let me go. If I lose my position as detective, I won't be able to do this kind of work for you, and we can't afford that. So I'll do everything that I can to be there that night, but I can't guarantee what will happen."

"Unless you're already working," Hawthorne said slowly.

"What do you mean?"

"The OT shifts for patrol." Hawthorne turned to look at me. "Sign up."

"That won't help," I argued. "I might technically still be Patrol and Street, but Vogle's all but formally transferred me. He'd never allow it."

"I know, but they would if they knew there's going to be a protest."

"Hawthorne, I don't know if that's—"

"No, hear me out – I'll call my contact and tell her to have some of her partners let the plans slip. The second someone on city council finds out they're planning to flood the downtown core, the CPD will have to start upping the staff. As it stands, Mallick is already concerned."

"Mallick is concerned about Halloween OT every year," I countered. "But that's beside the point. There's no guarantee that your contact will agree to let it slip, and even if she did, and even if I signed up, they'd station me in the city centre where it's going to be the most crazy. That will make it even harder for me to get to the docks."

"No, that might work," Orion interrupted. "Eridanus has a contact at the CPD."

"What?" Warren sounded surprised, and his displeasure was clear, but his father ignored him.

"They can get you stationed near the docks – I can set that up," Orion continued. "Then you can just pretend to have responded to something suspicious in the area, and you can call it in after we're clear."

"That could work," I said, nodding as I thought it through. "I could identify it as a disturbance. Maybe someone on your side can fire their weapons or do something else to create some commotion just before you leave. I'm sure Beckette's men will be armed. It won't be hard to create a scene – the more difficult part will be trying to prevent one until we're ready for it. We'll have to be careful and manage that, but calling it in would force them to open an investigation. The docks are federal land, so they can't just bury it as they did with the girls at Scott's house. If I call it in to dispatch from my radio, they'll have to respond, and that will give you the media attention that you wanted."

"It's done, then," Orion said as he turned to look at Hawthorne. "Contact your ally and have her leak the details of the protest today before 6 pm, but make sure she speaks directly to Kenneth at the Carneth Free Press. That will get it in the news before your regular shifts start tonight. Your friend is involved with the wildlife conservation efforts, correct?"

"Yes." Hawthorne nodded.

"Then tell her, 'the sun is rising, and soon the birds will sing'. She won't hesitate. Corvus, sign up for the additional patrols. Once the news breaks tonight, the CPD will scramble, and no one will question it if you add your name to the list. You won't be the only detective who does so."

I nodded.

"I'll contact Eridanus and tell them to make sure their contact gets you both posted close by."

"It shouldn't be too difficult," Hawthorne said as he folded up the map. He stood from the ground, towering above everyone. "I switched my patrol route. It's already down by the north side of the docks. I'll be placed there for the OT shifts regardless, so if this Eridanus person's CPD contact can pair Corvus with me, it's a done deal."

"What about Hernandez?" I asked.

"Our shifts got out of sync a few weeks ago with all those days I was working. He's still stationed downtown core. I've mostly been running solo."

"Alright." I nodded again, standing from the ground with Warren and Orion. "Then we have a plan. We'll focus our efforts on warehouse 236A, put the sensors near the road, compile a typical timeline for the security and staff, come up with a definitive plan of entry, and figure out the best way to get from Hawthorne's patrol route to the warehouse. I'll cross-check Sante Lumen Limited with the data we've collected so far. I'm sure 236A is the right place, but we'll see if we can link it to the company and find any ties back to the Beckette or Lionetti family. We'll put everything together on a disk and print some extra maps and plans – but I'm not sure if I'll be able to make any drops this week.

"My partner pulled me onto surveillance for another case," I explained. "I'll do what I can, but I have no idea how much time he plans to keep me out. As it stands, Hawthorne will be doing most of the work by the docks. I also can't do anything about weapons or gear for the night of, aside from the sort of stuff I've already been bringing. Our ammunition is counted and logged, so Hawthorne and I won't be able to fire our weapons if anything goes wrong unless there's a way to explain it, which isn't easy to do."

The monotone-looking female snorted at my words, and despite my best intentions to ignore her, I turned and glared.

"But that doesn't mean we can't effectively remove threats or help you," I said stiffly, and her eyes narrowed at me. "There are other ways to immobilize Reborn that don't involve firearms."

"Don't worry about gear." Warren's voice sounded to my right, and I turned to look at him. "We have other connections for that. We can spare you both rifles for the night so you won't have to use your firearms. They won't be new, but they'll work."

"Thanks," I said, my voice coming out much softer than I had meant it to. I cleared my throat, tugging my eyes away from him as a nervous flutter stirred in the pit of my stomach.

"I can make the drops this week," Hawthorne offered to Warren, and everyone in the cave turned to look at him. "I know it probably isn't your preference, but if Corvus can't make it, I can do it. At the very least, you're going to need copies of these maps."

My eyes flicked between the two men, silence ringing through the cave as Warren stared at Hawthorne, then, to my relief, slowly nodded.

"Alright. Do you remember the way here?"

"No," Hawthorne admitted, a sheepish smile crossing his lips. "She's the one with the good memory, but I'll pay attention when we leave."

"I can meet you closer to the road."

"Alright. I can drop off copies of all this tomorrow afternoon so you can start planning right away. Once we get more assembled, Corvus can coordinate another drop time."

"Okay," I said, nodding in agreement. "Then let's get to work."

We packed up our stuff, agreeing to keep in touch and play things by ear throughout the week while Orion worked with Eridanus to finalize the plan and Hawthorne and I did everything we could to help without drawing more attention to ourselves.

Orion told us he would have everything ready for Friday, and Warren would give us the final details.

I shook his hand just like last time, then turned with Hawthorne to leave. Everything was happening so quickly it felt surreal. I didn't feel ready, and I couldn't shake the uneasiness lingering in my bones. I was glad that Warren didn't seem to be angry anymore, and yes, it was great to know that he didn't hate me, but things still felt off.

I walked by Hawthorne's side toward the mouth of the cave, my helmet hanging loose from my fingertips, only for my grip to instantly tighten when I heard Warren's voice.

"Corvus!"

I turned, pausing just outside the cave in the rain, squinting through the dim light of the afternoon that filtered through the thick clouds and stung my face. Warren was moving toward me, and when his eyes flicked to Hawthorne, I felt him shift away from my side and saunter further out onto the rocks.

"I nearly forgot. I've got your gear bag," Warren said, holding up the empty canvas material. "It will save you needing to grab another for the drops this week."

"Thanks."

I took the bag and shivered as his warm fingers brushed against mine. I opened my mouth to say something, but I didn't know what to say, so I closed it. Even if we were completely alone with no one to hear our exchange, I still don't think I would have found any words.

We needed to talk about what had happened. We both knew that. I could see it written all over his face as we awkwardly stood there, his eyes circling my exposed face like he was hoping it might have some clue as to what the hell we were supposed to do now. I swallowed, wondering what he was thinking and if he, too, felt the desperate pull that made me want to reach for him.

"You should put your helmet on," he finally said. It felt like an odd thing to say, but then he took a small step forward, and his voice dropped lower. "I know it's the rainy season, Valya, but it still stresses me out whenever you take it off outside during the day."

"Alright," I said, and I couldn't help the small smile that touched my lips. "I will – but I promise you I'm fine. We don't burst into flames and instantly die if the sun comes out."

"Well, then you can explain all the technicalities of how it works to me," Warren said, giving me a small smile. "But later. You need to get some sleep. This is going to be a long week."

"I know." I forced myself to step back, even though I didn't want to leave. "I'll text you later."

He nodded, and I turned away, stuffing my helmet on my head but leaving the visor up so it didn't feel so suffocating as I moved toward Hawthorne's side. We walked across the rocks in silence, only the sound of the rain and wind tugging at our clothes filling the air until we hit the trees.

"So you really did patch things up with Aries then, huh?"

I frowned, not liking the teasing tone of his voice.

"Yes, I told you that I had."

"Mhmm," Hawthorne mused, flipping up his visor now that we were under the shadows of the trees so I could see his face as he turned to look at me. "But you didn't tell me that you guys were *that* friendly."

"We're not."

"Pfft," he scoffed. "Yes, you are."

"Aren't you supposed to be paying attention to the trail?" I countered. "You have to find your way back here on your own, you know."

"I'll be fine." Hawthorne waved his hand, turning to give me a sly grin. "Your human said he would come meet me by the road, which was rather nice of him considering how things went last time. What did you do? Talk me up? Tell him I'm not just handsomely good-looking but that I am, in fact, rather skilled and incredibly useful as a partner?"

"You're ridiculous." I rolled my eyes, but discomfort was starting to itch across my skin. "I told him you were a good asset to the mission, but now I'm seriously regretting those words."

Hawthorne laughed, and I mentally crossed my fingers that this would be the end of his prying, but it wasn't.

"So… you two seem pretty comfortable with each other."

"I've been working with him for months, Hawthorne." A tone of warning rang in my voice. "Of course I've gotten to know him."

"Does he always worry about you?" His words made me falter, my feet stumbling across the slick moss-covered ground as I fought to keep my face impassive. "Because it's sort of adorable and also hilarious that he thought you might burst into flames."

"He doesn't know that much about us," I said, voice stiff as I regained my footing and hoped he would just drop the topic. The last thing I needed was for him to think there was something going on between us, which there was, but that was beside the point.

"Maybe not, but he seems to know a bit about you."

I scoffed. "And how do you figure that?"

"Your reaction just confirmed it." He sounded pleased with himself. "So, do you two hang out when you drop off supplies or—"

"Can you cut it out?"

"Personally, I think it's rather cute that you like him so much," Hawthorne said, and even though his voice was light and laced with playfulness, all my muscles tensed at his words. "Though he is ridiculously short – but I suppose not for you. It must be nice not having to constantly look up. I'm going to have to watch it, or you're going to get a crush on him, and I really will lose my shot."

I stopped, memories from twenty-four hours ago flooding my mind. The taste of his lips. The feel of his warm hands against my skin. And the horrible mix of nervous excitement and sickness returned as if it had never left.

"That's not funny," I whispered, my hands clenching at my sides.

"Oh come on, Gorski, I'm just—"

"Stop." I turned to glare at him as my voice started to shake. "I asked you to stop. So just stop, okay? How hard is it for you to let this go? Why do you always give me such a hard time!"

My voice had risen, and I had all but screamed the last few words at him. He stopped moving, his body going completely still.

"I was just teasing, Valya."

He looked confused, and to my horror, my eyes started to burn. I wanted to throw up again. A part of me wanted to go back in time and stop that kiss from ever happening, while a huge portion of me wanted to see where it could have led if my partner hadn't called and interrupted us. I blinked, dropping my gaze to the ground as I tried to regain control. I really was pushing things—both physically and mentally—if I was about to cry two days in a row.

Reborn didn't usually cry, not unless severely injured, so to say this was concerning was an understatement.

"Valya—"

He stepped forward, but I stepped back, refusing to look up at him.

"Let's just go. We need to get back and get to work."

I made to leave, but Hawthorne grabbed my arm.

"Hey!" He pulled, and I glared up at him as he spun me around. "I didn't know."

"Didn't know what?" I spat, ripping my arm from his grasp. "That you're incredibly annoying?"

"That you actually like him."

I stilled.

"It's okay," he said, his voice cautious. He raised both hands as if he was trying to steady my racing heart. "I tease you all the time, and you've never once gotten angry about it because we both know I'm just screwing around, and it doesn't mean anything. I know you, and you only ever get angry when something truly matters to you."

I swallowed, my legs beginning to tremble as I watched him search my face.

"It's okay," he repeated, and I felt a tear break loose from the corner of my eye. "I wouldn't have said anything if I knew. I – I thought there was something weird going on after I met him because he seemed so horrible and you were so stressed out, but I didn't think it was this. I wouldn't have joked about it if I knew you liked him."

I nodded, dropping my gaze to his chest.

"I'm sorry."

"It's alright." I cleared my throat, forcing the rest of the tears down along with the bile that had come with it. "I'm fine."

"Are you sure?" He sounded skeptical. "Because you don't look alright."

"Gee, thanks."

"That's not what I mean," he said with a sigh. "I mean, are you – is it – do you want to talk about it?"

"No, I don't want to talk about it!" I groaned.

"Well, I don't know!" Hawthorne raised his hands again in defeat. "I've never been in this situation! I have no idea how to handle it. That's part of why I was teasing you about it because it seemed like such an insane scenario."

"I'm aware of how insane it is," I said, turning away from him to keep walking back to the road. "Thank you for highlighting that fact."

"Hey, I'm not judging." Hawthorne fell into step by my side. "They really don't seem all that different from us, and you've spent a lot of time with him, as you said. It just – it just seems complicated."

"No kidding," I muttered.

We walked in silence for a few minutes, Hawthorne no doubt questioning my sanity as I pondered if it was possible for a Reborn to die of stress.

"So, have you—"

"Do not ask that question."

"What? No!" Hawthorne sputtered, looking at me in shock. "I was just going to ask if you've told him or if he knows! And you say I'm the inappropriate one."

"You *are* the inappropriate one, and I don't know."

"How do you not know if you've told him?"

"No, I don't know if he knows," I said. "We haven't had the chance to talk about what happened."

He slowed, and I could feel his eyes on the side of my helmet again.

"And it was nothing like that," I said, turning to glare at him. "So get your mind out of the gutter."

"I didn't even say anything."

"You don't have to, I know how your brain works."

We walked in silence until we reached the edge of the woods and navigated toward my car. I tried not to think about the dried mud that covered both front seats as I opened the driver's door or how I hadn't even noticed that we were filthy when we'd left the ditch and raced out here. We'd been in such a hurry it hadn't even crossed my mind. I would need to clean this out, but I doubted I would have the time before work, so I'd have to just throw in a dozen air fresheners and cover the seats with a sheet.

I sighed, falling into my car and turning the key to start the engine.

"I wasn't lying, you know?" Hawthorne said as we both tossed our helmets onto the backseat.

"Lying about what?" I turned to look at him as I put the car in drive.

"About not judging you," he said, but this time his voice was low, and his expression had grown serious. "I don't. You're my friend, Valya, and I'll support you no matter what. I know you don't want to talk about it, and that's fine, but I am here if you want to talk about it. And I won't tease you about him again."

I stared at him in the refreshing dark of my car, a small, exhausted smile pulling at my lips.

"Thanks, Theo," I said, and his eyes creased as he smiled. "You're a good friend."

Countdown

The noise of a key scratching in the lock jolted my attention from the screen. My eyes went wide, my head turned, and my slow, steady pulse quickened as the door opened—only for it to relax as Hawthorne's voice filled the air.

"Hey, you're supposed to be sleeping," he said, dropping his small gear bag on the floor so he could unlace his boots. "Wasn't that the point of me going out to crawl through the disgusting ditch all by myself?"

"It's after 6 pm, Hawthorne," I said, pausing the video and stretching my arms above my head. I turned in my seat to face him fully, noting the mud that covered the legs of his dark black pants and his boots. The rest of him looked soaked to the bone. "I did sleep. I slept for four hours. I just got up."

He frowned. "That's not enough."

"Yes, well." I shrugged, not bothering to argue because he was right. "This week isn't enough to prepare, either, but it is what it is."

"Isn't that the truth."

"Besides, I don't have to go in as early tonight. Hakim confirmed we're taking the Wednesday day shift for the Morin stakeout, and that doesn't start until 9 am. I'll head into the precinct just before 4 am, so I can always take a nap before then."

"Uh-huh."

He didn't seem to believe me, which was fair. I would probably spend the remainder of my time crawling through footage for warehouse 236A and preparing the next set of information to be dropped off to Warren. Hawthorne let out a sigh as he kicked off his boots and made his way across the room toward me.

"So – did you do it?"

"Yes." I nodded, taking the hard drive he handed me and gesturing for him to sit down. It didn't matter that he was riddled in mud; my entire apartment had been a mess since our late return the day before. "Orion was right. I heard it on the radio on the drive in. I wasn't even in the building for two seconds before I saw a poster about the OT sign-ups. Mallick must have had his day cut short. He was probably into work minutes after it hit the evening news. I added my name to the sign-up list before I even headed up to eleven, then stopped at Vogle's office to let him know."

"Did he mind?"

"No." I shook my head. "He wasn't surprised, either. He knows I still have close ties to Patrol and Street and figured I would want to help support them. Besides, I wasn't the only detective to sign up. Apparently, a bunch of other "go-getters" volunteered. The city is going crazy over this. The news mentioned that the mayor is trying to get some emergency status passed to keep the streets locked down over the weekend, but the local businesses aren't having it because Halloween is their busiest night until the winter holidays and they rely heavily on the income, so the CPD is under a lot of pressure to ensure things stay under control. Vogle said as long as Hakim didn't mind, it was fine."

"And I take it Hakim didn't mind?"

I snorted, plugging the new hard drive into my computer to start the download.

"No – big shocker there," I said, and I was unable to keep the bitterness from my voice. It worked out well for our mission that he didn't care, but the reminder of how little he thought of me still stung. "He just told me to keep my phone on – that he would call if something happened and he needed my help, which I doubt he'll do. As much as he seems to love calling me in and keeping me late, I'm convinced that's only to try and drive me away, which sucks. Even after all this time, he's still just trying to wear me down and get me to quit."

"He's a jerk," Hawthorne said, his tone conveying even more dislike than my own. "But that's fine. It works in our favour."

"Exactly." I nodded. "Even if he didn't hate me, I doubt Vogle would have pushed to keep me on call anyway. With so many patrols scheduled, he isn't exactly expecting many murders or crimes requiring full-scale investigations. It will likely be petty theft, protest confrontations, and disorderly conduct, none of which will be considered an emergency if riots break out downtown with the protestors. The bigger issue is crowd control."

"No kidding." Hawthorne leaned back in his seat and ran his hand through his hair. He looked just as tired as I felt, but I knew he would never complain. "If the turnout is anything like what my contact seems to think it will be, the core will be packed. I just hope things stay peaceful."

"Me too."

"Any word on placement yet?"

"Not yet, but I'm sure I'll find out in a day or two."

"Well, let's hope that Eridanus's contact can pull this off," Hawthorne said, and I nodded in agreement. "Otherwise, Saturday is going to be even more difficult than it already is if you can't be there."

"What, you're telling me you couldn't handle breaking into a warehouse and freeing dozens of humans without me?" I teased.

"Of course I could." Hawthorne scoffed. "I just don't want you to miss out. Besides, Aries would probably be disappointed if you weren't there."

My eyes narrowed into a glare, but Hawthorne simply grinned.

"I'm joking."

"Ha, ha." I rolled my eyes. "You're hilarious."

"But in all seriousness," Hawthorne said, leaning forward to rest his forearms on my table. "We should come up with a plan in case that happens."

"I know," I agreed. "I've been thinking about that, but I really don't know what I can do. The cars have GPS trackers in them, so if I'm stuck in the city centre, I'd have to run down to the docks. Otherwise, they might notice it in the log files."

"That would be a far run."

"No kidding," I sighed. "I mean, I could do it. Maybe park my personal car near my patrol route and swap vehicles, but if someone noticed, it would raise some red flags or, at the very least, look bad on my service record. If anything happens on my route and dispatch puts out a call and I don't respond, at a minimum, it will look like an OT grab."

"Which is something Mallick is already harping about," Hawthorne said. "He called a floor meeting during the break last night – said if anyone was caught camping in their cars simply for the sake of getting OT, there would be repercussions."

"I can't afford to get fired, Hawthorne." I met his eyes with concern. "I won't be useful to Orion without my CPD access."

"That's not true," Hawthorne countered. "But maybe you should just go ask Mallick to be paired with me?"

"He never plays favourites." I dropped my gaze to the table, staring at the map as my thoughts spun. "But who do you think it is?"

"What do you mean – the contact?"

"Yes." I nodded, meeting Hawthorne's eyes once more. "I keep thinking about it, and it has to be a lieutenant in Patrol and Street, right? Otherwise, how would they be able to alter our patrol routes?"

"I wondered that too, but it could be someone in IT," Hawthorne pondered. "Or maybe Eridanus has more than one ally in the CPD."

"Or maybe Eridanus *is* the ally in the CPD," I said as I wondered just how much Orion's contact knew about Hawthorne and me. If they had access to the CPD and an inside person with the capacity to influence our shifts behind the scenes, it wasn't farfetched to think that both Eridanus and Orion now had copies of our files.

Perhaps that was why Orion had accepted our help…

"Did they ever say anything about him?"

"No." I shook my head. "Nothing – it might not even be a him."

"Maybe it's Mallick."

I snorted, smiling in amusement. "Could you imagine him breaking rules?"

"No," Hawthorne laughed. "But it would be the perfect cover."

I nodded, dropping my eyes back to the table.

The idea of Mallick being Eridanus or being an ally of Eridanus was insane. Thinking about it made me want to laugh, and yet the longer I stared at the map and my computer chugged along behind me downloading the files, the more I started to wonder if I was crazy for thinking it didn't sound so crazy. After all, that exchange with him in the elevator had been a bit odd. Though, maybe not. Mallick had warned me about the Detective Unit before he'd brought me up to meet Vogle. So maybe he just didn't approve of what happened in that unit. The man was incredibly clean-cut, and I couldn't see him ever allowing someone to rip pages from his notebook, let alone turn a blind eye to a federal crime.

"Do you mind if I use your shower?" Hawthorne's voice pulled me from my thoughts. "I can help you clean up the mud after."

"Go ahead." I gestured toward the bathroom with my hand. "I'll keep going through these old videos while the download finishes. See if I find anything related to Sante Lumen Limited."

"Nothing yet?"

"Not yet," I sighed. "Just the usual dock patrols, a few people in business clothes coming out to their cars, and the janitors coming by to clean the office area at the end of the night, but I'll keep you posted."

COUNTDOWN

WEDNESDAY, OCTOBER 28
1:23 PM

It was difficult to see. Between the sunshield and the sheets of rain that pelted against the car, everything blurred together, and I found myself sympathizing with the officer Hakim had kicked off stakeout duty. No wonder he didn't have anything noted down in his reports. He probably couldn't see a damn thing the entire time he was in his car, and I had no idea what Hakim was expecting us to find. Reborn didn't mind the rain, but we didn't venture out into the rainy season for fun either.

In the last two hours, only one car had driven by, and there wasn't a single kid in blackout gear to be found, which made sense. The gutters were flooded. The sewer system was at capacity, and school midterm exams were in the works. Even kids who hated studying would find it undesirable to step outside in this, especially with all the good skateboarding areas flooded.

I bit back a sigh, wishing that I was the one running the supply drop to Warren this afternoon instead of wasting my time in this car. I'd have to wait until I got back to the precinct to text Hawthorne. Drawing my secret phone out was out of the question with Hakim sitting less than two feet away. As it was, I had turned both phones to silent, letting Warren and Hawthorne know I would be MIA until the sun went down and we swapped shifts with the new officer Mallick had loaned out to the Jane Doe case.

While impossible in practice, a part of me was amazed Hakim wasn't planning to stakeout Morin's apartment during the night shift too. I was sure he would if he could, but he seemed pretty convinced that whatever Morin was up to, it was happening during the day. All our data agreed with that theory—times of death, when the bodies were found, where they were dumped, the footage of him getting on the train, and even Gloria Gilbert's recollection of when he came home.

Still, I found myself doubting we would catch him as my watch buzzed, and I dropped my eyes to note the time.

1:30 pm – no change

I marked the words in my notebook exactly the same as I had every ten minutes for the last four and a half hours. It was partly to keep myself awake but also because I wanted a good, clean record of everything, or in this case, nothing, that happened today.

I chanced a side glance at my partner, wondering how the hell he could sit so still and breathe so quietly. It wasn't like I was making much noise, but if not for the fact that he'd driven us here and I could see him with my own two eyes right now, I'd never have known that he was here.

A blur of movement in the side mirror caught my eye, and I sat forward in my seat, only to frown in disappointment when the car drove past us and Morin's apartment building. I watched the red taillights fade from view, then marked the time and noted it down in my notebook because I had literally nothing else to do. I'd already run through my mental map of the warehouse, gone over Hawthorne's plan for getting down to 236A without going through the docks' main gate security, and reviewed the security patrol routes.

Now I was left wondering how Orion planned to get his people out and whether Hawthorne would be waiting at my apartment with an outline of the plans.

Then again, maybe Orion didn't plan to tell us anything. Perhaps we were simply the muscle, instructed to show up at a designated time, get his people inside the building, and take out any guards or armed threats. It wouldn't surprise me if that was the case. Orion was a smart man. I knew he didn't have any issues working with Reborn, but that didn't mean that he trusted us, and I was sure he kept his cards close to his chest. This mission, and likely all the details of his and his allies' other activities, were probably strictly controlled.

Warren might be the only other person that knew everything going on and who was who within their network. With the exception of Eridanus, it seemed, who might very well be using code names and protective measures for their Reborn ally network too. It was quite possible that even Orion didn't know who the CPD ally was.

Headlights from the street ahead flickered into view, and I shifted, watching and waiting for the vehicle to drive by like all the others—but it didn't. I watched it pull to a stop along the side of Morin's building, and for the first time since we had parked the car, Hakim moved.

"Gorski—"

"On it."

I grabbed my binoculars, leaning forward and fiddling with the dial to get things in focus, as Hakim grabbed the camera.

"See anything?"

"It's a van," I said, moving my binoculars to track the person who had gotten out of the driver's side door. "One person, average male height – probably around seven feet five inches. Dressed in plain blackout gear."

I heard the click of the camera as Hakim took several photos.

"They're getting something out from the side of the van and – oh, it's just a vacuum." I readjusted the dial to read the open van door. "Jensen's Janitorial."

It felt oddly familiar, but I ignored the feeling in favour of returning my gaze to the unknown person, watching as they kicked the large rolling shop vac through a puddle toward the building, the motion drawing my eyes to their feet and the very distinct symbol along the shaft of their boot.

I stilled.

"They're wearing Ridgebacks," I said, the words coming out slowly as the unidentified figure returned to their van to grab a small bag. I dropped my binoculars and turned to look at Hakim, who stared at me blankly.

"The boots," I clarified, but he simply arched a brow. "They're a popular brand."

"So?" Hakim asked. "What's your point, Gorski?"

"My old patrol partner was really into fashion," I said, twisting in my seat to face him. "She used to talk about different brands all the time, and Ridgebacks are probably the most expensive boots a person could buy. My point is, how on earth could someone working the janitorial day shift in an apartment building like this afford to buy them – and even if they could, why the hell would they wear them to work in this weather?"

He stared at me for a moment, then nodded. Orion had been right in his words by the fire a month ago—even if it pained me to admit it—Reborn were classist, incredibly so. I had never really thought too much about it before meeting Warren. I knew it, as I'm sure we all did, but it was just so normal it was never a focus until I became Hakim's sidekick and started to see it everywhere. Until it was shoved down my throat in glaringly obvious ways that left me feeling sick.

A janitorial job simply wouldn't pay enough to afford someone Ridgebacks. Hell, it would barely pay enough to support a minimum standard of living, and no person who had enough family wealth to afford those boots and not care about keeping them clean would voluntarily be working the day shift cleaning up low-rent apartments.

That wasn't how Reborn worked, which meant something else was going on.

"Write it down," Hakim said, turning back to take more pictures as I pulled out my pen. "Capture everything. We'll open a search on Jensen's Janitorial when we get back to the precinct. I want a complete list of the staff and all the locations where they work."

"Got it."

I scribbled down my observations, but instead of feeling relief that we might have just caught a break, I felt my stomach churn as I realized why the name had seemed so familiar. Jensen's Janitorial was the same company that cleaned the office building of warehouse 236A.

THURSDAY, OCTOBER 29
10:17 PM

I unlocked the door to my apartment, slipped inside, and immediately stripped off my vest. I felt claustrophobic, which was a recurring and concerning theme as of late, and sitting in the car with Hakim all day had done nothing to help. It just made it worse, and I found myself tugging at the collar of my shirt as I kicked off my boots and made my way across the room toward my table.

We hadn't seen anything the entire day. Not Morin, not Jensen's Janitorial, and not even any residents from the building as the rain continued to pour, and Hakim sat there in silence, ignoring me completely. I let out a groan, stretching my arms above my head and rolling my neck. It felt good to be out of that car, and I was happy to be home so I could get to work on other things. Thankfully, I only had one more shift on stakeout duty until I was placed on Halloween OT patrol.

Yet that didn't really make me feel any better.

I still hadn't heard anything about my placement, and I hadn't been able to touch base with Hawthorne since Tuesday. Hakim didn't end our shifts until after 8:00 pm, then we had to go back to the precinct to drop off our gear. By the time I was free to head home, Hawthorne was already at work. He'd texted me to let me know that he had stopped by my apartment again, which I assumed meant that the second drop with Warren had gone well because that was what he had done while I was on duty.

Neither of us was stupid enough to text anything condemning, so after the first drop, he'd left me a note on my table detailing a summary of the exchange. I had read it when I got home yesterday, then destroyed the evidence. Tonight would be no different, except this time, I was hoping his note would include the plans.

The purpose of Wednesday's drop had been for Hawthorne to pass on all the latest information we had compiled—updated copies of our maps, a complete entrance plan for warehouse 236A, locations of all building exits, approximate head counts for everyone working in the office building based on the cars we had been tracking, camera locations, light locations, rough security schedules, boat schedules—you name it, we'd made copies of it all and Hawthorne had hand delivered it.

Apparently, Warren had thanked him, but aside from that, the first drop had been quick, quiet, and completely unremarkable. So I wondered if this drop had been any different. When I reached the table, I found Hawthorne's note among the organized mess of papers and quickly snatched it up.

The drop went well!

I told Aries about Jensen's Janitorial and how you think they might be tied into this. He said he would let Orion know. I gave him the bag of additional supplies, and he said they didn't need anything else. The plan is really close to being finalized. I guess Eridanus has a way to get everyone into the city and down by the docks. No idea how that's going to work. I asked, but Aries said he didn't know, though I doubt he would have told me even if he did. So I guess we'll just have to wait and see.

Or maybe we won't.

I don't know. They might just be there when we show up, but I gave him a copy of my patrol route anyway and told him that we're working under the assumption Eridanus's contact will pull through and we'll get slotted together.

I left some food in the fridge for you because I know you're going to start crawling through footage again and won't bother to cook anything. Make sure you eat it.

Also, Aries says hi.

I'm kidding. He didn't really say much of anything. Strictly business, per usual – but he did give me a code name! I asked if I could have one for the mission, and he said I had been assigned Vela. Not sure what that is? I'll need to find some time to look it up. Anyway, make sure to get some rest. Aries didn't mention anything about meeting again, so I'm planning to go swimming again tomorrow and get one last look to make sure nothing has changed.

Good luck creeping on Morin! I hope Hakim isn't too much of a jerk today!

A smile played on my lips as I finished reading his letter. I didn't know what Vela was either, aside from knowing it would be a constellation, but I was happy that he had finally gotten his code name. Not only because he wanted one and it would keep his identity safer on the mission, but also because it meant that he was now officially an "exposed asset" too, and that meant Orion had extended him some level of trust.

Which he deserved.

Hawthorne was a good friend and ally, yet despite him being in this mess with me, I felt my uneasiness grow as I made my way over to the kitchen to burn the note.

We were less than forty-eight hours away from those humans being shipped out on a boat, lost forever, and we still didn't have a plan. I didn't like it. I hated being kept out of the loop, but I would just have to trust that Orion and Eridanus knew what they were doing. After all, I wasn't in charge. This wasn't my mission. These weren't my people. My only role in this was to help them in any way I could, and I was already doing that. It wouldn't be my place to push them for plan details or try to take control.

I ignited the front element of my gas stove, setting the paper alight before I switched off the dial and made my way to the sink, paper in hand. I watched the edges curl, the flames growing brighter and hotter like the summer sun. The note was quickly scorched black, crumpling to ash in the sink as an emptiness settled in my chest. I dropped the rest of it when I felt the flame lick my fingers, then washed the remains down the drain.

I stood there for a moment, staring at the drain in silence before letting out a sigh. I might not know what was going to happen, but there was still plenty to do.

I grabbed the food Hawthorne had left in the fridge, then settled down at the table to review the information we had managed to pull on Jensen's Janitorial. For the most part, they appeared to be a functional and legitimate company. No issues of fraud, no complaints lodged with the Business Bureau, and they filed their taxes every year. We were still waiting on an employee roster, which would take longer because we had to go through the FIDA, completing a broad scan of all known Carneth residents to see if any had their employment listed at Jensen's Janitorial.

It wasn't ideal, and I knew we wouldn't get a complete list, but we couldn't exactly ask Jensen's Janitorial for their employment records and expect them to freely give it to us the way Dolan's had. And we certainly couldn't submit a formal query through the CPD without raising flags.

I shuffled through the pages, noting that the owner was identified as M. Longwurst, but the details were minimal. I frowned. It was yet another name I would need to chase down in this mess to determine if there was a connection to Natasha Lionetti, and thus the Beckettes. I let out a sigh, leaning back in my chair and pulling out my small black flip phone.

It wasn't too late yet. Warren was probably still awake, and I hadn't checked to see if he had messaged me yet. I opened the phone, punched in the pin code and smiled when I saw the unread messages from earlier in the day.

> A: Vela dropped everything off.
>
> Just an FYI, he's terrible at navigating.
>
> I saw him drive by twice before he found the spot that you usually park in.
>
> Finalizing things tonight, but O said your end should be sorted.
>
> I'll let you know as soon as things are set.
>
> How was your shift?

The last message had been sent two hours ago, the rest spanned across the afternoon, and I wondered if they had since managed to sort out the plan.

> C: Long.

I answered, wishing I could just drive out there and see him instead of sending fragmented messages. We still hadn't talked about what had happened, and it was starting to look like that wouldn't be in the plans any time soon.

> C: Glad it's over.
>
> I know V is. I'll work on it.
>
> Any update on the plan?

I set the phone back to vibrate and nearly jumped when it instantly buzzed.

> A: Yes.

My pulse quickened.

A: Time your surveillance route so you and V are by Capel Street at 9:50 am.

Take the maintenance road V identified down to the ditch.

Cross the bridge there. The cameras will already be disabled.

There will be an unmarked maintenance van between 234 and 235. Park beside it, and make your way to the fire escape.

We'll be waiting there.

"Okay," I breathed, knowing I was unlikely to get any additional details like how the cameras would be disabled via text.

C: Alright. We can do that.

That's our alibi? We saw the van go in?

A: Exactly.

Tell V to pop out tomorrow, and I'll give him a final copy of the plan.

C: Alright.

A: Any other news on JJ?

C: No. Details are still coming in. I'll have a better picture by Monday.

Did you find something on them?

Do you need something?

A: No. E didn't have anything.

But it's on their radar now.

C: Good.

There was a moment of silence as I sat there holding my phone, wondering what else to say. I had a thousand thoughts in my mind, and yet not a single one could be captured by text.

A: Did you get some sleep?

I stilled, staring at the message. It was a complete change of pace, and I found myself wondering if he'd sent it because he cared about me and was worried or if he was simply concerned about my health for Saturday. I supposed it didn't really matter. Both would be valid. It just all felt so confusing because I didn't have a clue where his head was after what had happened.

C: Yes, I did.

I answered, knowing it was the only thing I could say. Then I quickly added,

    C: Make sure you get some too.

    A: I will.

I stared at my phone in silence, then smiled when the next words came only seconds later.

    A: Goodnight.

       I'll text you tomorrow morning.

Friday, October 30
8:02 AM

The precinct was alive with chatter. A dull but vibrant buzz hummed throughout the building and infected every corner. It was impossible not to hear. Impossible not to linger in the hall on the way to the print room or stand a little longer in the bathroom washing my hands as everyone gossiped about the upcoming forty-eight hours.

Hawthorne's plan had worked, and Orion's desire for the atrocious misdeeds of the Beckettes becoming evening news would be the easiest part of the mission at this rate.

The impending rally of protestors this Halloween weekend was all anyone could talk about. The news outlets were speculating massive turnout numbers, likely causing more harm than good as they stirred people into a panic and warned the public to stay indoors. Many in the precinct were pissed because they had booked the weekend off to participate in the festivities and were now being asked to work OT. Others were excited about the opportunity to make some extra cash, while a good number were just adding fuel to the fire by outright debating the ag-gag bill and the legitimacy of the human rights advocacy groups instead of filing their reports.

Meanwhile, I was doing everything that I could to stay sane as I eavesdropped on the conversations, bit my tongue any time

I heard someone say humans weren't people, and turned away from anyone who was looking to *debate* their opinions. For the first time since joining on as his partner, I was thankful that Hakim didn't have any interest in speaking to me. I was happy that he shut our boardroom door so we could work, and I was positively thrilled that I would get to spend the next twelve hours in a car with him, away from all this chaos.

I closed my eyes, letting out a quiet sigh and reminding myself to breathe.

In twenty-four hours, Hawthorne and I would be patrolling the streets that neighboured the docks. Eridanus's contact had come through. When the email had been issued to the Patrol and Street Department last night outlining the shift schedule for the weekend, I'd found my name paired with Hawthorne's, assigned to his current route, and slotted in for day shift. The second 9:50 am hit, we would cross the small maintenance road, drive to warehouse 235, park near the unmarked van just as Warren had outlined, and weave our way between the warehouses toward the fire escape.

Then everything would change.

It was incredible how many critical moments my life had encountered recently, and I wondered how many more would be crammed into the next few days. Then I shook my head, blinking my eyes open to stare at the Jane Doe map one more time.

"Gorski."

"Yes." My head shot up, turning to look at Hakim, who hadn't bothered to look in my direction.

"Go get the gear," he said, his eyes focused on his notes, probably seeing a million trends and leads I would never be able to spot. "They're likely swamped down there, and we can't be late."

"Yes, sir."

I stood from my seat, making my way toward the door and ensuring that I closed it behind me so the blast of chatter that collided with my ears wouldn't deafen Hakim too.

"I can't believe you think they should actually be there."

"It's a free country, isn't it? I'm not saying I agree with them; I'm just saying we can't force them to leave the city core."

"Well, I just think this whole thing is ridiculous. I mean, could you imagine the prices if they passed that bill? Food is already too expensive."

I blocked it out the best I could, nodding to the detectives that I recognized as I beelined to the stairwell. I had no interest in getting stuck in the elevator with anyone, so I swiped myself out and made my way down the stairs. Hakim's theory was proven correct the second I stepped foot onto the second floor. There were way more people here than usual. Some were coming to return the equipment they'd had logged out so it would be available to the weekend OT shifts, and others were on the weekend OT shift trying to sign gear out early.

I made my way over to the cage, waiting patiently behind eight other people as two Reborn behind me drone on about the upcoming hunting trip. My fingers curled into the fabric of my pants as I fought to tune out their words. That was another problem that I had yet to resolve, but it would need to wait.

I shuffled as the line moved up two spaces, then stiffened when I saw who was leaving the cage. Her blonde hair was perfectly slicked back into a high ponytail. Her uniform looked freshly ironed, despite it being the end of shift, and her nails had been done up with festive orange and black paint. I took a tiny step to the right, hoping I might catch a break and she would pass by without noticing me, but I knew I would never be that lucky.

Her eyes caught mine, and they narrowed, a crease forming between her perfectly plucked brows as she slowed. I could see the muscles in her jaw moving, clenching and unclenching as she either fought the urge to say something or tried to decide what words would be the most cutting, but what she settled on surprised me.

"I saw you signed up for OT," Grace said, slowing to a stop just two feet away. Her eyes were cold and calculating, something burning behind them just out of reach.

"Yes." My response came out clipped, and her eyes narrowed further. "A lot of people did."

"And you got paired up with Hawthorne." She said it sweetly, but the tone just made me feel queasy. "How *nice*."

I didn't say anything back. I wasn't going to do this at work.

"Well, hopefully your shift goes well." She smiled, but it didn't reach her eyes, and it made my skin prickle. "I'd hate for you to find yourself in any more trouble."

If not for the people around me, I might very well have reacted. Instead, I remained silent, my fists clenched tight as I watched her turn and walk away. Then I waited another ten minutes in line before I got the equipment Hakim wanted and hauled it all back upstairs.

He didn't thank me, and I didn't care. All I could think about was Grace as we packed up and made our way down toward the parking garage. If Hakim noticed that I looked angry, he didn't say anything. I loaded our gear into the backseat of the undercover car, then made toward the passenger seat door as the engine roared to life. I yanked it open, intending to slide into the seat, only to pause as a cold shiver ran down my spine and the hair at the base of my neck stood on end. I turned, my eyes rapidly scanning the busy lot and freezing when they met the pale, cold, blue ones watching me from three rows away.

I swallowed, my grip on the door tightening as Grace held my gaze, the disapproval etched across her face as her eyes flicked to the driver's side, then back to mine.

"Gorski!"

I jolted, turning to look at Hakim, who was putting the car into drive.

"In or out – I'm not waiting."

"Sorry." I quickly climbed into the car, barely getting the door shut before he started to drive away. "I thought I might have forgotten something."

I buckled up my seatbelt, ignoring the irritated expression on Hakim's face as he weaved his way through the rows of cars toward the exit. I tried to clear my head, tried to focus on the long upcoming day of surveillance where I would need to stay alert instead of worrying about tomorrow. I tried not to think about what Grace had said or the look on her face as she stared at me from across the lot. But more than anything, I tried to ignore the sinking feeling in the pit of my stomach, and the dread that was building in my mind.

Infiltration

"Are you ready?"

I glanced at Hawthorne, watching his face carefully as we made our way across the underground parking garage toward a row of cars. I was so nervous I could barely keep my hands from shaking. I hadn't slept a wink in the last twelve hours, and I doubted if Hawthorne had either. He'd come by last night to give me a copy of the plan from Warren, and we had reviewed it for hours. After he'd left, I'd done nothing but pour over my notes and run through the plan, trying to commit every little detail to memory in the hopes that it might somehow help.

I could tell that Hawthorne was just as nervous. I could see it clinging to his body, making his movements seem stiff and awkward. Even he couldn't hide it as he turned and gave me a tight smile.

"Yeah," he answered as he pulled the keys from his pocket and unlocked vehicle number 209, then moved to open the trunk. "I'm ready. You?"

I nodded, my gloved fingers curling around the strap of my gear bag. I had packed everything we could possibly need: tape, bolt cutters, cuffs, and even medical supplies for the humans in case things went wrong. I'd also brought water, clean snacks,

412

acetaminophen, and a few wraps and sticks to use for splints since we had no idea what kind of condition the people we were trying to rescue would be in. They could be injured, dehydrated, or suffering from any number of things. For all we knew, they might not be able to walk. They'd been locked in a truck for the last three days travelling through cold rain, and we had no idea if they were ever let out for a break or if they'd been allowed to eat or walk around since they had been captured.

I still didn't know enough about their biology to feel confident in making any assumptions, but I did know that they didn't recover the way we did. If they had been cooped up for weeks with little room, food, or water, they would be in bad shape. This entire mission could fall apart based on that alone, but it was just something we would have to deal with when the time came. If we had to, Hawthorne and I would pick them up and carry them out.

I just hoped Orion wasn't planning on them walking anywhere as part of the evacuation.

I ran a quick mental check over all of my belongings for the hundredth time, making sure that I had absolutely everything. I was wearing my vest. Warren was bringing us rifles. My firearm was strapped to my hip, which I would use as a backup if I had to, but otherwise, it would remain untouched. The visor of my blackout gear helmet was freshly cleaned, and my boots were laced tight. I had everything, and yet I still could not shake the unease that clung to my bones.

But at this point, there was nothing else I could do to prepare. I just had to be ready.

"Yes," I answered as I tossed my gear into the trunk. I turned to look up at my friend, then did my best to give him a reassuring smile. "I'm ready."

We both got into the car. Hawthorne started the engine as my eyes scanned over the busy lot, looking for familiar blonde hair. I had told Hawthorne what had happened with Grace. It made him uneasy, too, but I hadn't heard a peep from her since. She wasn't signed up for OT duty, and I'd already checked the garage for her car.

She wasn't here. By all logical reasoning, she should be at home, setting up the rest of the decorations for her party, then grabbing some sleep before her guests arrived. It was hard to imagine that she would risk the success of her social gathering to follow us around, and it was instead much more likely that she had reported her suspicions to Mallick.

There was a very good chance that I would be under investigation starting Monday, and I knew that would damage things for my role as a detective even further. If Grace did report me, Mallick would be obligated to alert HR and inform Vogle, because he was my acting captain. And even though I knew Vogle *and* Hakim both drained, I didn't doubt they would throw me under the bus. Hell, Hakim would probably be happy. He'd probably use it as a way to get rid of me permanently.

I just hoped I was wrong about Grace, and maybe I was.

After all, Mallick hadn't even spared me a glance during the debrief, but then again, he was up to his neck in problems. The protests had started Friday evening, and they were already having issues. Fights had broken out, a dozen Reborn had been arrested, and nearly twenty people had ended up in the hospital with severe burns after failing to clear the square or put on proper blackout gear. They were expecting tonight to be much worse, so an accusation of employee draining was probably the least of Mallick's concerns.

I buckled my seatbelt as Hawthorne pulled from the parking spot and made his way toward the exit. It took a bit to get out with all the traffic, but we eventually hit the city streets, driving south through the rain toward the docks. We didn't speak the entire way. I kept my eyes glued to the mirrors watching for anything suspicious or any sign of someone following us. Twice I thought I saw Grace's car, but with the weather, it was difficult to know for certain.

I knew I was probably being paranoid, but I couldn't help it. I just couldn't shake the feeling of dread that continued to build in my chest.

At 8:10 am, we reported in, noting our location on Hawthorne's route and alerting dispatch that everything looked fine before heading off down the quiet and all but abandoned street. Hawthorne's usual route ran on the north side of the forest, through the mostly industrial streets parallel to the docks. Every once in a while, the trees would drop, the road would incline, and we would be able to see the water and the warehouses, but for the most part, the river remained hidden behind the colourful array of trees. Any chance we had to get closer, we took. Hawthorne opted to drive down a few service roads, then circle back just so we could scope things out, though it was challenging to see much through the rain.

The plan was to keep this up until 9:45 am, then we would head toward Capel Street, and take the little maintenance road at the end down toward the ditch. There was a small bridge there, gravel, unmanned and typically unused, but gated and monitored by cameras. We would cross it, make our way over to warehouse 235, and park beside the unmarked van—at which point, the clock would already have started.

Warren's people were using that service bridge to get in, according to the plans that Hawthorne had brought back, and while the docks were long and the cameras were many, it was still possible that security would notice the camera feed of the service road going blank. Hopefully, they would blame it on the weather and think nothing of it, but that wasn't a guarantee, so once parked, we would need to move fast and hope that Orion's plan for evacuating the captured humans was efficient, discrete, and thoroughly well devised.

Time seemed to slow and drag as we circled the patrol route. I found my eyes darting to the clock more and more, each minute an eternity. My fingers curled into the fabric of my pants, my eyes shifting back to the window and mirrors to look for anything strange, only to find nothing again and again, but that only made it worse.

I hated this.

That haunting intuition of something gone horribly wrong, yet absolutely no evidence to prove it. I fought the urge to text Warren and instead ran through the plan six more times until Hawthorne finally spoke.

"It's time."

My eyes flashed to his, then my hand moved to the radio.

"Dispatch, this is car number 209," I said, forcing my voice to remain steady.

'Received.' The noise crackled through. *'Status update?'*

"No change," I said as Hawthorne turned down Capel Street and made his way to the maintenance road. "Nothing to report. Things are quiet here."

'Confirmed. Next check-in one hour.'

"Confirmed." I put the radio back, making sure the call was disconnected before I twisted in my seat to face Hawthorne. "You ready?"

"I was born ready," Hawthorne said as he turned onto the narrow maintenance road. "Let's do this."

We bumped along the gravel for several metres, passing the fence and reaching the bridge to find that the gate was already up. We didn't stop. We simply drove through, trusting Warren that the cameras would be disabled and making for the main road that ran in front of the warehouses along the piers. I watched the buildings whip by, my fingers curling tighter and tighter as we got closer until 235 came into view. Then Hawthorne turned down the narrow unmonitored road between 234 and 235, and I undid my seatbelt, twisting around completely to grab our helmets from the backseat.

"There," Hawthorne said as we neared the end. "They're here."

They had parked in the perfect spot, between two large dumpsters and not easily visible from the main road. I tossed Hawthorne his helmet the second he parked the car next to the van. I didn't wait. I handed Hawthorne the radio, stuffed my helmet on my head and got out, making my way around the car and opening the trunk. I had my gear bag on in seconds and Hawthorne's in hand as he exited the vehicle and made his way toward me.

We didn't speak. I simply passed him his bag, then motioned for him to follow as he fixed the radio to his belt. We raced south toward the end of the narrow road, slowing when we reached the intersection of 234, 235, and 236A.

"Cameras?" Hawthorne whispered as I peered around the corner to the left.

"They've been pushed flush against the buildings," I murmured, squinting through the rain and the tint of my visor. "They've left us a clear path down the center."

"Eridanus and their allies came through again," Hawthorne said as he tapped my shoulder to confirm the opposite way was clear. "We'll have to thank them."

"If we ever meet them." I gestured with my head. "Let's go."

We made our way east between 235 and 236A, sprinting clear down the centerline, as Warren and his team must have done earlier, until we finally neared the northeastmost corner of 236A, where several of the cameras appeared to be completely disabled. The tiny little red lights were off, and I wondered if perhaps the Beckettes had turned off their own security to avoid catching the unload on film.

Maybe this wasn't Eridanus's doing at all?

I pushed the thought aside; it was something I would have to ask Warren about later. Right now, I needed to focus, and that meant making a right between 236A and 236B and cautiously making our way down to the fire escape.

We paused at the corner of our turn, Hawthorne checking our rear and left again as I peered around the edge of 236A to the right. Everything looked clear, but as we stepped around the edge of the warehouse and started down the alley toward the ladder, a familiar scent filled my nose.

Sweat.

I slowed as we passed the second alcove, keeping my hands empty, up, and clearly visible—the last thing I wanted was an incident of friendly fire.

"Aries?" I called as we neared the ladder.

He stepped out when he heard my voice, two of his eight allies covering him with their rifles as Hawthorne and I slowly approached. They were exactly where Warren had said they would be waiting, tucked into the fourth alcove, out of view, just beside the fire escape. All of them were wearing blackout gear, and if not for their size, they could have easily passed as Reborn on the street—if we gave them a set of skateboards, they would blend right in with some of the younger teens.

"Corvus." Warren's voice sounded from behind the tinted visor, and I let out a breath of relief. "Any trouble?"

"No." I shook my head, shrugging off my gear bag and handing it out for Warren to hold as Hawthorne removed his own and handed it to another one of the humans. A sour part of me sort of hoped it might be that monotone-looking girl. "All clear so far. Did you have any issues getting in?"

"No," Warren said as he took my bag and moved out of the way so Hawthorne could move beneath the fire escape. "Gate was up when you got there?"

"Yes," I said, then I gestured to the others who stood watch with their rifles. "Are we waiting on anyone else, or are you ready?"

"Everyone else is on evac duty." Warren's head turned to Hawthorne, who was now stretching his arms out and getting ready beneath the ladder. "A few are covering the other sides, and once we clear the office, they'll meet us at the loading doors to help."

"Okay." I nodded, then moved toward Hawthorne and planted my foot firmly into his cupped hands, bracing my own on the wall behind him. "It will only take me a second to get this down. I'll lead, then Vela will help everyone else up and take the rear for the climb. Once we get across the roof, we'll take point for entry. Make sure you hang back – if anyone is in there, they'll be able to smell you, and lights will be a dead giveaway. So try not to use them. We'll signal you when it's clear to move."

"Alright," Warren said, though his voice sounded unsure as he looked between me, Hawthorne, and the fire escape that was easily more than a storey above my head. "You're sure you can do this?"

"Oh, yeah," Hawthorne said, gripping my foot tight. "She's tiny. It will be like tossing a pillow. You good?"

"I'm good." I nodded, taking one last glance at Warren. "I'll see you at the top."

I looked up at the ladder as Hawthorne crouched low to the ground, the muscles in my body tensing in anticipation of what was to come.

"Three, two, one—"

Hawthorne stood, his movements so rapid I didn't even have time to breathe as he hoisted me up with his hands and launched me into the air.

The wall whipped by before me, but my eyes were focused on the bottom rung of the ladder. I outstretched my hands, straining to reach the metal, only for my gloved fingers to barely brush the surface. The throw wasn't going to be enough, but we didn't have time to keep trying. I dropped my gaze, rapidly scanning for something else I could use, as my body reached the vertex of Hawthorne's throw and slowed, the sinking sensation of falling creeping into my gut.

There was a lip, a small two-inch edge that ran along the warehouse just a foot or two below the ladder. I reached for it as my body dropped, the fingers of my right hand barely snagging it and breaking my fall before I collided against the wall with a thump. I bit back a groan as the muscles in my shoulder strained. I gave them a split second to mend, then adjusted my grip, using both hands to haul myself up and pressing my feet into the wall so I could launch myself at the ladder once more.

It was easy.

I caught the rung despite the water that coated the bar and quickly pulled myself up three more rungs and onto the tiny platform to let the ladder down. There was no way the humans would be able to reach it on their own from the ground, but Hawthorne lifted each of them into the air one by one, getting them all onto the ladder before he reshouldered his bag and jumped his way up.

The climb was quick, though twice I heard someone slip on the wet metal behind me as the wind tugged at our bodies. Warren was the last human to the top, and I helped him over the edge like all the others before taking back my bag. Once Hawthorne had joined us, Warren gave us each a rifle and a light, then pulled two leather holsters from his bag.

"Knives?" I asked, staring at the weapon with hesitation. I glanced up at him as I clipped the light to my belt, wishing that I could see his face, but he simply shrugged.

"They're quieter. Two flashes of light to let us know the room is clear – press the little button on the top."

He didn't say anything else, and I had no argument to counter his words, so I took the knife and strapped it to my thigh even though the idea of stabbing someone made me sicker than the possibility of shooting them.

I slung the rifle over my shoulder and across my back, then motioned for everyone to follow Hawthorne and me across the roof toward the access door. Opening it was easy, probably because they never anticipated anyone entering this way. It would have been impossible for Hawthorne to toss an average-sized adult high enough to reach the fire escape, so it likely wasn't considered a risk, especially with all the cameras. The lock never stood a chance—one solid whack with the butt of Hawthorne's rifle and the handle came right off.

I let Hawthorne take the lead, the sound of the storm following us inside into the darkness as we made our way down the concrete stairs. We stopped at the next door, each human pulling out their knife while Warren pulled a small black kit from his pocket. One of the other humans switched on their light, shining it at the doorknob as Warren fished out two tiny metal sticks and started to pick the lock. I strained my ears against the door as he worked, but there wasn't a sound save for the faint scratch of his tools. It took a few minutes, but eventually, the quiet *click* echoed in the concrete hall, and everything seemed to go quiet.

I waited for Warren to move out of the way, then motioned for his ally to cut the light.

My hand shook as I reached for the doorknob, every sound and every smell amplified by the adrenaline rushing through my veins. I twisted the handle, silently inching the door open and peering into the office. It was dark. The hallway was empty, and I couldn't hear a sound.

I drew my knife, ignoring the unpleasant tug in my gut as I did so, and nodded to Hawthorne. He slipped inside, knife held at his side, and I followed along behind him. The others didn't move. They waited as we made our way down the hall, stopping at each door, testing the handles, and clearing the rooms. Two were large offices, modernly decorated and highlighted with expensive furnishings. One was a supply room, and another looked to be used for meetings.

All of them were empty.

I shifted toward the end of the hall, a faint tapping sound making me slow. I motioned to Hawthorne, waiting for him to cover me before I carefully peered around the corner and surveyed the room. It was a large open space. A few cubicle desks with basic chairs and equipment were spread out across the floor, and a small set of windows that looked down at the warehouse floor ran along the far wall.

The room was empty except for the single Reborn sitting at a desk, hunched over his keyboard, typing away.

He didn't look like security. He was wearing a pale blue dress shirt, black dress pants, and decent-looking shoes. Not Ridgebacks, but it felt safe to assume that he made more than average pay, and he was lanky like most civilians. I watched him in silence for a moment, debating what to do before I turned back to Hawthorne and held up one finger. He nodded, and I pointed at him, motioning for him to go first and indicating that I would follow.

He moved without a sound, slipping around the corner into the farm of cubicles, making his way across the floor in a crouch. I followed behind him like a shadow, my Academy training taking over as I covered Hawthorne and watched the door on the other side of the room by the windows. Then, just as the smell of rain would have registered in the target's mind, Hawthorne moved, grabbing him by the neck and yanking him from the chair.

I caught the chair before it collided with the ground, setting it down gently as Hawthorne pulled the man to the floor and pressed his knee into his chest to hold him down. I quickly joined him, pushing my knife to his neck and holding his arm as Hawthorne held the rest of him still.

"Make a noise, and you're dead," I whispered, and the man instantly stilled. He didn't try to fight. It wouldn't have done much good if he did, and it was clear he knew that as he stared up at me with wide eyes. "Name?"

"Craig."

"What do you do here, Craig?"

"I'm just the accountant," he whispered, and I could feel the tremble of his body beneath mine.

"Who else is here today?"

"No one." The answer was much too quick, and I pushed forward on the knife until I felt it break the skin.

"Lie to me one more time, and I'll cut your head clean off. It won't grow back," I said, leaning down in his face. "How many other people are here?"

"Three."

I pressed harder, and a grunt left his lips.

"Where?"

"Warehouse – on the main floor by the south doors."

"We're looking for a container," I whispered. "One filled with humans. Where is it? Are they guarding it?"

"Yes," he hissed, his eyes pinching as blood started to trickle from his throat. "It's right at the front by the doors."

"Good." I kept the knife still and turned to look at Hawthorne. "So what do we do with him?"

"Let me go?" the man offered, and Hawthorne pressed his knee deeper, making the man grunt. "Please! Beckette will kill me if you leave me here. You don't know what you're dealing with. Let me go, and I'll disappear. I swear."

"Hard to believe that when you've already lied once," I muttered. I grabbed the light from my belt, flashing it twice at the hall to signal Warren before turning back to Hawthorne.

"We could tie him up here?" Hawthorne suggested.

"Then you might as well kill me," Craig groaned. "It's what Beckette will do when he finds me."

I heard Warren and his team approaching, and I saw recognition dawn in Craig's eyes as they filled the room and their dim lights lit the ground.

"Humans," Craig whispered, his eyes shifting back to my visor. "You're working with humans?"

"Be quiet." I pressed the knife harder against his neck, then turned to look at Warren. "His name is Craig. He says there are three men guarding the container by the main doors on the south side."

"Alright." Warren nodded, crouching by my side as his people moved to cover the far door that would lead down to the warehouse floor. "You're okay taking point for that?"

"Yes." I nodded. "But what do we do with him?"

"Take him out." Warren's voice was flat and cold, and I stiffened at the words. "Or is that a problem?"

"No," I answered, even though every bone in my body was rejecting the thought. I had known this was coming. It was an inescapable reality of my life, which I had been ignoring. It was the path I had chosen, and eventually, I wouldn't have a choice, and I would need to come to terms with that. But in this case, there was another option. "He's Beckette's accountant."

Warren stilled, and I knew he was debating what I had yet to say.

"He might be useful. We should take him with us."

"Then we have to make sure he's completely detained," Warren warned. "I won't risk this entire operation just to question some vampire who may or may not know anything."

I felt the man flinch beneath my knife, but his eyes widened with hope.

"I know stuff," he said, his gaze shifting to Warren. "But I'm not going to tell you here. You'll just kill me after. Take me with you. I can help you."

"Fine," I said, turning back to him. It was probably a lie, and I knew the final call would be made by Orion or Eridanus, but we could deal with that later. "Provided that you continue to prove useful and don't cause any problems."

I removed the blade from his neck, quickly shrugging off my pack and digging out my cuffs. He didn't resist when I banded his wrists or when I pulled out the tape and started winding it around his mouth. Hawthorne took over, quickly wrapping his legs and feet while I grabbed another set of cuffs to bind his ankles. Warren stood, moving toward his group and tapping one of them on the shoulder.

"Stay here with him," Warren said, gesturing to Craig. "Keep your rifle aimed at his head. If he moves, kill him. The second loading door is clear, we'll send someone up to help bring him down."

The person nodded, then shifted across the floor toward us as they unslung their rifle.

"Alright," I said, tucking my tape back into my bag and pulling it on. "Three more downstairs. We'll take the lead. You can cover us from the end of the aisle until we signal the all clear again."

Warren nodded. "I'll let evac know to get moving – we meet in five minutes."

Hawthorne and I didn't wait. We made for the door on the opposite side, keeping away from the windows, moving silently. This door was unlocked, and in a matter of seconds, we were descending a set of metal corrugated stairs toward the warehouse floor.

It was even bigger than I had realized. The bland exterior didn't do any justice to the massive stacks of metal shipping containers, crates, and boxes that lined the concrete floors in rows. We made our way along the wall toward the south end. It wasn't far, and soon we reached the final corner and peered around the edge toward the massive bay doors. I could smell cigarette smoke. The quiet murmur of voices echoed down the aisle and easily gave away the three men's position despite the distance. I leaned back against the end container, turning to look at Hawthorne and nodding in confirmation that the guards were there.

The quicker we dealt with this the better. My uneasiness had yet to fade, and if anything, it was starting to grow. Things had moved much too smoothly thus far, and I didn't like leaving a Reborn tied up upstairs with Warren and the others. I knew Craig would never rip through the tape fast enough to cause any life-threatening damage. The human Warren had left guarding him would shoot him well before that happened, but a gunshot would draw attention, and I didn't trust that there weren't other people here somewhere. Or that more wouldn't be coming at any time.

Sure, Warren said they had the outside covered, but I still didn't like it. I'd had no part in the planning. My job was limited to getting them in, taking out the threats inside, and helping them load. So my confidence that we were secure right now was pretty low. When this was all over, Warren and I needed to have a serious talk. Not just about that kiss but about everything.

I wanted in.

Completely.

I'd already said it, and Orion had accepted me, but I wanted more. I knew it wasn't my place to ask, and I had been trying not to overstep, but I wanted to meet Eridanus. I wanted to become part of their network. I wanted to be involved in the planning. I wanted to know what was going on. I hated that my part in this and the farm break-in had been so limited. I was still only barely engaged in the efforts, not able to truly help while an invisible barrier remained between Warren and me.

I let out a silent sigh, then motioned for Hawthorne to follow my lead, shifting back the way we'd come until Warren and seven other humans came into view. I waited for them to get close enough to see us through the dark, then led them back to the end of the very first aisle, where I instructed them to wait beside a stack of metal containers. Then Hawthorne and I made our way down the second row behind our targets.

They weren't expecting us, and that would be our advantage. The air was already damp and stale, so they wouldn't see us coming. As long as we could incapacitate all three before someone fired a weapon, this would be fine.

We slowed as the voices grew louder, both Hawthorne and I drawing our knives as we crept forward. I glanced through the spaces between the containers, watching the three men and confirming that they hadn't moved. The one smoking was leaning up against the bay door. The other two were standing in front of the container that must have contained humans. I could smell them. The sweat, the fear, and a hint of blood wafting through the tiny vents on the large metal box.

I tried to ignore it, focusing on what I was about to do as my hands started to shake.

I stopped at the last gap, checking to ensure it was wide enough for us both to slip through. Then I turned to Hawthorne, my heart in my throat as I stared at his visor. I wished I could have seen his face, to see if he was just as nauseous and horrified as I was. But all I saw was the warped reflection of my own helmet-covered face.

Maybe that was better.

Later I could pretend it was some nameless, faceless person that had done what needed to be done. I gripped my knife tighter. I could make out the words of the men now. They were talking about next weekend—about the hunt.

I swallowed the acid that was creeping up my throat, my hands trembling harder as I held up one finger, gestured to the large bay doors behind us, and pointed at myself. Then I held up two shaking fingers, gestured to the container before us, and pointed at him. He nodded. The message was clear, but neither of us moved. I could feel the seconds ticking by. Each beat of my heart grew faster and faster until I could hardly breathe and the claustrophobic feeling that had been plaguing my body for weeks returned in full force.

I wanted to rip my helmet off. I wanted to throw up. I wanted to go home and just go back to being ignorant. I didn't want to hurt anyone, not even assholes who might deserve it, but I knew if I didn't move now, I never would, and my inaction would ruin the rescue. These humans would die. Scott Beckette and his father would continue to decimate Warren's people's populations, and he'd ship them out like cattle to be used for who knows what.

Nothing would change. Warren and his team would get caught, and he would die like the people trapped inside the container.

And it would be entirely my fault.

Something cold traced down my spine, like ice had penetrated my bones as, suddenly, my hands went completely still. I stood from my crouched position, my heart rate slowing as every thought clouding my mind and halting my motions grew eerily silent and faded into a dark corner.

It was as if a switch had been flicked.

I couldn't feel anything. I couldn't think. I moved, slipping between the containers, my feet silent and quick, until I reached the end of the narrow gap and burst across the aisle. I heard Hawthorne break free behind me, followed by the startled noise of all three guards. I reached the cigarette man before he lifted his pistol, driving my knife forward into his chest and slamming his head into the door.

"CRAI—!"

His voice cut off in a groan of pain. There was a thud behind me, the sound of a grunt and fists, and I pulled my knife back only to get kneed in the chest. I buckled, the impact nearly taking the wind out of me as the man tried to shove me off and reach for his weapon. I didn't let go. I gripped him harder, kneeing him twice in the diaphragm before stabbing him with my knife once more.

This time, he stumbled, and my limbs moved quicker than I ever could have imagined. Like it was coded into my DNA. Like doing this was the most natural thing in the world as instinct took over, and a snarl left my lips. The urge to bite him rushed through my veins as I gripped the back of his head, pulled it back, then drove my knife through the exposed tissue.

It wasn't hard.

In fact, it was remarkably easy.

I watched the thick brown blood pour out and cover my gloves as his head fell to the side. I let go, his body slumping to the ground. His eyes continued to blink and look up at me while his neck tried and failed to heal, but there was nothing there for his skin to reattach to. I had completely severed it, so it would wither and regenerate over and over as he slowly died.

I stumbled back, turning to look at Hawthorne who had lost his helmet and rifle in the scuffle. He had the final man on the ground, head gripped tightly between his large hands as he slammed it into the concrete. Without pausing to think, I ran over, sliding to my knees and driving the knife down through the man's neck as Hawthorne yanked up. I heard his flesh tear until there was nothing left. Until Hawthorne dropped the severed head to the ground by his side with a thump and we both sat there panting for air. Until I raised my blood-soaked hand and shoved away my visor, meeting Hawthorne's gaze.

His eyes were wide, pupils fully dilated. He looked terrified, but exhilarated—his nostrils flared as the smell of stale, old blood filled the air—and I knew I looked just the same. Dangerous.

Monstrous. A perfect representation of everything Warren and his people feared.

We stared at each other in stunned silence until the sound of running footsteps registered in my mind, and we both scrambled to our feet.

"Clear!" I called, staggering back from the bodies and wiping my hands on my vest.

I shook my head, trying to shake the buzz from my bones as eight lights flicked on and the familiar scent of Warren's sweat filled the air. It made my mouth water, and that made me sick. I moved, grabbing Hawthorne's helmet from the ground and shoving it onto his head before shutting my own visor. The last thing I wanted was for Warren to see us like this.

To see me like this…

"Is the evac here?" I asked as the approaching group slowed.

"They're here," Warren said as he came to a stop and looked at the mess on the floor. He didn't say anything about it, but when his head turned back to me, I knew he was probably eyeing the blood that now covered my jacket. "Let's get this door open."

I nodded, not trusting myself to say anything else. I moved toward the large bay door, grabbing the latch at the bottom and yanking it free. Hawthorne moved to the chain on the right side, rapidly unhooking the wall latches before he started to pull and immediately let in the storm. Rain pooled across the concrete, the dark grey skies blocking out most of the morning light as two wheels came into view, followed by half a dozen sets of legs.

"This unit!" Warren called, motioning for the truck to back up into the warehouse once Hawthorne had the door high enough for the evac team to move in. They were all dressed in blackout gear, and from what I could tell, only most of them were human. "Pisces – grab someone and head back up to the office to bring that vampire down. Corvus – the container?"

"On it!"

I moved toward the shipping container and unslung my bag. I pulled out my bolt cutter, grunting as I cut the thick metal. I tucked the cutter into my belt as the lock fell to the floor, then tugged the latches free. Four other blackout-clad bodies came running over to help me yank the doors open, and when the metal swung clear, I felt all the air leave my lungs in a wheeze as if I'd been kneed for a second time.

Nothing could have prepared me for what I saw.

It was worse than the factory farm. Worse than the hunting trip. People were crammed into the container, too weak and emaciated to stand. Some looked better than others, but most of them looked absolutely horrible.

"Aries."

My voice wavered as I turned and called for him, but he didn't falter as he yanked off his helmet and moved toward the container.

"Get them out," he directed, his eyes trailing over the crowd of bodies. They lingered on the ones at the back who were most definitely already dead, and his eyes creased. "My name is Aries. I'm here with Orion, and we're taking you home."

Eridanus

I didn't hesitate. I moved into the container, grabbed the first person who couldn't stand, and lifted them from the ground. I carried them over to the truck, passing them off to what I assumed was another human dressed in blackout gear, then quickly returned to grab the next. Hawthorne came over to help, carrying people two at a time and lifting them into the truck. The ones that could walk did. They shuffled forward, some crying, some too shocked or exhausted to speak as Warren's people and allies loaded them up.

I made my way toward the back of the container, ignoring the filth on the floor and blocking out the odour as best as I could, to check over the motionless bodies, finding one that was still alive.

"It's okay," I said as I approached. "I'm here to get you out."

I had barely even kneeled at her side before her hands were on me, grabbing at my vest as her hoarse voice cried out.

"My daughter," she wheezed, her broken and bloodied fingernails digging into my jacket. "You have to find my daughter. Please – please! You have to help me find her!"

"What do you mean?" I asked, looking around the container even though I had no idea what her daughter looked like. "She's not here with you? Where did they take her?"

"I don't know." The woman's voice grew more desperate. "They separated us – they said one to port, one to local bid. Something about EC-D. I don't know where she is – but please. Please. I told her I would find her again. I told her not to be scared. Please, you have to help me find her. You have to help me find Lily. She's all I have!"

My heart faltered, a cold stone dropping into the pit of my stomach. Our worst fear came true. There were more humans here, and we had no idea where they were. They'd been separated intentionally, moved to another container to be bid out locally. I glanced back toward the flashing lights and dull voices, then found myself nodding.

"Okay," I said, helping the woman up and turning us toward the door. "I'll go find her. I promise, but we need to get you out of here."

I carried the woman from the container, rapidly making my way toward the truck and searching for Warren through the mass of bodies.

"Aries," I called before catching sight of him helping a younger boy into the truck. "Aries!"

He turned, quickly moving toward me as I carried the woman through the throng of slow-moving humans.

"What's wrong?"

"This woman," I said, passing her off to him. "She said her daughter isn't with her. They were separated – she's here, Aries. In the EC-D section in another container to be bid locally."

"Shit." He looped his arm around the woman, his head turning to scan the crowd of bodies. "Okay – okay – I'll get some people to—"

"No." I shook my head, stepping back from him. "You need everyone here. I'll do it."

"Corvus, EC-D is a huge section," Warren argued as he stepped toward me. "It's at the other end of the warehouse!"

"Exactly!" I said, double-checking that my cutters were still secured in my belt. "Vela can carry twice as much as me, and I can move twice as fast as both of you. It makes sense that you two and your team stay here and get these people loaded. I'll go start looking – I'll be able to cover more ground on my own. I promise you, we'll get the others too, but you can't risk these people's lives in the process. You have to get them loaded. We don't have time to debate this."

"Fine," he said, though he didn't look happy, and he quickly grabbed one of the radios off a passing blackout-clad human and handed it to me. "But take this. I'll have Pisces talk to Craig to see if he knew about this. Radio when you find them – the channel is already set."

"I will."

I didn't wait to see if he said anything else. I simply turned and set off at a run, lifting my visor so I could see better. I could still smell the sweat from all of those behind me, and I was banking on that being my guide as I ran down the first cross aisle I hit toward the north end of the warehouse, where section EC-D was located. Their container would need to be ventilated, so locating them by smell was the only thing I had to go on unless Craig gave up something good.

There would be no records of this shipment and no way to know exactly where they were being kept otherwise. If that woman hadn't heard those words, we wouldn't even have had a chance of finding that second container—assuming she'd heard them correctly.

As it stood, the odds of being successful were extremely low, and I had a feeling Craig would very quickly be eliminated.

I broke out into a full sprint, my feet nearly soundless as they collided against the concrete floors. Even at this pace, it would take me a few minutes just to get to the correct section, assuming the information Eridanus's contact had gathered continued to hold true.

I forced my legs to move faster, my breath coming quick and sharp behind my helmet, as I tried to remember the layout of the warehouse. There were doors on every side, but the main loading zone was the south end facing the docks. Section EC-D ran along the northern end of the east side of the building. There were a few doors there, three smaller loading doors and a handful of man doors. They all bordered warehouses 235 and 236B. We'd passed them as we'd made our way toward Warren and his crew. Both neighbouring warehouses were owned by Lionetti, so if I had to hazard a guess, the container would be in one of the first aisles, either on the north or the east, making it easier to unload and show to potential buyers.

Maybe Lionetti really had turned off her own security cameras to allow her clients anonymous access. Maybe we had used the same route of entry her buyers were planning to take, and maybe—maybe they had already been sold last night immediately after arriving, and we'd missed our window.

My stomach curled as my eyes scanned the orange plastic labels that numbered the support columns until I found the southmost row of section EC-D. Then I turned right, racing down a long row of stacked containers toward the eastern wall as I tried to think analytically. I knew the container would have a door facing the aisle, likely bolted and chained shut, and it would probably be on the ground. I couldn't imagine it would be stacked on top of anything or that containers would have been placed on it in the last few hours, so it might even be a single box.

At least it would be something to look for until I heard back from Warren on Craig.

I skidded to a stop when I reached the large main aisle that ran directly along the east wall, quickly checking that both ways were clear before I grabbed the radio Warren had given me. Then I turned left and started to make my way along the stacks of containers toward the north corner.

"Aries, this is Corvus," I said, pausing before a lonely container and skimming the surface for vents. "I just reached the southeastmost corner of section EC-D according to the labels. I'm looking for it now. It's got to be a lone, vented container, possibly located near one of the man doors on the east or north side for access, so I'm checking the east wall first."

'Heard.' Warren's voice crackled over the radio. *'Your captive insists he knows nothing about it despite Pisces pressing. We're almost done loading. Once they're clear, we'll head your way.'*

"Heard," I answered. "See you soon."

I reclipped the radio to my belt, abandoning the container I had been examining and moving forward.

I lost track of how many I touched, how many I smelled, and how many I knocked on to see if I heard any movement inside. They were all starting to blur together. The aisle was endless, and I was only in the first row. I had thought that they would place it here for convenience. I couldn't see why they would bury it in the center of the massive section, but maybe I was wrong.

Or maybe they were already sold.

I fought against my growing panic, forcing my feet forward and examining the suspect-looking containers as quickly as possible. I had nearly reached the north end of the warehouse, and my hope was starting to fade, when I froze. I turned, stepping closer to the nearest container and taking a deep breath again.

"Blood," I breathed, a tingle running over my skin as my pulse began to quicken.

It was faint. I could barely smell it among the cold steel, damp concrete, and lingering staleness of the warehouse air, but I was certain it was there. I set off again, rushing down the main aisle, the smell growing stronger and stronger, mingling with the scent of sweat, as I pushed my legs faster than they had ever moved before.

I could taste it now, and the smell made my mouth water as my stomach grew sick.

"Shit."

I skidded to a stop as the smell began to lessen, turning back to look at the long row of tall containers behind me. I doubled back, racing along them as my eyes creased. They were all stacked five or higher, and none of them had any vents. I paused, heart pounding as I looked at the wall of containers, then realized my mistake.

"They're in the second row."

Without pausing to think, I rushed toward the nearest gap I could find, pressing myself flat against the metal boxes and squeezing through. I all but tumbled out the other side, then immediately continued north again as the smell grew stronger once more.

"Come on, come on," I panted, racing down the narrower aisle as my eyes scanned each metal box. "It has to be here – it has to be here—"

Six more useless stacks of containers, then I saw it. A single, lone box tucked between two towers of four. There was a rusty vent on the front. A padlock on the door. And a pungent smell of human sweat and waste hanging in the air. I immediately sprinted toward it, my heart thudding so hard I could barely hear anything as I reached the metal and pounded against the side.

"Hello!" I called, grabbing the padlock and turning it so I could cut it. "I'm here with Orion – is anyone alive in there?"

I heard movement—a shuffle against the walls—then a tiny voice echoed back.

"We're alive."

Relief flooded through me like a wave, a heavy sigh leaving my lips as I set the bolt cutter against the lock and then gripped both handles tight.

"Aaargh!"

Pain jolted down my arms as I forced the cutters shut and snapped the lock in two. I let the tool fall to the floor with a clang, then grabbed the latch with shaking hands and heaved it open. I stepped back, grabbing both handles and yanking with all my strength, the groan of metal echoing with my own through the air as I tugged the door free and found myself face to face with more than two dozen terrified eyes.

Some were no more than a few feet high, while others looked to be teens, but they were all incredibly young. I swallowed; the rank smell was all-consuming and made it hard to breathe. They looked like they hadn't bathed in weeks. Their skin was sallow, faces gaunt like the others, and a few of them were bleeding. My eyes dropped to the youngest, who had a large cut running down their face, and I felt my heart break.

"Can everyone in here walk?" I asked, scanning the container, taking in the slow, quiet nods. "Alright, then come on."

I stepped back, clicking on the small light Warren had given me so they could see and motioned for them to step out, but they didn't. Every single one of them stood frozen, their eyes locked on my face, fear radiating from their gaze. I stiffened, quickly realizing my mistake of leaving my visor up after switching on the light.

I took another step back.

"I'm not here to hurt you," I said, keeping my voice low as I raised my free hand in the air. "I'm here to get you out. Orion and your people are waiting at the other end."

"And why on earth would we believe that?" one of the older girls whispered. Her tone was strong despite the terror that shone in her eyes.

"Because the sun is rising," I said, repeating the words I had heard Orion give to Hawthorne. "And soon the birds will sing."

The girl's eyes widened, and I could see several others looking at her for direction.

"I'm here to help," I said quietly, taking yet another step back as I kept my hands visible. "We're getting you all out. I swear on my life – I won't hurt you. But we need to go. We don't have much more time."

The girl who had spoken hesitated. Her eyes darted from me to the empty space around me and back to the container. Then she nodded, and they all started to move. I watched to see if anyone needed help. A few of them were moving slowly. One of them was limping, but they appeared better off than the first batch we had found and capable of helping each other, which was good, because I doubted they wanted me anywhere near them.

"Alright, take this." I held the light out to the girl who had spoken. She eyed me warily but took it before quickly stepping back. "Down this aisle." I pointed. "It's a fair distance, so if you need help, let me know."

The girl nodded again, shifting south with the group as I reached for my radio to call Warren.

"*Don't move!*"

The familiar voice rang out so fiercely the young humans before me flinched, and I stiffened.

"Take your helmet off and drop it on the ground."

"Gra—"

"Take your helmet off and drop it on the ground, or I'll shoot you right now!"

My fingers twitched.

"You have three seconds."

"Grace, I—"

"One."

I slowly raised my hands.

"Two."

I grabbed my helmet, slipping it off and letting it fall to the ground with a heavy thunk.

"Switch off your radio."

I debated grabbing my firearm instead, but that would only end in bloodshed for the humans around me. So I carefully reached toward my belt and turned off the radio.

"Turn around."

I started to twist, pausing instantly when her voice rang out once more.

"With your hands up where I can see them."

I spread my fingers, raising my hands up by either side of my head before I finally turned around. Her usually perfect expression was pinched with disgust. Her pale blue eyes burned with a hatred that rivalled that of Warren's people.

"What the fuck are you doing, Valya?"

I stared at her, a million thoughts raced through my head, and yet the only sentence that seemed to form coherently in my mind was probably the most useless thing I could have said at that moment.

"I'm making a difference."

"By trafficking humans?" Grace raised a perfectly plucked brow, her expression unbelieving. "Was this the only way you thought you could get out of your financial mess? How much trouble did you get in?"

"I'm not trafficking them, Lexie," I said, taking a very slow and cautious step forward. Her eyes immediately narrowed as she moved her firearm to point at my head, and I stopped. "I'm helping them."

She stared at me, and it was like she couldn't process my words. Her eyes flicked between me and the people standing just behind me, her brows knitting together as she struggled to find words.

"I'm not a drainer, Lexie," I continued, taking her silent battle as an opportunity to try and repair this. "I'm not in financial trouble. I haven't gotten involved in any gangs, and I'm not trying to ruin my life. I'm trying to help. I'm trying to put an end to this."

"You've got to be kidding me." She shook her head. "You're helping them? The bleeding-heart human activists? You actually support their bullshit?"

"It's not bullshit." I took another step forward. "These humans are people, Lexie. They're no different from us.

"Holy shit," she breathed, her eyes widening. "You're actually serious."

"Of course I'm serious!" I said, dropping my hands to gesture to the dozens of people around me. "Look at them! If not for their size, you wouldn't even be able to tell them apart from a Reborn."

"They're not people, Valya!" Grace spat. "They're humans. They're animals – you're going to throw away everything to try and save the lives of a few meat bags?"

"Meat bags." I stilled, my eyes searching her face for any flicker of compassion but finding none. "That's all you see? After you said that you hoped their conditions would get better on the farms?"

"Yeah, on the farms. Not out in the real world! Do you have any idea how insane you sound!" Anger etched across her features, like my being here had personally offended her. Like she was the one hurt, and I was the monster ruining her life and tearing the world apart. "Do you have any idea how stupid this is?!"

Her firearm lowered an inch, a painful, almost pleading look crossing her face. She hesitated, then took a small step forward.

"You can still fix this," she whispered. "You can call this in with me. We can report this together, and I won't tell anyone you were involved. You don't have to do this, Valya – I can help you."

My head was starting to shake, and I could feel my heart sinking further in my chest. She would never change. She would never understand. It was clear as night looking at her now. She was exactly the type of Reborn that Warren's people feared, and

I wasn't even sure if it was her fault. She just didn't have the capacity to care.

"I can't," I said, and I took a step back from her toward the people behind me. "I can't, Lexie."

Her grip on her firearm tightened as the hurt shone brighter in her eyes.

"You would give everything up for these humans?" Her voice wavered. "You would pick them over your own species? Over your family? Over me?"

"Yes." I lifted my chin higher, staring across the endless gap that had always existed between us, but I had been too stupid to see. "Every time."

Maybe I should have lied. Maybe I should have pretended to take her up on the offer, then tried to disarm her, but the words were so genuine they left my lips before I could even think, and the second I had spoken them, I knew the damage was permanent. Grace's face twisted into a mess as a snarl left her lips. I could hear two voices calling out through the warehouse. It was Hawthorne and Warren trying to find me, and we were out of time.

"GO!" I yelled as my hand reached for the firearm on my hip. "Down the aisle NOW!"

I heard the first shot as my fingers brushed against cold metal. The second, as I pulled my firearm from the holster. The third, as I raised my pistol into the air, and another two as I released the safety.

Then I felt the force of the impact.

It was like nothing I had ever experienced before, and my mind registered two things instantaneously: first, that her marksmanship was impeccable, and second, that Lexie Grace was using Reborn-grade ammunition.

Our vests are designed to withstand a direct hit, but not two in a row in the same location from such close range.

The first bullet collided with my chest like a battering ram, and the second ripped clean through the already damaged material of my vest, tearing into the tissue and taking large pieces of me with it as it burrowed into my core. I heard bodies fall around me. I knew others had been hit, but my brain seemed to paralyze as I stumbled backward, my legs shaking beneath me as my right arm went limp and my firearm dropped to the ground.

Everything around me faded out of focus, and my ears buzzed with emptiness as I met Grace's gaze.

Her eyes were burning. Her pupils dilated as the smell of fresh blood filled the air. I stared at her, an eternity of silence passing by in an instant, only for it all to come rushing back in like the rise of a raging storm. I dropped to my knees and fell backwards. I could feel something hot and wet covering my neck, and when I reached for my sternum, I found a large hole instead.

"Nobody move!"

The chaos around me stopped, and as my head lolled to the side, I could see two sets of dirty feet. I blinked, a horrible wheeze leaving my lungs as my head rolled back to look up at Grace.

I didn't recognize her. I didn't know this person. I didn't understand how it had come to this, and yet I couldn't help but wonder if this was always how my life was destined to end.

Then I felt the pain.

It rolled through my body like a wave—scorching, searing, the toxic combination of materials making my insides scream in unison. It burned like acid. The ache in my chest grew wild and furious, thudding through my veins as blood leaked out onto the floor. I tried to inhale but sputtered on the thick brownish liquid pooling in my throat as my eyes began to burn with tears.

I stared up at Grace. Her pistol was pointed at my head. Her hand was on her radio. My panic flared as the familiar static crackle filled the air, and all I could think of was getting these people out.

"Le-xie," I wheezed, coughing up more blood as my head rocked back and forth. "N-n-nno."

She didn't even look at me. Her eyes were cold as she pressed the small button and started her call-in.

"Dispatch," Grace said, her eyes locked to the humans standing frozen around me. "I have a—"

Her lips went still.

I watched through bleary eyes as her own went wide for a fraction of a second before dark red splattered through the air, the deafening ring of another gunshot echoing across the warehouse. I could see the mess on her shirt. The emptiness to her gaze as her hand dropped to her side. The radio clattered to the ground and then her body followed. Down, down, down, until I heard it hit the concrete. I knew there would be nothing left to the side of her head, but I didn't turn to check. Instead, my eyes traced to the right, toward the approaching figure.

My broken lungs rattled as I sucked in a ragged breath, then my eyes grew wide in horror as I saw who stepped into view, their CPD standard-issue firearm turning to me.

"Gorski."

I met his mismatched gaze, and suddenly it didn't matter that I couldn't properly speak because I was too stunned to utter a word. I watched him move before me as the tissues across my chest tried and failed to knit back together again.

"You only have a few minutes at best." His gravel voice filled the air. "You won't heal from that wound on your own."

I forced my right hand to move, sliding it through the slick that covered the floor in search of my firearm while the rifle remained useless and inaccessible behind my back. He stepped forward, and I heard him kick the weapon away, leaving me defenceless in a pool of my own blood. Images from that night in the woods filled my mind. My eyes darted to Lexie's motionless body on the ground, and I knew in my heart that this man would have zero hesitation killing me too.

Footsteps were rapidly approaching. Warren's voice sounded in the distance. That last shot had given away our location, and I knew he and Hawthorne would be here in moments.

"W-War – en—"

I tried to yell it, to warn them, but barely any sound came out.

"It would be best if you didn't do that," Hakim said as he looked down at me, his expression cold. "You'll only make it worse, and I have something else I need you to answer."

I glared up at him, shifting my arm through the blood again and finding his leg. I grabbed it. It wouldn't do much. I doubted I had the strength to cause damage when I could barely feel my fingers, but I gripped his ankle as tightly as I could anyway, hoping that maybe I could break it, as another bloodied wheeze left my lungs.

"It's a simple question, Gorski," he said, leaning in closer as the edges of my vision began to blur. "Are you in or out?"

I coughed, blood sputtering from my lips as I glared up at my partner in confusion.

"You and Hawthorne," he said, and more tears trailed from my eyes as they widened. "This is only the beginning. We still have a long way to go, and Orion isn't interested in people who get cold feet after they see how ugly this war is. It's great that you're here playing hero today, but it's only going to get more difficult. This – right now – likely won't be the worst thing you experience. So, I need to know that you're one hundred percent in. We can't afford any other changes in heart this year. There is no backing out. No changing your mind, and no exit off this train."

"H – How?" The word was so raspy it was barely audible, but he seemed to hear it just fine as he crouched down by my side, his mismatched eyes all but boring into my soul.

"I am Eridanus."

His voice was like the low rumble of thunder, and my heart stuttered at his words.

"So what will it be, Gorski?" Hakim asked, pulling a small bottle from the pocket of his vest as he kept his pistol trained on my face. "Are you willing to do whatever it takes to see this through until the end? Are you Corvus, or are you not?"

I could hear a dull thrum, and in the back of my mind, it registered that the noise was starting to slow. I couldn't feel my legs, let alone the rest of my body. I had no idea if I was still gripping his ankle or not. Everything hurt. It was hard to think. And yet even in this state, I knew the answer to his question, because who I was meant to be and who I would become had been etched into my bones the very night I'd set foot on that farm by his side. It was burned into my skin the morning I met Warren and cemented in my heart the instant I abandoned my duty as an officer of the law to do the right thing.

"I-I'm in."

The words came out as a wheeze as more blood trickled from my lips.

"I am Corvus."

THANK YOU

Thank you for supporting my work and taking the time to read SYNTH. I hope that you enjoyed the story.

Please consider leaving a short review on <u>Amazon</u> or <u>Goodreads</u> to share your thoughts.

Honest reviews help readers discover new authors and find the books they're looking for—even a sentence or two is greatly appreciated! You can also share your reading experience on social media with the hashtags #TheRebornSeries #SynthBook and encourage others to read the story too!

ACKNOWLEDGEMENTS

I am incredibly grateful for the love and support I received while completing this book. Hundreds of hours went into plotting, writing, editing, formatting, and planning - and it wouldn't have been possible without the help of so many people.

To Dan, who is more incredible than words can describe. Thank you for listening to my ideas, supporting my goals, reading my stories, and always encouraging me. You are my everything, and I could not do this without you.

To my family, who continually supports me. I am incredibly lucky to call you my family. Thank you for being my biggest cheerleaders, for reading my books, and for everything that you do. Mom and Dad, for teaching me how to work hard and never give up. Julie, for being my trusty beta reader. John, for your edits and support. Jeff, Nelly, Gayle, Rob, Nic, Heather, Laurie, and everyone in Book Club (I'm sorry we haven't read anything in a while!). And Grant, for our inspiring walks and for always lending a keen and fuzzy ear.

To my friends and readers, your support means everything, and I am filled with gratitude. Devon, Jade, Tessa, and Jamie, thank you for your help.

To Mandi, I'm so happy to have met you and incredibly grateful for your help. Your edits were marvelous, and without your hard work, I would never have been able to finish this book to the same level of quality (or as quickly).

To Alex, for being so patient with me and designing a beautiful cover that I absolutely love.

To Ginny, thank you for being my developmental sounding board. You helped me to get my thoughts in order and ensure everything made sense. Without you, this book would not be what it is. Thank you for never allowing me to cut corners and for always pushing me to put my best words forward.

And to Henry, thank you for bringing so much happiness into my life. I love you more than anything.

About the Author

Engineer by trade, P. J. Marie has always been a storyteller at heart. Inspired by the captivating tales that her Ukrainian grandfather used to tell about life on the Canadian prairies, P. J. has always looked at life through a narrative lens.

An avid creator, P. J. loves the design process from start to finish and is always working on projects that meld the structured world of engineering with her creative passions. Whether world-building, crafting cosplays, or building custom bookshelves for her ever-growing collection of novels, manga, and terrible monster movies, P. J. is always working on something.

In her spare time, she enjoys collecting new skills, drinking copious amounts of tea, and spending time with her family and adorable doggo.

Sign Up

Visit https://www.pjmarie.com and subscribe to the newsletter for updates on upcoming works, release dates, and events.

Also By P. J. Marie

Veles Saga:
Veles

For weekly updates, bookish content, recommendations, writing advice, and more, be sure to follow P. J. Marie

@authorpjmarie

www.facebook.com/AuthorPJMarie.Page

https://www.goodreads.com/pjmarie

Ingram Content Group UK Ltd.
Milton Keynes UK
UKHW040819200723
425383UK00030B/115/J